Trevor...

"I like you, Carolina." I couldn't believe the words were coming out of my mouth, and yet, it felt good. I felt free. But she didn't say anything. Crap! Why didn't I just keep my mouth shut? Then I realized there was a tear in her eye. Which I didn't understand. But it disappeared and just glistened a bit. And then that smile happened again and she said—

Carolina...

"I like you too," I said. Oh. My. Gosh. I said I liked a boy. To his face. And he had said he liked me. What did this mean? I MUST KNOW WHAT THIS MEANS OR I WILL DIE.

D1016533

FOREVER
FOR A YEAR

b. t. gottfred

SQUARE
FISH

Henry Holt and Company

NEW YORK

SQUARE FISH

An imprint of Macmillan Publishing Group, LLC
120 Broadway,
New York, NY 10271
fiercereads.com

FOREVER FOR A YEAR. Copyright © 2015 by b. t. gottfred.
All rights reserved. Printed in the United States of America by LSC Communications,
Harrisonburg, Virginia.

Square Fish and the Square Fish logo are trademarks of Macmillan and are used by
Henry Holt and Company, LLC under license from Macmillan.

Our books may be purchased in bulk for promotional, educational, or business
use. Please contact your local bookseller or the Macmillan Corporate
and Premium Sales Department at (800) 221-7945 ext. 5442 or by
e-mail at MacmillanSpecialMarkets@macmillan.com.

Library of Congress Cataloging-in-Publication Data

Gottfred, B. T.
Forever for a year / b. t. gottfred.
pages cm
Summary: "Two young teens fall in love for the first time, and discover it
might not last forever"—Provided by publisher.
ISBN 978-1-250-08003-5 (paperback)   ISBN 978-1-62779-192-2 (ebook)
[1. Love—Fiction.]   I. Title.
PZ7.1.G68Fo 2015   [Fic]—dc23   2015000935

Originally published in the United States by Henry Holt and Company, LLC
First Square Fish Edition: 2016
Book designed by Anna Booth
Square Fish logo designed by Filomena Tuosto

5   7   9   10   8   6

I asked Carolina who this book should be dedicated to, and she said:

"To soul mates, obviously, but not just the ones that have each other,
or even the ones that lost each other, but, gosh,
you also have to dedicate it to the ones that
never found each other at all."

Part One

STRANGERS
FOR A WEEK

1

Carrie will now be Carolina

IT WAS MY IDEA FOR US TO START USING OUR FULL NAMES. It was going to help us take ourselves more seriously now that we were starting high school. It's like I used to be Carrie, this awkward eighth grader, but now I was going to be Carolina, this amazing freshman. Oh my gosh, this sounds so dumb when I say it like that. Never mind.

Wait a minute. Just because I didn't want to be geeky Carrie anymore didn't mean Carolina wasn't going to be a good student. She was. I mean, *I* was. Obviously. I mean, school was still the most important thing. By far. And if you ask me, I wasn't really a geek in junior high. I'm super normal. It's just that other people thought my best friend, Peggy, and I were geeks, so we didn't really argue with them. Can you even do that? Argue with popular people on how they categorize you? Maybe you can, though it probably would have just made us even bigger geeks in their eyes. Gosh! Why was I worrying about this NOW? It was the first day of high school and I had to get ready! I mean, I was totally ready. I had been waiting by the front door for twenty minutes for Peggy and her sister to pick me up. But, you know, get ready in my mind. Because this year was going to change my life. I just knew it.

So I sat and pictured ("envisioned" might be the better word) how today would go in my head. Except the horrible stuff that happened with my dad earlier kept popping into my brain and I got mad at him again, and suddenly I felt like I was going to cry (again) and if that happened, I was sure my first day would be ruined, which might ruin my entire existence. Wait a minute! I reminded myself that I'm in control, that I'm super smart, that my dad was part of my past, not my future, and then I felt better.

And then I heard the honk. And even though nobody could have gotten out to the car faster than I did, Katherine honked again. Katherine is Peggy's sister. She's not very patient. Or nice. In fact, she's kind of a lunatic. But she has a car, and if I did everything she said, I wouldn't have to take the bus. And taking the bus is for losers. At least that's what Katherine said.

By the way, Peggy's new name is Marguerite. It's not her new name. It's on her birth certificate, just like Carolina is on mine, but nobody knows it's her name. Except me, because we're best friends, remember? Peggy wouldn't go by her longer name unless Katherine said it was okay. See, Katherine was a junior, and always tan and really pretty when she wore lots of makeup, and—most important to Peggy (and maybe me)—Katherine was super popular. Maybe the most popular girl ever to go to Riverbend High School. And since Peggy wanted to be cooler in high school even more than I did, Peggy wouldn't go by Marguerite unless Katherine said it was okay. Which she did.

I would've become Carolina no matter what Katherine said. Because I was ready.

"WHAT'S WRONG?" PEGGY ASKED AS I GOT IN THE BACK seat of the Civic, which Katherine had painted CRAPMOBILE on the side of with nail polish. (I'm gonna have to learn to call Peggy Marguerite in my head, aren't I?) Anyway, Peggy/Marguerite knew something was wrong even though I had hoped I was over it because Peggy has known me since before time began. (Actually, fourth grade.) I should stop exaggerating for effect. I'm in high school now. High schoolers don't do that. Maybe they do. I don't know. But they shouldn't. They should be mature enough to just tell the truth as it is. Which is what I'm going to do.

I said, "Nothing," to Peggy. She knew it was not nothing, but she also knew my "nothing" meant I didn't want to talk about what was wrong right then. I mean, I kind of did, but not in front of Katherine. I wanted to tell Peggy ALL about how my dad had ruined my first/last/only morning before my first day of high school. But Peggy knew to drop it for now, because she's amazing, and changed the subject.

"Guess what? Katherine talked to her friend Elizabeth Shunton, who's the older sister of Shannon Shunton, and told her to tell Shannon that she should be our friend this year."

Katherine, who was driving like a person who thought looking at the road was optional, grinned. "I'm gonna make you two the hottest chicks in the freshman class. You watch. You will love me."

I smiled at Peggy, pretending to be excited about being friends with Shannon Shunton. Because I was so *not* excited. Shannon Shunton was the most popular girl in eighth grade, and I suppose she would be the most popular freshman, but I didn't care about being popular. (Okay, I'm lying! I totally already admitted I wanted to be popular.) But, and I mean this, I don't care about it if it means pretending to want to be friends with Shannon Shunton. Who is the meanest person ever. She could make you cry just by rolling her eyes at you. How could you be friends with someone like that?

Katherine started giving us a lecture on how we should walk through the halls, where we should sit in the cafeteria, what boys we should talk to (soccer players yes, football players maybe, band members no), and how she knew we were both good students, but maybe we shouldn't try too hard or it would make us look geeky. This is the dumbest thing ever said. But probably true. This is why I shouldn't care about being popular! Or boys! Or any of it!

Riverbend High School, which most kids call The Bend, came into view as we turned right past the bank onto Kirby Street. It looked huge. Peggy (I mean, Marguerite) and I came here most of July for soccer camp, but it was empty during the summer, like a ghost school. But now we were pulling into the parking lot and there were so many cars and kids, and they were so tall, and looked like they were thirty years old even though they could only be four years older than me. My stomach started eating my insides. This is what happens when I get nervous. My stomach becomes an alien and eats all my organs and I almost die. Yes, I exaggerated, okay! I'm sorry. Gosh.

"Now, Carrie," Katherine said, turning back to me as she parked.

"Carolina," Peggy said. A big mistake.

Katherine's face jumped two feet in the air as she screamed: "YOU MAKE YOUR FRESHMAN DORKS CALL YOU THAT; I CALL YOU WHATEVER I WANT, PEGGY! PEGGY! PEGGY! PEGGY! OKAY, PEGGY?"

See? Lunatic. But she was my best friend's sister and my ride. So I listened as she began again.

"Carrie, listen to me. My ugly sister Peggy hit the jackpot the past four months, in case you didn't notice." Katherine pointed at Peggy's boobs. Which had grown from super small to SUPER huge in 114 days. It was amazing. Like when you add water to a scrunched-up straw wrapper, but not that fast. Obviously. We started measuring them every day, laughing like it was the funniest thing ever, until one day she cried from her back hurting and I cried because I was still flat. Peggy slunk down in the front seat, her face becoming one big freckle of embarrassment. Katherine continued, "And she still has skinny legs. She doesn't quite get it even though I've told her, like, every day, but every dude with a penis, even the gay ones, are gonna stare at her, want to talk to her, ask her out, and kiss her just so they can reach up her shirt. Trust me, I know this, and this is so true. But your boobs are still small and you dress like a boy, so we are going to have to come up with a thing to make boys like you. I can't put my reputation on the line for you if you aren't willing to make boys like you. So I'm thinking you should learn to talk dirty. Like they do in porn. Guys love it. This college guy, Nick, would go nuts when I would say certain stuff. And they'll never expect you to talk like that, because you're such a goody-good girl. It will make them see you as someone new. So I want you to learn to say things like, 'I get turned on thinking about you.' So go ahead and say that right now." (Except she didn't say "turned on"; she said something so embarrassing I don't want to even think it.)

She beamed her big saucer eyes down at me. Making me feel one inch tall. And like she stole my ability to talk even though she wanted me to say something. No, no, no! I was not going to say that ever. I'd walk to school. I'd even take the bus! Ugh. I hate Katherine. Hate her. Hate her. Hate her.

"Say it or I'll know you're a big waste of my time and you'll stay a loser like you were in junior high."

I didn't care. I'd be a loser. Life is one hundred years. High school is only four.

"Don't be a loser, Carrie!"

Ugh. This was so unfair! "I get turned on thinking about you." Except I said it her gross way. I know I said I wouldn't, but Katherine is crazy and sometimes you have to do what crazy people say or they get even crazier. And, OBVIOUSLY, I know what it means. I'm a teenager and there's this thing called the stupid internet.

"Good job," Katherine said, grinning as she looked at herself in the mirror. Pouting her lips and narrowing her eyes like movie stars do on red carpets. She continued, "Marguerite and Carolina, yeah? Okay. Okay. I got your backs. Let's rock this." She swung open her door. Peggy and I slinked out of the car and fell in line behind her as she marched us toward the northeast entrance. (And I know I'm supposed to call her Marguerite! I'm sorry, okay? I had a really difficult morning.)

Wait a minute.

Wait. A. Minute.

I was starting high school.

2
Trevor doesn't give a . . .

"TREVOR."

"Dad," I said, but I pretended I didn't know why he was talking to me.

"Trevor."

"Dad."

"Trevor!"

"Dad!" I knew that would be our last back-and-forth name calling. I was right. My dad stepped—in two giant, super-loud steps—across the room from the doorway toward my bed. I was still lying in it. It was seven thirty or something. Classes were starting in twenty minutes. I was going to be late. I hadn't overslept. I'd just overstayed in bed. Staring at the ceiling.

Thinking.

Thinking about how there was another Trevor in another dimension who was happy. A Trevor who had gotten up on time, was excited about school, and had friends, a girlfriend, and a reason to live. Then I was thinking about how this Other Dimension Trevor would be clueless, and I would hate him for being clueless. Because I might not have any of those things Other Trevor did—friends, a girl, a reason to live—but at least I wasn't clueless. I knew what the world was really like. I had seen its dark, corrupt core, and I couldn't and wouldn't unsee it.

My dad didn't care about Other Dimension Trevor. He didn't care much about This Dimension Trevor right now either, because he was mad. He didn't get mad very often. So when he was mad, you could tell. And right now, as he sat on my bed, you could tell he was very, very mad.

He grabbed my shoulder and turned me toward him. I didn't fight it. He's not evil. He's just ignorant. Ignorant that everything is bullshit. "Trevor, this is a new school and a new year. Don't you want to start off on the right foot?"

"That's a cliché, Dad. 'Start off on the right foot.' I no longer comprehend clichés. Try again."

"Trevor. No smart-mouth. Get up. I'm driving you."

"You're going to be late for work."

"Don't worry about me. Get up. Lily refused to get on the bus since you were still sleeping. Now she's late too. So get up now. We leave here in twenty minutes."

"Mom can drive me."

"Your mother is sleeping."

"Are we sure she's sleeping? She might be dead." This was a joke. You don't understand it, because you don't know my mom overdosed on sleeping pills over a year ago. Maybe you don't find it funny now that you know. Neither did my dad. He gave me that look where I feel I'm the worst son ever born.

"Okay, fine," I said, but I didn't move. So he didn't move. "Fine. Okay. I'm up." I kicked off the blankets and sheets, which also dislodged him from my bed. A bonus. He didn't leave the room until I walked into my bathroom.

Yeah, I have my own bathroom now. My little sister, Lily, who's seven but talks like she's forty, says this is the best part of our new house. "We really should be grateful, Trevor. Not many children get their own bathroom. We should be grateful for a lot of things, I believe. Our family really needed the fresh start." She's right. She's super smart. She was smarter when she was five, but then the crap happened with my mom and now she tries too hard. But she's still the smartest seven-year-old ever.

I turned on the shower, sat down in the tub and just let the water rain down on me. I love sitting in the shower. Usually do it for forty-five minutes. Just sit and think and sometimes don't think, which is just as nice. Lily says it's bad for the environment, wasting all that water. I tell her it's not wasting water; it's saving my soul. Then she says, "I have such a strange brother," and walks away.

My dad pounded on my bathroom door less than ten minutes into my shower escape. I almost pretended not to hear him, but I decided to be nice. His year has been pretty crappy too.

MY MOM GREW UP IN RIVERBEND, ILLINOIS. THAT'S WHY we moved back here from Los Angeles, to be closer to my grandma and Uncle Hank and his family. My grandpa, who was super cool because he just listened and didn't try to impress you, died a few months before my mom overdosed. He had a stroke, didn't like being weak, stopped eating, and just died. My grandma blames his death for my mom's depression. My dad agrees, which is total denial. My mom's been depressed my whole life, so it has nothing to do with my grandpa dying. Just a good excuse. I don't blame her for being depressed. Life is pointless. I'm sorry. It is. But I am pissed at her for trying to leave us behind.

I was going to be a freshman this year. I was a freshman last year in Los Angeles too. But about two weeks in, I'd said screw this, I'm not going to school anymore. My mom had just come home after months at some fancy loony bin resort, so my dad thought I wanted to stay home to make sure my mom was okay. But I didn't care. I mean, I cared about her. I still do. But I didn't care about stopping her from trying to kill herself again. Because, guess what? You can't stop people from hurting themselves. Impossible. So I'm smart enough to never try. I'm also smart enough to know my dad wasn't going to fight me about going to school last year. But after twelve months of video games and a move halfway across the country, he was fighting me this time.

"Trevor! We are walking out this door!" he yelled from downstairs. I threw on some jeans, Chucks, and a blue T-shirt that just said FREE YOURSELF. All my T-shirts say crap like that. People are so gullible. Free yourself from what? Exactly.

I hadn't gotten a haircut since my mom's thing. That's a lie. My dad made me get a trim two days ago, but my hair was still pretty long. Below my ears. I couldn't quite put it in a ponytail, at least not a cool one. But soon.

When I got in the back of my dad's BMW, Lily handed me a bagel with cream cheese and a bottle of water.

"Why don't you say thank you, Trevor," my dad said.

"I was about to, but you didn't give me a chance," I said. "Thanks, Lily."

"Do you know what I was thinking might be a fun activity this weekend for the whole family?" Lily started. See? Like she's forty! She's blond like my mom, tall for her age, and probably will be the most beautiful woman ever by the time she's a teenager. If she becomes president someday, we'll all be lucky. "I think we should drive into Chicago, shop on Michigan Avenue, and then have dinner somewhere nice. We haven't done that yet, and we've been here a whole month. I really think that could make us feel like we belong here. What do you both think about this idea?"

"I think that's a great idea," my dad said. He likes Lily better than me. I can't even be angry at him for this. I like Lily better than me too.

I said, "Sure, Lily. But only if I don't have tons of pointless homework that I must do for no reason."

"Trevor, I think you're going to like high school this year. I really do," Lily said. She's always trying to be my life coach.

When we stopped outside Skvarla Elementary, Lily turned to my dad and me and said, "Both of you have wonderful days," and then hopped out and sprinted toward the entrance, her hair swishing and backpack spinning on her right arm. Only when she ran like that did you remember she was seven years old.

I think it reminded my dad of the same thing, because he mumbled, "I should walk her in on her first day," and then jumped out of the car and ran after her. Later, watching him walk back to the car, he had this smile that only Lily can give him. That smile was gone by the time he got back behind the wheel. He had to deal with me now. "Get in the front, Trevor."

"I prefer you being my chauffeur."

"Trevor. Now."

Lecture time. Yay. I climbed over the seat and slid headfirst into the front passenger seat before twisting around and seat-belting myself in.

"I know the move, and all the stuff with Mom, has not been easy.

13

But in four years colleges aren't going to care how rough you had it, so you have to start buckling down. Work hard. Working hard can help you forget about things."

I almost said, *Like working hard helped you forget your wife hated life so much she tried to off herself?*, but I didn't. Just because. Sometimes it's easier to ignore my dad than argue with him, even though ignoring him makes him think I'm listening. Which makes him think he's wise. Which annoys me. Because he's not.

He continued talking, telling me he'd put a call in to the football coach to see if I could play even though they'd started practice a couple of weeks ago. I used to love football. I have a pretty good arm. Played quarterback in eighth grade for the park district team. But football just doesn't interest me anymore; it's so serious and ridiculous at the same time. Dad just wanted me to make friends, which I suppose would have been nice if I could snap my fingers and have supercool friends who weren't full of crap. But the long-drawn-out process of making friends, being fake and generic so you don't scare anyone off, just seemed like such a headache. I'd rather play video games and talk to Lily.

When Dad stopped outside Riverbend High School, he said, "I love you, Trevor," and for a second he seemed real and vulnerable and awesome, so I said, "I love you too."

But then he added, "Keep your head down and work hard," which was a cliché and meaningless and pointless. So I didn't hug him, just flung open the door and walked inside without looking back.

I HAD TO GO TO THE FRONT OFFICE SINCE I ARRIVED AFTER first period started. The lady behind the desk asked why I was late.

I wanted to say something clever and over her head, but I couldn't think of anything, so I just said, "Missed the bus."

The office lady asked if I had my class schedule. "Yeah, of course," I said, only to realize that I didn't. I had left my backpack at home. Or maybe in the back seat. "Actually, can you print it out?" She nodded and handed me a copy of my schedule, a map of the school, and a hall pass. Hall passes. So insulting. Just let kids go where they want and figure it out. Or give adults "life passes" so they can't wander off. Because I guarantee you, right this second, more adults than kids are in places they shouldn't be.

Riverbend High School had two major wings, east and west. The east seemed to have all my classes, including first-period biology. Connecting the wings was a long hall, with the cafeteria and library on opposite sides. The gym, pool, and auditorium were north, down another long hall.

When I found the biology classroom, I thought about not going in. What was one more day, right? Then I thought: Exactly. What was one more day avoiding the inevitable? Might as well get this crap started and over with. So I walked inside. All the kids, in eight rows that were four desks deep, turned to me. The teacher kept talking, not noticing or caring that I was entering or that the rest of his students had stopped paying attention to him. Mr. Klenner was old with greenish skin and a baggy neck, like some giant frogman. Maybe I just thought that because he was a biology teacher.

There were two empty seats. Remember when I said all the kids looked my way? Well, that wasn't exactly true. One didn't. At least not for more than a second. A girl with brown hair. One of the two empty seats was next to her, and for some reason I decided to sit by her even though it was closer to the teacher.

After I sat down, I realized everybody was back to taking notes. Which I couldn't do. Because my bag was in some undetermined place. I didn't care. I'd just daydream about better stuff.

Then two sheets of paper and a pencil appeared on my desk. It was the brown-haired girl, but by the time I turned to mouth *thanks* she was already back to staring ahead. As pathetic as this sounds, what she did was one of the cooler things anyone had done for me in a long time.

I felt I almost had to start taking notes or else it would be an insult to her cool thing. So I did, even though it made me a robot brainlessly writing down crap a teacher said so we could regurgitate it to him later. Pointless! Why can't people see this? Someone should realize how absurd school is and make it better.

I would do it if I cared. Which I don't. But I do care about being cool back to people who are cool to me, like the brown-haired girl. I'd have to figure out a way to repay her.

3

Carolina's first day doesn't go according to plan

OKAY, LISTEN: EVEN THOUGH SCIENCE IS MY WORST subject, first-period biology—my first class of high school ever—started perfectly. As it should have, since I had been envisioning it all summer. Most other classes come easy to me, like Spanish, or I find them really interesting, like history, but I knew I was going to have to work extra hard and pay extra attention in biology.

Which I was totally doing until this boy showed up late to class and sat right next to me. He was a new student. Definitely didn't go to junior high with us, which most kids at Riverbend High School did. And he didn't have a bag or a notebook or anything, so I gave him a pencil and some paper to take notes with. Not because I cared about him—I mean, I'm nice, but the real reason I did it is I just knew if I didn't give him paper, I would be thinking the whole class how he didn't have any, and then I wouldn't be able to concentrate.

So why couldn't I concentrate now? This was sooo frustrating. It was the first day of classes; I needed to start off good! Start off WELL, I mean. . . . See, I was a mess! What was going wrong? I was so prepared! Wait a minute. I totally know what was happening: The new boy was staring at me. He had to be. Definitely.

But when I glanced toward him, he was staring ahead at Mr. Klenner, even writing stuff down. Ugh. Why did I feel so weird? Was there something weird about HIM that made me feel weird? I stole tiny, bitsy glances out of the corner of my eye. Mmm. Okay, he was cute. That's just a fact. He had dark skin and a chin that looked like a sculpture. Oh, what a corny thing to say. Though I guess it's true. But there had to be something about him besides being cute that was making my brain unfocused. He probably looked like someone I knew. Or maybe I met him once. That had to be it, right? He just felt sooo familiar. . . .

Oh my gosh. Wake up! Just listen to the teacher, Carolina! Listen. Listen. Listen.

Which I totally did, except when I was thinking about the new boy and what his name was and where he was from and if he was going to thank me for giving him sheets of paper at the end of class.

Which he didn't. Because after class ended, I lingered there at my seat for an extra couple of seconds, even though I'm usually fast to leave so I can get to my next class on time. But he was even faster than I was, so he left and didn't say anything.

I didn't care. I didn't. Boys are horrible. All of them. New ones with nice hair and even nicer forearms. And old, dumb ones too.

"CARRIE!" MY DAD CALLED OUT AS I WALKED INTO THE kitchen that morning at 6:40 a.m. More like he sang my name. Waving, with a big smile on his face. He liked to do this—sing your name when he was saw you, especially me—because he thought it would make everyone forget he was a big jerk. I would never forget. Never.

"My name is Carolina now, and WHAT ARE YOU DOING HERE, DAD?" I screamed because his being here ruined everything. Everything, everything, everything.

"Please don't scream at me. What made you decide to start going by Carolina? I like it." My dad talked like he was the mature one. Which he isn't.

"Why are you here?" I whined. I hate when I do that. I'm too old to whine now. Oh no, I could feel tears forming. No, no, no! I would not cry. I would not let him ruin this day. I'm strong. I'm amazing. I'm a grown woman now.

He said, pretending to be a good parent, "It's your first day of high school. I wanted to see my little girl off. I know your mom had an early shift, so I'm here."

For, like, maybe one tiny little second I thought this was true. I mean, maybe part of it was true, but for just that tiny second I thought it was the only truth. And I remembered when I loved him, before he hurt my mom. When he was my best friend who I could talk to about anything, and we flew to New York City, just the two of us, just to see a new musical, and he was so wise and interesting and funny and the best dad ever, and . . . NEVER MIND. I hate thinking about that stuff now. Because then I noticed he didn't have shoes on. He noticed that I noticed.

"Carrie . . . Carolina," my dad started, smiling, always thinking he can smile away all the problems he causes. "You're right. I don't have shoes on. Which means I spent the night. You don't miss a thing, do you?" He laughed really big. Like it was sooo cute that he couldn't trick me. "Please don't cry. Oh, my princess, please don't."

I didn't know I was crying until he said it, which made it worse. My motivational pep talk in my head didn't work. This made me cry more. Why couldn't I be perfect? I wanted to be perfect!

19

I would be. I WOULD BE. I would be.

Tears were wiped away. Big breath. Chin high. "Scott . . ."

"Scott? You've never called me that before. So I'm Scott and you're Carolina? High school already marks some big changes. I prefer Dad, but I respect your choices."

Ignore him? Definitely. "Scott, I will have a discussion tonight with my mother, your ex-wife, about her mistakenly letting you back into her life last night."

"We're not divorced. We're not getting divorced. Stop talking like that. So cold and stilted. That therapy-speak makes you sound brainwashed, not mature, like you think."

"I only saw a therapist because of youuu!"

"Carrie, you're being mean. You haven't let me see you all summer. Can you please sit down and talk to me? I want to hear about your new school year."

"Scott, first off, I'd really appreciate it if I didn't have to tell you again that I'm going by Carolina now," I said, calm, perfect. "Second, I am going back to my bedroom, where I will get my bag, go over my checklist one last time, and then come back here to have breakfast. I am requesting that you be gone when I return so I may enjoy breakfast before my first day of high school in peace."

He looked down. My dad never cried when he was sad; he just looked down and stopped trying to charm you. I felt bad about making him sad, but then I remembered he ruined my life, and walked back to my room.

After I closed the door to the bedroom, I looked in the mirror. I had been so proud of myself for regaining my composure and speaking to my dad the way I did, I assumed my reflection would show this amazingly powerful young woman. Like a beautiful TV lawyer in a tastefully sexy suit admiring herself before a big case.

But the person in the mirror was just me. Red-eyed and puffy-faced me. Carolina Fisher. Calves too big. Boobs too small. Baggy clothes to hide both. The same shoulder-length brunette bob I'd had since the first grade.

My brother had gotten my father's good looks. I was athletic like my mom. It should have been the opposite. Only now that Heath was in college did his being terrible at sports stop mattering so much to the other boys. And junior high would have been so, so, so much easier if I was popular and all the boys liked me. I wouldn't have liked them, but, well, you know.

I called my mom. She wouldn't pick up, I knew, because she was working, but I felt like leaving a message to let her know she was in trouble. "Mom, I just saw Dad. You and I are going to talk when I get home from school today. I love you, but . . . Okay. Bye."

After going over my checklist, which I had completed six days ago but kept because I liked seeing completed checklists, I walked back toward the kitchen, deciding whether I was going to use "therapy-speak" again on my dad or just yell at him. Thinking, thinking, thinking. I was going to yell. Definitely. It made me a bit excited, even. Which was weird and bad, I know, but it just did.

Except when I got to the kitchen, my dad was gone. Aaah! Aaah! Aaah! I hated him for leaving before I could yell at him. Which was stupid since I had told him to leave. But you know what? You know what? I didn't care that it was stupid. I still hated him.

"WHO WAS THAT GUY WHO SAT NEXT TO YOU?" PEGGY ASKED after we left biology.

"Who?" I said, even though I knew she was talking about the new boy I gave the paper to. Why do people do stuff like that? Ask things like *Who?* even though they know exactly who people are referring to? I'm going to stop doing it. I really am.

"You think he's cute, don't you?" she said. Sometimes it's frustrating not being able to lie to Peggy. It's also, obviously, amazing. No matter what else turns bad in the world, I'll always have Peggy, the *best* best friend ever.

I whispered so nobody in the hall could hear except Peggy. "Yes, but he's a jerk. And a jerk can only be cute for a few days." Then Peggy and I hugged good-bye, and I walked toward my second class.

During Spanish and then third-period literature, I didn't think about the new boy from biology at all. It probably helped that he wasn't in either of those classes, but I was also sure I was back to my normal, focused self.

But then, guess what? We had fourth-period world history together. I made sure to sit in the front center so he wouldn't sit next to me. Because handsome boys always like to sit in the back. But then, guess what? He totally did sit next to me.

Oh.

Wait. A. Minute.

Did this mean he liked me? It must, right? Why else would he sit next to me? What should I do? What should I say? This was impossible. I hated this. I wanted to go to an all-girls school so I could just concentrate on getting good grades and going to a good college and anything besides what a stupid new boy thinks of me!

Wait a minute, Carolina. Silly, silly Carolina.

Obviously he sat by you. Want to know why? Because he needs more sheets of paper. He wants to use you. Some girls get used for sex stuff; I get used for my school supplies.

Without looking at him, I tore two sheets (a neat tear—I hate jagged sheets of paper) and put them on his desk. Only I did it just as he was putting down his own notebook. A new black one.

Oh, my face must have turned sooo red. I felt sooo stupid. I looked like such a clueless geek, right? I AM a clueless geek. Never interact with any boy, ever, ever, ever again. Ever. But then the new boy said, "You're awesome. Thanks. But I went to the school store after biology so I could pay you back." Then he slid back the two sheets I just gave him PLUS two more empty ones to replace the ones I gave him during first period.

Did I hear that right? He called me awesome, right? He totally did. My gosh. This definitely meant he liked me, right? I wanted to throw up. I wanted to move seats. I WANTED to say something back. I really did. But it needed to sound cool, fun, smart, amazing, and like something he would remember the rest of his life, and my brain couldn't think of anything. Nothing. So I just smiled. It wasn't even a good smile. I'm sure it looked like a mean smile. Like a Shannon Shunton smile. Which is the worst smile ever. The worst.

And then the teacher, Mr. Rivard, started talking, so I couldn't even whisper something simple back like *thank you*. Oh, why couldn't I have just said *thank you*? That would have been so nice if I just could have said that. It would have made everything great; it would have saved everything from being ruined.

Mr. Rivard talked for the whole class because that is what teachers do. Which I usually like in history, especially teachers who get so excited about all the stories from the past that they pace and even sweat a little bit. Mr. Rivard was definitely sweating too, but I couldn't hear a word he was saying. I mean, I was writing a bunch of notes down, so I must have sort of heard it, I suppose, right? But it had to be only the tiny part of my brain that tells my hand what to do, because what

I was really thinking about was what I would say to the new boy at the end of class to make up for my stupid, snobby smile that I totally didn't mean but was now the only thing he knew about me. Yes, he knew I gave him the sheets of paper, but that was sooo long ago. The terrible smile was the last thing he saw, and he was going to hate me just like all the boys in eighth grade.

Maybe that's why I was obsessing about him. Which was so against my rules to NEVER OBSESS ABOUT BOYS and so unlike me. But, see, he was new, you know? He didn't know anyone from eighth grade. He didn't know that all the boys didn't like me or talk to me. He didn't know there was, like, this secret rule that you couldn't like Carolina Fisher.

But I totally messed that up.

Which was fine. Yes, Carolina, it's fine. It's better this way. School. Soccer. Peggy. No distractions. I was fine. It was fine. Everything was amazing. Always. Definitely.

4

Trevor follows orders

"WHAT UP, TREV," MY COUSIN HENRY SAID AS I SAT NEXT to him and some other freshman football players at lunch. Henry is my uncle Hank's son. He's a year younger and always looked up to me when we were kids, even though we'd only see each other once a year. But now we were in the same grade. At his school. Where he knew everyone. Was friends with everyone. And I was this new, strange kid who everyone probably labeled as the boy with the mom who tried to kill herself. My dad said Henry promised his parents he wouldn't tell anyone, but who knows. You know? The two times I had seen Henry since we'd moved to Riverbend, he'd acted strange. Like I didn't really belong there. Which I didn't. I don't belong anywhere.

Henry turned to his friends and said, "Guys, this is my cousin Trevor. But his last name is Santos, not McCarthy. My dad and his mom are brother and sister. So that's why his last name is Mexican and not American." What Henry said was true. I still wanted to beat his face in. In Los Angeles, I was half white and nobody cared. Here, I'd be half Mexican and everyone would care even if they pretended they didn't. What nobody knew unless they met my dad was that he acts whiter than most white people. His name is Robert Santos. He was born Roberto but dropped the "o." He's a sellout like that.

"So why aren't you on the team? Are you not a good athlete like Henry?" one of the kids asked.

"I'm okay," I said. Truth was, I was better. Henry knew it but just sat silently. "My dad said he might call the coach and see if I can play even though you started practice already." Why was I saying crap I didn't want to say?

"No way Coach Pollina would go for that, Trev. First game is Friday. Sorry," Henry said, not looking at me.

"No worries." Whatever. I wished this day was over. Just wanted to go home and sleep.

"Have any hot girls in your classes?" another kid asked. His name was Jake. He was over six feet tall. Maybe six feet wide too. But baby-faced like a fifth grader.

"Yeah, I suppose," I said back.

"You like one already?" Jake said. "Who? Who? Who? Tell us and we'll let you know if it's okay."

Don't say anything, Trevor. But I couldn't listen to my own self. I suck. "She's brunette. Really pretty."

"What's her name?" Jake asked. Now all twelve freshman football players were looking at me.

"I don't know her name. She's cool." Though she ignored me in history. Probably knows how beautiful she is and doesn't want to be nice to every guy who tries to talk to her. Girls are always playing games like that.

"What class do you have with her?"

"Why's it matter?" I asked.

"Because how else are we supposed to know who she is?"

"Biology and history, but that probably won't help—"

"Carrie Fisher," another kid said. He was wearing a white hoodie, and I think people called him Licker. He was in my history class. Figured that out too late. He added, "I heard she wants to be called Carolina now."

"The Princess!" Jake screeched, cackling like some gremlin jumping in gold coins.

"Carrie Fisher's a loser, Trev," Henry said. Matter-of-fact. "You can't like her."

"Oh. Okay," I said. Just accepting Henry's order as if he were my goddamn lord and master. What was my problem? This was my idiot younger cousin who used to throw crybaby hissy fits when his parents put vegetables on his plate at Thanksgiving. This was why I hated school! Makes you think crap matters when it doesn't! Makes you listen to idiots! Makes you act like someone you aren't! Get me out of here!

But I didn't say anything. I didn't go anywhere. Just sat there nodding, or maybe I didn't move at all. My brain was turning dark. Hot. Ready to explode and blow up the entire school. But my body must have been still. So still. I must have seemed so calm. Nobody can tell anything about anyone. We are all a big mystery to one another.

Jake kept saying stuff like, "He thought the Princess was cute! She's so ugly! So ugly!"

Then another kid said, "Carrie and Peggy Darry are lesbians. Everyone knows that."

So Licker added, "Yeah, I know a girl who saw them making out in the bathroom last year."

Jake felt it was a good time to say, "Has anyone seen Peggy Darry this year? Her tits got huge!" And the whole table leaned in and smirked, whispering just how huge.

Henry then said, "I might pretend to like Peggy just so I can feel her up."

And that's when I decided I hated my little cousin. But I didn't say anything. Because he was the only person I knew at this crappy new school in this crappy new town. Him and Carolina Fisher. But I didn't really know her. Just that she was cool to me. But not cool enough for me.

5

Carolina makes a vow

So I TOTALLY RAN OUT OF HISTORY CLASS THE MOMENT the bell rang, without looking at the new boy, because I knew he hated me for not saying thank you. I didn't blame him—I would hate me if I were him. I mean, I did hate me, and I *was* me.

Fifth period was lunch. I was supposed to meet Peggy in front of the cafeteria and wasn't really paying attention to anything except getting there when this really, really, really weird thing happened. So weird! This boy leaned up against the lockers like he had been waiting there all day, and said, "Hey, you." I looked at him. I wish I hadn't, but I did.

I shouldn't even call this boy a boy, because he was definitely not a freshman. His face had scruff on it and he wore a thin black tie. Who wears a tie to school if they don't have to? He wasn't handsome, not really ugly either, but with his wide chin and long forehead he kind of looked like he should have lived one hundred years ago. Like on that HBO show about gangsters from the 1920s. He should have had a toothpick in his mouth, but he didn't. "You're the freshman who wrote that article in the *Riverbend Review* last spring?" the scruffy boy with a tie on said. He didn't blink when he looked at me. His eyes looked very mature and very fast. Like he was taking photographs with them. Like he was having dirty thoughts. Gross. I wanted to run, but instead—

I said, "Yeah," even though I should have said no. But I don't lie. Almost never, anyway. Because I *had* written an article for the *Riverbend Review*. The local paper had asked me, after the junior high principal recommended that they ask me, to write an article about what it meant to be a kid in Riverbend. Except all the horrible stuff with my dad had just started, so all I could write about was how kids didn't get to be kids very long in the world now. Obviously, I didn't talk about my dad directly. Just that every secret about sex and life was just a Google search away. That sort of thing. I didn't think anyone had read the article besides my mom and brother. Especially not some weird man-boy.

"My name is Alexander Taylor. I'm a junior. You interest me." He talked slowly, so intense, like he was trying to brainwash me. Then he said, "Your name is Carrie Fisher, right?"

"Carolina Fisher."

"Interesting. You're too young for me right now, but maybe I'll say hello again in a few months to see if you haven't been turned into one of the masses. Until then, Miss Carolina." And then he nodded at me and walked away.

I wanted to take a shower just for having been near him, and I told myself I would never speak to or look at Alexander Taylor again. Such a weirdo.

I MET PEGGY JUST AS WE PLANNED, AND WE WENT INSIDE the cafeteria, which had puke-yellow walls, and found a table near the food line, which is where the freshmen sit because it smells like dead animals and soap. Only seniors are allowed to drive off campus, so there were, like, nine hundred people stuffed inside, and it was sooo loud, like everyone in the room was screaming at the exact same time. Groups like yearbook club and chess club met in classrooms during lunch, and some people had lunch sixth period, so I'm probably exaggerating about there being nine hundred people. And I promised not to exaggerate. I know. But sometimes it's just how it FEELS, even if it's not how it is, you know?

Seven other freshman soccer players joined us at our table, also just as we planned, and then some other freshman girls that we didn't know too, but they sat at the end and just looked at their phones. Soccer season wasn't until the spring in Illinois, but we'd all gotten close during summer camp practices. Peggy and this girl Kendra, who was the best goalie I had ever played with, were both on the fall club team with me, and our mothers were going to rotate driving us to practice.

I spent the rest of lunch talking mostly to Kendra. She was quiet, and new like the new boy, except she was at summer camp, so she wasn't new to us. She's black. Or African American. I wish I could ask her what's the better way to describe her. Or I wish we were all the same color. The best, however, would be if we were all a million different colors. The best. I know it's impossible, but I think sometimes you have to think about impossible things.

My dad would always tell me I was a "thinking addict," because I would ask him questions about everything. And then he would give me an answer, and I would ask two more and then three more. Even when I realized that he didn't know any more, I kept asking because I wanted him to go find out and tell me because not understanding drove me crazy. I used to love when my dad called me that because he

31

said it with such pride. He said it was our greatest bond. He said it was how he knew I was his daughter. But now that I hate my father, I kind of hate that I'm a thinking addict.

Near the end of the lunch period, Katherine—you know, Peggy's whack-job sister—stomped over to our table, pointed at Peggy and me, and said, "You two, come here."

I really wanted to say: Nobody tells me what to do! But I didn't. I always do what people say, sort of, which is pathetic. I want to change this about myself, but I didn't know if I could start right then. So I just got up and followed Peggy, who followed Katherine to a lunch table on the other side of the cafeteria. Shannon Shunton was sitting there with the four other most popular eighth graders. Emma Goldberg. Jean Booker. Raina Bethington. And Wanda Chan, who used to be a geek like me until she started to dress like a slut. You know, super-short skirts and super-high boots. I suppose all these girls were the popular freshman girls now. Does it work like that? You just get to carry your membership from one grade to another? Even one school to another? DO NOT CARE ABOUT THIS! This is dumb. I just wanted to go back to the soccer table. I thought I was going to faint standing there, waiting for Shannon Shunton to yell at me or not look at me or something just as mean. My whole head was turning into bumblebees that wanted to fly out of my eyeballs and kill me.

Even though I really did feel sick and about to die, I ALSO felt, and this is so lame to admit, that I was actually cool for just being there, near Katherine and Shannon and all of them. That just by being included in their little lunch table atmosphere, I was, like, one of them. Anointed cool. And I thought people could see us there and would think we were special. So LAME, right? But I couldn't help it. It's just what I felt.

Katherine said to Shannon and the others, "Peggy's my sister, so if you want to come to our parties and for me to introduce you to junior guys, you have to be friends with her. And Carrie's her best friend. So you have to be friends with her too. One more thing. Call them Marguerite and Carolina. Okay?" Katherine pronounced my name like the state (Caroliiina) and not how I like it (Caroleena), but I didn't correct her because I didn't want her to kill me.

All the girls nodded, except Shannon Shunton.

"SHANNON!" her sister Elizabeth yelled from down the table, where she sat with a pack of junior girls, who all looked like they should be in college or working at the Macy's perfume department. Elizabeth and Katherine were best friends. Probably because they were both very pretty, popular, and liked to yell so loud it made your body convulse.

Shannon Shunton finally smiled and said, "Great, can't wait." What she really meant, obviously, is "Not great, could wait forever," but Peggy said thanks so I did too, and then there was the most awkward moment. Like, were we supposed to sit down and start talking? Or leave? Or make plans? Or exchange phone numbers? Or just wait in silence? Which is what we did, until Katherine yelled, "Stop standing around like freaks! Go to class already." Peggy and I quickly scooted back and made for the exit. Then Katherine must have felt bad because she started yelling at Shannon, Emma, Jean, Raina, and Wanda too.

"That was . . ." Peggy said as we left the cafeteria. For the breath it took her to finish her sentence, I wanted her to say, "That was stupid; let's totally not be friends with them," but then I realized how much I liked the idea of other people knowing we were friends with Shannon Shunton. Which is sick. Just sick. So sick. Why am I so sick? Then Peggy finished her sentence, ". . . so amazing." "Amazing" was Peggy's favorite word. It was mine too. I want to use it less, though. Feels too immature, I think. Don't you?

Except then I said, "It *was* amazing," and giggled, and then I saw Kendra walking by herself to class and thought we should make Shannon be friends with Kendra too. But I stopped thinking about Kendra when I saw the new boy walking down the hall with Henry McCarthy, who dated Shannon Shunton in seventh grade and was not very attractive, but he was still the most popular boy all through junior high.

Not that I was surprised. Obviously, the new boy would already be friends with the popular boys. Obviously. Obviously. Obviously.

Wait a minute. I might be popular soon too, right? So that means the new boy and I could . . .

But then I stopped thinking these stupid things. Sooo stupid. High school and popularity is sooo stupid. I want to be grown-up and mature and never have to stress about this relationship stuff ever again. Ever. So I made a vow to think only about school the rest of the day. I'm usually pretty disciplined when I make a vow.

SIXTH PERIOD WAS ALGEBRA. HAVING A BORING CLASS, LIKE math, after lunch is the worst. Even though I'm a really good student, I really am, it's sooo hard not to fall asleep after lunch. My dad says they should give nap periods at school, and at work for adults. I told him naps are for little kids. But my head kept nodding during algebra anyway.

Seventh period was health class, which you only had to take for one semester. It was an elective, but only sort of since you had to take it by the end of sophomore year. So I just decided to take it right away. Why postpone things? The teacher, Mrs. Maya, went over the syllabus and said yes, we would be talking about sex, and then everybody giggled, even the sophomores in our class. And then she said, "I'm even going to use the words 'penis' and 'vagina.' " And then everyone laughed, but not the sophomores as much. And then she said, "Let's all say those words now so we can get the giggles out on the first day. First, let's all say 'penis.' One, two, three," and half the class said "penis" and half the class just laughed. I said it, obviously, because I'm mature for my age. Sort of. Then Mrs. Maya counted down and everyone said "vagina," even the still-giggling freshmen.

Well, everyone except the new boy. He didn't laugh or giggle or say the words. Luckily, I had not thought of him since I made my vow. I barely even noticed he was in the class. That's just a fact. I'm glad I'm not going to be one of those girls that goes boy bonkers and thinks dating is more important than school because it would be embarrassing to be in health class with him and have to talk about sex.

When the bell rang, I decided to look toward the new boy because, well, just because. But he ignored me, probably because by now he's figured out he's too cool to even be my friend.

Which is fine. Totally. Because I don't care. I don't! Really.

EIGHTH PERIOD WAS GYM CLASS FOR ATHLETES. SO IF YOUR sport is in season, like football players in the fall, you just go to the locker room and head out to the field. Since girls' soccer isn't until spring, Kendra, Peggy, and I had club team Monday, Wednesday, and Friday and then study hall on Tuesday and Thursday.

My mom was waiting for the three of us in front of school to drive us to club practice in Highland Park. I totally forgot I was mad at her about having Dad spend the night when I saw her. Maybe that's because I just needed to tell someone about my first day of school.

After practice, my mom drove us back home, dropping off Kendra first since her house was farthest from mine. She lived in the nicest area of Riverbend, in a development called Covered Bridges. It was for rich people. The houses were really big, and the streets looked newly paved even though Covered Bridges was built almost five years ago.

Once Kendra was gone, my phone beeped with a text. It was from Peggy, who was in the back seat. For a second I wondered why she didn't just speak actual words, but then I read it:

PEGGY

My parents are going to the lake this weekend. Katherine is throwing a big party at our house Friday and said we get to come!

I glanced back. She was so excited that I texted back:

ME

Yay!!

Even though the idea of going to a big high school party with upperclassmen made me queasy, stressed, and miserable. Peggy and I never got invited to parties in junior high. Obviously, we wanted to be invited; who wants to not be invited? But guess what? We usually spent the weekend watching movies or talking about a hundred million things, and never once did I think we would have more fun at some party. But now that Peggy's sister went to the same school and made us be friends with Shannon Shunton, we would have to do things like go to parties. Being cool would be hard and not always fun, I imagined.

Then I wondered if the new boy would come to the party.

No, I didn't.

Okay, yes, I did. But I hate that I did. I hate that I broke my vow. Nothing is going as I planned it. Nothing. It's all ruined.

Possibly.

6

Trevor figures it all out

EVEN THOUGH I DESPISED HENRY AND SORT OF DESPISED myself for agreeing to never like Carolina Fisher, my brain must have followed what he said since I didn't think about her again until I saw her in seventh-period health class.

Mrs. Maya had organized the room in a circle, boy-girl-boy-girl. The way it worked out, we were across the room from each other. Carolina didn't look at me the entire class. Me? I didn't look anywhere else. Like barely blinked, I bet. I was trying to figure out how I could have been wrong about her being pretty. I must have been, since all the guys were so sure. I didn't care if Carolina caught me staring. Maybe I wanted her to. Now that I knew everyone thought she was a loser, I didn't worry about her judging me. Did I just really think that? Maybe I'm an asshole just like Henry. I hope not. This world sucks. It does. But I don't want to make it any worse than it already is.

So the longer I looked at Carolina, the more some really deep stuff started to come together in my head. Like understanding-the-universe deep. I don't even know why or how but then it all came apart again, and I wanted to run a hundred miles until it came back to me. But I didn't. I doubt I even stopped staring at Carolina for more than a few moments. And even though all the really deep stuff vanished from my brain, one thing remained: I think I was starting to understand why someone like Carolina would be so unpopular.

First off, she was smart. Probably really smart. The junior high I went to in Los Angeles (which actually wasn't in Los Angeles but in this small town called La Cañada Flintridge near Pasadena) was super elitist; every parent there was a successful doctor, lawyer, or businessperson. So the cool kids were just as smart or smarter than the not-so-cool kids. But Riverbend was more like the cliché you see on television: the athletes and partiers were popular, the smart kids were geeks, and everybody else fit somewhere in between.

Second thing, she was so serious. More serious than my dad even. Just watching her in health class, while everyone else was laughing at Mrs. Maya talking about sex, she was writing down every note, not smiling once. She had the look of someone who thought everyone else was doing pointless stuff and she was the only one doing important stuff. It was awesome, her giving me those sheets of paper in biology, but to be so caught up in school and being the perfect student that she couldn't even say one word to me in history? Not that awesome. And probably intimidating to most people, especially the ones making the popular-kid lists.

Third and last thing: Carolina didn't wear any makeup, she wore these green square glasses during class, and she dressed like my seven-year-old sister. Either she didn't want to look like high school girls did on TV or she didn't watch TV at all. So unless you gazed at her like I did, you might think she was plain or boring-looking. Maybe Henry, Jake, and the rest of the freshman football guys at lunch weren't as blind as I initially thought. Maybe they just weren't looking at her close enough. Because Carolina Fisher was beautiful. She just was. If experts on faces, with no bias against being smart or serious or not wearing makeup or not being popular, were to come to Riverbend High School and pick the prettiest face, I'd bet every dollar I ever make that Carolina Fisher would be number one. Everything just looked like it was in the right place, and it glowed. Her eyes were so deep. Golden brown. And her eyebrows were so dark, and eyelashes so long. Each eye was like a mini-painting. That sounds lame. But it's just what I saw. And then she had these cute brown freckles, and this one bigger mole high on her left cheek. Someday, she would look at those girls on TV, realize she was just as pretty or prettier, and learn how to use makeup to highlight what was there naturally. Then everyone who ever saw her would see what I was seeing right now.

My dad has a younger brother, my uncle Ernesto (he's trying to be an actor), who just had his ten-year high school reunion. He told me there was a girl nobody paid attention to back in high school, even though everyone knew there was something special about her. Well, he said, when she showed up at the reunion, nobody could look at anyone else, even the married guys. My uncle Ernesto told me to look out for that girl, because every high school has at least one, and the guy smart enough to find her will be the one guy the girl could fall for.

When health class began, I planned to talk to Carolina again. Just to show her that I didn't care that my cousin Henry said she was a loser. (She didn't know Henry said that, but that's not the point.) But after staring at her the whole period, fixated on who she was every second, I started to think that Carolina was the most beautiful girl in the world, not just the school—the world—and that she was my soul mate and insane things like that, so then I couldn't say anything to her because it was too damn important to say just anything.

She sorta turned my way as she walked out of class, but I looked the other direction. I hoped she thought I was ignoring her. I wanted her to feel insecure and unstable, like I felt. But there's just no way she did. She was perfect, wasn't she? I wanted to be above all these petty teenage social games, but I wasn't. I was a total fake. Weak. Listening to Henry like a brainless follower. But Carolina was above it for real. Didn't care what she wore, didn't care what people thought.

Then, out of nowhere, I got mad at her. Carolina had everything figured out and never had a moment of doubt about who she was or what she wanted in her life. Screw her.

MY LAST PERIOD OF THE DAY WAS GYM CLASS. THE TEACHER, Mr. Pasquini, said that the scheduling office must have screwed up because only kids who were on sports teams should have gym for eighth period. (My gut says my dad marked that I'd be in a sport when he registered me.) Mr. Pasquini said I could go to the office and try to switch my classes around so I could take gym earlier in the day or I could join a sports team. Most teams were already set, as tryouts took place before classes started. There were only two teams that let everyone join: football and cross-country running. Mr. Pasquini told me I could go talk to Coach Pollina about joining football or I could join the cross-country team. Part of me wanted to join football to shove it in Henry's face, not just since he said I wouldn't be able to join but also to show the other guys I was pretty good. But then that sounded like so much effort, and so petty. And clichéd.

Cross-country was for losers. So no way was I doing that. Not losers. I don't want to label like that. But let's just say it's not for me.

So I went to the front office and said I needed to change my schedule around. The lady rolled her eyes. Whatever. Adults always take their crap out on kids.

When she came back and showed me the new schedule, gym was where history was, history moved to biology's spot, biology to health's, and now health was last period. I stared at the schedule a long time. The lady even asked me if everything was okay.

I didn't tell her yes. I didn't say no either. What was going through my mind was that I would now have no classes with Carolina Fisher. None. If I had gotten this schedule before today, I would have never met her and it would have been no big deal. But now to move everything . . . to not have any classes with her . . . I don't know. I didn't like it.

Crap.

Life is pointless. I've said this, but even I have to delude myself once in a while into believing it's not one hundred percent pointless one hundred percent of the time or I would just melt away. So maybe one of those few times where life had a point (or at least I wanted it to have a point) was when I was put in Carolina Fisher's biology class, on the first day of school, with no backpack, and she slid two sheets of paper to me without me even asking.

I don't know. I don't even know what I'm talking about anymore. Who cares? I should just switch the classes. Right? She's a snob, thinks she's too good for me, all that. Right?

"Mr. Santos, is the new schedule okay?" the front-office lady asked again.

7

Carolina gets a request

"CAROLINA," MY MOM SAID AS SHE STOPPED THE CAR ON the side of the road even though we were still a block away from our house.

Before she even said another word, I started crying. Why would I start crying? I didn't even know what she was going to say! Maybe my first day was more stressful than I realized, but THEN I realized I knew exactly what she was going to say. I just did.

"I've told your dad he can move back in."

"But, Mommy," I started. Mommy? I never call her that anymore! Wake up and grow up, Carolina! "Mom, he hurt you so much. He doesn't deserve you."

"Don't say that. He's been a very good dad to you. He loves you and your brother so much. He's just made some mistakes. We all make mistakes."

"But some mistakes shouldn't be forgiven!" I screamed this, without meaning to, but I really needed my mom to understand.

"Calm down," she said, "calm down, okay? If he ever hurt you in any way, I wouldn't forgive him. But—"

"He did hurt me!" Then my crying just exploded. I didn't even know who I was—it was like I was a tiny monster baby who couldn't speak, only scream and cry. But I *could* speak, so I did, but I couldn't stop crying. "He hurt me because he hurt you! And I know he'll do it again and you'll be even sadder and I'll have to take care of you again and who will take care of me?"

Then I stopped talking and my whole chest just heaved up and down. I couldn't breathe. But I could, obviously—it just felt like I was going to suffocate from so much craziness pounding under my skin.

Then my mom said, "Okay. Okay. I won't let him move in."

Then she didn't say anything. I didn't either. My breathing was almost normal again. I wiped my snotty, teary face with my sweaty soccer shirt. It was drenched.

"He did ask . . . to bring dinner over tonight. Is that okay?"

My face wanted to cry some more, but I was too tired. I didn't want to see my dad, I didn't, but I didn't want to make my mom's life harder. She's fragile, you know? So I nodded yes, it was okay. Then my head, without me even telling it to, fell across the seat onto her chest. She laid her chin on the top of my head.

My mom works as a nurse in the emergency room at the Leary County Hospital. When I was eight, my dad lost his job at Northwestern University, and for a while my mom supported the whole family. How could a man hurt a woman who supported him like that? The worst part is that we were all so happy when he got a new job at Northern Illinois University, not knowing the new job would ruin everything. See, NIU was almost two hours away, so some days he would stay the night near the school. And eventually he stayed more than he used to. I tried not to think about it, but my mom kept getting sadder and sadder. On nights he didn't come home, she would make me food but not eat any herself, then watch TV in bed when she used to read next to me while I did my homework.

When my brother, Heath, came home for spring break last year (he goes to college in Colorado), my dad made sure to be home the whole week—because he really does love his kids, I think. But my mom couldn't turn off her depression anymore, even though she kept saying everything was fine. Heath talked to my dad, who then talked to my mom, who then talked to me, and I was the one who cried the most and yelled at my dad, who couldn't say anything to me, couldn't even look me in the eyes, and I told him to leave and never come back, and he left, even though my mom never officially kicked him out.

WHEN WE PULLED INTO THE DRIVEWAY, MY DAD'S CAR WAS already parked in his old spot in the garage. My mom squeezed my hand before we went inside and said, "I'll tell him he can't spend the night. A really big favor to me would be if you were nice to him, Carolina. For me. Please?"

I didn't say yes, and I didn't even nod, but I decided, maybe, I would try.

Then we walked inside, where my dad had set the table, which he never did, and put out Indian food, which he picked up a lot before I kicked him out. When he saw me, he sung my name: "Carolina!" Hearing him, and seeing him there making the house warm before we got home, and singing Carolina not Carrie, and my mom smiling even though she didn't want to smile, made me smile even though I didn't want to either.

While I went to the bathroom my mom must have talked to my dad about not staying over. Because when I came back to the kitchen, he was not quite as jumpy/singing happy as when we first came home. But he tried to pretend he was and kept hugging us while we ate, and I told him about my first day of school. About the classes, not about Shannon Shunton or the new boy. My dad thinks popularity is even dumber than I do, so he would just make me feel dumb for caring or even mentioning it, probably, or convince me to not become friends with Shannon, which I sort of wanted to do, even though it *is* dumb.

As I talked, he especially hugged my mom, petting her almost. And this made her giggle, and it was cute, but, I don't know, I didn't want her to fall in love with him again. But then I realized she probably never fell out of love with him, so she couldn't help it, and I decided to not think about it. And just let them be for tonight. They were both grown-ups, right? Well, at least my mom was. I'm kidding. I can be funny, even though I'm smart.

My dad did the dishes and then he got ready to leave, even though he looked like a sad dog who didn't want to go in his cage.

"Bye, Scott. Thank you for dinner," I said, and then hugged him for only a second.

"Carolina, I really enjoyed hearing about your first day of school," he said, and I could tell he would keep talking so I went to get my laptop from my bedroom, leaving my mom to say good-bye to my dad alone. When I came back and he was gone, the house felt so hollow, like a tornado had sucked out a whole room.

I set up my computer in the living room. For the first time in a long time, my mom got a book and read next to me on the couch.

After I finished my math homework, which I always do first because it's so dull, I gave myself five minutes to look at Facebook, which some people say isn't cool. But I think people are just trying to be cool by saying it's not cool because everyone still uses it. Maybe in, like, the future when cars fly nobody will use it, but they probably will.

So after I signed in, I saw a new friend request.

From Trevor Santos.

Who I totally didn't know.

Wait a minute.

Until I clicked on his page.

And saw it was the new boy.

Wait a minute!

THE new boy.

Oh. My. Gosh.

8

Trevor runs even though it's pointless

"Who coaches cross-country?" I asked Mr. Pasquini, the gym teacher, after I had the front-office lady switch my schedule back. Just in case. Right?

"Well, that happens to be me," Mr. Pasquini said. One side of his long-bearded mouth lifted up into a grin. He was a strange dude.

"And it's just running, right?"

"Oh no, young man, cross-country is not merely running. It is pushing the limits of the human spirit."

Whatever. Don't overthink this, Trevor. So I said, "Okay, I'll run."

Pasquini did another freaky grin thing.

I didn't have any running stuff with me, so Coach Pasquini lent me some old gym-class T-shirt and shorts. It was as disgusting as it sounds. And dorky, epically dorky, which I tried not to care about. But I just did. What made it worse was that after I changed, I joined the team out on the steps of the gym and discovered that not only was every boy on the team a total outcast or nerd, but the girls' team practiced with us too. I don't even know what to say about that.

Two years ago, I'm quarterback of my eighth-grade football team, I have a pretty girlfriend named Dakota (who was super nice; a bit superficial, but super nice and super pretty), my mom at least pretends to be happy, I'm basically the king of junior high, and I'm in California, which is where everything happens. Now I'm in smelly, old, torn gym clothes that are riding up my butt crack and strangling my neck, I'm on the cross-country team with girls and geeks, my mom wishes she was dead, and I'm stuck in Bumblefuck, Illinois.

And I swore I wouldn't be judgmental anymore, except I feel like judging everybody, so I feel like crap for that on top of everything.

"Gentlemen! Ladies! Gather up!" Pasquini hollered like he thought he was some kind of Civil War general. "We have a new warrior in our midst! You treat him with respect. You encourage him. You challenge him to be the best runner and human he can be. Stand up, Trevor."

Please just kill me. But I stood up and Pasquini led the team in applause, which only made me feel like a bigger idiot. "It's Murder Monday, runners. Murder Monday. Five miles. Down Kirby Street, up Jeske Ave, back down Fridell Road, and then through the practice fields. Up! Up! You go! You go hard! You never stop moving, you never cut corners, and you never stop fighting! Go! Go! GO!"

And then the lot of us—probably forty kids, from freshmen to seniors—just started running. I had no idea where the hell any of these roads were, so I just followed the pack. Not that I would have wanted to lead even if I did know where I was going. Because I know sports are just another way to pacify the masses. One hundred percent. Watch 'em. Play 'em. Either way, they exist to distract people from their empty lives. You think you're better than someone because your

NFL team won or you beat someone in a five-mile run? Then you're an idiot. Why are we so competitive? What's wrong with people? Why can't people just be chill? It's because everyone is insecure. So pathetic.

Except I couldn't stop myself from wanting to stay near the front, just behind the leaders. Want to know why? Because I'm more pathetic than anyone. I know it's all BS, yet I can't stop myself. Moments like this, where I just have to stay at the front, when I can't let anyone see me as weak, even if it's a bunch of strangers, remind me how weak I am, even if I'm fooling everyone else into thinking the opposite.

By the time we made the turn onto the forest preserve bike path, there were only five of us in the lead pack. The senior captain named Randy Chung, who had a shaved head and tattoos of Bible verses on his arms. A quiet freshman named Conchita Piniayo with thick black hair down to the middle of her back. And the other senior captain, Craig Billings, who looked like he should be related to the Kennedys.

But it was clear to me that the best runner was this junior named Todd Kishkin. He was no taller than five six, with rounded shoulders almost pointing to the ground and a beak for a nose. If I had seen him in the hall, I would have pegged him as a violin player or a math club president who had never seen a sport on TV, let alone played one. But this kid could run. My chest was burning, my legs were going numb, and this Todd Kishkin looked like he was just floating above the ground. When we turned down Fridell Road, he said, as if getting off an elevator, "I'll see you guys in a bit." And, pow, he went into another gear and out of sight.

I wanted to ask Craig about him, but I didn't have the energy to speak. Eventually Randy and Craig pulled away from Conchita and me, and I made sure to stay side by side with her. Couldn't lose to a girl. But then, as we crossed the practice fields, just when I should've been able to outsprint her since my legs were twice as long, I had nothing left. She cruised ahead as if I were cemented in place. Everything hurt so much. I wanted to drop this pointless sport, get another gym period, forget about Carolina Fisher anyway. Who does this crap? Run five miles for no reason? This isn't a sport! It's torture!

But I never walked. Never. Might as well have, but still. By the time I got to the steps of the gym where we started, two sophomores had caught me. Then a half dozen others. Didn't care. Couldn't care. I collapsed to my knees, hard into the gravel of the cement. If you had asked me in that moment if I would ever, ever run with the cross-country team again, I would have said, "Fuck no."

But Pasquini walked fast toward me, mumbling, "I thought so, I thought so." Then he crouched down because I was on my hands and knees, dry heaving, and lifted up my chin and said, "You don't know what the hell you're doing, but when you do learn, you might be dangerous." He was giving me a compliment in his way. It felt good. I wished it didn't. But it did.

I was planning on taking the late bus home, but when I finally had the energy to stand up, and after Pasquini had given the team a cornball pep speech, I saw my mom's Infiniti SUV waiting in the parking lot. Unfortunately, it had not driven itself.

9

Carolina will stop boy obsessing tomorrow

"I-HAVE-TO-CALL-PEGGY-I'LL-BE-RIGHT-BACK," I SAID TO MY mom exactly one second after I saw the request from Trevor Santos. I went to the basement laundry room because my room was too close to the living room and no way did I want her to hear my conversation.

"He sent me a friend request!" I said, except I probably screamed it, as soon as Peggy answered. Why was I screaming this? This is not a big deal. Not. At. All.

"Who?" she said.

"The new boy!" I screamed again. I was out of control. I didn't know who the heck I was anymore. "His name is Trevor Santos."

"I can't hear you, hold on." In the background, I could hear Katherine yelling at their mom. They were always yelling at each other. Peggy found someplace quiet, then said, "So what's his name?"

"Trevor Santos."

"That's a sexy name," she said.

"I know," I said, even though I hadn't thought about it and didn't even know what would make a name sexy. "What should I do?" my voice felt almost normal. I was starting to calm down instead of acting like some hysterical girl in love with a boy band.

"About what?" said Peggy, who was having a "space-out night," which sometimes happened. Especially when her sister and mom were yelling a lot.

"About the friend request he sent, Peggy."

"Accept it, right?"

"But . . . Okay. Yeah. But . . ." Should I admit it? I had to. Even though it completely ruined my vow. Just ruined it. So I said, "What if I like him?"

"Then for sure accept it, right?"

"But . . . maybe I should wait."

"Maybe you should," Peggy said, not really listening. Or listening but not really thinking. Peggy was the greatest friend, except sometimes she just told you what you wanted to hear instead of real advice. So I changed the subject to talk about homework, and then about her sister's party, and then we said good-bye. After I hung up, I really wanted a new friend. Not to replace Peggy, but a second friend, so I could have someone else to call when something so major was happening, like now. With Trevor Santos. Maybe his name *was* sexy.

I said it out loud—"Trevor Santos"—but I felt like the silliest person ever and couldn't bear to spend one more second alone with my own brain.

So I called Kendra, because I had her number, and because I talked to her the second most today.

"Hello," she said, her voice very quiet, like always.

"Kendra, it's Carolina."

"Hi."

"So what did you think of our first day of high school?"

"It was good." Kendra spoke her words really fast, like she didn't like the way they tasted and wanted to get them out of her mouth as soon as she possibly could.

"You ever have a boyfriend?"

She didn't say anything. I almost said my mom was calling, which would be a lie, it's just that Kendra was not easy to talk to like Peggy, even when Peggy was being space-out Peggy. But then she finally said, "No, I've never had a boyfriend. Have you ever had one?" Which was the exact question I wanted her to ask.

"No. Never. But this boy I met today. I might like him. And he sent me a Facebook friend request. What do you think that means?"

"He likes you."

"Really?"

"Yes."

"REALLY?"

She was quiet again. I felt stupid for getting so excited. Which I should. Because it was stupid. The stupidest. Definitely. Then Kendra said, "Why are you so excited?" And I felt one hundred times more stupid, until Kendra somehow said the most amazing thing ever. "It's just that you're so pretty. Lots of boys must have liked you before."

I couldn't breathe for a second, and my eyes got watery, not sad but happy, so not tears, just so emotional because no had ever called me pretty before. I mean, my mom and dad had, and my brother, Heath, but no one else, ever. Even though Kendra was a girl, it's almost better to come from a girl, because boys can be morons a lot, but girls are usually very smart. Then I said, because I didn't want her to think I was conceited, "You're so pretty too." And this was TOTALLY true! You should see Kendra. She has skin with no pimples, and lips that old actresses have to pay for, and big, bright eyes, like they could be white suns, but smaller. Duh. But I worried she wouldn't believe me because I said it right after she said it to me, and then I worried she thought I liked girls in a romantic way, and then I was silent.

But she said, fast but nice, "Thank you," and then changed the subject, which was great, by saying, "So are you going to accept his friend request?"

"Yes. I don't know. Maybe. What do you think?"

"If you just want to be his friend, do it right away. But if you want to be more than friends, then you could wait. Boys like girls more when you make them wait. That's what my dad says. But it makes sense."

"It DOES make sense," I said, and I was sooo happy I called Kendra, and was sooo excited to have a new friend, especially one who was really smart and gave good advice.

"Have you done the history homework yet?" Kendra asked, which was great, because it let us talk about school and not just boys, but then we talked about boys again, and Kendra said she had only kissed three boys, which was two more than I'd kissed. And the one I kissed was in sixth grade when kids still had birthday parties, and I was still invited, and we played Spin the Bottle, even though it was a shoe not a bottle, and I kissed Nicholas Durant, who was not very cute. Everyone calls him Licker now, and I don't even know why. It was fine that it was my first kiss, I just wish it wasn't my only kiss.

I wondered if Kendra had done more than kiss boys. Shannon Shunton, supposedly, had had sex with a senior over the summer, but I only heard it once from Peggy, who heard it from one of Katherine's friends, who hates Elizabeth Shunton, so it might not be true. But it was definitely true that Shannon and the other popular girls had done more than kissing, like letting boys go up their shirts and down their pants. But I didn't ask Kendra about this because I worried I would want to talk about it forever, and I would never get my homework done, and then I would fail out of school and not be able to see Trevor Santos ever again.

So we said good-bye and then I ran upstairs to talk to my mom, but she wasn't on the couch anymore. She was watching TV in bed, which made me think she was missing my dad, and I felt bad because if it wasn't for me, she wouldn't have to be missing him.

Yep. Okay. Gosh. Okay.

Maybe tomorrow morning I would tell her it was okay to let Dad move back in.

I WENT BACK TO THE LIVING ROOM TO FINISH MY HOME-work, except I couldn't stop thinking about the new boy. Snap out of this, Carolina! You must do your homework! You are a good student! You are not going to become one of those dumb girls who only feels good about herself because boys like her!

But I just couldn't stop thinking about him. I so wished I could. But I couldn't.

Tomorrow, I promised myself, I would stop with the boy obsessing. I really would. It was a new vow. I never broke two vows in a row.

So I signed back on to Facebook and went through and looked at all of Trevor's pictures, even though he had, like, only twenty, and most of them were grainy, and some not even of him or people, just dead birds in front of windows, but there was this one picture where he was sitting with a little girl—his sister, Lily, the caption said. And he had this look in his eyes, facing the camera, that he just could see through you and everyone and was probably the most interesting person ever born. Plus, he looked sooo attractive. Like he could be a model for some mysterious new designer. But even better than that, because he was probably smart and deep.

I wanted to message him that I was in love with him and for him to message me back and tell me he loved me too. But then I realized I would never do this, and if I did, he would never message me back: He would laugh at me and tell Henry McCarthy and the rest of the stupid boys that always hated me and made fun of me. And then I realized Trevor Santos was probably a horrible person just like them, and that I should just do my homework.

I also realized no way—NO WAY—would I let my mom let my dad move back in. Never. Never. Never.

10
Trevor doesn't want to hear it

NONE OF THE BOY CROSS-COUNTRY RUNNERS SHOWERED after practice. Strange. But whatever. So I didn't either.

First thing my mom says to me when I get in her SUV? "You smell, Trevor."

"Thanks, Mom."

"Do they not have showers at the school?"

"My first day at school was great, Mom. Thanks for asking," I said.

"I'm sorry. How was your first day?"

"Can we just go home, please."

"I'm sorry. Please tell me about your day," she said as she started driving back toward our house. Except I refused. She kept asking me to talk, saying sorry over and over, but I just ignored her. Sometimes that was the only weapon I had against her.

MY MOM WENT TO RIVERBEND HIGH SCHOOL. SHE WAS A legend twenty-five years ago. A cheerleader when it was still cool to be a cheerleader. Lead in the musical. (They did *My Fair Lady* just because of her.) She got straight As. She didn't win homecoming queen, but trust me, it wasn't because she wasn't pretty, but probably because she was a bit of a snob. She was valedictorian, and she gave a speech about how life is too precious not to believe in your dreams and follow them no matter what. Everyone in our family, and everyone in this town, expected her to become a famous novelist or the first female president, except she wanted to be an actress. She didn't go to Princeton University, even though her parents wanted her to. Instead she went to New York University and eventually dropped out to move to Los Angeles because she wanted to be a movie star and that's where people move to become movie stars.

Nobody has ever told me this, certainly not her, but I think she just assumed she would be this super-famous actress-celebrity right up until she was about twenty-nine. Then, boom, I think she panicked she would never make it, so she found my dad, who was this boring but successful business guy, and she quit acting, got married and pregnant with me before she turned thirty.

My mom told me the reason she stopped acting was that her first love, before high school, was writing, and she wanted to get back to that. I've seen her scribbling in a notebook a bit but she's never finished anything except a couple short stories that she won't let me read. So I think my mom tried to kill herself because she knows she failed. She gave this big speech at the end of high school about following your dream, yet she gave up following hers. And knowing that made her want to be dead.

I will tell you, there is this picture in her senior yearbook that I've studied a lot. You should see it. It takes up a whole page when nobody else even got a half of one by themselves. In it she's reading a book in an empty auditorium, spread over three chairs, her long blond hair all glowing. My mom looks so beautiful. But more than that, she looks like she's so in control. Anything she wanted, all she had to do was ask and she would get it.

When I think of that picture, I feel sorry for her. Must be hard to think you can accomplish anything you want and then one day wake up and think you'll never accomplish anything at all.

"Trevor?" she said, for, like, the twentieth time.

"It was fine, Mom. It was boring but not too painful."

"What was your favorite class?"

"Biology probably."

"Did Henry introduce you to his friends?"

"Yeah, but Henry and his friends are assholes."

"Don't use that word," she said. Except then she smiled and said, "My brother is an asshole, so you're probably right about Henry."

I smiled too. My mom is the greatest at moments like this. When most adults would keep pretending to be mature and know-it-all, she can let the truth out. For the first time in a long time, and just for a second or two, I felt safe with her.

By the time we got home, which was only ten minutes later, my mom said she was exhausted and needed to rest. I'm sure she hadn't been up for more than four hours. But whatever. She asked me to walk down to our neighbor's to get Lily, which I would've wanted to do anyway.

Except after I started walking, I realized that Lily had two new friends on our block. (She made friends faster than anyone.) So I walked back in to ask my mom which neighbor and she was on the phone in her bedroom. I wanted to yell to interrupt her phone call, but I didn't. Instead, I got really quiet. I don't even know why, but I stayed that way and kept inching closer to her bedroom door. That's when I heard her, very clearly:

"I miss you too. . . . I can't visit. . . . You know I can't. . . . Because I need to stay in Chicago with my family . . . Of course I love them. . . . It's different with you. . . . I have to go. . . . No, I can't Skype again. . . . I have to go. . . . Bye, Dylan."

Then the phone call ended. And I waited. For a couple seconds but it felt longer. Like my whole life just fast-forwarded to the end and then rewound. Then I yelled, "Mom!" And I opened her bedroom door.

The look on her face let me know what I thought I knew. But I didn't want her to say anything. I couldn't stand to hear it just then. So, super quick, I said, "What neighbors? The Thuressons or the Hammans?"

"The Hammans," she said. She opened her mouth to keep talking, but I just turned and walked away.

"HI, TREVOR, DID YOU HAVE A GREAT FIRST DAY OF SCHOOL?" Lily said the moment she saw me, strapping on her blue backpack. Then she turned back to our neighbors and her kid friend, and said, "Thank you so much for hosting me, and you have a wonderful home. I'll see you soon, I'm sure."

After they closed the door, I said, "Where'd you learn to talk like that?"

"I'm being gracious."

"It's strange that a seven-year-old girl talks like that."

"I think people like it."

"They do."

"So then why shouldn't I do it?"

"You should. It's just strange having your younger sister talk like she's older than you."

"You're hilarious, Trevor. Enough about me, how was your first day?"

"Mostly pointless," I said, but then I realized I was bored with talking about things being pointless and Lily was the best to talk to about important stuff. Except I couldn't talk about Mom's phone call I just overheard. I just couldn't do that to her. She wouldn't even understand. So instead I said, "I think I met a girl."

"Really? Really!" she screeched, jumping up and down and acting like a seven-year-old for once. "Goodness! What's her name? Is she as pretty as Dakota?"

"Her name's Carolina. And she's pretty, but in a different way than Dakota."

"This is very exciting! I want to meet her. When do I get to meet her?"

"Well, we didn't really talk yet." I shouldn't have brought Carolina up. Big mistake.

"But why not? You just have to talk to her, Trevor! Don't be afraid."

"You don't talk to boys."

"Yes, I do. Don't be hilarious," she said. (She was using the word "hilarious" all the time lately, even when it didn't make that much sense.) "But I don't like them yet because I'm seven. I'll like them when I'm ten. Are you Facebook friends?"

"Facebook isn't cool anymore," I said.

"But you look at it every day," Lily said. I didn't say anything back. "Just ask her to be friends on that. I think she would like that."

"Okay, I'll think about it."

"You're so hilarious." And then she made herself laugh, which made me laugh, which made her laugh for real, which made me forget all the shitty things that happened today.

Lily was magical that way.

11

Carolina dies of a heart attack

"Point him out," Katherine said after she followed Peggy and me to our first-period biology class Tuesday morning. Peggy had told her about Trevor Santos's friend request, so then Katherine said she would decide for me whether I should accept it. What kind of person does that?

So originally I didn't accept his request right away because Kendra and I decided it was better to make a boy that you like wait to know that you like him back. But then after thinking about it longer and my whole body hurting at the thought of him, I realized that Trevor was probably just asking me because he wanted to collect girls' friendships but not really care about any one of us. So I couldn't be his friend if I thought that, right?

But then I just wished I'd gone ahead and accepted it so that Katherine couldn't make it a million times worse. But it was too late for that.

I saw Trevor turn down the hall, walking right toward us. The worst part? He looked so amazing, like he was in a music video and moving in slow motion. Gosh, I'm even thinking like an airhead because of this boy. Everything's ruined.

Peggy whispered to Katherine, "That's him," but I couldn't look anymore. I had to turn away. Just let this be over, please. Please, please, please.

What felt like an hour later, Peggy finally said to me, "He's inside, Carrie." I didn't even care she used my wrong name.

Katherine said, "He is hot. You really think he likes you? Never mind. You can be his Facebook friend, but don't talk to him until I find out more about him." Then Katherine left.

I looked at Peggy, wanting her to tell me that her sister was mean and crazy and I should ignore everything she says, but Peggy just shrugged and went inside biology. I hated Peggy for one second, even though I knew she had to live with Katherine's insanity everyday.

I just felt so small and invisible. Like I could get sucked into the crevices between the lockers at any moment and no one would even remember I existed.

Biology was horrible because Trevor was there and I didn't even get to sit next to him. I tried not to think about him or look at him but that was impossible. Then Mr. Klenner called on me when he must have known I had no idea even what my name was or what planet I was on, and so I said, "Huh?" and the class laughed, or at least it felt like it, and then he asked the question again, except I still had no idea, and then he gave the answer and gave me that look that says, "Don't be a bad student," which I had seen teachers give to so many other people but never to me.

I wanted to die and never come back to school, though I suppose if I was dead I couldn't come back to school anyway. The embarrassment did make me pay attention, so I guess teachers embarrassing students must work, but it is a horrible thing to do and should be against the law.

Trevor didn't sit next to me in history either, which was fine. Just fine. I was thinking of him less by the minute. Lunch was fine too, though near the end, when I was talking to Kendra about our game Saturday, Peggy got up without telling me and went over to talk to Shannon Shunton and those popular girls. When I finally found her, she was walking away from their table.

"What were you talking to them about?" I asked as we walked to algebra.

"About the party Friday," she said, and suddenly my throat felt like it was swelling because I wondered if Peggy would become Shannon Shunton's best friend and not mine, then I realized that would never happen and just smiled so she wouldn't know what I was thinking.

IN MATH CLASS, HENRY MCCARTHY SAT BEHIND ME, which I didn't think about because everyone has to sit somewhere. Except then, when the teacher had his back to us, writing some weird math equation on the whiteboard, Henry leaned up and whispered into my ear. I jumped a little, but maybe only in my mind, because no one turned in my direction.

What did he whisper? This: "I heard you were going to the Darry party Friday." Darry was Peggy and Katherine's last name. But he also said, "You should come to the freshman game first. It starts at three thirty. I'm the quarterback. I'm going to throw touchdowns." And then he stopped talking. I nodded because I didn't know what else to do. Had Henry McCarthy just invited me to come watch his football game? He had, which was almost as weird as when that junior

Alexander Taylor, with his tie and his odd eyes, stopped me in the hall yesterday. Boys in high school were already much different than they were in junior high.

When the bell rang, Henry said, "You better come," which maybe he meant as charming, because he tried to smile, but it felt like a threat because Henry had always been mean to me before and it was hard to rewire my brain to accept that maybe he was being nice to me now.

I was telling Peggy about this in the hall after class, and she was saying how amazing it was, though I'm not sure if it was amazing or just really confusing. Then we saw Shannon Shunton and Wanda Chan, and they stopped us by stopping right in front of us.

Shannon spoke directly at me, which I don't think she had ever done before. "Do you want to borrow some of my clothes?"

I wanted to cry and I didn't even know why, but I didn't cry, which was a relief.

Then she said, "For the party."

"Okay," I said, only I didn't know if I meant it. Shannon Shunton always dressed in short skirts—because she had these amazing thin, thin, thin legs—and tank tops or very, very tight T-shirts, usually black or gray ones. My favorite colors were green and yellow and I liked to wear baggy clothes and pants because my body was horrible. Just horrible.

"Cool," she said, "I'll bring some stuff to Marguerite's house."

"Do you still like Henry McCarthy?" I asked her. Peggy looked at me like I was from Mars for asking Shannon this, but I didn't understand why this was a bad question, and aren't we supposed to be friends with her now? And I still didn't know why Henry was asking me to come watch his football game.

"Uh, no," Shannon Shunton said, and then, "he's a freshman." Except she might as well have said, *He's a squirrel,* and her voice suggested she might even have dated a squirrel before she'd date a freshman.

Then Wanda said, "We hung around some seniors this summer and it's just hard to relate to freshman boys anymore." Then they both smiled, but cool smiles that didn't feel like real smiles at all, and then they both left.

"You shouldn't ask Shannon questions like that," Peggy said after we had started walking again.

"How come?"

"I don't know. It just feels like we shouldn't," Peggy said.

I didn't know what else to say about Shannon Shunton, so I said, "Trevor hasn't talked to me at all today."

"My sister said she was going to talk to him at lunch about you."

Whaaaaaaaaaaaaat!

Huh?

No.

Wait a minute. Wait a minute. Wait a minute.

"What?" I said after my brain stopped being a huge giant fireball.

Peggy said, in a calm voice that annoyed me, "Katherine talked to him. At least she said she was going to."

"What was she going to say?" Oh my GOSH! My heart was beating really fast. So fast.

"Just ask him why he liked you. I don't know."

"BUT WHY WOULD SHE DO THAT?"

"Shh! Don't yell, Carrie!"

"My name's Carolina!" I sort of yelled. Because I was so mad. So mad I couldn't breathe! I couldn't see! I couldn't exist one more second without EXPLODING!

"I'm sorry. But shh. Katherine is trying to help. She knows more about boys than we do."

"I can't go to health class."

"Why not?" Peggy asked, even though she's my best friend and she should know why and obviously I WAS HAVING A HEART ATTACK.

"Because Trevor's in my health class!"

"Will you stop freaking out?"

"I just can't handle this. It's too much. I can't—" I stopped walking and sat down. In the middle of the hallway. Oh my gosh, why did I do that? Peggy pulled me up to my feet and pulled me over to the side so I wouldn't get trampled.

And then she said, "Guess what? You're amazing. And if he's smart, Trevor will like you. And if he doesn't like you, then he's stupid and you won't like him."

This felt like it should make me feel better, but I didn't feel better. Then because I thought I should, I think I did, a little. Peggy hugged me, and I hugged her back.

Then Peggy said, "I have to go to history now," and she walked off. I wanted to tell her I loved her, maybe not out loud, but maybe just by telling her she was amazing, but by the time I turned to say it, Peggy was already with Shannon Shunton and Wanda Chan and then all three of them disappeared among the crowd.

Gosh.

Anyway, I repeated what Peggy said in my head, decided I probably wasn't going to have a heart attack, and went to health class. I was the last one to arrive, and there was only one seat left . . . next to Trevor Santos. As I walked from the door to the desk, my face turned so red, I mean, it must have, and my skin itched, but I was also excited, with the good butterflies in my stomach, so I sat down but didn't look at him.

Again, I had the weirdest sensation during the whole class, being close to him like that, which was that we knew each other. I started to believe we knew each other from a past life, except I think past lives are silly. It's just that there's always been, like, this separation between me and other people. I didn't ever think there was, not really, until right now, when I thought that this separation that I never realized was there wasn't there with Trevor . . . it was like I had always lived in my own bubble and no one else had ever been in my bubble until him.

EXCEPT I DON'T KNOW ANYTHING ABOUT HIM! And I'm crazy and I'm so tired and I don't know who I am anymore. But I couldn't convince myself to be sane so I thought I just *had* to speak to him. The last twenty minutes of class I only thought about what I could say, and I had fifty different ideas but I didn't pick one until the bell rang.

I said, "Did Katherine say something to you?"

And he said, "Yeah," except it was more like he said, *You and your friends are horrible, disgusting people, never talk to me again,* all in that one little "yeah" and then he walked out of the classroom.

I kind of did die of a heart attack then, but not from it going too fast. Instead it just stopped and dropped into my stomach, where it shattered and turned into nothingness.

I didn't really die, obviously, but you understand. So even though we get in big trouble for using our phones in school, I took mine out and signed in to Facebook, which I never do at school because school is important, but I couldn't stop myself. I wanted to accept his friend request because I was sure that would make up for whatever Katherine said and whatever bad things he was thinking I was.

Except, you know what? When I signed on and looked for his friend request, it was gone.

Like it never even existed.

Don't cry, Carolina.

Please don't cry.

12
Trevor wakes up burning

MY CHEST BURNED WHEN I WOKE UP TUESDAY MORNING. All my muscles felt wrenched an inch closer to my bones. What was strange is I liked it. Liked the ache. Liked the pain. I must be screwed up in the head to like pain.

Dad didn't have to wake me up. Whether it was my body or my brain that did it, I don't know, but I was up at 5:40 a.m. First thing I did was check Facebook. Hated that's what I did, but I can't lie and say I didn't do it.

Carolina still hadn't accepted my friend request. Not a big deal. But . . . never mind. Just not a big deal. But then I started looking at her pictures. Didn't do it yesterday because, well, it's a stupid thing to do, but now it was so early and she hadn't become my friend and, I don't know, I just wanted to look at her pictures.

The truth was she didn't look that great. She dressed mostly like a boy, never stood up straight, and always smiled like taking photographs was torture. This might be another reason she wasn't popular. Because of stupid Facebook and iPhones, how good you looked in pictures mattered as much as how pretty you were in real life.

But then there was this one photo of her playing soccer. Carolina was concentrating so intensely on the game, she couldn't tell anyone was taking the picture, so she didn't know to be uncomfortable. Instead she looked like an Olympic athlete that would be in commercials because she was beautiful and amazing at sports. She was striding across the grass, two opposing players behind her, anguished they couldn't catch her. Her eyes were so sharp you had the feeling she could see right through you and the ground and into whole other worlds. The muscles in her arms and legs were tight, reminded me of how I felt right this second, and for that second I thought again we were soul mates. You know, like the one person that would make me feel not so fucking alone.

Then I stopped thinking that because I don't believe in that crap. But maybe I didn't stop thinking it as much as I wanted to.

CAROLINA ACTED STRANGE AS I WALKED TOWARD BIOLOGY. She looked at me, so did her friend and some older girl, but then she looked away. Suddenly I felt like she was annoyed I had sent her that friend request. So I sat in the back of class, far away from where we sat yesterday. I did it to punish her, but it probably only punished me.

At lunch, the older girl who was with Carolina before biology marched over to our table, pointed at me, and said, "You, come here," like she was a teacher disciplining me. I wasn't going to move. I didn't know this chick, and I certainly didn't like being told what to do.

But then my cousin Henry said, "Dude, that's Katherine Darry. She's, like, the hottest girl in the school. Go, go."

"Thanks for telling the new kid here what's up," Katherine said, winking at Henry like he was her best friend, only to turn her gaze cold as it descended back on me.

Screw it. I got up, followed her out of the cafeteria into the hall. Not sure why Henry thought Katherine was that attractive. Yeah, she knew how to walk so that her butt moved back and forth and she knew how to wear makeup like girls on reality TV, but there was nothing pretty about her at all. Her face was puffy and angry, her eyes small and panicked.

"Do you like my sister?" Katherine asked after she stopped, spun, and shoved her head six inches from mine.

"Who's your sister?"

"Oh. My. God. You retarded or are you just retarded? My sister is Peggy. She looks like me, but not as, you know, mature, except her boobs are huge, which is why you like her, don't lie!"

"She's Carolina's friend?"

Katherine opened her mouth but didn't say anything while her brain tried to catch up. "Listen, new kid. I know how stuff works. You're super hot, but nobody realizes it yet because you're new. Not even you, apparently. So you can't like Carolina. It just won't work. So you can like Peggy maybe, because I don't want her dating any of my friends. So you think about it, and I'll talk to Peggy. But leave Carolina alone. She's not your type." Then she tapped my ear with her hand two times. "Okay?"

But I didn't say anything. I sure as hell wasn't going to agree with her, but I didn't have the balls to tell her off either. Then she left and I just stood there, not quite sure what this really meant. When I turned around, Henry was standing there, Licker and baby-faced Jake behind him. They stepped fast into my space before I could do anything about it.

"What did she say? What did she want?" Henry asked.

"I don't know."

"Don't lie! Just tell us!" Jake whined.

"Something about her sister, Peggy. Wanted to know if I liked her."

Licker said, "Katherine must think you're going to be cool, which means you probably will be."

Henry's face scrunched up when Licker said this. Then my cousin said, "You can't go out with Peggy because I was going to go out with her. Sorry, Trev." Then he walked away, Jake and Licker following after him.

This. School. Sucks. For the next minute, all I could think about is how much I hated my mom for making us leave California and come to this crap-hole place because she's so malfunctioning in the head. Then, I don't even know why, I decided to take out my phone and take back my friend request to Carolina. It wasn't until after I did it that I realized why: For at least a few minutes this morning I thought she was my soul mate. I thought she was different and I was different and we could be different together, but then with all this Katherine and Henry BS, it was clear that she was a part of their game. She wasn't different like me. She was the same like them.

AFTER HEALTH CLASS, CAROLINA TRIED TO SAY SOMETHING to me. I'm not even sure what—I was concentrating on ignoring her—but I let her know with one look that I knew she and her stupid friends were trying to manipulate me and I wanted nothing to do with any of them.

Except, after I walked away, the look on her face kept creeping back into my memory. It wasn't the look I expected. What did I expect? I don't even know now. Maybe for her to roll her eyes or give me a wicked grin like Katherine, or something that would have made it easy for me to think she was one of them.

But her look was so vulnerable, and deep—like her whole being could see me, not just her eyes—that I left wondering if maybe I should have listened to what she had to say.

No. No. No.

Trevor. Listen: Nobody will ever understand you. Nobody will ever make you feel you're not alone. Stop trying to trick yourself into thinking anything else. You'll be a lot happier when you accept that you'll always be miserable.

13

Carolina makes some important decisions

So, like, study hall on Tuesday . . . yeah, okay, remember that I have study hall last period on Tuesday and Thursday because we have club soccer practice the other days? Anyway, so I was kind of excited about study hall because, you know, it's not a real class, and we could get homework done, and it would be Peggy and Kendra and maybe some new people but people just like us. It would be this society of student-athletes. I would belong to something, you know? All summer Peggy and I talked about how amazing study hall would be. It sounds stupid to think study hall would be amazing, but we thought it anyway.

But after Peggy sat between me and Kendra, right away she said, "I'll be right back," told the teacher she needed to go the bathroom, took sooo long, and then when she came back she sat next to this soph-omore volleyball boy named Thomas something. Peggy and this Thomas kept whispering to each other. I knew this because I was star-ing at Peggy the whole time. I mean, I was having a major crisis with Trevor caused by HER sister and she was talking to some boy I didn't even know she knew existed? Huh? What?

About halfway through study hall, the teacher said, "Shouldn't you be getting some work done?" Right! To! Me! I was mortified. Oh my gosh. Mortified. I mean, Peggy was flirting with a boy, I wasn't saying anything, and I get in trouble? Oh my gosh. Everything was ruined.

So I pretended to do work, but I couldn't concentrate, so it wasn't real work. It was just me writing a long letter to Peggy that I knew I would never give her even before I finished.

After study hall, we met Katherine by her car in the parking lot. She would be driving us home on Tuesdays and Thursdays. Which was great. I mean, it was better than the bus, but even better than that would have been if I could have gone home with Kendra and her mom.

Anyway, the first thing Katherine said as she walked toward us at the car was, "So I talked to the new boy—"

I KNOW YOU DID, I screamed from behind my teeth, but I was silent. Obviously. I would never yell at Katherine, unless I wanted my face broken.

"Turns out he likes Peggy," she said, just like that. Like it was nothing. Like those words could have been anything. Like those words didn't just destroy ALL MY DREAMS AND HAPPINESS AND EVERYTHING.

"He does?" Peggy said, confused, but also smiling. It was a super-small smile. Most people wouldn't have noticed. But I was her best friend so I could see it. I could see her smiling because the first boy I had ever really liked . . . liked her instead.

Don't cry, don't cry, don't cry. It didn't matter that I told myself a gazillion times not to cry. I did.

"Carrie, goddamn," Katherine started, rolling her eyes, "you can't cry over boys. Seriously. There's a million of them."

"Yeah, Carrie, there's a million of them," Peggy said. I nodded and tried to stop, but all I could think was that Trevor Santos, this boy who was supposed to be different from all the boys in junior high, was the same as them. No, it was worse. Because in junior high the boys didn't like Peggy either. So at least we were geeks together. But now I would be a geek alone.

I got in the back seat of Katherine's car, buried my head against the window, and ignored them. They probably didn't even try talking to me. They probably forgot I even existed by the time we pulled out of the parking lot.

WHEN I GOT HOME, MY MOM WAS ALREADY IN HER BED- room watching television. There was a note on the fridge that said there was leftover pizza from her lunch but that she was tired and would probably fall asleep soon. It wasn't even four o'clock. I mean, she worked a five a.m. morning shift, but still, my mom never went to sleep this early.

I called Kendra, just to hear someone's voice, but I didn't tell her about Trevor liking Peggy, or about anything I was really feeling. When I thought I would cry again—for no reason!—I got off the phone. Then I just started bawling. I was such a mess. It was only the second day of my entire high school career, and nothing, nothing, nothing was what I wanted it to be.

ON WEDNESDAY MORNING BEFORE KATHERINE AND PEGGY picked me up—which I was looking forward to not at all!—and after my mom had left for work, my dad stopped by with donuts even though I've told him one thousand times that donuts are terrible for me. But I ate two in, like, two seconds anyway.

"What's wrong?" he asked, which I hated, because I hated him and hated him more because he knew something was wrong just by the way I ate donuts.

"Nothing, Dad," I said.

"You called me 'Dad,' so now I know something's wrong." He did his big-smile thing, and it sort of worked even though I didn't want it to.

"I don't want to talk about it."

"I know you think I'm a terrible person . . ."

It made me so sad to think I thought my dad was a terrible person. And for him to know it. But it was true. So how could I stop thinking it just because it was sad?

". . . but you are, without question, one of the best people. And the best people care a lot about a lot of people, and when you care a lot about a lot of people, you get hurt more."

"Then maybe I shouldn't care so much!" I said, and because I'm a crying machine the tears started falling.

"No, Carolina, no," he said, calling me by the right name even though he just found out about it Monday. "I know you are hurt and you feel vulnerable, but caring as much as you do will eventually give you strength—real, lasting strength. Not the fake strength that being mean gives others."

"Oh, Dad," I said, and then leaned toward him to let him know it was okay for him to hug me. And he did. And it felt so good, like when I was a kid, but even better because I thought I would never let him hug me again and yet here we were. My dad was so smart and wise and amazing and then I remembered he was also horrible and then I didn't know what to think anymore so I just let him hug me until I felt calm. Really calm. Calmer than I had since, I don't know, maybe ever.

"Do you want me to drive you to school?" he asked while still hugging me, which was the perfect thing he could have said, and I nodded without really moving my head. When I texted Peggy to say I didn't need a ride, I felt good, like I didn't need her. I don't know. I don't want to not need her but I don't want to need her either. Everything's complicated now.

As my dad dropped me off in front of school, he said a really weird thing, but he liked to say weird things so I guess it wasn't weird for him. He said, "In high school, everyone is figuring out who they're supposed to be. You just be who you want to be instead of who you're supposed to be and you'll know something no one else knows."

"Okay, Scott," I said. I don't even know why I didn't say "Dad" after he had been so nice, but sometimes when my dad tried to say smart things it made me frustrated because I wish he would just act smart (mainly with my mom) instead. I did give him a quick hug—really quick—before jumping out of the car and heading into school.

So. Okay. I made a decision as I walked to biology. A couple of decisions actually.

One: I really wasn't going to think about Trevor, or any boys, at all. Maybe after I got accepted to Stanford when I was a senior I would think about them again. But not until then. Now that I knew Trevor didn't like me, it wasn't as fun to think about him anyway.

Two: I was going to talk to Kendra more. Peggy was still my best friend, but, you know, I thought it would be a good idea if I talked to Kendra lots too.

Three: I wasn't going to listen to anything Katherine said about anything. I would pretend to listen because she would go psycho on me if she knew I was ignoring her, but I wouldn't really listen.

YOU KNOW WHAT? I DID A REALLY AMAZING JOB AT DOING all three things on Wednesday. And Thursday. And Friday. Like, really, by lunch on Friday, I couldn't even remember why I would have even wanted to like Trevor. I mean, he was cute and all, but he was just, I don't know, a boy. What could be so special about him? There were a million boys, right? (Yes, Katherine said this, but she said it before I decided to ignore her.) And I had ignored her! She kept telling me to wear more eyeliner and stuff my bra and chew gum to make me look less intense, but I didn't do any of that.

Kendra and I started becoming really close. She was just so nice, and even though she was quiet and maybe a little boring sometimes, she also really listened when you talked. Peggy started being more like old Peggy by Friday too. I think she started to see that Kendra and I were becoming better friends and didn't want me to become too good of friends with her. Maybe. That's mean for me to think. It doesn't matter. What matters is by the end of soccer practice on Friday, everything seemed almost normal. Not perfect. Okay, definitely not perfect. But normal. Like I could understand it. Like I was in control of my life again.

But then Friday night happened.

Oh. My. Gosh.

The party at Peggy and Katherine's.

My first high school party.

It changed everything.

It didn't ruin it. No.

(I'm going to stop saying everything's ruined unless it's really ruined. I really am. I need to stop being so dramatic. Really.)

So not ruined.

But changed.

Because suddenly I was not in control of anything. Not ANYTHING at all.

(I'm one thousand percent not being dramatic!)

14
Trevor decides not to give up on the world

"TREVOR, DO YOU NEED TO TALK?" LILY SAID AS IF SHE were my therapist, except she said it while holding a Barbie doll that was wearing a shirt but no pants. It was Tuesday after school, and I was thinking about moving to Europe or someplace awesome.

"No," I said, then went back to sitting by myself in the basement, where we went only to watch TV, except I hadn't turned on the TV. Lily ignored my "no" and climbed onto the couch next to me. She didn't say anything. Just sat there, nestled close, combing her Barbie's hair with her fingers. My sister just understood people. I don't even think she knew she understood, but she understood them anyway and that's what made her goddamn magnificent. So eventually I said, "You making friends at school?"

"Yes, I'm very good at making friends. Not everyone likes me, which is okay. Because Mom says if everyone likes me, then that would mean I was trying too hard."

"You've been talking to Mom?" I asked. I can't remember the last time I saw the two of them have a real conversation.

"You're hilarious. Of course I talk to Mom!"

"That's good. But, you know, Mom doesn't know everything."

"Duh. I know."

"No, Lil, some kids have moms that they can always trust. But we don't."

She stopped looking at me, stopped fiddling with her Barbie. Even though Lily never said she was sad, hell, she never cried—seven-year-old girls should cry!—after I said what I said about Mom, I could almost see her spirit deflate. Even if it was only for a second. Seeing that made me sad. Almost made *me* want to cry. She's a little kid, not forty like you always think, Trevor! Just let her pretend our mom is a good mom.

So I said, "That girl I said I like, Carolina . . ."

Which made her perk up, sit on her knees, and face me. Excited. Which was why I said it.

"She's not as cool as I thought."

"Trevor! What happened?" Lily asked, still thrilled to be a part of my personal life even if my personal life was depressing.

"Her friend, or maybe it was just her friend's sister, came and told me I couldn't like her."

"Why?"

"I don't know. That's why school sucks. People just say stuff and try to control you and don't have any real reasons."

"Did you ask her why her friend said you couldn't like her?"

"No, Lily, that's not how it works."

"Why?"

"Because once someone says something, that's just the way it is."

"But Carolina didn't say it," Lily said, trying to act like she knew what she was talking about, but I knew she didn't.

"Forget it, Lily. Carolina's a loser."

"Don't call people names, Trevor."

"Goddamn it! You're just a kid! You don't know anything!" I pushed myself up from the couch, didn't look at Lily again, and went up two flights of stairs to my room. By the time I slammed my door shut, I knew I had been an asshole. Lily was just being Lily. But I didn't apologize because then I would have to really admit it.

When I opened my door for dinner a couple hours later, there was a folded piece of red construction paper in front of it. It was from Lily. Of course. I picked it up, opened it. There was a drawing of a girl and a taller boy. You know, like a seven-year-old would draw. And then, in her seven-year-old handwriting, but with her super-wise soul, it said: *I love my big brother forever.*

And then, crap, I did cry. Not *cry* cry. But tears formed. I fought them, but a few fell down my cheek anyway. Crap! This whole world sucks, but my sister is so goddamn special I can't give up on the world. Not yet anyway.

So Wednesday and Thursday were just a waste of time, but they weren't a waste of time in an interesting way. Carolina never looked at me; I never looked at her. Which was fine by me. I kept having lunch with my cousin Henry and his friends even though I didn't like any of them, except Licker was sort of cool.

After Thursday's cross-country practice, which again ended with me collapsing to the ground and telling Coach Pasquini to go fuck himself in my head, he sat down on the curb next to my splayed-out carcass and asked, "You ready to hear a few things, or should I let you keep punishing yourself?"

This felt like a setup, so I didn't say anything. Lungs still being on fire might also have made it difficult to speak.

"You like pain," he said, then paused. I remained quiet. Pasquini locked his eyes onto mine, like some possessed general from ancient history, and continued, "That wasn't a question. It's a fact. Which is good. Not good for your life, sorry to say, but it is good for running. To be a great runner, you must understand how to control the pain. If you always make running painful, you'll never know when to use your high threshold for pain to win. When you can control pain, you'll love the pain for what it gives you, not just what it makes you forget. And when you love the pain for the rewards, you'll love running, and then, and only then, will you be great."

"Okay," I said before I could tell my mouth to ignore him.

"Okay," he said with that twisted grin of his. "Okay. Good. Tomorrow, your new life starts."

"Okay," I said, and crap, you know, I actually believed him. Even stranger, he turned out to be right.

15

Carolina tries on a new dress

So Peggy's mom, Mrs. Darry, picked us up from school on Friday and drove us to soccer practice. Peggy's mom is insane, like Katherine, so I always make sure to be nice to her. Like, if you're not careful, boom! She'll just start yelling at you for rolling down the window or doing your homework in the car or something no one would ever get mad about except her. Gosh.

Anyway, after practice, Kendra and I were in the back seat and Peggy was in the front with her mom when Kendra answered a phone call from her mom.

Mrs. Darry just exploded. Like almost for real, I think: "NO CELL PHONE CALLS WHILE DRIVING! IT'S THE LAW!"

"Gotta go, Mom," Kendra said, then hung up. She looked at me, wanting me to tell her that she'd done nothing wrong. Which she hadn't. But I couldn't open my mouth or Peggy's mom might have murdered me. Obviously it's only illegal for the driver to make cell phone calls while driving. But Mrs. Darry just likes to yell at people, so she will make up reasons to get mad. For a couple seconds, I did feel sorry for

Katherine. I mean, if I had a mom like Mrs. Darry, wouldn't I be crazy too? Probably. You know, it's actually amazing Peggy is normal like me. Then I stopped feeling sorry for Katherine because she ruined my life. Then I remembered I wasn't going to say things were ruined, so I thought about what color Gatorade I would have when I got home.

After we dropped off Kendra at her house, Mrs. Darry said, "Must be nice to be rich. I'd probably think I could answer phone calls in other people's cars too."

Neither Peggy nor I said anything. We both knew to stay out of her mom's way when she got like this. If we were in Kendra's mom's car or my mom's, Peggy and I would text about the party, but neither of us would touch our phones in front of Mrs. Darry. Oh my gosh, no.

MR. AND MRS. DARRY WERE GOING TO LEAVE FOR THEIR timeshare condo in Wisconsin right after soccer practice, so after I got home, I took a quick shower, packed a bag, waited for Peggy to text me that her parents had left, and rode my bike over to her house.

"Carrie," Katherine said as I walked in, "in high school, only tools ride their bikes."

What could I say to that? I mean, nothing. Right? I just went upstairs to Peggy's room, but when I got there it wasn't just Peggy. Shannon Shunton, Emma Goldberg, and Wanda Chan were there. Wait a minute! They didn't belong here! I mean, yes, we were becoming friends, and trying to be popular, okay, but Peggy's room was like my second room and now there were these OTHER GIRLS in it! My heart just froze in my chest, and I searched for Peggy, who was bouncing on her bed in a dress that made her boobs look like cartoons, and she was giggling even though no one was saying anything. She just looked so happy to have new, cool friends, which made me so sad.

Shannon and Wanda were in their underwear—not even wearing bras!—holding up dresses to their bodies. They both were so skinny and perfect. I mean, you could see their ribs and the bones in their shoulders like models. Gosh. I would never have a body like that. Never. Why would any boy like me if there were girls like that? Emma was smoking a cigarette by the window and even though she was blowing the smoke out the window, I wanted to puke.

"What up," Shannon said, and Wanda and Emma both said, "Hey," and then Shannon grabbed one of the dresses that was splayed on Peggy's bed and held it up to me. "You'd look awesome in this." She pressed it into my hands until I grabbed it. It had black-and-white stripes, and it was one thousand percent shorter and tighter than anything I had ever worn. No way would I wear it in public. No way, no way, no way. All their eyes turned to me, and I guess that meant they were waiting for me to try the dress on, but I'm like, I'm not getting undressed in front of these popular girls with their model bodies. Peggy had seen me naked a million times, but she was like a sister, and . . . oh my gosh, they kept looking at me. I wouldn't even be able to escape to the bathroom, and I didn't know how to talk to them or to Peggy in front of them, so I just turned a bit to the side so I wouldn't have to look them in the eyes, and I quickly, like so quickly, took off my shorts and sweatshirt and put on the dress.

"Yeah, that looks fucking awesome," Shannon said.

"You look amazing," Peggy said.

"Yeah," Emma said between puffs.

"Like, really, I expected it to look like a nightmare, but yeah, you look hot," Wanda said.

So I was terrified they were tricking me or maybe just trying to be nice, but when I finally looked in the mirror, it was, I don't know . . . good. Yeah. My gosh. I looked, I don't know, cute. Even . . . sexy? Maybe. I don't know. But I didn't look silly, which I was sure I would. You know, I have these huge calves and muscular arms and no boobs, so I didn't look like a model or Shannon Shunton, but I looked better than I thought I could look. I looked like an athlete. You know, like a soccer player, but one of the not-so-ugly ones. And everyone always says how pretty they are on TV, so maybe I could be a pretty athlete. Maybe? I don't know. My brain couldn't stop spinning, couldn't make sense of what I looked like in the mirror with what I always thought I would look like in a tight dress.

"Now put these on and walk around," Shannon said, throwing a pair of high heels at my feet. This sounded like a simple thing until I put on the shoes and I could barely move in the dress and I was sure I would fall over after one step. But I tried anyway, and I didn't fall, but Emma giggled, and you know who laughed even louder? Peggy. This made me want to cry, but I think I had cried enough already this week to last for the rest of my life, so I didn't cry even a little. I just felt stupid, so stupid, until Shannon said, "You have to place one foot directly in front of the other, swivel the hips. It feels demented, I know, but it works. And keep your shoulders back; it will make you look like you have boobs," and I hated her for saying I had no boobs—only I should be able to say that!—but I did what she said anyway, and then Shannon said, "Yeah, that's great. You got it. You're a rock star."

"You're amazing!" Peggy said, and leaped up to hug me, only she fell down from her tight dress and everyone laughed at her, except me. I just helped her back to the bed. "I'm such a klutz in this!" she said, and she sounded like an airhead even though she's smart and a good athlete.

Then Shannon sat next to us and said, "You guys are cool," and I don't know if she meant it like we were always cool and she could see it now that she was getting to know us, or as if she was deeming us cool now that we were her friends. But the weirdest thing was that I actually, oh my gosh, liked her. Like, I thought she was being really nice to me. And she found me a dress that I liked and she taught me how to walk in high heels, and, I don't know, she was amazing.

So eventually Shannon and Wanda found dresses they wanted to wear from the hundred they brought over, and then we all put on some makeup—yes, I did, okay, I don't really like makeup, but I just wanted to try new things, so I put on just a little, okay?—and then when we were all ready, I felt like we were going to walk down the red carpet at the Academy Awards, except we just walked down the stairs to Peggy's living room, which had one new brown couch, one old red couch, a glass coffee table with fake-gold legs, and a television that was probably worth more than their house.

I sat on the couch next to Shannon and Wanda, Emma leaned against the wall, and Peggy sat on the floor after she put on a fashion reality TV show. And then we waited. I felt so silly, but worse, I thought the popular girls would get bored and leave even though this is where the party was, and then, just when my leg started bouncing because I was nervous, Katherine came back home. With her were three junior girls, including Shannon's sister Elizabeth, and two senior boys, and the boys carried two big beer kegs, and all four of the girls carried plastic bags filled with bottles of vodka and tequila and maybe rum. I don't know how to recognize alcohol bottles very well.

"Don't the young'uns look smokin'," Katherine said as she walked past us, though it didn't feel like a compliment. She led all the older kids into the kitchen, and Shannon, Peggy, Wanda, and Emma followed them so I did too. I mean, I wasn't going to sit in the living room by myself, right?

16
Trevor meets Mr. Pain

DURING THE TEAM STRETCH BEFORE FRIDAY'S RUN, COACH Pasquini squatted next to me and talked. Quietly. Almost stealthily. But everyone could see him and hear him. So it was odd because the dude was odd. But, Jesus, I was starting to like him. I don't even know why. Maybe I'm odd. Whatever.

"So, Trevor Santos. My Mr. Pain. You ready?"

I nodded. Two seniors who ran cross-country just to look good on their college applications laughed at Pasquini. I tried not to look at them.

Coach said, "Every day you go out running with the lead pack. Todd placed sixth in the state meet last year. Where did you finish last year at state?"

"I was in California, and I wasn't running cross-country," I said, feeling like a complete fool.

"There, I can see it, you feel stupid. That's you punishing yourself again. Stop it! I'm glad you weren't running last year. Because if you were, some other coach would get to feel like a genius for turning your physical gifts and stubborn-ass determination into something special.

Now I'll get to take all the credit while you do all the work." He did his grin thing, then said, "My first new rule for you. Start being nice to yourself. Got it?"

I nodded again, though I didn't really get it. How was I supposed to be nice to myself? It didn't make any goddamn sense.

He continued, "Todd's All-State. Randy and Craig were All-Conference. Everyone else in the lead pack has run for years. When you try to stay with them from the start, you hurt your body and you hurt your spirit. Setting yourself up to fail. Because you are Mr. Pain. And I know you think if Conchita, a freshman and a girl, can stay with them, you should too, but that young lady has been winning races in her age group since she was nine. She knows more about running than the rest of us jokers combined. Yeah, that includes me. I'd let her coach if I didn't need to pay for my kid to go to college. So rule two. Find runners at your level. Where it doesn't hurt fifty meters in. Perhaps, just perhaps, where you even enjoy running for a short while. Got it?"

I nodded.

"You fast?" he asked.

"I think so."

"I know so. Even though I've never seen it because by the time you get done with the run, you're so blasted, you can barely walk, let alone kick the finish. You've got long legs and a good stride and a lot of anger. All that will make you the best miler I've ever coached, but that's track. This is a different beast. Oh yeah. Cross-country is five thousand meters. It requires strategy. Who beats you every practice?"

"Todd and Randy—"

"No. Have you been listening? They don't beat you because they are playing tennis while you're playing Ping-Pong. Maybe someday you'll be playing the same game. But you have to work your way there. Who beats you who's running the same race?"

"Aaron and Tor," I said, motioning toward the two sophomores that passed me at the end of Monday's run and passed me sooner every practice since.

"Closer. But still out of your league."

"Edward and Michael," I said, pointing to the seniors that laughed at Pasquini. When they ran by me at the end of every run, Michael would say, "Crawling works too."

"Exactly," Coach said, then turned to the seniors, "Hey, you two, Mr. Pain here is going to run with you today." They whispered into each other's ears and laughed. At me? At Pasquini? I don't know. Who cares? I cared. But who *should* care? No one. Pasquini leaned in close, really whispering this time. Only I could hear him. He said, "You stay on their heels. Don't think about anything else. Find a rhythm. Linger. Wait. What do you want? You want to beat them. Right. I know you do. I can see it. But linger behind them. Keep them in sight. Which means, be okay with being behind. You don't need to attack right away. Don't need to feel pain right away. Just be there. And then, when you sense the right moment, you go get what you want. Got it?"

"Got it," I said.

I HAD BEEN THINKING ABOUT CAROLINA TODAY. A LOT, okay? She wore her hair in a ponytail, and as soon as I saw it in biology, all I wanted to do was run my hand through it. So cheesy. I know. And it didn't matter. We sat on the other side of class from each other now. Because I didn't like her. She didn't like me. We had nothing in common.

It was hard letting Todd, Craig, Randy, and Conchita run off and not trying to stay with them. Really hard. Felt weak. Felt like a waste of space. But I let them go. Settled in behind Edward and Michael. Pasquini was right. Didn't feel pain. Not the physical kind. But, man, was I bored. Tried to stop thinking about being bored, though. Tried. Edward and Michael kept talking about all the girls they wanted to have sex with, and it was obvious to me they would never talk to these girls let alone kiss them or anything else. People are so delusional.

Then I thought: Maybe I should just talk to Carolina. Just to . . . say I did it. That's pointless, Trevor. Shit. If she liked you, that Katherine girl would have said so. Instead, she steered you toward Peggy. Maybe go out with Peggy to get close to Carolina? Why would you do that? That's so fake. And cruel. And pointless. No.

The run was a 5K. There was no race tomorrow, so this would be our practice race for the week. About halfway through, not feeling even half as tired as I usually did, I had the urge to speed ahead. Maybe just to stop having to listen to Edward and Michael babble on. But I didn't. I lingered. Like Pasquini said. Linger until . . .

Actually . . . damn. I should talk to Carolina. Even if I don't talk to her, I should stop avoiding her. Walk by her. Sit by her. Smile. Screw that. I'm not going to smile. That's lame. But walk and sit by her? Yeah. Linger . . .

With a mile left, Edward and Michael stopped talking. Both too tired. At the half-mile-to-go mark, they lost a step, then a second, and that's when I knew it was time. Moved around them and added to the pace. It hurt. Legs shook. Lungs scorched. Head boiled. But I liked it.

Then I did something so strange. After I left the seniors long behind me but still wasn't near the sophomores, I said to myself, but out loud, "Nice to meet you, Mr. Pain," then I smiled like I was some mental patient. And then I ran even faster. Move. Move. Move. Yes. Yes. Yes. The sophomores, Aaron and Tor, were slowing. Or maybe I was getting faster. I said, not out loud this time but in my head, "Mr. Pain, Mr. Pain, Mr. Pain, Mr. Pain . . ." And . . .

I didn't quite catch them. With about one hundred meters to go, they sensed me nearing fast and gave it a last kick that I couldn't outdo. But I was close. I knew it. They knew it. Pasquini, and that damn grin of his, knew it too. Know what I didn't do? Fall to the ground. Remained on my feet. I could have run another mile. Or run that last mile faster.

Pasquini approached, looking like he was bursting to talk, but he just shook his head with that crooked mouth of his and went to talk to Edward and Michael, who were on their butts, and who I had beaten for the first time.

WHEN WE WERE DOING OUR POST-RUN GROUP STRETCH, during a lull in the conversation, I spoke. I had never said anything at cross-country practice before, not to the group.

"Anyone going to the Darry party tonight?" I asked. I asked because I wanted to go. Because I knew Carolina would be there. And maybe I liked pain. Or maybe I liked what pain could give me.

17

Carolina doesn't and does take a shot

So, ANYWAY, BY THE TIME I ENTERED THE KITCHEN, there wasn't much room—Peggy's house is not very big—so I just leaned next to the door frame. Katherine got a bunch of red plastic cups out from under the sink, had one of the boys open the vodka, then started pouring just a bit for everyone. These were shots, I guess. One by one, everyone got a red plastic cup and then the second boy passed one to me and I said, "I'm okay," and didn't take the cup.

The second boy called out, "Kat, this freshman is not partaking in the pre-party shot."

Everyone stepped aside so Katherine could look at me with her big eyes, and she looked so angry, like I just punched her in the face, and then I noticed Peggy had a red plastic cup in her hand even though we both promised we wouldn't drink until college, and then Katherine said, "You do the shot or you get the fuck out of my house," and everyone laughed because they probably thought she was joking, except I knew she was not joking at all.

Then things got quiet when Katherine didn't laugh, and then, one second before I was going to leave, or maybe I should just do the shot, but I was probably going to leave, Shannon said, "I'll do her shot for her," and took the cup meant for me.

"Shut up, bitch," Elizabeth Shunton said to her sister.

"No way—" Katherine started, but then the first boy said, "It's cool, Katherine. Come on. Drink yours. Let's have a good time," and he grabbed her butt, and she finally laughed.

"To the best year ever!" Katherine called out, raising her cup. Everyone else did the same, and I felt invisible, like I didn't belong here or anywhere in the world, and then they all drank their shots and screamed. Shannon drank the one meant for me, and I wanted to hug her except she probably would think I was a freak, so I didn't. Then everyone (except me, obviously) did a second shot, even Peggy, and, I don't know, I felt silly in my dress and these shoes and in this house and in high school. I wanted to go back to junior high and be in eighth grade forever.

But then Kendra arrived, because I invited her even though Peggy didn't want me to, and they offered her a shot, and she said no, and suddenly I felt I wasn't so alone even though that's a stupid reason to not feel alone. No one, not even Katherine, made fun of Kendra for not drinking. This was probably because they were all white and Kendra was black and they were afraid of coming across as racist even though it's actually racist not to make fun of someone just because they are different. I didn't really care why they didn't make fun of her or yell at her, because I really wanted her to stay at the party.

MORE PEOPLE STARTED SHOWING UP AFTER SEVEN, AND IT was actually really fun for a little while, because all the freshman girls started dancing after Shannon started, and even though she looked so sexy, like they do in perfume commercials, she said *I* was a great dancer. I didn't think I was, but I liked her telling me that anyway. But then some junior boys started trying to dance with Shannon, and she stopped, so I stopped, and then Kendra did too, but Emma, Wanda, and Peggy decided to let the boys dance with them.

Then more and more people showed up, and no one could walk without bumping into someone, and the music got louder even though no one had room to dance, except four sophomore girls jumped on the couch and tried until Katherine yelled at them.

Kendra and I decided to step outside because we wanted to breathe actual air. "Are you having fun?" I asked.

"Yeah," she said, though I don't know if I believed her because I knew I wasn't having fun anymore. I hadn't seen Peggy since the boys started dancing with her, and Shannon had disappeared into the back-yard with some of the upperclassman stoners, and Kendra and I had just been standing in a corner, people-watching, and not able to talk because it was too loud. Then Kendra said, "I still feel like I'm in junior high and just pretending to be in high school," which was EXACTLY how I felt, or at least really close.

That's when I saw a group of four boys walking toward the house under the shadows of the trees, and I don't know why I cared about these four—I mean, there were a million boys in the house, but I just kept watching them until they stepped into the light.

Then he looked at me. The boy in the back.

Trevor.

Gosh. He looked so handsome outside of school, and I wanted to cry, but actually, not really, what I really wanted to do was go talk to him, and pretend I was cool, and like I didn't care that he liked Peggy, but I didn't know how to open my mouth.

Then—what was happening?—Kendra said, "Hi, Trevor," and he said, "Hi, Kendra," and THEN he said, "Hi, Carolina," and even

99

though he said my name like the state, I fell back in love with him. Not really. I mean, maybe. I don't even know what that means. I guess I really just wanted him to like me again after not caring for three days.

He followed the boys he was with, who I didn't recognize, into the house.

"How does Trevor know you?" I asked Kendra.

She must have sensed I was all twisted up inside because Kendra said, "We're in math together. He's really nice. I thought you didn't like him anymore?"

Then I told Kendra what I hadn't admitted to anyone except my own head. "I just stopped liking him because he stopped liking me."

"How do you know he stopped liking you?"

"Katherine told me he likes Peggy."

Then Kendra whispered something I had told myself (but apparently myself didn't listen as well as I thought). She said, "I don't think you should believe anything Katherine says." And that's when I thought that even if Trevor really did like Peggy, I would much rather find that out from him instead of spending the rest of eternity wondering if Katherine had lied.

"Will you help me go talk to him?" I asked.

And Kendra said, "Of course," which was amazing, so amazing . . . gosh. Just amazing. Then she took me by the hand, and we walked back into the party. Except there were now, literally, a gazillion people in the house—yes, I'm exaggerating, but, you know, probably not by much—and I was sure there was no way we would find Trevor.

But then, through the cracks between the twelve people that stood between us, I saw the side of his face. So we moved in that direction, but by the time we got to where he'd been standing, he had moved, and we had to spin around until we saw him, this time near the stairs, and we walked that direction, except halfway there, Henry McCarthy and his big friend Jake stepped in front of us, and Henry shoved his finger in my face. "You didn't come to my game!" he yelled. Everyone had to yell to be heard at the party, but his yell wasn't very nice.

"I had soccer practice," I said.

"I don't care!" he said.

Jake said, "Girls shouldn't play sports!" And he laughed, and Henry laughed too, and I realized that even if Henry was the coolest person in the world and the only boy who would ever like me, I'd still rather be alone and a geek.

"We have to go," I said, and tried to step by him.

"I think you owe me a kiss. We lost because you didn't show up."

"She doesn't owe you anything," Kendra said.

"Who do you think you are, new girl?" Henry said.

"She's my best friend," I said, and I didn't mean to say "best," but maybe I did.

Then Jake said, "What happened to Peggy? You get jealous because she's having sex with Carl Zerrela?"

"She is not!" I yelled, and hit him, even though I'd never hit anyone.

Henry didn't say anything, but his face made me so sick to my stomach—he knew something, something about Peggy—so I pushed by him, holding tightly on to Kendra. We got to the stairs, and there was Trevor, and he smiled at me, I think, but I was too worried about Peggy so I said, "I have to go check on Peggy," and then . . .

Trevor said, "I'll help you," which was weird, but then I thought, well, obviously he wants to help because then he gets to see Peggy.

I let go of Kendra's hand as I ran up the stairs, but she ran just as fast, and Trevor was right behind both of us, and I turned and flung open Peggy's bedroom door and there on the bed was Wanda with a junior boy. The boy's shirt was off and Wanda only had on her underwear and bra. And Peggy was on the floor with the same junior that she had been dancing with. He had pulled off her dress strap so that her right boob was hanging out and her skirt was hiked up to her belly button. Peggy was so pale, and her makeup was smeared over her face like a clown.

"Are you okay?" I asked.

The junior boy on the floor said, "Get out of here!"

"Peggy!" I screamed, and got down on my knees next to her. "Are you okay?"

"I'm fine!" she yelled, swatting me away, but I could see in her eyes—because we had been friends forever—that she wasn't fine.

"Get out of here!" the junior boy said again. He stood up and tried to grab me, but Trevor pulled him away from me. Trevor was taller than he was, and the junior boy wasn't quite as brave anymore.

"Carrie?" Peggy said. "I don't . . ." And then she threw up on her carpet. It was brown, with tiny chunks of pizza she had eaten, but mostly hot and liquid.

"Fucking gross!" the boy said, grabbed his shirt and left. Wanda and the boy she was with also picked up their clothes and disappeared. I picked up Peggy, or tried to. Kendra helped, and we took her to the bathroom. She was moaning, then she threw up again, and started crying, telling me she was sorry and how much she loved me. But then she went silent, like she was sleeping with her eyes open, and she looked so sick and scared. We wet a towel and cleaned her face, then wet another and put it against her forehead. Then I laid her down on the bathroom floor and Peggy fell asleep.

"Do you think she's going to be okay?" I asked. Kendra shrugged. I was scared. I called my mom, who answered, and I was so happy my mom was a nurse even though sometimes I hated how much she worked. I told her what happened to Peggy. I was worried she was going to yell at me for being at a party with alcohol, but my mom actually never yells, and she was calm and had me check Peggy's breathing and pulse and eventually she said Peggy would be fine. She just needed to sleep.

So Kendra and I helped Peggy back to her room, and put sweatpants and a sweatshirt on her, and turned off the light. Kendra whispered, "My mom's here to pick me up. Do you want a ride?"

I said, "I think I should stay a little while longer."

Kendra said, smiling, "I think you should talk to Trevor." I had—honestly!—forgotten about him after Peggy started throwing up. Kendra and I hugged, she left, and I watched Peggy sleep for a long time, maybe ten minutes, before I thought she was fine and maybe I should see if Trevor was still at the party.

So I closed Peggy's door behind me and put up a Post-it note that said KEEP OUT so no boys would go in there, and walked back downstairs. It was still so crowded, and I thought, even if Trevor was here, I would never find him, and he probably went home anyway and that's when I heard a police siren, saw the spinning red lights, and someone yelled, "COPS!"

And whoooosh, all the gazillion people started running toward the doors at once, and jumping out the windows, and people screamed from getting smushed, and something crashed. Luckily, I was on the stairs, and so I just stepped backward and watched everyone flee as if the house were on fire. I didn't run because, well, I thought someone shouldn't.

By the time two police officers stepped through the front door, I was the only person there.

"You live here?" one of policemen asked.

"No," I said. "This is the Darrys' house."

"Where are the parents?"

"On vacation in Wisconsin."

"What's going on?" a voiced yelled, stumbling out from the basement. It was Katherine. She was drunk, and angrier than usual. Which is a lot. The senior boy that had grabbed her ass before was behind her, shirt off, but when he saw the cops he ran out the back door even though he didn't have shoes on.

"You live here?" the first policeman asked Katherine. She rolled her eyes, stumbled over to the couch, and collapsed into it.

"Yes, I fucking live here. Shit. This sucks."

"You should leave, miss," the second policeman said to me.

"I can't. Peggy's sick. She's passed out."

"Where is she?"

"In her bedroom." I pointed up the stairs.

"We'll make sure she's okay," the policeman said. "Do you have someone to take you home?"

"She has her fucking bike!" Katherine said, then cackled and swore under her breath.

"I can walk her home," a boy's voice said, stepping into the house from outside. Everyone turned except me since I was already facing him.

It was Trevor.

You know how I said I didn't really love him because I didn't know what that meant? Well, now I knew what it meant. I really did. And, gosh, did I love him.

18

Trevor does his own party loop

WHEN I ARRIVED AT THE PARTY, MY EYES LOCKED WITH Carolina's. I didn't stop to talk to her, because I'm a wimp, so they didn't stay locked for long, but for that one moment . . . I'm not going to say any generic, fake-romantic crap. No. It was just that, I knew . . . Crap. I don't know. Maybe I just I knew I liked looking into her eyes and wanted to do it again as soon as possible.

But I followed Aaron and Tor and their friend they called DJ into the house. We had to push our way through an endless, thick wall of people. Why? I don't know. Because at parties you have to move around so you look like you know what you're doing, I guess. Stupid. Whatever. But halfway across the living room, I realized I was only getting farther away from where I wanted to be. So I let the sophomores keep doing their party loop, and I stopped and looked back. Carolina and Kendra had stepped inside. Carolina was looking for someone. For me? Probably not. But maybe. Yeah. Why not, Trev? Why's it always have to be someone else? Why couldn't it be you? So I started moving back toward the front, but I lost sight of them and by the time I got near the door, in front of the stairs, I had totally lost them. Looking outside, I considered leaving. Just because. But then I waited. Just because.

When I spotted Carolina again, she was talking to my cousin Henry. He was hitting on her. He was goddamn hitting on her. Told me I couldn't like her, but here he was, making a move. Everyone's a liar. Or an asshole. Or both, like my cousin. Then I noticed Carolina's face. She didn't like Henry hitting on her. Not at all. And I couldn't stop being happy for a second, even though I hate being happy.

Then something changed, and Carolina walked toward me, and I was nervous until she said, "I have to go check on Peggy."

And not even knowing what I was thinking, I said, "I'll help you," and followed her up the stairs. We found Peggy drunk, getting felt up by some creepy upperclassman. When he tried to push Carolina away from helping Peggy, I stepped between them. I'm not brave. Never been in a real fight in my life. But I don't know. Hard to describe. Just did it and wouldn't have backed down no matter what. Didn't need to. Peggy puked and that cleared the room. Carolina and Kendra helped their friend to the bathroom and closed the door.

I lingered in the upstairs hall, but then felt like I was stalking her and she needed private time with her friends, so I went downstairs. The screaming and drinking and claustrophobia of the party all looked so boring. Truth? It didn't look boring; I felt I was boring looking at it. The more people at the party . . . the more alone I felt. Man, I'm lame.

Went outside. Thought about going home. It was a good night. I had done what I hoped. Saw Carolina. Even helped her help her friend. Yeah. I might have even looked brave in her eyes, maybe? So a good night. I should go home. Not ruin it. Not stalk her. Not look desperate and strange. But I couldn't get my legs to start walking home. So I went and leaned against a big tree and stared back at the party. Stalker! I'm such a freak! If my life were a horror movie, I would be the serial killer about to kill every kid at the party. But I'm a good guy. Right? I just didn't fit in. But I didn't want to leave either. So I was an outsider standing outside. I guess I was where I belonged.

Then I heard a siren, and police lights flashed. A cop car stopped in the middle of the street, someone yelled, "COPS!" inside the house, and then, crazy-town, every kid flung himself or herself out of the party. I just stood there, smiling at how funny they all looked sprinting in fifty directions out of the house, like baby mice escaping a sinking ship.

Most of the kids had fled by the time the two policemen got out of the car. One of them said to me, "Go home."

And I said, "I'm waiting for someone."

He didn't like how I talked back to him, so he repeated it: "I said, go home." But he didn't know I knew I wasn't doing anything illegal. Also, I knew he was probably just another screwed-up adult who only pretended he knew what he was doing. So I ignored him, and the police forgot about me and walked inside. Through the open front door I could see her.

Carolina. Standing on the stairs. She hadn't run.

I started moving toward the front door. Maybe to get a better look at her. Then I heard a cop say, "Do you have someone to take you home?" And I had my moment. So I walked inside and said, "I can walk her home." And Carolina looked at me. And I looked at her. And our eyes locked for more than a moment. I almost thought, "they locked forever," but that would be just the fake-romantic crap I hate, so I didn't think it.

CAROLINA LED A COP UPSTAIRS TO SHOW HIM PEGGY AND came back a minute later with her bag. We didn't say anything, but we did both look at Katherine Darry at the same time. She was crying to the other cop, and saliva and snot were running down her chin.

Then we turned and left through the front door. Together.

We started walking down the sidewalk. I was leading, I suppose, but I didn't know where she lived, so maybe I should ask that. But I didn't want to say anything. Which was so stupid. But I didn't. Then I noticed her wobbling on her heels and I said, "Do you have other shoes in your bag?"

She looked at her bag, thinking. "Yes," she said, "but they would look dumb with this dress."

"No, they wouldn't."

Then we didn't say anything or move for a long time. At least ten seconds.

She said, "I left my bike. . . ."

"Would you rather ride home?" I asked.

"No!" Then she took a deep breath. "I'll come back tomorrow and check on Peggy, and I can get it then." We stood there again. Another super-epic ten seconds. I grabbed her bag, unzipped it, took out her sneakers, and I don't why the hell I did this, but I got on one knee. Helped take off her heels and put on her sneakers one at a time.

What the hell, Trevor?

I was clearly not normal in my brain. But whatever. I liked helping her. When I stood back up, she had this smile on her face. She was trying to not smile, which only made the smile that much more pure. Goddamn, she was pretty. But I had to stop thinking that or else I'd say something dumb.

19

Carolina . . .

So. Like. Wait a minute.

Wait.

A.

Minute.

I didn't know what was happening. Really. He was on his knee, helping me change my shoes, LIKE I WAS CINDERELLA, but, you know, instead of a glass slipper, it was my sneakers. This was a movie. But it was my life! But it was a movie, but so perfect I almost didn't believe it, even if it was a movie, so how was I supposed to believe it was happening for real?

Gosh.

But, you know, it was happening. It really was. And then, after he changed my shoes, and I finally managed to say, "Thanks," without exploding from happiness, we started walking again. We were going the wrong way to my house but no way—no way!—was I going to tell him that.

Neither of us could talk. Why didn't I talk? He will think I'm so boring if I don't talk! Talk, Carolina, talk, talk, talk, talk, talk . . . But my mouth didn't say anything, and I hated it because he was going to hate me for not saying anything.

20

Trevor...

CAROLINA LOOKED SO GODDAMN PERFECT IN HER DRESS and sneakers, and walking with such grace, and here I was, not able to think of anything to say to her. Why couldn't I think of anything? Just say something, Trevor. Say anything. Don't just walk next to her, acting like an uncool tool. But . . .

Nothing. Nothing. Nothing came to my head.

This is why you shouldn't have stayed. She's going to realize what a loser you are. If you had left, maybe gotten hit by a car and died on the way home, she would have thought forever how you were so great for helping her with Peggy. But now? Now she was going to see how lame you are.

Say something, Trevor!

But.

Crap.

Crap . . .

21

Carolina . . .

EVEN THOUGH WE WERE WALKING SIDE BY SIDE, I KEPT turning my head so I could look at his face. He was just so attractive, and he was walking with me. ME! And even though he might never talk to me again after I was being so boring, I would remember this as the most amazing night of my life. Except then, when I still couldn't think of anything to say, I suddenly couldn't stop thinking Trevor was just being nice to me so he could impress Peggy. It made nooo sense, but my brain couldn't stop thinking it anyway, so I finally said, "Do you like Peggy?"

I should never, ever, ever, ever, ever, ever, ever have said that. I ruined everything! But then Trevor said, "No. Katherine said I should. I thought she told me to like Peggy because you told her to tell me that."

"No!" I burst out, though I didn't mean to be so loud. I wanted him to know I liked him, or at least that I didn't want him to like Peggy, but I didn't want him to know I wanted him to know so much. So I calmed myself down, super calm, and said, "I didn't tell her to say that at all. Katherine is . . ."

"Not cool," he said. I had never heard anyone call Katherine not cool. Crazy. Mean. Bitchy. But never not cool.

"She's the most popular girl in school," I said. Why did I say this?

"Being popular has nothing to do with being cool," Trevor said, and he sounded sooo cool saying it.

"Thank you for walking me home," I said, because I didn't want to tell him I liked him unless he said it first, but he would never say it because he was silent again because he was so cool and so in control and—

22

Trevor . . .

I LIKE YOU, CAROLINA. EXCEPT I DIDN'T SAY IT. ONLY THE biggest dork on earth would say something so obvious. But maybe I should say it because it would be real, not fake, not like all those dumb TV shows and movies where people pretend not to like each other forever, and a bunch of dumb things happen just because neither the girl nor the boy was smart enough to just say what they feel.

Goddamn. Yeah. Screw it.

"I like you, Carolina." I couldn't believe the words were coming out of my mouth, and yet, it felt good. I felt free. But she didn't say anything. Crap! Why didn't I just keep my mouth shut? Then I realized there was a tear in her eye. Which I didn't understand. But it disappeared and just glistened a bit. And then that smile happened again and she said—

23

Carolina . . .

"I LIKE YOU TOO," I SAID. OH. MY. GOSH. I SAID I LIKED A boy. To his face. And he had said he liked me. What did this mean? I MUST KNOW WHAT THIS MEANS OR I WILL DIE.

No, Carrie. No.

Wait a minute. I should say to myself . . .

No, Carolina, no.

You will not die. Because you are a grown-up now. You are in high school. You went to a high school party.

And now a boy was walking me home. An amazing boy who liked me and I liked him and I would spend the rest of eternity with him. That was so silly, but it was true. Even though it was impossible, it was so true.

Part Two

A COUPLE
FOR A MONTH

24
Trevor meets the other man in her life

AFTER WE HAD WALKED A LONG, *LONG* TIME, CAROLINA explained we were going in the wrong direction. I'm an idiot. But she, because she's perfect, could tell I felt like an idiot, and she said, "It's my fault! I should have said something, but I just was, you know . . . enjoying walking with you, so I didn't say anything."

"That's why I didn't ask," I said, and then we both didn't say anything. Until I said, "I can call my dad to see if he can pick us up here."

"He won't be mad?"

"He'll probably be mad, but it's almost midnight."

"I can call my dad," she said.

"He won't be mad?"

"I'm mad at him, so he knows he can't be mad at me." So Carolina called her dad and told him to pick us up in front of the town library, which had been closed for construction since I moved here.

I asked Carolina why she was mad at her dad, and she opened her mouth but then stopped herself. I shouldn't have asked. Just because someone likes you doesn't mean you should ask about her family. In fact, if you like her, you *shouldn't* ask about her family. I know I wouldn't like it if Carolina asked me about my mom.

"It's okay," I said, before she could decide to tell me or not, "I get mad at my parents too." She shook her head, but not really up and down or side to side. Shook it all directions. So I asked her about how she liked her first week of school, and even though it was a boring question, I could tell she appreciated it. She told me about her classes as if I wasn't in half of them, but I didn't mind since I liked hearing her talk. Then she asked me what I thought of school, and I pretended it wasn't pointless, because if she knew how much I hated it she probably wouldn't like me. That makes me a liar, but I don't know, I hope that Carolina will make school not as pointless, so maybe I won't be a liar in the future even if I'm a liar today.

HER DAD ARRIVED SOONER THAN I WOULD HAVE LIKED. I wasn't going to kiss her—I liked her too much to kiss her so soon— but I would have liked to just be close to her, just by ourselves, for longer. Her dad drove a Prius, the old model, and it had a big dent in the side and no hubcaps. I guess Carolina's parents don't have that much money. I suck. I shouldn't think about that. But I can always tell how rich people are by what their cars look like and then I can't not think it. I don't care that Carolina's family doesn't have as much money as mine. They're probably a lot happier without it. Money sure as hell never made my mom happy.

"Scott, this is Trevor. Trevor, this is my dad, Scott," Carolina said as she got in the front seat and I got in the back. Had to push aside three fast-food bags and some books so I could sit. Calling her dad

"Scott" made Carolina seem really mature. Maybe I should call my parents by their first names.

"Nice to meet you, Trevor," her dad said, then started driving. "What part of town do you live in?"

"Covered Bridges," I said, and I hated that I had to say it. It was the wealthy part of town. Carolina was going to think I was a snob, which I probably was because I suck, but then she said, "Kendra lives there! It's very nice. Scott, isn't it really nice?"

"It is very nice. Did you grow up in Riverbend, Trevor?" Carolina's dad had longer hair for a grown-up. Not as long as mine. But a lot longer than my dad's. It looked cool. It also made him look younger. He wore jeans and a T-shirt—not old, boxy jeans and shirts like my dad, but designer stuff. Hip. He must be a fun dad. Don't see how Carolina could be mad at him.

I said, "No, we just moved here from California over the summer. My mom grew up here, though."

"I grew up in Gladys Park, the next town over. What's your mom's name?"

"Ashley Santos."

"Is that her married name?"

"Oh yeah. No. Her name was Ashley McCarthy," I said, and as I said it Carolina's dad grinned. I didn't like that he grinned. He knew my mom when they were kids. I didn't like that he knew her. Not at all.

"I knew your mom," he said. Yeah, Scott, I knew that already. "She was so beautiful—"

"She still is," I said. Why did I say that? Who cares? I wanted out of this car. Not away from Carolina. No. We should run away together, forever.

"I bet she is. Tell her Scott Fisher from Midnight Dogs says hello. She'll know what that means." No way was I telling my mom hello for him. But I would. I'd have to. Carolina and I were going to be . . . Yep. I'd have to.

Carolina, always knowing the right thing to say, said, "Trevor and I have three classes together."

"Well, Trevor," he said, "I hope you can help Carolina take school a little less seriously."

"I like how Carolina does everything," I said, which I didn't mean. Maybe I meant it. But I didn't know for sure. My brain wasn't focused. It was tied up about Scott and my mom. And I don't know. I couldn't really . . . I don't know. Carolina liked what I said, though. She smiled at me from the front seat. This glow surrounded her. Like she was an angel. That's lame. Like she was a ghost. A ghost angel. I don't know. It all sounds lame. But she and her glow were the opposite of lame.

"I stand corrected," her dad said. "I respect that. Okay, then." We had turned into the Covered Bridges development. I told him what turns to make to my house. You know how many covered bridges are in Covered Bridges? Zero. Yep. Zero. That is why this world sucks!

Never mind. It's boring to be so negative. I don't want Carolina to see that. I'm going to be more positive. For her.

AFTER SCOTT STOPPED IN FRONT OF MY HOUSE, I THANKED him and said to Carolina, "Thanks, Carolina," even though I don't know what I was thanking her for. Not literally. I got out of the car, started moving toward the front door, and it felt wrong not to hug her good-bye. Damn. My body just wanted to hug her. But I couldn't hug her in front of her dad. Not after our first date. This wasn't even a real date! Trev, you probably are imagining that any of this will mean anything. By Monday, everything will probably go back to what it was. Strangers. Or worse.

But then I heard a door open and turned. Carolina ran toward me. Not fast. But faster than walking. And she was embarrassed, and could barely look me in the eyes. She opened her arms and wrapped me in them. And I hugged her back. Tight but not so tight. Then she pulled back a little, and we were staring at each other. So close. Her face was so close. Her lips were so close.

She wanted me to kiss her.

Crap.

Did she?

What if I was wrong? I couldn't be wrong about this!

Help!

Kiss her!

No.

Don't. So dumb, Trevor. She smiled, said, "Thank you," and turned before I could kiss her, or before I could not kiss her longer, and got back into her dad's car.

AFTER I GOT INTO BED, I LAY THERE, STARING AT THE ceiling, thinking about Carolina. About kissing her. About holding her hand. About her being my girlfriend. After thinking about this, obsessing about it actually, I realized my mouth had been stuck in this dorky frozen smile. Man, I'm such a loser. But I still went back to thinking about her. I sure as hell wasn't going to sleep.

25

Carolina gets a text

"HE WANTS TO KISS YOU, CAROLINA," MY DAD SAID AS I watched Trevor walk toward his front door.

"No, he doesn't. Shut up," I said. Trevor had such a nice house. It was fifty times bigger than ours. Gosh. He wouldn't like me anymore once he saw how we weren't as rich as he was.

"Look how slow he's walking."

"Shut up, Dad!" But I liked that he said it. My dad always treated me like I was his friend, not like a little girl. Which was amazing. Sometimes.

"Just go hug him good-bye, you'll see."

"No, he'll think—" But then I stopped talking, opened the car door, and ran after him. But I didn't want to look too nervous, so I think I slowed down, but I was too nervous so I'm not sure what really happened. I hugged him because—wait, gosh, what was I doing? This was so weird. I'm so weird! I don't know how this works! He's going to be able to tell and then my life will be over. STOP BEING SO DRAMATIC, CAROLINA. I just hugged him for two more seconds, and then I pulled back a tiny, tiny, tiny bit. Because if we were hugging we wouldn't be able to kiss. Wait.

Wait.

Wait a minute. He was going to kiss me. Our faces were, like, an inch apart, we were the only people in the universe, except I couldn't stop thinking about how my dad was watching, and maybe his parents, and how I would tell Peggy then Kendra, or maybe Kendra then Peggy, and then, wait . . .

Wait a minute.

He wasn't kissing me! He didn't like me! He didn't like me at all! Wait a minute.

He was nervous. Oh. Gosh. He was as nervous as I was! Which was amazing. That meant he really liked me, didn't it? But I couldn't say anything. I couldn't kiss him first. So I said, "Thank you," and then turned before I died from love or something.

"I GUESS I WAS WRONG," MY DAD SAID WHEN I GOT BACK IN the car.

"No, you were right. He was just nervous."

"How could you tell?"

"Because . . ." And I was going to say, *we're in love*, but that would sound crazy, even to my crazy dad, and then I was going to say, *because I know him*, but that felt like I wouldn't know what I was talking about even though I did, and so I said, "I just can."

After we had driven across town, my dad stopped in front of our house. I had almost forgotten he didn't live with us. So I said, "Mom and I are going to have sushi tomorrow night. Do you want to have it with us?"

"If you think your mom would like me there, yes."

"Of course she wants you there. You were really nice to me this week. So I want you there too."

"I love ya, kid," he said. And I almost told him I loved him too, but instead I hugged him and went inside.

WHEN I WOKE UP IN THE MORNING, THERE WAS A GIANT thing in my stomach that sort of felt like it could be pain but then I thought it was excitement, and then, I don't know, it was maybe both. I didn't look at my phone for as long as I could stand because I wanted to give Trevor as long as possible to text me, so, like, twelve minutes later, I finally looked at my phone. There was no text. This was sooo horrible I wanted to cry, but instead I breathed deeply, told myself it was okay and that everything was fine. I'm really getting better. I am.

I called Peggy, but her phone went straight to voice mail. I remembered she had been sick, and the police, and felt selfish for wanting to talk to her about Trevor. So I called Kendra and I told her what happened and then she asked, "So is he your boyfriend now?"

Oh. My. Gosh. Maybe? Oh. Maybe. "I don't know," I said.

"You should ask him."

"You can't ask someone that, Kendra!"

"Then how are you supposed to ever know if someone is your boyfriend?"

This was a stupid thing to say!

Then I thought about it.

Maybe it was an amazing thing to say. Kendra was so smart. I'm smart. So is Peggy. But Kendra was smart in a way I had never seen before. "You're right," I said. "I'll ask him. But, like, in two weeks. He might not even like me anymore today."

"I think he likes you a lot," she said.

"Me too," I said, then giggled without making a noise. After I hung up with Kendra, I saw there was a text message. It hadn't beeped. I held my breath and opened up the text and—

It was from him!

I sound like I'm ten. Gosh. I'm not ten. So I went mentally back in time and when I saw the text, I tried thinking: "That's nice that Trevor texted." But that sounded like a robot, so I stopped pretending I wasn't me and just read the text.

It said:

TREVOR

Hope you have a great Saturday, Carolina

Which was so kind. And sophisticated. But also like HE WAS A ROBOT and I wasn't going to respond right that second because I didn't want him to know how much I wanted to respond, but then I typed:

ME

You too :)

And pressed send before I could do anything else. Then . . . he didn't respond. And I was going to explode. I hated myself because I never listen to what my smarter, older self says, and I knew I would ruin everything I ever wanted, but then—

He texted back. It was a minute later. That sounds like a short time, but it was forever. Trust me.

TREVOR

Thanks ;)

The ;) made me think he was flirting with me—WHAT ELSE COULD IT BE?—so I didn't even pause and texted back:

This is weird but suddenly
I'm so much more excited about
school on Monday

This was super insane for me to text, because it basically said, "I love you, Trevor," but, you know, I don't care. Or maybe I couldn't stop myself even if I did care. So I don't care because I can't stop.

And then? He texted back (and reminded me it was Labor Day so we wouldn't have school until Tuesday, but it was cute how he told me) and it was amazing and I texted him and then he texted me, and guess what? We texted, like, the whole day, and by the time dinner came around, we had texted back and forth three hundred and nineteen times. I counted. How did people get to know each other before texting? It must have been so hard.

SUSHI WITH MY PARENTS THAT NIGHT WAS REALLY NICE. My dad was being amazing. And my mom was so happy, and she was so happy for me for being happy, and I was happy for her being happy because I was so happy. I mean, maybe Trevor and I getting together would save my parents' marriage. It could. We were that amazing together.

Then I said, "Dad knows Trevor's mom from high school," except my mom didn't like hearing it.

"We were just friends," my dad said. He was lying. I can always tell when Dad lies because he leans over and opens his eyes very wide and tries really hard to prove he's telling the truth by not blinking as he stares right at you. My mom can't tell when he lies, which is good, because I want my mom and dad to get back together. I want to have a normal family so Trevor doesn't get scared away by all our problems. My dad learned his lesson. Right? Anyway, now that I know what love is, I can explain to my dad how to not hurt my mom again.

And I don't care if my dad and Trevor's mom were, like, boyfriend and girlfriend fifty years ago. If they were serious at all, they would have gotten married. But I do think it was just another sign that Trevor and I were meant for each other.

WHICH IS CRAZY.

But amazing.

So Trevor and I texted all day Sunday. I was hoping he'd say something like, *Want to go study at Starbucks together?* or call me even, but texting was still great.

I didn't hear from Peggy until Sunday evening. She called and said, "Hi."

"How are you? You okay? I was so worried." And I was worried, I was, I just hadn't thought about how worried I was because of Trevor. I'm a horrible person.

"My mom is taking away my phone, but she went to the store, so I'm using it now."

"Is she super mad?"

"Yeah, but she's always super mad, so I don't care. But I'm never drinking again. You were so smart. I'm sorry. I was so sick yesterday. Last week was so strange. I can't wait for things to go back to normal. You're the best friend in the world, Carrie."

I didn't correct her. But I did say, "You are too, Marguerite."

"I'm sorry. Carolina," she said.

"I don't care." I did care. But I didn't want to make her feel bad.

"Don't you think our new names sound dumb? I think we should just go back to Peggy and Carrie."

"Those were our junior high names."

"Don't you wish," Peggy said, then stopped, then started again, "we could just go back to being in junior high? Things were so much better there."

"Yeah," I said, but then I said, "but I like high school. I think it's good that we got older."

"I want to be Peggy," she said, and I could tell she was mad at me.

"Okay. But I want to be Carolina."

"I want to call you Carrie." This made me mad. But I had done a horrible job of calling her Marguerite both in my head and to her face, so I just said, "Okay, but I want everyone else to call me Carolina."

"Like Kendra?" she said.

"Yes. And . . . everyone." I didn't even want to tell her about Trevor. She was in the worst mood ever.

"That's fine. I'll be special. I'll be the only one that knows the real you." This used to make me feel so good, but Peggy didn't say it to make me feel good, I don't think. We talked a little bit more, about unimportant stuff like homework, and then we hung up and I felt really sad and I didn't really know why, but then I saw a text.

TREVOR

Are you free next Saturday?

So I texted back within one second:

130

ME

Yes :)

TREVOR

Want to hang out with me?

ME

Yes :)

TREVOR

;)

So. Like. (Don't say "like" so much, Carolina. Really.)

So. Next Saturday would be . . . a date, right? Yes. My first high school date. My first real date, EVER.

This was the most amazing thing in the history of the universe. I'm exaggerating, but I'm doing it on purpose because I'm funny. But really. It was really the most amazing thing that ever happened to me, and my dad says we each live in our own private universes, so it's funny and true, sort of. Never mind.

But really! I had a date! But it was literally six billion years away. I could never wait that long. I'd think about it every second and not be able to study or walk or probably even breathe. Gosh. Really, Carolina. Stop being such a silly little girl who makes such a big deal out of everything. You'll be fine. It's just a week. Six days.

OH MY GOSH. That's so amazing. And forever.

26
Trevor has a seat saved

On the way to school Tuesday, despite Carolina and I texting constantly all weekend, I was sure, just goddamn sure, that when she saw me again in biology, she was not going to like me anymore. Or forget what I looked like. Not who I was. But more like, "Oh, wait, you don't look anything like the boy I said I liked on Friday night."

Yeah, I'm sort of obsessed with worst-case scenarios. You know why? Because it's a lot better than thinking everything is going to be great and then something, anything, going wrong. You know why else? Because bad stuff always happens!

But you know what? After I got off the bus, as I was walking through the front doors of the school, my phone beeped with a text.

It was from Carolina:

CAROLINA

**I got to class early and saved
you the desk next to me.**

My face snapped into the goofy-ass smile. How. Did. I. Find. The. Most. Awesome. Girl. On. The. Planet? Then, because I'm the weakest, worst jerk on the planet, I started thinking that when I saw Carolina I wouldn't like her. I'd be like, "Oh, wait, you don't look anything like the girl I said I liked on Friday night." Crap. Crap! This was gonna happen, I just knew it.

So I closed my eyes as I walked into class, just not wanting to face the truth, and then—

Crap.

Craaap.

She looked even prettier than I had ever seen her look. Her eyes lit up the room. Cliché! Do better, Trevor!

Her eyes were . . .

Her eyes were . . . beams of white and brown, pulling me toward her, calming my mind and inspiring my heart. . . .

That's terrible. Like, the worst poetry ever written. Screw it.

Her eyes just made me want to look at her. Okay? Look at her and no one else. Couldn't see the big-ass wall behind her. Nothing. Nothing else. Just her.

I sat next to her. She smiled. I smiled. I could have sat next to her, like this, not saying anything, just us looking at each other, all day. All week. All year. Man, I'm insane.

"Hi," she said after a bit.

"Hi," I said back. I should have said "hey," it would have been cooler, but screw it, I said what I said and she didn't mind. Carolina made everything better. Even school.

AT LUNCH, I SAT WITH MY COUSIN HENRY AND THE REST of the freshman football players. Carolina sat with Peggy, Kendra, and the rest of her usual freshman girlfriends. The tables were on opposite sides of the freshman section of the cafeteria. I would have asked her to sit with me, or us, but how do you ask that? Do you just say, *Let's sit together at lunch*? Shouldn't you be able to communicate some of this stuff without words?

I wasn't paying attention to anything Henry or the others were talking about until Jake elbowed me in chest. I looked at him, but he pointed at my cousin.

"Is it true?" Henry asked.

"What true?" I said back.

"You and Carrie Fisher. You're going out? Licker saw you two in history. Said you whispered something to her." My cousin said it as if I had broken some law. As if he were a powerful judge about to condemn me. I didn't like Licker any better than the rest of them anymore. And I was liking the rest of them even less by the second. Yeah, so I whispered to Carolina. Whispered, "History is my favorite subject." Felt stupid, but I couldn't think of anything else, and I wanted to lean close to her. Cheesy. I know. But I did it anyway. And that whisper, I guess, was all Licker needed to see to know. All that was needed to make whatever Carolina and I were public. I could deny it. Yeah. But . . . screw it.

"Yeah," I said.

"I thought I told you that you couldn't go out with her."

Licker said, "I think she's much cuter this year." Okay, I liked Licker better again.

"That's not the point, Licker!" Henry yelled. "The point is we are supposed to be like brothers, and how can we trust each other if we don't listen to each other?"

My cousin was talking like a moron. I knew this. Did anyone else? It's hard talking to a moron, especially when he's the lead kid of the popular freshman boys. Because whether you talk moron back or you don't talk moron back, you're probably going to piss him off, and if you piss him off, you're probably not going to be part of the group anymore.

"Trev? Dude. Don't just sit there and say nothing. Tell me what's up. Tell me you're not going to go out with her so that I can trust you. So we can all trust you."

27

Carolina doesn't sit with Trevor at lunch

KATHERINE DIDN'T SAY ANYTHING ABOUT THE PARTY when she picked me up on Tuesday morning. I wasn't going to say anything. Obviously. But Peggy didn't say anything at all. Then I noticed Katherine wasn't saying anything at all. And so, the three of us just drove to school in silence. Sooo uncomfortable.

Peggy clung near me on the way to biology, which was fine, but you know, she hadn't sat next to me half the time last week, and now I knew she was going to sit next to me in class and I wanted to be a good friend, but I also wanted to sit next to Trevor because . . . because, I just did. Even if he wasn't my boyfriend, we did say we liked each other, and you sit next to people you like, right?

But Peggy was my best friend forever and so I decided I would sit between them. Which was not as complicated as I was thinking it would be, but then I put my folder on the desk to my right after we sat down and Peggy said, "Who are you saving that seat for?"

"Trevor," I said as I got out my phone.

"Who are you texting?"

"Trevor," I said. And even though all I did was say his name twice, Peggy knew I liked him again and he probably liked me and not her. She also knew I hadn't told her about it, which best friends are supposed to do.

She said, "I think he found out I was into upperclassmen like Carl." Carl was the junior who was molesting her at the party right before she puked. I'm surprised she even remembered his name. I'm sure Carl wishes he could forget her name. I'm being mean. Gosh. I shouldn't be mean about Peggy. I love her, but I kind of hated her right then.

"Yeah, I don't know. Maybe," I said, and I said "maybe" because it was the nice thing to say, even though I knew Trevor never liked her and Peggy was being such a liar.

"You're being really strange, Carrie," Peggy said, which was her way of saying—right then—she hated me too. And this made me sad but then Trevor walked into biology and he looked at me like I was the most beautiful girl he had ever seen and, gosh, I didn't care if Peggy hated me forever as long as Trevor looked at me like that. That sounds horrible. Horrible! But it was sooo true I wanted to scream it right at her face. But I didn't. Obviously.

Trevor didn't ask me to sit with him at lunch. Maybe I should have asked him. But Kendra said, "Let him make some of the first moves or he won't feel good about himself," and I wasn't sure why me asking him to sit with me at lunch would make Trevor not like himself, but Kendra sounded really confident, so I listened.

But at lunch, I wished I hadn't because I couldn't focus on anything Peggy was saying or Kendra or the other soccer girls. It was about school and sports and stupid stuff and all I wanted to do was be next to Trevor. We wouldn't have to say anything, just be there, and, I don't know, smile and let everyone know that we were together and . . .

Ugh. This is really hard, combining friends and school and liking boys. I wish I could have an on/off switch in my brain so I could think about things only when I wanted to or needed to and then I wouldn't think about things I wanted to when I needed to think about something else. That makes sense, right? I think so.

Anyway, so I was trying not to look across the cafeteria toward Trevor. It was impossible to see him through all the people, so it was really just staring at nothing except the idea of where he might be sitting, and what he might be doing, and thinking, and saying, and then—

Wait a minute. No, more than that:

WAIT A MINUTE!

He was suddenly taking three last steps toward our table, his tray in his hand, like he had just appeared out of fog, except that is silly, but really, it was like he had superpowers that allowed him to just materialize and, whoosh, there he was. He looked so amazing, and tall, and handsome, and best, best, best of all, he was looking right at me and he said, "Mind if I sit by you?"

And Peggy—because she had been taken over by an evil witch!—said, "This is our table." Oh my gosh, I despised every inch of her whole stupid body, but I didn't say anything to her, I just focused on Trevor and I said, "Of course you can sit here!" I wish I hadn't said it sounding like I was five years old, but Trevor liked it, I could tell, and then he sat next to me. Kendra was on the other side and Peggy sat across from us. She was still possessed because she said, "What's wrong with your table?" But before I could say, *He just wanted to be close to me*, I stopped myself because I would have sounded so dumb, and anyway, Trevor said, "I think I need new friends." But it sounded cool and tough, not desperate or pathetic like I probably would have.

Then I said, "I'll be your friend," which, obviously, sounded pathetic. But maybe Trevor didn't think so because he gave me a super-small, almost secret smile, like he was a spy who had out-smarted everyone.

Kendra said, "I think Trevor wants to be more than your friend," and I almost died, but all the soccer girls besides Peggy laughed. Then the second it got quiet (well, quiet at our table, the cafeteria was the least quiet place ever), Trevor said, "That's true." Which was sooo cool. My boyfriend is cool! Not just nice and attractive and amazing. Cool. (I know he's not officially my boyfriend, but, well, you know what I mean.)

Peggy said, "I have to go," and gave me this super-intense look that said, *You are such a bitch,* and then stood up and left. We never give that look to each other, so it made me super nervous and con-fused. Like, what was I supposed to do? I would have followed her and made things better every day of my life except today. Because TODAY Trevor was sitting next to me, and to get up and go after Peggy would be to leave Trevor by himself and I couldn't do that. Just couldn't. So I let Peggy walk off, and just when I thought I might cry, Trevor asked, "Is something wrong?" and touched my back with his hand. Oh. My. Gosh. I love him so much. I know you think I couldn't possible love him already. But I do. I do. I do. I do. I do. I do. I do.

"Carolina?" he said, and he said it perfectly.

I do.

28
Trevor makes cereal twice

ON WEDNESDAY MORNING, WHEN LILY AND I WERE EATING cereal, my mom walked into the kitchen and asked, "Where's your dad?"

Lily responded faster than I did, mostly because she cares more about our mom not feeling like an idiot. "He flew to Los Angeles very early for work, Mom. Remember?"

"Oh. Right. I remember. When's he coming back?"

"Thursday," Lily said.

"Oh," my mom said, then leaned against the kitchen island. She was feeling stupid, and I felt bad about not caring.

"Don't worry about us. We can take care of ourselves, Mom," I said, which was supposed to help her feel less pressure, but it only made it worse.

"I'm going to make us dinner tonight," she said, proclaimed actually. Like she was announcing she was running for president.

"Do you want me to stay home and help?" Lily asked. Most kids might have said that because they wanted to skip school. Lily said it because she knew our mom had never cooked a real dinner in her life.

"No, Lily. I know you think your mom can't do anything—"

"No, I don't!" Lily said. Yes, she did. And so did I.

"But I'm not a bad cook. Just an unmotivated one. But I'm motivated today." She walked over, leaned down, and put her arms around Lily. It was awkward, but it was still almost a hug. My mom hadn't hugged us since she tried to kill herself, except when my dad was around and he basically ordered it. (In his nice "ordering" way.)

Then my mom looked at me. Crap. I think she wanted to hug me now. Not going to let that happen. So I looked down at my cereal bowl until she stood back up, walked away from the table, and turned on the coffee machine. My mom could maybe fool Lily, because Lily wanted to be fooled, into believing she was not a total failure of a parent. But no way could she fool me.

AT LUNCH, CAROLINA AND I SAT TOGETHER AT HER TABLE with the soccer girls. I felt a little stupid sitting with only girls, but I'd rather feel a little stupid with Carolina than a total fraud with Henry and the rest of them. But maybe I should find new guy friends too.

I TOOK THE LATE BUS HOME AFTER PRACTICE TO FIND LILY home alone. Yeah, she's super mature for seven, but she's still seven freaking years old and shouldn't be home alone. Ever. "Where's Mom?" I asked.

"She wasn't here when I got off the bus," she said, sitting on the floor of her room, coloring. She always stayed inside the lines.

"You hungry?"

"Mom's making us dinner."

"Are you hungry?"

"I'm going to wait for her to make dinner, Trevor! And so should you. We have to be supportive." Yep. That's my sister. Thinking it's her job to be a cheerleader for her mom.

"It's five thirty now. At seven, we're both eating whether she's here or not."

"Maybe," she said, then refused to look up from her coloring book again.

When I called her cell, my mom didn't pick up. Goddamn. Worst mother in history.

AT SEVEN TWENTY-FOUR, I POURED LILY A BOWL OF Cheerios with a cut-up banana. Only thing she would consider eating. Said it would be a snack before our real dinner.

Three minutes later—exactly three minutes, actually—my mom walked into the house from the garage. She carried two big plates with tinfoil over them.

Lily cried out like it was stupid Christmas morning, "I knew it!" Dumped her cereal in the sink and jumped in the air next to my mom trying to see what she carried.

"Trevor," my mom said, "there is one more plate in the car. Can you grab it for me?"

"Where were you?" I asked, as if my mom had stayed out after her curfew.

"I was cooking!" Mom raised the plates in the air before setting them down on the dining table.

"She was cooking, Trevor," Lily said, pulling off the foil to reveal a plate of grilled chicken garnished with charcoaled cherry tomatoes and yellow peppers. The other plate held seasoned sweet potatoes. The food looked great. Too great.

I said, still pissed and still wanting Mom to pay for it, "Lily was here for two hours alone after school."

"Lily, you were okay, weren't you?" my mom said, not looking at me.

"Yes! I'm always okay. Mom told me she wasn't going to be home."

"Lily, don't lie!" I cried out. Frustrated. Like a baby. God, I hated how my mom made me like this. "Your seven-year-old daughter is lying for you, Mom!"

"Trevor, I want this to be a fun night. Can we please make this a fun night?"

"Apologize."

"I'm sorry," she said. Fast. Too fast. She didn't mean it. And I didn't want to let her off the hook so easily.

"No, Mom, this is not okay!"

"Trevor!" Lily screamed. She never screamed. So I shut up. "She said sorry and she made us dinner!"

"Did she? Did you, Mom? Did you make all of this? Why are you carrying it in? Shouldn't food you made ALREADY BE IN THE KITCHEN?"

Lily collapsed onto the floor, hit her palms over and over against the floor, retching out some animalistic cry. Never seen her do anything like it. And I had made her do it.

"Trevor," my mom said once Lily's noises subsided enough for her to be heard. "I cooked at Grandma's. I wanted to do it with her. Is that okay or do you want to yell at me more?"

"But—" I started, because my mom still hadn't looked me in the eyes. I always knew she was lying when she couldn't look me in the eyes. Only Lily jacked up the volume of her first-ever temper tantrum. That made me stop talking. Lily was smart even when she was acting crazy. I turned toward the garage.

"Aren't you going to eat with us?" my mom asked.

"You said there was another plate in the car." Flung open the door. Aaaaaaaaaah! But the scream was just in my head.

FOUND THE LAST PLATE OF MY MOM'S "COOKING" IN THE back of her Infiniti. Chocolate and peanut butter brownies. My grandma's specialty. What probably happened was my mom told Grandma that she needed to cook something for dinner, and Grandma volunteered to help. Then she probably ended up doing the whole thing. Mom went off and did who knows what all day.

And probably not alone.

Crap. Man. It was just that one phone call. . . . Maybe my mom didn't cheat. Crap. Forget it. Forget it all. Don't care about Mom, Trevor. Don't care about her at all. Care about Lily. And Lily wants to like Mom.

No! I won't let her!

I picked up the plate of brownies and walked back into the house, ready to tell her I knew Grandma had cooked everything, only I found Lily giggling with wonder at the table as she smelled the food. She acted like it was the greatest meal she had ever seen.

Screw it. I put the brownies down next to the other food.

"Brownies, Trevor!" Lily called out. "Your favorite! This is MY favorite dinner ever!"

Double screw it. I pretended to be a monster, with a deep, gargley voice, and said, "Food so good. Food so good," and picked up a chicken thigh and gnawed at it, made a mess of my face and the table, but it made Lily laugh. Made my mom laugh too. I can act goofy for Lily, but not for anyone else.

See, life would be so simple and fun if I could pretend it wasn't bullshit.

BECAUSE LATER, AFTER WE ATE THE CHICKEN AND SWEET potatoes and vegetables, for some idiotic reason, probably because the brownies made me weak, I decided to tell my mom about Carolina. She tried to be interested, but it was hard for her to really care about anything except her own problems. Then—because, I don't know why, maybe because I wanted her to pay attention for real—I told my mom that Carolina's dad knew her from high school. She asked his name.

And I said, "Scott Fisher," and then this thing descended on my mom. A memory. I don't know. Whatever it was, it made me sick. I hated that memory of hers as much as she loved it. I hated that she knew Carolina's dad before I knew Carolina. She might have poisoned our thing thirty years ago and I couldn't do anything about it.

29

Carolina goes shopping

So Trevor had his first cross-country race Saturday morning. I asked about it one thousand times on Thursday so he would invite me to come watch, but he never did, which made me think he didn't like me as much as I liked him, but I tried not to really think that because everything else was so amazing.

Well, except Peggy. We sort of talked a little on Wednesday, but not about anything that made us hate each other. I didn't even hate her anymore, I just didn't love her. I mean, I did. I would forever. But I didn't really know what to say to her. How could I tell her about Trevor if she was going to be a poophead about it? I never say "poophead." Gosh. Something's wrong with me. Anyway, Peggy and I were still best friends, but right then we weren't really *friends* friends.

On Thursday, I went to the bathroom during study hall because I didn't want to look at Peggy any more than I had to. It's always so bizarre going to the bathroom during class periods. I never usually do because I don't want to miss anything, but I wouldn't miss anything in study hall except Peggy's stupid face. WHY WAS I BEING SO

MEAN? Anyway, the school feels like a deserted planet and any sign of life is very exotic, so I didn't see anyone walking to the bathroom but then when I got into the bathroom, there was Shannon Shunton. See, exotic. She was smoking. It was pot, I think, because of the smell, but it was the first time I had ever smelled it so I can't be one hundred percent sure.

"Hey," she said.

"Hey," I said.

"You—?" Shannon offered her cigarette. Or joint. Gosh.

"No, thank you."

"Crazy end to the party, huh?"

"Yeah."

"I heard you stuck around, faced down the cops like a superhero or something."

"Oh, not really. Peggy was sick."

"Still super cool of you. First time I drank, I got sick too. I had no idea what I was doing. I must have been nine. I was such a crazy kid," she said, talking like being a kid was something that happened fifty years ago. I wanted to hug her. Or maybe leave, but instead I went into the stall.

"Thanks for doing the shot for me," I said after I flushed and started washing my hands.

"No problem. I respect you doing whatever you got to do." Shannon was the hardest person to figure out on the planet. Seriously. I'm not exaggerating! Was she a bitch? Was she cool? Was she totally messed up? Was she the wisest freshman in history? So, so, so complicated. If I were to write a novel, I'd write one about her. It would be so interesting to know what goes through her brain.

"Maybe we should do homework together after school sometime. . . ." Why was I saying this? It felt like I was asking her out on a date. It's just . . . maybe she wanted a friend, and she had helped me with the dress and the shot and maybe—

"Aww, yeah, maybe, but I'm, like, an idiot. If I get a C, I throw myself a party. I bet if you got a C, you'd have a coronary."

"You're not an idiot," I said. "You're really smart."

"That's cool of you to say . . . but what are you doing Saturday night? Me and Wanda were gonna chill at her place."

"I have a date, but maybe—"

"A date? Yeah? With who?"

"Trevor Santos, he's new—"

"He's in history with us?" Shannon said. I nodded. "He looks like a good dude. So many dudes suck, like, fucking suck, so that's awesome. Happy for you."

"Maybe we could all go out sometime?" I didn't even know what my mouth was saying.

"Yeah," she said, laughed, then coughed, then continued, "sure."

ON FRIDAY, I FINALLY TEXTED TREVOR THAT I WANTED TO come see his race. I really just wanted to see him. I don't really understand cross-country. I mean, in soccer running is something we have to do as punishment. Why would you do it as the only thing? Anyway, I still wanted to see the race because I want him to know how much I love him without actually ever telling him I love him. Until after he tells me he loves me first. Then I'll tell him right away and every day. That will be amazing.

But Trevor texted back that cross-country races are boring and that he was not very good, which meant I couldn't come. I don't know how I felt about being a better athlete than my boyfriend (well, my future maybe boyfriend), but I guess there was always a good chance

I would be a better athlete than any boy because I'm really, really good. I don't mean to brag. It's just that, you know, I worked really hard at it. Okay?

The only good part about not going to his race was that I could prepare for our date that night. I'm sort of kidding. I mean, what could I do for twelve hours? I did all my homework and I talked to Kendra, who kept saying, "He's going to kiss you, he's going to kiss you," but she said it in this super-cute way that made me really excited, and nervous, but excited that I was nervous. Kendra was not as boring on the phone anymore. Which was weird. I thought I knew everything about her.

My dad had slept over at our house every night this week. It was amazing. I don't know what else to say. It's like we were suddenly this perfect family. Even more perfect than before he hurt my mom. He drove Kendra, Peggy, and me to practice on Labor Day morning. He did the dishes when my mom cooked and picked up bagels when she worked in the morning. Gosh. He was the best husband ever. And he was my best friend again. (Well, besides Peggy and Kendra and, I don't know, could Trevor be my best friend too?) My mom didn't know how to talk to me about boys. She would tell me all the boring stuff, like how I should get to know him "very, very well" before I got serious (she meant sex, which I wasn't having until college anyway), and that I shouldn't be alone with him in his house if his parents weren't home, and that I should never allow him to be mean to me. (I wanted to tell her that she let Dad be mean to her, but I wanted even more for her to forget that ever happened so we could be the perfect family forever.) My dad would ask me all the great questions, like what we talked about and what I liked about him, and if

I was excited to have a first boyfriend. Gosh. I totally loved my dad again and I felt sooo lucky.

I TEXTED TREVOR WHEN I KNEW HIS RACE WOULD BE OVER and asked him how it went, except he must have done poorly since he just responded, "Fine," and then, "We can talk about it tonight." It sounded so serious and sad, and I didn't want to talk about it at all. Except I did, because I wanted to be the best girlfriend ever. Gosh, I know, maybe the best not-his-girlfriend-yet ever.

So Trevor didn't tell me what we were doing Saturday night and Kendra made me promise not to ask more than once, and I didn't ask—well, only three times, but it wasn't obnoxious, I don't think. I JUST REALLY WANTED TO KNOW WHAT MY FIRST DATE WAS GOING TO BE. Kendra said that boys don't plan things well, or at least her dad doesn't, and neither does my dad, and so I'm like, I plan things very well, so maybe I should plan the date? But Kendra says I couldn't do that until we were married. I laughed when she said that. But I listened. I didn't try to tell Trevor anything. And then, in health class, the LAST class on Friday, Trevor said, "Let's meet at Lou Malnati's Pizzeria in town at seven p.m. and then, after we eat, we can walk back to my house. My dad agreed to drive you home at midnight, if you can stay out that late again."

I loved this plan, though I almost said we should have dinner at five because then I could see him sooner and wouldn't have to wait so long, but I bit my tongue (not literally), and said, "I can't wait."

Which was true. Because I really couldn't wait. Except I did. And then it was six thirty and I was having my dad drive me to the restaurant even though it would only take two seconds to get there and I would have to wait even more.

So I never talk about what I wear because my clothes are so boring, but ever since the party at Peggy's where Shannon showed me I didn't look that horrible in a tight dress, I thought about clothes a little bit more. So on Thursday night, I had my mom drive me to Marshalls to look at dresses. That's where we buy most of our clothes, which is fine, but, you know, it would have been nice to go to Macy's or someplace a little nicer for my first date. But I didn't want to make my mom feel bad for being poor. We aren't poor. We're just not rich. Gosh, I hope Trevor's not going to think I'm so boring for wearing clothes from Marshalls. But I pretended he could never tell and I found this black dress that had some lace at the bottom, and straps that made my arms and shoulders look toned, not big. And I looked good, not quite as good as at the party, but maybe it was better this way since I'm really a classy girl.

My mom said, "It looks . . ." And I could tell she bit her tongue, like, for real, and then she said, "You look grown-up. It looks very . . . adult. How fancy will this date be?"

"I don't know, he hasn't told me."

"I'll need to know where before you go."

"I know, Mom." Gosh.

"Okay, well, do you really need a new dress if you end up going for pizza?" she asked. (And knew!)

"It's my first date ever, Mom!" She saw my point and bought me the dress.

Except now I was sitting on the green bench by the cash register and every other person in the pizzeria was in shorts and sneakers and I had this black dress that made even me look like I had boobs and my legs were crossed and I had fancy black shoes with small heels so we could walk to his place after and . . . my gosh, I'd made the worst decision ever. I almost thought about calling my dad to come back and pick me up so I could change, but then I thought I would be late, and if I was even one minute late, Trevor might think I wasn't coming and then, I don't know, I could text him, but still . . .

Carolina, I said to myself, you look pretty. As pretty as you can look, at least. I'd even put on some eyeliner after my dad said I should. I'd said, "But Mom never wears makeup," and he'd said, "Guys like girls who wear makeup. Not a lot. But some. It makes us think you want to look beautiful for us." Did that mean Mom didn't want to look beautiful for him? I stopped thinking about that before I could even tell myself to stop thinking about it.

So, anyway . . . maybe Trevor was going to see me looking so silly and turn around. But probably not. He's really nice. But he'd still think I looked silly all dressed up for pizza and I'd be able to tell and I'd cry and I'd never want to go on another date again.

But at six forty-six, which was super early, but not as early as me, Trevor walked in. And he was wearing jeans, but he also had nice black shoes on and a button-down shirt AND A SPORTS JACKET. Oh my gosh, he got dressed up too. I stood up and we hugged, and I felt like we were so grown-up. Except I'm sure grown-ups never feel grown-up, they just are. I don't know. Doesn't matter.

We both wanted to look nice for our first date because we both wanted our first date to be amazing, and it was amazing that we both wanted it to be amazing.

30
Trevor doesn't stick to the plan

So even though Coach Pasquini told me how great I was running, he screwed me over for the race. I had been finishing every practice the past week right ahead of or right behind the sophomores Aaron and Tor. So I was one of the top-ten fastest on the team, and that included Conchita, who would, of course, run the girls' race.

Cross-country teams are made up of seven runners, and the top five placements count toward your team's total. You want the lowest score because first place counts as only one point, second place two points, and so on. I thought there was a small chance I would run varsity even though that was the top seven runners. I thought maybe Pasquini would decide to make a big bold choice, like they do in sports movies, and then I would win or finish just behind All-State favorite Todd Kishkin, and a new star would be born.

Even if that stupid fantasy didn't happen, and Pasquini made the more obvious choices for varsity, I thought for sure he'd have me run with junior varsity. That only required me to be top fourteen, and I was one of the top nine boys!

But nope. Nope. I was put with the freshmen. The freshmen.

I couldn't look Pasquini in the eye after he announced it on the bus to the meet Saturday morning. I said, in my head, "Screw this," and I decided I was going to quit after the race. My coach hates me! How am I supposed to be a part of a team where the coach hates me?

I'd win. I knew it. I was better, by far, than every other freshman at our school, so I knew I'd be better than all the freshmen at Barrington and Libertyville too. Pasquini kept trying to corner me before the race, but I avoided him. No reason to talk. I just needed to race. So after they fired the gun, I started out fast. I ignored Pasquini's strategy to have me always fall behind the lead pack. No one kept pace with me. I'd show him. I'd have a faster time than anyone on junior varsity and all of varsity too, and then Pasquini would feel like such crap when I quit the team. I could have been his best runner ever, and he lost me because he betrayed me.

Yeah.

Except . . .

I couldn't keep up my pace. I hadn't expected to run that fast the whole race, but I started slowing sooner than I'd thought I would. How fast had I been going? Maybe too fast. Maybe way too fast. A little freshman named Kareem, maybe five feet five and looking like he could be Lily's age, ran past me not even one-third into the race. I tried to match his strides for a bit, but . . . no way. The kid was Olympic quality. I slowed. Let him go. Then the lead pack hunted me down and I tried to stay in front of them, then in the middle, then at the back. Nope. I wasn't staying behind the lead pack today. Not after I blew my legs on that sprint at the start.

So I finished the freshman race in eleventh place. I couldn't walk afterward. My legs hated me too much. I had to sit on my butt in the middle of the grass and just let everyone else hover over me, hugging their parents or friends, celebrating what a great job they'd done. I'd told my parents this was just another practice and I had no friends. So no one hugged me. Or talked to me. Carolina had wanted to come. But I would have hated her if she'd seen me run like such a loser.

Pasquini finally managed to talk to me. Couldn't avoid him if I couldn't get off my ass.

He said, "That's why I ran you with the freshmen."

"Because I suck?"

"No, because you needed to learn that even if you're the best run-ner in the race—and YOU WERE—if you don't stick to the plan that made you good, you're going to lose."

Whatever.

But. Yeah. Okay. I won't quit. Not yet.

WHEN I GOT HOME, CAROLINA TEXTED ME, ASKING ME about the race. She was really nice. I thought about calling her up and talking to her about how I messed up, what Coach had said. I might have suggested we meet earlier. Why spend the whole afternoon alone if I could be with her? Then I thought she would have other plans and would tell me no and I'd feel even worse. So I just texted her that we could talk later. It made me sound cooler, I think. Or at least less interested in her, which is cool? I don't know. Whatever.

I went into my room and decided to lie down. Maybe I needed . . .

Yep. Napped. Great nap. Woke up, panicked that I had slept through my date, but I still had an hour. I got to see Carolina in less than an hour. Our first real date. My brain did not know how to han-dle how excited the rest of me was.

My dad drove me to Lou Malnati's in downtown Riverbend, gave me five twenties even though the pizza and sodas and even a salad wouldn't cost more than thirty. He'd never ask for change, which was good, because I was saving money in case I needed to start a new life. I might. If Carolina stopped liking me, and Lily stopped being the best (she wouldn't, but let's just say), then I really would run away. I'd be in control for the first time in my life.

As I walked toward the entrance of the restaurant, I couldn't believe I wore a sports jacket. So dumb. So pointless. So uncool. I would take it off once I got inside. But Carolina was already there. Sitting on the bench in the prettiest black dress I had ever seen. When she saw me, she leaped to her feet and hugged me. I liked her body being next to mine. It felt so comfortable. Even though it shouldn't. It should feel strange to hug someone; it should feel awkward and claustrophobic. But not with Carolina. Our hug felt even more natural than standing by myself. That sounds stupid. But screw it. It was a fact.

"You look really nice," I said.

"You do too," Carolina said, and the way she said it with her eyes so big and alive made me feel like I could do anything as long as she liked me. Then I couldn't think of what else to say, so I turned to the host and asked for a table. He led us to a back table by the window. All the other people at the restaurant were families and old people (like, in their twenties). Maybe I should have taken Carolina to a nicer place for our first date. But I didn't want to seem like a snob. Most fancy food doesn't taste nearly as good as it should. But pizza is always good. The best. Especially Lou Malnati's. It's deep-dish, which Chicago is famous for. The only good part about Chicago so far. Besides Carolina.

After we sat down, we both looked at our menus. I would look at her over the top of mine and she would see me looking at her but instead of glancing back down she would laugh a little laugh. It made me laugh all three times it happened. I never laugh. I felt like an idiot but I liked it, and I didn't know what that meant.

We ordered a small salad to share, then a Coke, a Diet Coke, and a medium pepperoni and mushroom pizza. And then . . . we had to talk. Crap. What would we talk about? She was smiling, seeming so happy, but it wouldn't last forever. If I didn't find something interesting to talk about, she would stop smiling.

"I, uh . . ." I began. Why did I open my mouth if I had nothing ready to say? But then Carolina saved me.

She said, "This is really special."

"I could have taken us someplace nicer for our first date—"

"This is perfect."

Goddamn, she was good at this. I didn't know what the hell to say, and she was saying all the right things. Say something. Crap. Say something.

But Carolina spoke first. "So how did your cross-country race go? We don't have to talk about it if you don't want to."

"No. We can. I got eleventh."

"That's great!" she said. She was so positive. Maybe too positive.

"I should have done better. I screwed up and started too fast and then couldn't keep up the pace."

"That sounds so hard."

"Yeah . . . it's, I don't know, I'm not sure I even like it. Do you always like soccer?"

"Yes. I mean, not every second. But I love it. Plus Peggy and Kendra are there, and they're my best friends."

"Are things with Peggy and you okay?" I asked, but regretted it. I shouldn't ask personal stuff. She would think I was prying and hate me.

"Yeah," she said, and nodded her head quickly, but she couldn't look in my direction. I should have never asked about Peggy and then Carolina said, "It's hard to talk to you."

CRAP. I totally screwed up everything. Fix it, Trevor! "I'm sorry. I just wanted . . . No, I suck, I'm sorry . . ."

"No, I love that you asked. You have this great ability to know what's wrong and I want to talk to you about it, because I want to talk about stuff that's not just easy stuff to talk about. But I want to sound composed for you, and I'm always so emotional, and I don't want you to think I'm a mess but I also don't want to be fake so that's why it's hard . . . Oh my gosh, I'm talking so much."

"I like it," I said.

"You do?"

"Yes. I like how fast your brain works."

"You do?" she said. Tears, happy tears I think, welled in the corners of her eyes.

"Yeah."

"You're sooo nice to me, Trevor. I don't know if it's real."

"You're so nice to me," I said.

"But you're so easy to be nice to!"

"Only because you're so easy to be nice to first."

Carolina took in a deep breath, as if she were about to jump off the diving board, "Trevor, I really, really like you."

"I really, really like you, Carolina." I knew we were being so cheesy I'd throw up if I was watching this on TV, but I didn't care. It felt really good. "Carolina . . ." I started.

"Yes?"

Except I didn't know what else I was going to say. Was I going to tell her I . . . No. Not going to say that. That would be fricking crazy. Dammit. Calm down, Trevor. Say something else now. "I want to hear everything you have to say about everything," and this sounded pathetic, but she liked it. Maybe when someone really likes you, you can't say anything wrong. Who the hell knows.

SHE TOLD ME ABOUT PEGGY. HOW THEY WEREN'T TALKING now and that it was because of me. But she made sure I knew that it wasn't my fault and that she wouldn't trade anything for me. I told her about Lily, how great she was, and almost told her about my pain-in-the-ass mom, but decided not to. Maybe I'd tell Carolina about my screwed-up family someday, but only after I was sure she would never stop liking me.

CAROLINA OFFERED TO PAY FOR SOME OF THE PIZZA, BUT I wouldn't let her. I felt like a gentleman even though it was my dad's money. Then we started walking home. I had been planning the walk home since Thursday, so nothing would go wrong.

First thing: after we left the restaurant, I would take her hand into mine and we would walk holding hands. Except as soon as we left Lou Malnati's, she crossed her arms. Maybe she was cold. Or maybe she didn't want me to take her hand. Probably. Who knows. No matter what, no way I could do it now.

Second part of my plan: we were going to walk home through the park, then over the train tracks, and then, when we were on the train tracks, I was going to stop her and say, "Can I kiss you?" This girl I kissed last spring in California—Lisa—I had asked her, and she laughed at me and said I should never ask a girl, but I don't know. I like to ask. Isn't it polite to ask? And the train tracks would be very memorable, I thought. Except I hadn't thought about her being in heels and she couldn't walk on the gravel along the tracks, so we had to turn around and walk back to the crossing on the street, which was too busy with traffic. I wasn't going to kiss her with a bunch of cars driving by and who-knows-who watching.

So then we were in Covered Bridges and it felt stupid to kiss her in this cookie-cutter village, and I worried I would never kiss her. As I was obsessing about this, Carolina nudged closer to me and grabbed my hand and . . .

Make your move, Trevor!

We walked for a dozen steps or so. It felt so right. So powerful. Like we were two people joined together to take on the world, even though we were walking in a stupid safe suburban development. Then I stopped walking, but I couldn't look at her. *Just ask her! This is strange to stop and not look at her!* So I turned toward her, and her eyes were waiting for me.

"Carolina . . . can I kiss you?"

31

Carolina gets her second kiss

"Yes," I said, or I think I did. Wait a minute. Did I? Maybe I just nodded. But even though I had said it or nodded or something, HE STILL HADN'T KISSED ME! So I said, "Yes, you can kiss me." That sounded so terrible. Like I was a queen or a prude. But maybe not that much time had passed since he asked and maybe I don't know what I said because suddenly he closed his eyes and started moving his head toward mine, and—I should close my eyes, right?—I closed my lips too and then, because I couldn't see anything, I waited the longest one second ever, and then his lips touched mine. And we pressed our mouths together, and I didn't know what else to do and I don't think he did either, so we pulled away and opened our eyes.

I said, "That was amazing," and it WAS but only because it was a kiss with a boy I liked so much, because, really, it was nothing like I imagined. It felt very weird and not romantic and like we had just pressed our lips together but hadn't really kissed. Just dry and like kissing a friend's cheek. But maybe that's how it feels? Oh my gosh, that will be so sad. I'll never want to kiss any boys that much and then I'll be alone and, maybe—

"Carolina?" Trevor asked. "I don't think . . . I'm sorry . . . I was . . ."

"Why are you sorry?" I said, calm, but really, I was like: HE WAS SORRY HE KISSED ME!

"I had this plan and I didn't do the plan so I think I was nervous, it didn't feel right and so . . ."

"What are you saying?" Don't cry, Carolina. Don't cry. He's about to tell you he doesn't like you anymore because your kissing was so terrible so be ready and DO NOT CRY.

"Can I try kissing you one more time?"

"Oh my gosh, I thought you were going to say something else. Oh my gosh, yes. I want to kiss again." And then he kissed me while I was talking and his lips were opened this time and so were my lips and so it wasn't like they were just pressing into each other, but instead our mouths were wet and they slid across each other, and over each other's lips, and then our mouths closed and then opened again and kissed again, and now I could feel his tongue, so I pressed my tongue against his, and gosh, this was so intense, I felt like our mouths were eating each other but it was exciting and I wanted to eat him more and him to eat me, and my head got light and I grabbed on to his shoulders so I wouldn't fall, which pulled us tighter together, and he put his right arm around my back and pulled me even closer than that. And we kept kissing, our mouths rolling into and over each other, and our tongues touching, and I could feel saliva going down my chin but I didn't care, I just wanted to keep him near me.

I opened my eyes, which you're not supposed to do, I read, but I wanted to see his face, and his eyes were closed and he was so close, like we had two bodies but one brain, and it was sooo weird, but also sooo nice to feel so close, and then he opened his eyes and our eyes stared into each other from one inch away and our kissing slowed down, and we just hovered close to one another.

"Hi," he said.

"Hi," I said.

"That was better," he said.

"That was the best kiss in the history of the world," I said.

He laughed. "I like you so much, Carolina. I didn't even know it was possible."

"Me too," I said, and kissed him, but just a little one, then pulled away. He had saliva on his chin, and I wiped it away with my hand without even thinking about it.

WE FINISHED WALKING TO HIS HOUSE, HAND IN HAND. I imagined us being grown-up, and being married, and walking to our own house. This was silly to think about, but I couldn't help it.

When Trevor and I walked in, it was just after nine p.m. His little sister had been sleeping on the floor by the front closet, a pillow under her head and an iPad on the floor, still playing a movie. She had snapped awake and onto her feet by the time we walked into the hall. She was wearing pink flowered pajama bottoms and a blue pajama top with golf clubs on it.

"Hello, Carolina, my name is Lily, I'm Trevor's younger sister. Welcome to our house," she said, and said my name correctly, and I didn't know what to say because she sounded more mature than I did.

So I said, "Hi, Lily. I'm really excited to meet you."

"Follow me, let me introduce you to our parents," Lily said, taking my hand in hers. I followed her into the living room.

Trevor said, "Lily likes to pretend she's an adult."

"Trevor, don't be hilarious," she said, then pointed to a handsome man with dark skin, black hair, and thick eyebrows. He wore gray slacks and a tucked-in green sweater with a collared shirt underneath. He stood as I entered the room. The woman, Trevor's mom, was blond and curled into the couch, a book in her hand. She was the prettiest mom I had ever seen. It took her an extra few seconds, but she rose as well. Both his parents came over and shook my hand.

"We're glad to have you here, Carolina," his dad said.

"You're adorable," his mom said, which was nice, and I'm sure she meant it nicely, but I wanted to be beautiful like her, not adorable. She had long, thin fingers and thin arms, and I had big biceps and tough hands and I felt like such a little girl or even worse, like a tomboy. She was sooo feminine. Trevor's mom had everything figured out, I could tell, and she had this very handsome husband, and huge house, and lots of money, and the most sophisticated daughter ever, and then, obviously, Trevor, who was the best boy in the universe. I wanted her life. I wanted to be perfect like her. Gosh. I wanted it so bad I almost stopped breathing.

"We're going to watch TV downstairs," Trevor said.

"I'm coming!" Lily said.

"You need to go to bed," Trevor said.

"Trevor's right," his dad said. "Lily, it's bedtime. But I think you two should watch TV up here in the family room."

"Why?" Trevor asked. I knew. The family room was connected to the living room, which meant they could keep an eye on us.

"Robert," his mom said, "don't be old-fashioned. They don't want to watch TV with us overhearing everything they're saying. Go on downstairs. Nice to meet you, Carolina." She shook my hand and sat back down on the couch. His dad wanted to argue, but instead he said, "Okay, Lily, say good night."

"Good night, Carolina. I'd watch TV with you except it's past my bedtime."

"Next time, I'll come over earlier," I said.

"Would you?" Lily leaped into the air.

"I promise." And then she wrapped her arms around me and I loved her instantly. I wanted to marry Trevor tomorrow. Not really. But I would if he asked. He had the family every kid dreams of that you don't think exists. But it did. And Trevor had it. And I had Trevor.

32
Trevor gets too excited

I LOCKED THE BASEMENT DOOR BEHIND US. LILY MIGHT sneak out of bed. My dad may decide it was his job to check on us. This way they couldn't. We'd be alone. Not that we were going to do anything wrong. We were just going to lie on the couch. Watch a movie. And maybe kiss more. That's all.

Our basement has the biggest TV in the house, and it's always warm and comfortable. The couch is a big L and very deep so you can sleep on it, which I had done a couple times after falling asleep watching *Saturday Night Live*.

Carolina sat down, putting her feet up on the red coffee table. I grabbed the remote and sat next to her, our shoulders and hips pressed against each other. There was a thin, soft throw blanket that I covered both our legs with. It was strange looking down, knowing all four of our legs were under the same blanket. That sounds dumb. But it was really interesting, cool, whatever.

"What do you want to watch?" I asked.

"I don't care," she said, then slipped her right hand into my left hand and squeezed. Man. She always did these little things at the exact right moment that just made me feel so good. Like she was just happy to be here with me and nothing else mattered. I had never felt that with anyone, except maybe Lily. But she's my little sister, and little sisters always want to hang out with their big brothers. Carolina could be a hundred places right now but chose to be with me, alone, in my basement.

"Do you like *Game of Thrones?*"

"I've never seen it," she said. "We don't have HBO."

"It's like *Lord of the Rings* but with more sex and blood."

"That sounds cool," she said. I pulled up on-demand, started the first episode from season one. I had seen it four times. I sat pretending to watch for two minutes, but by the time the opening credits ended, I turned to her and kissed her again. I worried she would just give me a tiny peck back because she wanted to watch the show, but no, she started kissing me right away. Even more than I was kissing her. She was so . . . aggressive. Which was good. Great. Awesome. It just made me so excited, too excited, and I was aggressive back and our mouths were just so wild that I worried I looked dumb. But I couldn't stop. It was fun and my heart was beating crazy fast and I wanted to be closer and closer to her. Closer. Closer than we could get and then I leaned into her and she leaned back onto the couch, and then I was on top of her and then . . .

Oh. Crap.

33

Carolina stops kissing Trevor

WAIT A MINUTE. WAIT A MINUTE. WAIT A MINUTE.

I stopped kissing him. I almost laughed. THANK GOD I DIDN'T LAUGH. Because I was scared. I was too young to feel what I just felt! I mean, maybe not if Shannon Shunton was having sex, but this was . . . I don't know. But it was something! Right? What did this mean? Does this always happen when you kiss boys?

"I'm sorry," he said, and pulled away, off of me, and sat up. He looked so sad. I made him feel so sad!

"I . . ." But that's all I could say. Carolina, say something so he doesn't feel so sad!

"It's just that I like kissing you. . . ."

"I like kissing you." And I did! But then—

"I didn't think it would happen," he said.

"You're the first boy I've ever really kissed, Trevor."

"I kind of thought that," he said. Oh, he thinks I'm so immature. I shouldn't have stopped kissing him! I should have just pretended I knew what I was doing!

"I'm sorry," I said.

"Carolina, you shouldn't be sorry. I just don't want you to think . . . I don't know. I like you."

"I like you!"

"And I was thinking it . . ." His eyes glanced down toward his pants. ". . . wouldn't get like that because we would just kiss. Just romantic kissing."

"It's not romantic to you?" I asked. He didn't think it was romantic kissing. Why was I such a dork?

"No, it was . . . but it was also really exciting. Really, really exciting . . ." But he said the word "exciting" like he hated it, but I think I was starting to figure out what he was feeling. Which was amazing. It was almost like I could read his thoughts.

"I like that you, it, got like that," I said, and tried to be really serious but I think I laughed a little, which was good, maybe, because he laughed a little.

"I know I'm a year older, but I've only had one girlfriend . . . and it would get like this but only after we had been dating, like, four months. We never kissed this way. It was different."

"Do you want to kiss the way you did with her?"

"No! No, no, no . . . Carolina, I mean I didn't realize how much I liked kissing until now that I've kissed you," he said, and this was the BEST THING ANY BOY, I am sure, HAS EVER SAID TO ANY GIRL EVER, and I couldn't breathe, and I wanted to cry, but happy cry. But I didn't want him to think I was crazy, so I just sat there and looked at him because I loved him so much I wanted to die. But not die! To live forever and ever with him.

"You're the greatest boy in the world, Trevor," I finally managed to say, and it felt so emotional it made me vulnerable, but I decided I didn't care.

"You say perfect things, and do perfect things, and look perfect, and I can't believe you like me," he said.

"That was the perfect thing to say!" I said.

"We are so lucky. I've never felt lucky in my life, but I feel so lucky. . . ."

"Me too." Then we stared at each other, and I loved looking into his eyes in the dark, with only the light of the television. It made me feel we were in our own world. Then we didn't say anything again for a long time and I wondered if we entered a dream, but that was silly, and then Trevor said, "Can I kiss you again?"

"Yes." And then I said, "But is it okay if we only kiss?"

"Oh, I never . . . I would never . . ." Trevor felt horrible. He couldn't look at me anymore.

"I know. I know," I said, and I didn't know what else to say and I didn't want him to be sad again, so I leaned in and kissed him. I'd planned to kiss him slower, but I didn't like kissing him slower, I liked kissing him fast, because it made my whole body tingle and my head light, which was okay because I was lying down again, and he was on top of me again and then I felt it against my leg again. . . .

Okay, I'll say it. Gosh. I feel so stupid saying it, but if I'm going to grow up, I should say it, I guess. I felt his . . . penis . . . which, you know, was excited . . . against my leg. . . . Gosh. That is SO WEIRD TO SAY! But I'd read about this a lot, and yes, I'd seen stupid porn. I'm not, like, a baby, but, you know, it's just different when it's actually happening. And even though he had his pants on and we were still just kissing and he hadn't even touched my boobs—would I like if he touched my boobs? I didn't even know, but I was glad he was waiting—and anyway, this was a very big deal that I felt my first penis even if I only felt it with my thigh and not my hand and he still had pants on. Then I paused from kissing him, because his penis made me think, which made me say, "Why haven't you asked me to be your girlfriend?"

And Trevor said, "Oh, I, uh . . ."

He didn't want me to be his girlfriend. Oh, oh, oh, oh, but I didn't want to lose him, so I said, "It's okay, we don't have to call each other 'boyfriend' and 'girlfriend'—"

But then HE said, "No, Carolina. I just thought you were my girlfriend probably before we even talked. I definitely want you to be my girlfriend. Will you be my girlfriend?"

"Yes," I said, and tried to swallow my excitement before I jumped up on the couch and danced or something, and then I kissed him, and he kissed me, and gosh.

34
Trevor can't be careful

BY THE TIME CAROLINA AND I FINISHED MAKING OUT, OUR faces were red and wet with sweat and spit. It would have been gross to outside people, but to us, I think, it was great. I didn't know what the hell to do with all my stupid smiling, so I just ignored it and hoped Carolina didn't find me too dorky doing it.

As she put her shoes back on, I said, "It really sucks I have to wait until Monday to see you again."

"Let's meet tomorrow and study together," she said the instant I was done talking.

"I love how you just say things."

"Gosh, I'm sorry. I just say what I say sometimes without thinking."

"No, Carolina, I really love it," I said, scooting next to her and taking her hand in mine. I don't even know why, but whatever. Screw it. I knew why: I didn't want her to feel bad about herself for even one second. Not one second.

"Kendra says boys don't like it. They like to be in control."

"Yeah, no . . . I think boys that aren't strong like to be in control, but boys that are strong, they like strong girls." I stood up. Maybe to feel tall. Or strong. I don't know.

"So you like strong girls?" she asked, standing up next to me, looking at me as if she really wanted to know the answer.

"I like you, and you're like the strongest girl I've ever met."

"Thanks . . ." But she wasn't that excited at being the strongest girl I've ever met, so I said, "You're strong with your mind and your personality, but you're also super pretty."

"I like when you say that," Carolina said.

"I mean it."

"No one—I mean, my dad and brother have, but no boy—has ever called me pretty before."

"You're the prettiest girl I've ever met, Carolina." She kissed me quick on the lips, then engulfed my body with her arms and just held on. I didn't let go. It felt like we just stood there, silent, hugging in my basement for hours. But it was only a few minutes. Then my dad pounded on the basement door and said it was time for Carolina to go home. We got in his BMW, which I wanted Carolina to think was cool but then I didn't and then I did again.

Her house was in the older part of town and was small, but it was nice. Maybe. I could only see it from the outside. It was one story and had only one outside light and a one-car garage behind the house. It's sort of stupid that kids get to live in nice houses if their parents are rich and have to live in smaller houses or no houses if their parents aren't that rich. Stupid and confusing. Whatever.

After we parked, I walked Carolina to her front door. I kissed her and hugged her good-bye. We didn't say anything, but maybe we didn't need to. We just knew what we had was awesome.

As I walked back to my dad's car, I felt like my body had been chopped in half. I know how that sounds. Trust me, I'm the last person that would think he would get all gushy and strange about falling for a girl. And, crap, you know what? I have to just admit it. I loved her. If this wasn't love, I don't what else it could be, right? I literally felt my skin itch to run back and grab her again. My brain couldn't stop thinking about her or imagine not being with her. It was flooded, like, really flooded, like, I could feel it gushing and overflowing with thoughts and images of her. Things she said, the way she looked at me, little things. Everything. If that's not love, what the hell is it? Tell me! Because I don't want to be in love! Man! Why did I do this to myself! She's going to stop liking me or start being mean or die or hurt herself and then my life will be worse than it ever was. So much worse.

Man, please . . . stop, Trevor . . . stop thinking so much bad all the time. . . . Come on. Stay positive. Don't wreck this, please. . . . Please, Trevor . . .

"Trevor," my dad said in the driver's seat, halfway back home.

"Yeah?" I said, but could only half listen with my brain filled with only Carolina.

"Things can go pretty fast with a first love, so just be careful. For both of you," he said, and I hated him saying it. For one, why did he think this was love? And screw him for being right, and screw him for telling me what to do. But I didn't say anything. I just nodded so he wouldn't say anything more to piss me off.

What I want to know is how are you supposed to be careful when you feel like this? If I pretend I don't want to see her every stupid second of every stupid day, then she'll think I don't like her and I'll lose her or be a liar or both . . . so how? How can you? Because I don't see how I can do anything but just be with her and think about her and kiss her and everything else whenever I can. If I were to try to do anything else, if I were to be "careful," I should just kill myself because my love for Carolina was the first thing in my entire existence that felt real. And true. And worth it.

When I got home, I texted:

ME

I like you so much

Because I had to text her something. Had to. Just as I had to breathe, I had to text her something. But I didn't want to text her "I love you" because I didn't want to freak her out. And then I waited for her to text me back, maybe she would say *I love you* because Carolina is so bold like that, but she could also text me back how much she likes me or anything, even just a smiley face, but she didn't . . . she didn't text me anything.

Something was wrong. Something I said. What did I say wrong? Crap! Oh man! I thought about calling her, but I didn't. I just sat there, staring at my phone, waiting for her to text me, but nothing came. Maybe she fell asleep. How could she sleep? No way she could sleep. She was mad at me.

All my insides scrunched up in this ugly small ball. It hurt. Real pain. Pain. No way would I ever sleep. I just thought about what I could have said wrong. What I did wrong. Everything. I did every-thing wrong. I got a stupid erection. So dumb. *Game of Thrones?* That's a guys' show! So much cheesy words and lame everything. And then I didn't say anything to her when we dropped her off.

Oh man . . . I lost her. I lost the one person I wanted. The one person I needed. I could have gone through my entire life without any-one else but her and now I had lost her. . . .

35

Carolina goes to Starbucks

WHEN I WOKE UP, THERE WAS A TEXT FROM TREVOR. IT
said how much he liked me, and I texted back within the tiniest second
ever that I liked him so much too, and then I thought about how last
night was the best night of my life. Did I think last Friday was? Maybe.
But last night was definitely better. My gosh. Maybe that's what love
is—maybe every new day is more incredible than the last. It was. With
Trevor, it was. Oh my gosh, I can't believe this is happening to me.

Trevor texted me while I was thinking about him, which was always.

TREVOR

I sent that text last night

This felt like a weird thing to text, and I started breathing fast
because I don't know why, so I texted:

ME

**I just woke up or I would have
texted you back the second
I got it last night!**

Then I waited, until he texted:

TREVOR

I think I like you too much

My heart stopped. STOPPED. He was going to dump me! He was afraid and he was going to dump me and never see me again, but then he texted:

TREVOR

;)

And that wink face was all my heart needed to start beating again, and then I texted back that we should meet and do homework together at two and then he said noon and I said yes, obviously.

I called Kendra and told her about last night. I wanted to tell her about how Trevor's penis got, you know, but I didn't want to sound like such a dork. My dad and I watched this documentary last Christmas vacation before I kicked him out about a twelve-year-old girl in New York City and how sophisticated and knowledgeable she was about sex. I was so much older than her but the way this girl talked made me think I was one hundred years younger. She could talk about blow jobs and take Facebook pictures with sexy eyes in just her bra. After watching it, I got in bed with my computer, pulled the covers over my head and looked at porn for the first time. Everyone I knew, even Peggy, had watched porn by then and would talk about it and I would just nod, like I knew what they were talking about. But, I don't know, to be honest, I was scared. My mom had said to me, "Carrie, I can't stop you from watching it, but once you watch it, you eventually are going to see things that disturb you and you will never be able to unwatch it." This was the most terrifying thing my mom had ever said, it made me feel like watching pornography would alter my brain and I would be corrupted forever. But after seeing that twelve-year-old in the documentary, and feeling like such a little girl, I knew I had to grow up and watch porn even if it totally messed me up. So I did. And, so, anyway, it didn't shock me. Not like I thought it would. Gosh, what you can see in movies and music videos and even commercials was kind of sexier anyway, it's just these people were naked and having real sex, except they looked fake, and I don't know, they acted so silly. They just banged and almost never kissed. The shapes, and all the penises and vaginas were definitely super weird and I had to look away and I got this sick feeling two times or maybe more, but I didn't think my brain melted or anything. Maybe it did screw me up, but I only watched porn one other time with Peggy over the summer and we both laughed but then got uncomfortable and turned it off.

"When we were kissing," I decided to tell Kendra, "his penis got a hard-on and pressed against my leg."

"That means he likes you," she said.

"Really?" I said, but already knew this.

"But don't have sex with him yet."

"Kendra! I'm not having sex until college."

"Yeah, right," she said.

"Why don't you believe me?" I had planned this out very carefully!

"Because no one waits that long anymore except really religious people, and they only wait because they fear God will send them to hell if they don't."

"Well," I said, "I'm definitely not having sex until I'm a junior, then."

Kendra didn't say anything, which made me think she didn't believe me, which made me think everything I planned was going to change now that Trevor was my—yes!—boyfriend. It was scary, but I was becoming mature very fast so it wasn't that scary. Right?

MY MOM DROVE ME TO STARBUCKS AT ELEVEN THIRTY-SIX a.m. On the way, she said, "Don't let this boy get in the way of your schoolwork."

"I'm going to meet him to do homework, Mom."

"Okay, just make sure you get work done."

"I get straight As, Mom!"

"I know."

"Why can't you trust me?"

"I do. But boys . . . love . . . they can make us make bad choices," she said, and I could tell she was talking about herself, and this made me sad because I thought she was happy with Dad now, but I didn't want to think about her being unhappy again, so I said, "Trevor and I, we're soul mates," and then I wish I didn't say it. Why did I say that? Because it's true and I wanted to say it out loud! And your mom should be the one person you can say things to!

"Carrie," my mom said, calling me by the WRONG name, "you met him two weeks ago."

"When you meet your soul mate, you know after two seconds! He asked me to be his girlfriend last night!"

"Just slow down."

"I'm happy! You want me to slow down from being happy?"

"No, please don't yell. . . . I just know feelings can change very fast at your age. I don't want you to get hurt."

"Trevor would never hurt me, and I would never hurt him!" I didn't really know if Trevor would never hurt me. Maybe I did! But

I would never, never, ever hurt him, I was one million percent sure, but I told my mom this because I needed her to shut up.

"Okay, okay," my mom said, taking in deep breaths, strangling the steering wheel. She was upset. Why was she upset? She was not being supportive the first and only time I would ever fall in love! She kept talking. "Just know you can talk to me about anything. If anything ever comes up."

"Why would I want to talk to you about Trevor if you are going to be so unsupportive, huh, Mom?"

"I'm not . . ." But she didn't finish her sentence. She just drove. So I didn't talk either. And then she stopped in front of Starbucks, and I said, "Don't worry, I'll find my own way home," and I said it like a brat, but I didn't care. I cared a little. But I didn't apologize, I just went inside, and even though it was only eleven forty-four, Trevor was already there and he looked up, and he saw me and I saw him, and our eyes shot laser lights into each other and our bodies rose up off the ground and flew into each other's arms, but obviously that didn't really happen but maybe I ran toward him, or maybe he ran toward me, and I had the biggest smile ever and then we kissed and I wanted to scream, *I LOVE YOU SO MUCH I AM GOING TO EXPLODE*, but I didn't say anything, I just sat down next to him at the table where he had already gotten me an iced tea, and took out my homework but as soon as I looked at it I knew it was so unimportant compared to Trevor and love and soul mates and being his GIRLFRIEND.

If I told my mom this, she would think she was right, but she was the opposite of right.

36
Trevor tries to watch a movie

CAROLINA AND I KISSED AT STARBUCKS, BUT WE DIDN'T really kiss. Not that that's what I wanted to do. I did. But it wasn't the only thing. I wanted to talk to her and be with her. And it was really hard being so close to her but not able to be even closer. We were like . . . LEGO pieces that couldn't connect, but were meant to, and would soon, but just had to wait even though it was so obvious we should be put together. That's a dumb metaphor. Sorry. I'm just trying to explain how much we wanted to be as close as we could be all the time.

At five, I walked her home even though it was two miles away. We didn't mind. It meant more time to spend together, and it was nice to hold hands. When we got to her house, she invited me in. The house was dark; it didn't have many windows and the curtains seemed to block the light even when they were open. All the furniture was older. Like it had been bought used. But it was clean, or at least vacuumed. Her dad had driven out to Northern Illinois University for his classes the next morning, but Carolina's mom was on the couch watching television. Her hair was cut short, like a boy's but wavy, and she was wearing pants that were too big for her and big brown glasses that might have been in style in the 1990s. She seemed really tired, like she hadn't slept for weeks. Maybe years.

"Hi, Trevor," she said, "I'm Mrs. Fisher." She paused the TV and raised her hand without standing.

"Nice to meet you, Mrs. Fisher," I said. Felt like a puppet. Wish I could say hello to adults with more originality.

"I'm going to show Trevor my room," Carolina said.

"I don't think that's a good idea," her mom said. Carolina ignored her, grabbed my hand, and pulled me down a short hall.

As we walked out of the living room, I whispered, "Your mom is going to hate me."

"No, she won't. She's just in a bad mood because my dad is gone for two days."

"Are you sure?"

"She doesn't understand how important you are," Carolina said.

"My dad doesn't understand how important you are to me," I said. We both squeezed our hands tighter as we entered her bedroom.

"This is my room," she said, and she spun around in the center. It was small, about half the size of mine. It had pink carpet. On the wall were magazine pictures of girl and boy soccer players. Including David Beckham, who always made me feel ugly. Above her desk was a collage of photographs with Peggy and her that said BEST FRIENDS FOREVER. On the bed was a pink blanket and a rainbow of stuffed animals. There was one framed poster, of Stanford University, between her closet and the window.

Carolina closed the door behind us and kissed me. I kissed her back. I grabbed her. She grabbed me. And we acted like we were going to swallow each other. I couldn't even think when we kissed. It was just so intense my brain turned off and my body took over.

There was a knock on the door, and we yanked ourselves apart. Both of us wiped our mouths dry, and Carolina opened the door. It was her mom. Of course.

She said, "Leave the door open," turned around, and disappeared.

I walked home a little while later because when my dad was home we always had dinner at seven Sunday through Thursday. Carolina said her mom could drive me, but I didn't want her to hate me any more than she already did.

We texted during my whole walk home so it felt like Carolina was still with me, even if only in my head.

That week at school, Carolina and I went everywhere together. We held hands. We kissed in the hall. We texted between classes. During lunch period, we spent half the time with her friends at the cafeteria table, then half the time in the hall, sitting on the floor, our sides pressed tightly against each other. She called me on Monday night, so I called her Tuesday night. Then we video chatted Wednesday, which was awesome but uncomfortable—so much pressure to look cool because we couldn't touch each other; when we could touch each other we didn't worry about looking cool—so we went back to texting Thursday night.

At practice Thursday, Tor said, "I see you got yourself a girlfriend, Pain," because that had become my nickname.

And I said, "Yep."

"You had sex yet?" one of the seniors, Edward, asked, then laughed as if what he'd said was a joke.

"No," I said.

"Better find out if she's a prude now so you don't waste too much time with her," he said. I wanted to beat Edward's face in. But I didn't do it. Of course not. I'm not a psycho in real life, only in my head. I hate that I'm a psycho anywhere. Maybe Carolina will make me normal.

I didn't care if Carolina was a prude. She wasn't. But I wouldn't care if she were. Can you be a prude with someone you love? I don't know, but I don't think so.

WE WENT AND SAW A MOVIE FRIDAY. HER DAD DROVE AND dropped us off. He was super relaxed, which made him easy to be with. Like he was in high school, but not immature. My dad is so uptight about everything. I always feel like I'm doing something wrong around him even if I'm not doing anything. My life would be a lot better if Carolina's dad was my dad. Mr. Fisher probably would have been a better husband to my mom too. Maybe he would have made her feel like she didn't have to be perfect. Who the hell knows.

Sitting next to Carolina in the theater was . . . different. Made me a bit nuts. The right side of my body did this tiny shake the entire movie. All my skin cells wanted to jump off me and onto her. She didn't notice. We had never sat next to each other for two hours without talking or kissing. Just wound me up, more each minute. Voom. Voooom. Voooooom. I couldn't really concentrate on the story, but Carolina has this cute laugh where it starts in her nose, she tries to stop it with her hand, and then it comes out the side of her mouth as part of a big smile. I concentrated on that.

Afterward, my mom picked us up. As much as my dad makes everything tense with his seriousness, I still would rather deal with him than my mom. At least my dad knows when to be quiet. But she had insisted.

"Why don't you sit in front with me, Carolina?" my mom said as I opened the front passenger door. Before I could protest, Carolina said, "Okay!" and jumped in past me. I sat in the back. Sulked. I was primed to watch my mom find a way to destroy the one thing that had made life tolerable since she tried to kill herself.

And . . . I don't know. My mom asked generic questions about Carolina's family. And school. And other crap I know my mom didn't care about. But Carolina loved it. I could see it in her expression even from the back seat. Now I worried that Carolina would like my mom, they would become friends, and I'd have to tell her that my mom was this broken person who couldn't be trusted. Then Carolina wouldn't trust *me*. And then . . .

Come on, Trevor. Breathe. Breathe. This fake, overfriendly conversation is driving me insane! Aaaaaaahhhhh . . . Okay . . . Relax . . .

As we were walking down the stairs into the basement, Carolina said, "I love your mom. You have the best mom I've ever met," and for a second I hated Carolina. And I hated my mom more than ever for making me hate Carolina.

"What's wrong?" Carolina stopped, made me face her. But I couldn't look her in the eyes.

"Nothing," I said. I wasn't going to talk about this. No way. I'd rather slam my head through the wall.

"Trevor," she said, softer, taking both my hands in hers. "Are you mad at me?" And as soon as she said it, so sincere and looking at me with so much care, not with this emptiness my mom always had, I stopped hating her and loved her more than ever.

"I'm not mad at you. I'm . . . I . . . you're the best thing in my life," I said. Seriously, if you told me I'd be saying this stuff two weeks ago, I would have jumped in front of a train.

"You're my best thing too," she said, and kissed me. It was nice. I kissed her back slowly. Which was not usual for us. But I didn't want to swallow her up right now. I just wanted to be connected and make sure the connection stayed strong, and I could only do that if my head wasn't dizzy. So we tried kissing slow, and it calmed me. We lay side by side on the couch. Our legs stacked my right, her left, my left, her right, and my right arm was under her body, her right arm rested along my side. We didn't use tongue, not much. Didn't close our eyes. Just kept kissing every few seconds, like we were nibbling at each other. Not in a gross way. But like we wanted to taste each other, savor each other. That still sounds gross. But I swear it was really sweet. Now it sounds stupid. It was great, okay?

After a while, we stopped kissing and just gazed at each other. Deeper, longer than we ever had. I could see everything inside her, and I think she saw me too. Then Carolina said, "You're crying." And crap, I realized my eyes had started tearing. I wiped them away and looked down. "Is something wrong?" she asked.

"I'm happy," I said.

"You cry when you're happy?"

"I guess I do, sometimes."

"Me too, sometimes," Carolina said. She kissed the corners of my eyes. Of course she did.

37

Carolina has a new dream

SO, WAIT A MINUTE. OKAY?

I wasn't this girl who only dreamed of getting married someday, and planning my wedding day, all that stuff. No. Not me! At all! Even before my dad cheated on my mom and I had to kick him out, it's not like I thought marriage was this amazing thing that should be my number one dream. Even when I was, like, five, I knew I wanted to be my own boss and do great things. For a long time, I thought I would be a doctor. Just because they were so important and I watched them tell my mom what to do and I knew I wanted to be the one telling other people what to do. I know this sounds like I'm a bitch, but I'm not. I just know I have really good ideas and I'm nice and I work very hard. Shouldn't those types of people be in charge? I think so. Anyway, then in junior high I took science and I wasn't very good at it. My mom said not all doctors have to be great at science, but I started thinking I would be a soccer coach instead. My mom told me women coaches can't make very much money, and it's not like money is the most important thing, but if I'm going to work as hard as I do, I want to make sure my family doesn't have to worry about money like my mom does. (My dad doesn't worry about money. He says he's more concerned with his soul and his brain, but I think he can only worry about those things because my mom worries about the money.)

So at the end of eighth grade, it was no to coaching and probably no to being a doctor. And then I started hearing about women like Marissa Mayer and Sheryl Sandberg, and I realized that I wanted to do what they do. Be in charge at a big company where I could be on television and be an example to other girls of a woman who is smart and strong. I didn't want to be famous like actresses are—just for being pretty. I wanted to be someone people respected and listened to because I sounded wise, but in a humble way.

And that's totally still true. But ever since Trevor and I became a couple . . . gosh. I also thought about getting married and having kids and going to birthday parties and on vacation as a family. Like I was sure Trevor's family did. It just sounded so fun and easy. I'd still work, obviously, but I would teach high school or something and then I'd have lots of time off to be with my family. Trevor could work the same job as his dad, and we would make plenty of money. We would be so happy. So happy. Oh my gosh, I wanted to be twenty-four and married and living in a big house right now. Right! Now!

WAIT A MINUTE. OKAY? I WASN'T THAT SERIOUS.

A little bit.

Okay, maybe a lot. But I wasn't going to say anything to Trevor. It had only been, like, three weeks since we became girlfriend and boyfriend. But already every freshman knew we were together, and even though neither of us was the most popular by ourselves, Kendra said we were the most popular couple in ninth grade. Not that popularity is that important. It's not. But just like Marissa Mayer and Sheryl

Sandberg were changing the world because they're famous (which is just being popular on a really big scale, right?), maybe Trevor and I could use being the most popular couple to make the school a better place. Like, show people how nice we were and what love can do and . . . yep, for sure, right?

We would change the school, then go to college together, and get married, and have kids, and by being perfect, amazing parents, our kids would grow up and change the world. I could see it. I could see it even more clearly than I ever saw being CEO of a big company or a doctor or any other dream I've ever had.

Homecoming was October 13, which was only two weeks away, and Trevor hadn't asked me yet. I wasn't that worried. I mean, maybe if my life was a horror movie where the girl falls in love with the greatest boy in the world who spends every day talking and texting with her only he's secretly a crazy mean monster planning on dumping her after every other person has a date, then I would be worried. Would that even be a horror film or just a really sad Disney Channel movie? I didn't know. It didn't matter. I knew Trevor was going to ask me. It was just when, and WHY WAS HE MAKING ME WAIT SO LONG? But really, it was okay.

And then, on Saturday morning, my mom woke me up and said there had been a delivery for me. Oh. My. Gosh. I mean, I had gotten stuff from Amazon before, books mostly, but never a delivery for me from someone else. So I put on some sweatpants and ran to the front door and there, waiting on the front steps, were two dozen red roses and a big note that read, *Will you go to homecoming with me? —Trevor* and I screamed, and even my mom smiled. I always thought flowers were such a dumb gift, like how could I use flowers to have fun or be smarter? But now that I'd gotten my first flowers from a boy, I could see why they were such a great thing to get. I can't explain why. I mean, maybe because they were so beautiful, and soft, and alive, and could only mean that a boy loved you? Maybe. I loved them even if I couldn't think of why I loved them.

Then I called Trevor even though it was seven thirty a.m. and he was already on the bus to his race and he answered and I SCREAMED into the phone and said yes, yes, yes, yes, like, six hundred times, and he laughed. I said I couldn't wait to see him at his cross-country meet (he finally was letting me come and watch), and then I said, "Good luck, best boyfriend ever," and we hung up.

I turned to my mom and dad (who had gotten up because no one within a hundred miles could sleep after my screaming), and I was crying from being so happy, and I said, "I love him." And my dad said, "Really?" but with a smile because he thought he was funny. And my mom said, "I know. We're happy for you."

"Really?" I said, but not being funny.

And she nodded. I ran and hugged them both at the same time, which I hadn't done since I was a baby or at least forever. It felt amazing.

THE CROSS-COUNTRY RACE WAS AN INVITATIONAL WITH twelve other schools. It was a big deal. Even though Trevor didn't tell me it was a big deal, I could tell. He was running junior varsity after winning the freshman meet last week, which was a big deal, but again, he didn't tell me it was a big deal, I just could tell. What was weird was that after he told me he had won the freshman race and told me without even being excited, I started thinking he was a really good athlete, like as good as I am or maybe even better. And even weirder? I didn't like it! Oh my gosh, how could I be competitive with my boyfriend? Shouldn't I want him to be the best in the world, even if it's a hundred times better than me? I should! I should! But I was jealous and worried that he would go on and be this famous runner, like at the Olympics, and I would be just his girlfriend who hadn't done anything and nobody cared about. . . .

Carolina, don't be silly. This was dumb. So dumb.

Anyway, the race was at this huge park in Naperville, which was a long drive. So Mr. and Mrs. Santos picked me up in their fancy SUV, and Lily was in the back seat, and I felt like I was part of their family. I dressed up a little, but not much. I just wanted Trevor's mom to think I was pretty enough for her son. Gosh, that sounds terrible. But it's true so I can't lie and say it's not.

On the drive to Naperville, Lily asked me a million questions (like, literally), and I loved answering them because every answer I gave she thought was so interesting. Mr. Santos would laugh sometimes at us, which I liked, but Mrs. Santos didn't laugh at anything and was quiet and I thought she didn't like me anymore. I tried not to think about it, even though I kept thinking about it the whole time.

When we got to the race, all the runners were warming up by running with their teams in small laps. Lily grabbed my hand and made me sprint toward Trevor and the other kids from Riverbend.

"Trevor!" Lily yelled, and my face turned red because I felt like maybe both of us looked like we were seven. "Your sister and your girlfriend are here to watch you!"

Then the other boys started laughing, and one of them yelled in a mocking little girl's voice, "Trevor! Your sister and your girlfriend are here to watch you!" And everyone laughed even louder, and I felt so stupid, like I wished I hadn't come, but then Trevor broke away from his team and ran toward us and Lily leaped into his arms and he kissed me on the cheek. Gosh. He knew how to make me feel so good no matter what was happening. SEE WHY I HAD TO MARRY HIM?

All the family and friends (and girlfriends!) gathered in the center of the big park and the junior varsity runners took off their sweatpants and gathered near the starting line. Trevor was wearing these very short shorts and a tight tank top. Even though we had spent at least one weekend night (and the last weekend both Friday and Saturday) making out on his basement couch and he had touched my boobs (well, he touched my bra and it wasn't that big a deal; I mean, it was, but I don't know) and I had touched his bare chest and even his penis (not his bare penis—do you call it a bare penis?—just his penis through his jeans), seeing him there with so few clothes on, it made me feel weird. Maybe it was a good weird? His muscles were very lean. He was thin but not skinny. He was so handsome. I knew this from the first second I saw him, but I never thought about him having a nice body. Tall and toned and so . . . hot. Gosh. My boyfriend was hot. I suddenly got insecure. I didn't want him to be hot! Handsome, yes, but hot was . . .

I wasn't hot. Maybe I was pretty. Trevor had convinced me I was pretty. But he never called me hot. No one would ever call me hot, I was sure. But Trevor, gosh, he was hot. And so many girls would want him and he would become a model and become famous and he would leave me for another model and I would be alone and I'd cry every time I saw his picture in a magazine looking so hot. . . . I wished he was handsome but fat. Not fat. Chubby. Just a little. I'd feel much better about being so in love with him if he wasn't so perfect.

38
Trevor has a race

EVERY DAY THAT TICKED BY, TICK-TICK-TICK, AND CARO-
lina didn't dump me or wasn't mean to me, but just kept being this
fucking perfect girl and girlfriend, I started to think more and more
that I didn't understand who I was or what I was supposed to be.
I knew—*knew*—that life was meaningless, I did, but now I was wak-
ing up . . . excited. Excited to go to see her, talk to her, text her. But
also excited to go to school. And excited to go to cross-country practice. And excited for stupid crap like dinner with my parents. An alien
had taken over my soul. And the worst part? I liked it.

I couldn't talk to Carolina about it. Was I supposed to tell her that
before we started dating my existence was pointless? How would she
take that? She'd either think I was way too negative before or way too
dependent on her now. So I just had to pretend that this guy she had
fallen for, this boyfriend she liked so much, who smiled all the time
and sent cheesy-ass texts like "thinking of you every second," was who
I had always been. What if I couldn't keep it up? What if the darkness
came back? What if the real me came back and she saw it and dumped

me, and I'd know for the rest of my life that I'd lost the greatest girl in the universe because I couldn't just stay happy after I had found her?

Screw it. Who knew? Who cared? Of course, me, that's who. But I couldn't do anything about it. So screw it twice. Three times. Infinite times. Screw the Trevor who realized everything was bullshit by the time he was ten. Who could see my mom's epic sadness even if no one else could. Who could see my dad totally detached from the deeper truth of everything around him. Who could see how every kid was clueless about their parents being messed up and pretending they weren't. Adults lying about their kids or about their jobs or about everything. That ten-year-old Trevor could see it all. Fuck him. Die. Sick of you. He almost liked when Mom tried to kill herself. Psycho! He made me think I knew everything. He made me think I was better than everyone because I was real and I was true and I could see right through everyone else. Screw every moment of my life that happened before Carolina. Screw it and forget it. This, my life now, was good, it was so goddamn good, and I didn't want anything destroying it, not even the real me.

AARON, THE SOPHOMORE RUNNER WHO WAS BECOMING MY closest friend on the team, told me that I shouldn't see Carolina on the nights before cross-country meets.

He said, "Save that juice for the race." I wasn't totally sure what he meant, but I listened to him. It was probably good for our relationship to have an excuse not to see her. Otherwise Carolina would realize I was so stupidly in love with her and she might lose respect for me.

But I invited her to the first big invitational of the season. In the dual meets since that first freshman race, I had been running smarter and better. Coach Pasquini would point out the runner in the race he wanted me to draft behind, and I'd just fall in after him and kick when I saw the finish line. I stopped thinking about winning, stopped thinking anything when I raced actually. Not true. I'd think about Carolina. I would see her eyes and her smile. Not her voice. Not anything. Just a close-up of her face in the shadows of my basement. Maybe that's not thinking. Maybe that's just obsessing. I don't know. It worked. Got third twice and won the freshman race last week.

So on Thursday, Pasquini told me I'd run junior varsity this Saturday. Told me I'd run behind Aaron and Tor during the race. That's when Aaron told me not to see Carolina last night. I invited her to the race to make up for canceling our Friday night plans. She understood. She always understood. We video chatted and texted the whole night. Maybe Aaron was right, I would have gotten tired kissing her like we usually do. I got tired just wanting to kiss her.

But now that I was at the starting line, waiting for them to fire the gun, I wished I hadn't invited Carolina. I'd forgotten how dorky these uniforms were. I could see her holding Lily's hand and waving at me, but she must have been thinking she wished I played football. Football uniforms are cool. Football players are cool. What high school movie ever had the cool hero run around in big circles for three miles? Even though I was starting to like cross-country, maybe even really like it, maybe I should quit. Carolina was too great to have a boyfriend who was a dorky cross-country runner.

Bam.

Starter fired the gun. Brain went simple. Found the back of Aaron, looked at his shoulder, and ran. Ran. Ran. Didn't notice anything else. Trees, I guess. Grass, then sidewalk, then grass, more grass, dirt, grass again. But really I just hung behind Aaron. Lingered, remember? That's what I did. Carolina's face painted itself on the insides of my eyeballs. So that was there. That would always be there, wouldn't it? It would. Carolina. Carolina. Carolina. Carolina. Carolina. Carolina. Carolina. Carolina. Carolina. Carolina. Carolina. Thought it every breath. Twice. Breathed it in, breathed it out.

Aaron was slowing. I didn't feel a thing. Not pain even. I felt like we had just started.

"Go, Pain, go," Aaron said to me. "The kid from York, get in behind him." So I moved around Aaron to the right, didn't even see Tor—he must have fallen off a long time ago without me noticing. There was a thirty-yard gap between Aaron and the lead pack of five kids. Kid from York was in the back. I kicked it to catch them. The space was empty and foreign. Free but lonely. That's when my legs whined. I liked it. Liked that I could still feel pain. Carolina. Carolina. Carolina. Caught the lead pack quick. Settled in. Waited. I would see her soon. Couldn't stop seeing her in my head. Never wanted to stop seeing her in reality or fantasy.

Everyone rounded between two planted flags. A long straight stretch came into view. The finish was there. Was she waiting? Was she cheering for me? Go, Pain, go. Kicked in a second time. Whoosh, whoosh, whoosh, whoosh, I went by four kids from the lead pack within twenty strides. The kid at the front had started his kick before I realized a kick could be started. He was skinny but strong, with perfect form, and could probably run another fifty miles. But I only needed to make it another two hundred meters. Go, Pain, go.

Kicked harder, toes clawed into the ground. Catching him. Catching him. Carolina. Pain. Catch him. Carolina. Go. Pain. Go. Carolina. Get him. Get her.

Got him.

Won.

Outkicked them all.

Fell hard. Couldn't breathe. Coach Pasquini fell on his knees beside me, held up my head, and said, "You special son of a bitch," then let my head drop back down into the dirt. He left as Lily fell in his place by my side. She was crying.

"Is he hurt? Are you hurt, Trevor?" Lily was screaming. Then I saw Carolina behind her, then down on the ground beside her. Beside me. Her knees were touching my legs. I could feel it everywhere. Carolina was grabbing my hand, squeezing it.

She said, "He's not hurt, Lily. He's just tired because he ran the most amazing race ever."

"He won! Trevor, you won!" Lily started slapping my chest.

I said, "I had to, you were watching."

Carolina squeezed my hand again.

39

Carolina panic googles

WHEN THE SANTOSES DROPPED ME BACK OFF AT MY HOUSE after the race, I went to my computer and typed into Google "How do I make sure my boyfriend loves me forever?" All the answers were terrible. Either about feeding him or making sure you were good in bed. The smartest answers basically said, "You can't," but that didn't help me right now! My boyfriend was going to be a model and an Olympian and the most amazing person in history. I needed to make sure I kept him happy and loving me for the rest of eternity START-ING NOW!

"How was the race?" my dad said after knocking on my door.

"Trevor won. He beat everyone. He told me it was just the junior varsity race, but he's only a freshman, and he was the best, and he's going to be famous and I probably have to be famous to make sure he stays my boyfriend."

My dad laughed.

"It's not funny, Dad!" I called him Dad. Gosh. I must be super stressed.

He sat on my bed next to my desk. "Kiddo, that's great that Trevor won. Hopefully he does become a great, famous runner. Which will be good because when you are a famous soccer player and doctor—"

"I don't want to be a doctor anymore! I just want to be with him!"

"Carolina," he said, grabbing my hand. "Healthy relationships require people to have passions outside of the relationship."

"Can you just leave me alone?" I said because I didn't want ANY advice about healthy relationships from him.

"Are you okay?"

"I'll be fine. I just love him so much."

"Have you told him that?"

"No."

"Why not?"

"BECAUSE HE HASN'T SAID IT TO ME! You are making it so much worse!"

"Okay. I'm sorry. I love you, you know that?"

"You have to. You're my dad. He doesn't have to love me. And when a million other girls love him, why would he love just me?" Oh boy, I think I started crying. Why did I cry about everything?

"Carolina," my dad said, laughing again. Laughing! My dad found my future broken heart funny! "I bet right now, Trevor is thinking, 'Carolina looked so pretty at the race. That's why I had to win. So she would love me. So she would think I was worthy of her love.' I bet he's thinking that."

"He is not!"

"Call him."

"I'll text him." So I did.

ME

**I can't stop thinking about how
amwazing you were today.**

199

And then I waited. Forevvver. But my dad stayed and waited with me, so it must not have been that long. Then my phone beeped and it said:

TREVOR

I can't stop thinking about how amazing you are EVERY day.

"Oh my God! Dad! See! See how he's the greatest person in the world? See why I love him? See why I can't ever lose him?"

"Was I right?"

"Yeah, I guess, SORT OF," I said, because he wasn't one hundred percent right. Maybe he was. But Trevor's amazing text didn't prove it totally. Just mostly.

"I was right. You know it. Which means your dad is the wisest person on the planet. Which means you have to trust me when I say: That boy is the luckiest boy in the world to have you and he knows it."

"Oh, Dad . . ."

"I know, kiddo."

"I love you," I said, which I had not said for a looong time, even before I kicked him out. He smiled. I could tell it made him feel so good. It was nice to make him feel good after he did basically the best thing he had ever done for me. Ever.

My mom drove me over to Trevor's at five. She asked, "Why don't you two ever come to our house?"

"Because they have a basement where we can be by ourselves."

"Your dad and I can go to the kitchen or our bedroom."

"Mom, that's, like, three feet from the living room. You would hear everything."

"Carolina, you're not having sex, are you?"

"Mom! No! We just talk!"

"You don't just talk. I'm not an idiot."

"We kiss! Okay. Gosh."

"All you do is kiss?" she said. She didn't believe me. I mean, yes, we went up each other's shirts and we kind of caressed each other over our jeans and stuff, but it was really just kissing—I mean, not really just kissing, but it wasn't sex or anything like that, so I said, "Yes! Just kissing! You think I'm a ho? I'm not a ho, Mom!"

"Ho? I've never heard you use that word before."

"Other kids use it. I never do because I've always done everything you want. And I still do, but you make me feel bad about myself."

"I'm sorry," she said, and her face grew very still, like she had been slapped. I hate when I make my mom feel hurt.

"Mom, I'm growing up, but I'll be okay, I promise, okay?"

"Okay."

"You are the greatest mom. You give me lots of good advice. I promise. Okay?"

"Okay," she said. She was too sad to talk anymore. Only my dad and I could make her like this. My brother was always so nice to her. He never hurt her feelings like this. But I couldn't stress about both making my mom feel better AND making Trevor love me forever, so I just drove with her in silence until she dropped me off.

AFTER WE ATE INDIAN FOOD WITH LILY ON THE MAIN floor (Trevor's parents had gone out to dinner and left us to babysit), we watched *Finding Nemo* on DVD with her and then Trevor told her it was time for bed.

"Okay, I'll go to bed," Lily said, "but, Carolina, can you please tuck me in?"

"Of course," I said, and she took me by the hand upstairs to her bedroom. Her room was a hundred times bigger than mine with new fancy furniture and for a second I was jealous, but then I didn't want to be jealous so I stopped. After Lily got into her pajamas, she leaped onto the bed, flung up the covers, and slid inside.

"You're my favorite girl in the world," Lily said.

"You're my favorite too," I said, which was true. I think.

"Are you going to marry Trevor so we can be best friends when we are grown-up?"

"Maybe. We are only freshmen." I couldn't possibly tell her that I wanted to MARRY HIM TOMORROW.

"I know. You're right. I'm so hilarious," she said. "It's just that Trevor was so sad before he met you. All the time. And now he's happy, and I want him to be happy forever."

"He makes me so happy too," I said. I wanted to ask why he was sad before me, but I couldn't say the words. I don't even know why. Maybe I didn't want to know? Why wouldn't I want to know?

"I love you, Carolina. Good night." Lily hugged me and then flopped down onto the bed.

"I love you too." I then patted down the covers and turned off the light.

By the time I got down to the basement, Trevor had fallen asleep. At first I was upset because I thought it meant he didn't want to spend time with me. But then I remembered he'd had a big day and I liked that he could rest with me there. We were so close he could sleep in front of me. It made me feel so mature. I watched him sleeping for a long time, maybe a minute, and thought about how much I loved him, and then I wanted to be near him and not just watch him. I lifted his arm up so I could snuggle next to him. Except that woke him up. He jerked up, embarrassed.

"I'm so sorry, I . . ."

"You look cute when you sleep," I said as I sat next to him and wrapped my arms around him.

"Thank you for being so great with Lily," he said.

"I love her," I said, which felt weird to say to him. We hadn't told each other "I love you," but I was saying I loved his sister? And while I was thinking about this, he kissed me. Oh gosh, I loved kissing Trevor. But tonight I was going to do more than kissing.

40
Trevor has a talk with his mom

AFTER THE RACE, MY PARENTS TOOK CAROLINA AND LILY home. I had to stay and watch the varsity meet and take the bus home with the team. Todd Kishkin got third in the varsity race. His time was better than mine by over a minute, but I still won and he finished third. I didn't say anything except in my own head. Both varsity and junior varsity teams finished second out of twelve teams. On the drive back, Pasquini told us it was the best our school had ever done at the invitational in the thirty-two years we had been going.

Back at school, my mom was waiting for me in her Infiniti. By herself. No Dad, no Lily, no Carolina.

"Where's Carolina?" I asked.

"We dropped her off at her house. You'll get to see her tonight."

"Where's Dad and Lily?"

"I wanted to talk to you alone," she said. Fantastic. My mother wanted to "talk." Alone. I didn't even know what that meant to her.

"What about?"

"It's not a bad thing, Trevor. I . . . just wanted to talk about some stuff I know your dad won't talk to you about." Now I was getting frustrated.

"Like what?" She made everything so goddamn difficult.

"Can you please not be so defensive? I'm trying to be a good mom. But also . . . a mom that's not clueless."

"Fine. Let's talk. Talk."

"Let's get something to eat. What do you want?"

"A roast beef sandwich."

"Great." My mom then drove us to a deli in Northbrook that we had never been to before. After we ordered at the counter, we waited in silence until they handed us my sandwich and two drinks, then we sat in a corner booth away from the windows. I didn't want anyone seeing me having lunch with my mom. I don't know why, I just didn't.

"Are you ready?" my mom said, breathing in deep and laughing at the same time. She was so freaky!

"Just talk."

"Carolina . . ." she began, then stopped.

"Yeah?" If she tells me to not date Carolina, I might never speak to her again.

"She's great."

"I know she's great, Mom."

"You're speaking so coldly to me."

"You're being really strange!"

"I'm sorry. We don't talk much. I'm bad at it. And I know you think I'm a pathetic person."

"I don't."

"You do. It's okay. I'd hate me too if I was you."

"I don't hate you." Which was true. I just didn't . . . trust her.

"Trevor . . . you're getting older now. I can see it. You're smart. Different smart than most kids. Like me. Like I was in high school—"

I wanted to say, *I'm nothing like you,* but now I didn't want to say anything to her.

She continued, "So I feel like we can have more mature conversations. No one ever treated me like an adult when I was in high school, so I acted even more adult than I should have to prove I was an adult. Does that make sense?"

Not at all. But I just shrugged.

"Okay. Let me start over. Carolina . . . She loves you."

"She likes me, she hasn't said—"

"She loves you. I can see it. She is so in love with you, she can hardly function."

"I love her, Mom! And I'm not going to stop!" Why was I yelling?

"I know. I know. I'm not saying you should. I'm saying let's talk about what's happening."

"She's my girlfriend."

"I know, Trevor. I meant, let's talk about what's happening emotionally and . . . sexually."

Crapping fucking crap, this was a "sex talk"? My mom is so goddamn awkward I want to punch myself in the face.

She continued, because I sure as hell wasn't saying a word. "Trevor, your dad thinks you know better. He thinks when he says, 'be careful,' to you, that is all you need to hear so you'll wait until you're married to have sex."

"We're not having sex!" I yelled but in a whisper.

"Okay, okay. That's good. It has only been a month. That's good. But you're not going to wait until you're married either, are you?"

"Mom, crap. God, can we not talk about this?"

"Let me be more direct. You're definitely not going to wait until you're married. Your dad doesn't really think you will either. I was making a point. He thinks you'll wait until college like he did. But that was a different era, and he's a different person. His parents were very religious and he grew up in a very poor neighborhood, so he had to do whatever he needed to do to get out. That meant not even thinking about girls until he got to college. Your dad is also different from you. He thinks because you are both boys that you're the same, and that Lily is like me. But Lily is her father's daughter. Very linear and measured. You and I are ... creative ... and passionate. ..."

"Mom," I started even though I didn't have anything else to say. I just wanted her to stop. My brain was filling with anger and images too quickly for me to control. I had to stop eating. I felt nauseated. I was going to puke all over the table.

"I got a boyfriend my first month of freshman year too. His name was Mark. He was a senior. I thought I was so special. Too special for anyone my age. Plus Mark was the captain of the basketball team, student council vice president. It made so many girls jealous. Which I loved. My parents thought he was great. His parents were very well-off. So my mom and dad thought I was suddenly so grown-up. Which I also loved. But Mark wasn't very nice to me when we were alone. He'd tell me I was stupid. That I wasn't pretty. That I was immature. Especially if I didn't do what he wanted."

"Mom ..." I said, again not really knowing what else to say. Then I did. "Did he ... ?"

"Oh ... not ... that. No. He didn't force me ... physically. But we had sex on our third date. He had made me feel that if I didn't, I would be worthless without him. It was painful and I cried when I got home that night. He never cared how I felt. Never cared about if it was pleasurable for me. We must have had sex a hundred times my freshman year, and I hated it every time. I loved him. I told myself I did. A girl has to love the boy she's having sex with or she'll hate herself. Mark dumped me before he went to college. I cried, but even then I don't think I was sad about being dumped. Just sad about everything. After Mark, I'd either date boys who were so boring and weak I could control them or I'd date 'cool' boys who treated me like garbage. I was dating college boys by the time I was sixteen and thirty-year-olds by the time I was in college. But it didn't matter how old they were, they would either bore me or hurt me."

Why. Was. She. Telling. Me. This.

"Your first love . . . is important. Very important. That's what I'm trying to communicate. It will shape how you choose every future relationship."

"Carolina and I are going to be together forever."

"Trevor, I know you think that—"

"WE ARE, MOM!"

"Great. Okay. Great. I hope you are. It's still just as important that you treat her with respect."

"I DO!"

"Please don't yell, Trevor. I'm sorry I'm bad at this. I'm trying to tell you that . . . in some ways, you have Carolina's whole future in your hands. You're going to want to have sex with her soon. Sooner than you realize. And she'll want it too. She'll want to be as close to you as possible even if her body isn't ready to enjoy it. Because she loves you. You're a wonderful person, but it will still terrify her."

"Oh my God, Mom, can we please end this conversation?"

"Not yet. Last bit of what I want to say. Talk to her about things. Okay? Don't not talk about it just because it's awkward. If you want to do things sexually, ask her how it makes her feel first. Ask how it feels during it, ask her how it feels afterward. This might sound easy now, and in the moment it's going to seem impossible, but it's very important. Trust me."

She stopped. It felt like she had been talking for five hours. But she finally stopped. I'm not even sure I understood half of what she said. But once she stopped, I stopped being angry and uncomfortable almost as fast.

When we got back in her car, she reached into her purse and pulled out a box of condoms.

Condoms.

My mother was handing me a box of condoms.

"We aren't having sex," I said, but quiet. Not yelling. Not even mad. Just . . . overwhelmed.

"I know. But when you decide you are ready, when both of you decide, I want you to feel prepared. Any parent would love if their child would wait until they were older. But I always promised I'd be a parent who wouldn't put my head in the sand. You're in love. She's in love. If I didn't make you aware of what's going to happen, you might not be prepared when it does happen . . . and then mistakes can happen."

"I'm not going to get her pregnant, Mom."

"I know. You're very smart and responsible. I was a very smart and 'mature' girl when I was a freshman. I didn't think it could happen. My parents never talked to me about it. They didn't talk to me about anything. And I did . . . get . . ." She stopped, sucked in two deep but quick breaths, then continued, "I never told my parents. Mark stole money from his parents, and we drove to Wisconsin to have the abortion. I don't even know why we drove to another state. I think I just wanted it to be far away."

"I'm sorry," I said, the words coming out of my mouth before I realized they were. My mom started crying. I hadn't seen her cry in a long time. She looked so young. So fragile. I felt like I was the parent.

"It's okay, Trevor. I'm okay. I never told anyone. I can't believe I told you. Your father doesn't know . . . and I don't think he'd understand. So let's not tell him, okay?"

"Okay," I said. What was strange was . . . suddenly, I don't know, I understood my mom. At least a little bit. And that made me trust her. A little bit.

SHE TURNED ON THE CAR AND DROVE US BACK HOME. WHEN we were in the garage, before she opened the door, I said, "Thank you for the talk, Mom. I'm sorry I was cold and angry. I don't . . . I'm just . . . I'm happy you said everything. I don't think many moms would say what you said . . . and I'm glad . . . you did."

She nodded, sort of smiled, then got out of the car and walked toward the door to the house. I almost tried to catch up and hug her before she went inside, but I didn't.

41

Carolina talks to Peggy about hooking up

AFTER I GOT THE FLOWERS FROM TREVOR ASKING ME TO homecoming, I started thinking about who we would go with. See, you have to go with a group to homecoming. At least, that's what Katherine had told Peggy and me over the summer. I didn't freak out about it then because I never thought I would go to homecoming freshman year, and if I did, it one hundred million percent would be with Peggy and two boys who wouldn't matter. But then I met Trevor and now I was going and Peggy and I were barely talking and Kendra said she didn't want to go and Trevor didn't have any friends, so Trevor and I would have to go by ourselves. Which made me super sad. This was going to be the most important date of my life and it would be ruined. So after my dad cheered me up this afternoon, I texted Peggy:

ME

Trevor asked me to homecoming :)

I didn't even think she would text me back. At least not right away. But she didn't JUST text me back, she called me, like, one second later.

"That's amazing!" she said, and it felt so good to hear her voice. "Henry asked me last night, so we should all go together!" Henry McCarthy? Trevor's cousin? I didn't even know he and Peggy talked to each other, and now they were going to homecoming together?

But I said, "That's so amazing! It would be so amazing to go together!"

"I know. After he asked me, Carrie, I thought about you so much, and I know we got mad at each other but that was stupid."

"I agree," I said. "I miss you."

"I miss you!"

"So Henry's your boyfriend?" I asked.

"Katherine said to call someone your boyfriend is not cool, but we hooked up last weekend and then we hooked up again last night. He asked me afterward."

"After you hooked up?" What did "hook up" mean? DID PEGGY HAVE SEX WITH HENRY MCCARTHY?

"Yeah, it was romantic."

"That's amazing," I said even though I had no idea if it was amazing or not.

"How did Trevor ask you?"

"He sent roses to my house with a note."

"Oh," she said, then was quiet, then said, "that's nice. It's, like, old-fashioned. It's nice."

"Yeah," I said, and wasn't sure if I was mad at Peggy for calling it old-fashioned or at Trevor for being old-fashioned. I just knew I was starting to feel mad.

"So you two haven't had sex yet? Everyone says you're having sex because you can't stop touching each other at school, but I said that Carrie wouldn't have had sex and not told me."

"No! No. We just kiss."

"You only kiss?" she said, like I was a silly five-year-old.

"No! I mean, he touched my boobs and I've rubbed his . . . thing." Gosh, it was hard to say the word "penis." Even to my best friend. Peggy was my best friend again, right?

"So you gave him a hand job?" Peggy asked. Wait a minute. Did Peggy just say "hand job"? We had never, ever talked like that. At least not like it was nothing.

"I mean, sort of."

"Have you touched it or not, Carrie?"

"I've touched it through his jeans."

"You guys are practically married and you haven't touched his dick? Carrie, I know you always talked about waiting, but you can't be a prude or boys won't like you." Peggy was talking so fast and using language that she never used. It made my head want to pop off my body.

"Have you had sex with Henry?" I asked, then held my breath because if she said "yes," I would cry because that would mean she hadn't told me, which meant she wasn't my best friend and maybe Trevor would leave me if I didn't have sex with him.

"No!" Peggy yelled. Which made me feel sooo much better. "We've only hooked up two times."

"So what does 'hook up' mean exactly?"

Peggy laughed. Laughed at me. Gosh. She said, "You are still so immature, Carrie. You need to hang out with me more so I can help you grow up." Last time we had really talked, Peggy said she wanted to go back to eighth grade. Now she was telling me to grow up. I had a best friend who used to be nice to me all the time and now she wasn't nice to me that much at all.

But I said, "Okay." I think I probably looked like my mom looks when she gets hurt.

"'Hook up' just means you did stuff with a boy. All these junior boys asked me out but Katherine said I couldn't go out with anyone her age. So last Saturday, Henry and I just French-kissed and he went up my shirt and he put my hands down his pants. And then last night we did the same stuff but I gave him a real hand job."

"What's a real hand job?"

"Where the boy goes at the end. You're so out of it, Carrie!"

"I'm sorry," I said. I felt so dumb. I wish Trevor and I lived on an island by ourselves and could just kiss and maybe when we were married. . . . Never mind. That's so dumb. I need to grow up. Peggy was right. I almost asked Peggy how to give a real hand job, but she would make fun of me even more and then I might hate her again and I wanted to go to homecoming with her, so I just said, "You're the *best* best friend, Peggy." It sounded fake, but Peggy didn't care because she said, "So are you. I'm so excited about homecoming."

"Me too." Which was true I guess. We talked a little more but all I could think about was that I needed to look up on the internet how to give a real hand job so that Trevor didn't think I was a prude like Peggy says.

So. Anyway. That's what I meant when I said I wasn't *just* going to kiss Trevor tonight. But now we were in his basement and I was thinking about what Peggy had said, and what Lily had said about him being sad, and what my mom had said, and how I wanted Trevor to love me forever. . . . I didn't know what to do. The internet gave horrible advice. I even watched a porn of a hand job, and oh my, gosh, it looked so weird and how could that feel good and how would I even start?

And I liked kissing him sooo much. Why couldn't we just kiss? I liked feeling his weight on me. And grabbing his head and his shoulders. I liked how he had his hands around my back.

And then he stopped kissing me and I was, like, positive he was going to say that I was a prude, but instead he said, "Does this feel good for you?"

Oh. My. Gosh. He's the most amazing boy ever. He is. He is. He is. "Yes, so good. I love kissing you. Trevor, oh, I just love it. Do you like it?"

"Very much." And then we kissed more. And then I stopped.

I said, "I just want you to be happy."

And he said, "I just want *you* to be happy." Because he is perfect and too perfect and I have to be perfect or I'll lose him.

So I said, "Do you want to do other stuff?"

He said, "I like just kissing you." Which was the exact right thing to say. Because kissing felt good and not scary and everything else felt scary in my head. But then he stopped kissing me again and said, "Do *you* want to do other stuff?"

Which was nice, but it made me think he didn't want to just kiss. Maybe he did. Maybe he was just being super nice. But why would a girl want to do anything besides kissing? What could I say? I didn't want to be a prude. I DIDN'T KNOW WHAT TO SAY! So I said, "I just want you to be happy," again.

And he said again, "I just want you to be happy." Then we went back to kissing, except I wasn't that happy anymore and I don't think he was happy, so I stopped our kissing. Again.

"Trevor . . ."

"Yes?"

"I . . ." But then I kissed him, fast and wild, and turned off my brain and turned off the brain in my hand and then it reached down along his stomach and my fingers stopped at the top of his jeans. Just inside. I could feel the edge of his underwear. Oh. My. Gosh. Then I kept pushing my hand until it was just under his underwear. Oh. My. GOSH. And he was kissing me harder and it felt exciting and I couldn't see anything and I don't know.

42

Trevor . . .

STOP HER, TREVOR. STOP HER. YOUR MOM TOLD YOU TO talk to her. So talk to her. Stop her. But feeling her fingers against my skin, under my underwear . . . It tingled everywhere. My whole body shivered, but didn't shiver, just shivered under my skin, inside my body. My breath stopped. I sucked in my stomach. Because of the tingle. And maybe because I wanted to give her hand more room to move, to go farther. If I undid my jeans, she would have more room. But I could never do that. That would be such a jerk thing to do. So I should stop. My mom was right. My mom is not as broken and pathetic as I thought. She's smart, she knows things . . . I should stop Carolina . . . but her hand feels so good, her hand hasn't even touched it but it feels so good having her fingers so close. . . .

43

Carolina . . .

I TOUCHED THE TOP. WEIRD! FEELS WEIRD! IT WAS smooth . . . wet. Maybe sticky? Oh my God, did he pee? No. No. Maybe he went already? I don't know. I don't know!

His hips were gyrating faster than usual. He liked it. He liked it. Oh my gosh, I was doing a good job. I reached farther down and my fingers went along the side. Weird, weird, weird. And then I grabbed it. And he grunted. Grunted? Or was that a moan. What's a moan? Why is there not a big instruction manual about this!

It felt very soft. I mean, it was . . . you know . . . hard . . . but the actual skin of his . . . penis . . . it was soft. So soft. Not like other parts of his body. Or my body. So weird. It felt like an alien. Maybe that's wrong. Like, I'm sure it's normal. But it was different. So different. I just held it. I didn't know what to do. In the porn, the woman moved her hand, but I couldn't move my hand because my wrist was pinned by the waist of his jeans. Not really move it anyway. And wouldn't that hurt? So I just held it. And he was moving back and forth on top of me, so I guess my hand was moving a little. Or it was moving a little inside my hand. . . .

This is a hand job, right? Right? I was doing it, right? Right?

44

Trevor . . .

CAROLINA WAS . . . GRABBING IT. IT FELT SO . . . INTENSE . . .
so intense . . . My head was draining of all thoughts and all its brains
and all that was left was that tingle, the tingle in my body filling my
head, getting bigger and bigger and bigger . . . I needed to move, I
needed to kiss her, I needed to move . . . I needed to grab her, so my
fingers gripped her under her shoulder blades—did that feel okay for
her? . . . I needed to move . . . move, move, move, move, move, move,
needed to move so that I could . . .

I KNEW, FROM WHAT I'D READ ON THE INTERNET, THAT
most boys my age were masturbating a lot by now. At least they were
saying they were. But . . . And yeah, I had looked at porn a bunch,
but, and this may make me sound like a dork or whatever, it didn't do
anything for me. It was cool. I guess. I don't know. But, like, I didn't
get an erection. Is that strange? How could I really know? You can't
talk to your friends about this and I hadn't had any friends, not real
ones, for almost two years because of my mom and moving. So I just

played video games and kissed only that one girl between Dakota and Carolina. With Dakota I never felt anything like this, but I was thirteen and I didn't really care about doing anything with her.

Crap. Okay. Listen. So. I guess what I'm trying to say is that I had never . . .

I had woken up three times in the morning after . . . a wet dream. What a lame name for it. But it's not like I remember it. Not really. But besides those wet dreams, I had never . . . come. Cum. Come. Whatever. I mean, I had erections and I touched myself, but just never all the way . . . Am I a dork? Who knows? Who cares . . .

It's just that right now, right this very second, my whole body was like a speeding car going two hundred miles per hour and I swear it was levitating off the couch and the only thing that was holding me down from floating away was Carolina and her hand around my . . . that's . . . I should stop . . . No way, no way, just move and move and move and move and . . .

45

Carolina . . .

HE WAS THRUSTING FASTER AND FASTER, AND I STARTED TO get a little scared, like he couldn't control it and I couldn't control him and I almost let go but then I was worried about letting go, so I just held on and didn't do anything but grip it tighter and tighter as he moved faster and faster until . . .

He grunted really loud and then, gush.

Oh my GOSH. It went into his underwear, but also on my hand. It was hot and really gross. So gross. But don't think it's gross, Carolina. But it was, and he stopped thrusting and his whole body was shaking, like he was sick, so I reached my free arm around and pulled him close. To steady him. He was scared too. Which I liked. Then he stopped kissing me and then he said, "I'm sorry."

"Why . . ." was he sorry? But I couldn't finish the sentence.

"I . . . just . . . are you okay?"

"Yes, I mean, yes . . . are you okay? Did I do a good job?" Oh, please, let me have done a good job!

"You did, oh my God, Carolina, it felt better than anything I have ever felt in my life."

"Really?" Really!

"Oh yeah. So—yeah . . . Yeah. So good. I just . . . I feel great, I mean, it felt great, but I want to make sure you feel okay. . . ."

"Yes," yes, yes, yes. Trevor was so nice, he was making me less nervous by the second. So I said, "Can I let go?"

"Oh yeah, sorry," he said. Then I pulled away my hand, which was sticky, so I wiped it on the cushion, but subtly so he wouldn't notice. He slid off of me and onto his shoulder. I turned so I was on my shoulder, facing him on the couch. He looked at me in a way he had never looked at me before. He was scared. More scared than I had been. Oh my gosh. I was so mature. Wasn't I?

46

Trevor...

"CAROLINA, JUST BECAUSE . . ." I STARTED, BUT THEN, CRAP. My mom was right. This was hard to talk about. Do it, Trevor! You didn't talk about it before or during like you promised your mom and yourself, so talk about it now. Do it! "Carolina . . . just because we did that, it doesn't mean we have to have sex."

"Oh . . . I . . ."

"Not that that's the same or close. But what we did was more than kissing. Right?" I wished I could change my underwear.

"Yeah," she said.

"What we did was a big deal. Right?" Maybe it wasn't a big deal to her. Maybe she thinks I'm such a dorky prude.

"Right," she said. Okay. Good.

So I said, "But sex is even bigger."

"I agree."

"Is it strange that I'm talking about this? I feel so stupid talking about it."

"I like that you're talking about it," she said, which made me feel like such a great boyfriend. So mature. I can't believe my mom's advice was so smart.

I said, because I couldn't stop thinking about how she had made me feel, "I really, really liked what you did." Maybe I hoped by telling her how much I liked it, she would want to do it again. That's manipulative. Don't do that, Trevor.

"Really?" she said again. How could she be surprised? She was so perfect at this and everything.

"Oh yeah. So much. But we don't have to do it ever again if you don't want." Oh man, that would suck so bad if we never did that again, but I love her, so yeah, right, it would be okay. But it would suck.

"I would . . . we could . . ."

"But we wouldn't have to," I said. Stop saying that! But no, it's the right thing to say. What else is the right thing to say?

"I like making you feel good," she said.

"I love you, Carolina," I said.

"Oh my gosh, I love you, Trevor."

Part Three

LOVE FOR
THE HOLIDAYS

47

Carolina goes to homecoming

Oh my gosh, if someone had looked at my phone, or Trevor's, they would have seen a gazillion texts that said "I love you" and "I love you so much" and "I love you so, so, so much" and "I love you more than anyone else has ever loved anyone" and a gazillion more just like those. I'd been copying all of our texts onto my computer, then e-mailing them to myself so in case my phone got lost or stolen I'd have the texts saved. Because someday, like twenty years from now, when Trevor and I are the greatest couple anyone has ever seen in history, we might want to read what we texted to each other when we first fell in love.

So, anyway. After I told Trevor that we were going to homecoming with Peggy and Henry, he wasn't that excited. He didn't say anything, I could just tell. So I asked him if he wanted to invite any of his friends to be in our group. But I only said this because I knew he didn't have any friends . . . except Trevor *did* have friends to invite. Which freaked me out because I didn't want to upset Peggy. How come I was so worried about Peggy? Trevor texted me that Aaron and Tor, two sophomores from the cross-country team, would also be part of our group. Ugh. Disaster. I didn't know what to do, so I texted Peggy about Aaron and Tor. Then she texted me back that that was fine because Licker and Jake were coming as well with their dates. (What desperate girl would go to homecoming with Jake? But that's mean, so I didn't really ask that.) Then two days later, Peggy texted me and said that Katherine was getting a party bus and they needed more people to help pay for it, so suddenly our group for homecoming was, like, half the school. I'm exaggerating. But it's for effect. So when I texted Trevor about the bus, he texted me that we should just go with his cross-country friends because they won't want to go on the bus. Oh my gosh! My boyfriend wanted me to ditch my best friend! I didn't text him back right away and he realized I was upset, so he texted me a second time that the bus would be fun. He didn't mean it, but I texted him back,

ME

I love you sooooooo oooooooooooooooo much

And he texted me back,

TREVOR

I love you too

Which I could tell was not very enthusiastic, which I think meant he was upset about the bus, but I think sometimes both people can't get what they want and best friends (Peggy) are more important than new friends (Aaron and Tor). So I didn't feel bad about getting my way.

ON THE NIGHT OF HOMECOMING, PEGGY WANTED ME TO come over and get ready with her. But Trevor wanted to pick me up.

He had just gotten his driver's permit, so he was allowed to drive as long as one of his parents was in the car. This was really difficult for me. I loved Trevor more than life itself, but I didn't want to hurt Peggy's feelings. So I asked my parents at dinner for their advice, which was so weird since I never asked them for advice at the same time.

"You have known Peggy a lot longer. I'm sure Trevor will understand," my mom said.

But my dad said, "Didn't Trevor agree to go on the party bus for you?"

"Yeah . . ." I said.

"So I think it would be a good compromise to let him pick you up. When a boy first gets to drive, it's very important, and he wants to share that with you." Gosh. My dad was brilliant. He was right. I'm so lucky to have him as my dad. And, you know, I think this is why it's important for kids to have both dads and moms. So they can give you advice on the opposite sex. I mean, I'm, obviously, supportive of gay marriage because we are all equal and everyone should be able to love who they love. But I'm just saying that it might be hard for two lesbian moms to give a girl advice on teenage boys and how they might like to drive a car for their girlfriend. But, you know, I bet if my mom were a lesbian then my other lesbian mom wouldn't have hurt her like my dad did. So maybe no parents are perfect no matter what. I don't know. Never mind.

SO ON THE NIGHT OF HOMECOMING, I WORE A STRAPLESS dark green dress and black high heels that showed my toes. My dad bought the dress for me because my mom thought I could just wear the same dress I had for our first date at Lou Malnati's. She just didn't get it. It doesn't matter.

It was the first time I was wearing a strapless dress since I was, like, ever. But last weekend, Trevor and I had hooked up in his basement again and he was great, and we talked about how we wanted to feel our skin closer to each other so I took off his shirt and he took off mine (but I said I wanted to keep my bra on and he was super nice and said whatever I wanted). Anyway, he kept saying what a sexy body I had, and I said, "My shoulders are so big," and he said, "They are so toned and sexy," and he said I had a better stomach than he did and I guess that was nice, but really it was my shoulders that I liked being called sexy. I guess that's what made me get the strapless dress. Even though now that I was waiting for him to pick me up, I felt naked.

It didn't help when my mom said, "It looks like lingerie." Oh gosh, I wanted to change that instant before I stopped breathing, but my dad said, "Our daughter looks very, very beautiful."

"Trevor's going to think sex thoughts," my mom said.

"He's a teenage boy; he would think them if she was wearing sweatpants."

"Ugh, fine. You do look beautiful, Carolina. Your mother just . . . isn't ready for you to grow up, I guess."

WHEN TREVOR ARRIVED IN HIS DAD'S BMW, HIS DAD WAS in the passenger seat and Lily was in the back. I guess his mom was sick or something. Anyway, Trevor stepped out of the car in a tux with a thin black tie and he looked so, so, so, so amazing. Like there should be photographers taking pictures of him everywhere he went. Like he was worth a million dollars.

"He is very handsome," my mom said as we watched him walk toward our house. Lily raced behind him even though her dad was yelling at her to get back in the car.

When I opened the door, Lily screamed, "Oh, Carolina, you look so incredible. I can't even believe it." My parents laughed. They had never met Lily, but you could tell they loved her the second she said that. It's impossible not to love Lily. Then she said, "Trevor, doesn't Carolina look like the most beautiful girl you have ever seen?"

"Yes, Lily," he said, then leaned and kissed me on the lips. I was worried about my lipstick smearing, but then I thought that was dumb so I didn't worry about it and just enjoyed kissing him. We took a bunch of pictures, by ourselves and some with Lily, then I hugged my parents good-bye and got into the front passenger seat. Trevor got behind the wheel. He looked so old. Like twenty.

"Look behind you before you put it in reverse," his dad said from the back seat.

"I know," Trevor said.

"He knows," Lily said, hopping up and down on the back seat, waving at me.

"Seat belt, now," Mr. Santos said to Lily.

"You're right, Dad. I wasn't thinking because I was so excited about Carolina and Trevor's big night." Gosh, I love her.

WHEN WE GOT TO PEGGY'S, TREVOR AND I GOT OUT OF THE BMW, hugged Lily, then waved as she and Mr. Santos drove away. We were the first ones to arrive besides Katherine and Peggy. Because, duh, they lived there.

As we walked to the front door, I noticed my bike was leaned against the side of the house where I left it a month ago. I had never gone back to get it. Seeing it there, it didn't even seem like my bike anymore. Maybe I should get it back someday, but maybe I'll just leave it here forever like an artifact of a different time in history. Now that

Trevor drove (well, at least sort of), I might never ride my bike again anyway.

Mrs. Darry opened the front door. I'd forgotten to warn Trevor about Peggy's mom. You know, that she's the craziest adult in the universe. But she seemed to be a good mood, which was rare. When it did happen she would laugh after everything she said. So as long as you laughed a little too, it would be okay. "You must be the infamous Trevor," she said, and giggled as she let us into the house. Gosh. But I laughed because I had to. Mr. Darry, who never said anything, was watching sports on the TV and drinking a beer. I didn't want to leave Trevor alone with the Darrys, but I knew Peggy would kill me if I didn't go upstairs to her room.

"I'm going to check on Peggy," I said, then kissed him on the cheek.

"No teenage kissing in my house!" Mrs. Darry yelled. Even though she meant it to be funny, it made me feel bad. I still smiled at her because, you know.

"HI," I SAID AS I OPENED PEGGY'S DOOR.

"You look amazing!" Peggy said, and ran over from her mirror to hug me.

"You do too!" I said even though her dress was cut so low I thought her nipples might show. And she wore so much makeup. Purple eyeliner and super-dark lipstick and foundation even. Gosh. She looked so old, like, nineteen, but, I don't know, not as pretty as she did when she looked like a freshman. But maybe I was being mean. Or maybe I was jealous that her mom let her wear so much makeup. I was hardly allowed to wear any. It was like I didn't have any on at all. But I guess Trevor loved me without it so it was okay. But really you also want to look pretty for girls, not just boys. And at homecoming maybe even more for girls than for boys. Maybe. I don't know. This was my first dance ever. It was exciting. But also a little scary.

So EVENTUALLY EVERYONE ARRIVED, AND THE FRESHMEN gathered into a big group together, including the popular girls, Emma Goldberg, Jean Booker, Raina Bethington, and Wanda Chan, even though their dates were upperclassmen. I guess they were still the popular girls, though I didn't really think about it much anymore. Maybe that's what love does: makes you forget about being popular. Shannon Shunton was supposed to come, but she was late, I guess. It was weird, but I missed her. Not missed. How can you miss someone you barely knew? But, I don't know, I just think Shannon Shunton is interesting and I wanted Trevor to get to know her.

Trevor was nice to Henry, Jake, and Licker, even though I knew he hated them. They kept talking about their football game and how hard Henry had tackled this one boy on Glenbrook South's team after Henry threw an interception. The freshman team had lost by like twenty points today and had only won one game all season, so I don't know why Henry kept talking about their team as if they were good.

So I said, "Did you know Trevor might run with the varsity at next week's meet?"

"That's cool, Trev," Licker said, which made me remember he was the first person I ever kissed and now he was talking to the second person I ever kissed. So silly to think about that.

"Yeah, but it's cross-country," Henry said, and Jake laughed. Ugh. Now I remembered why I hated them. Trevor didn't say anything. I wished he would say something. I hated how he never talked back to jerks. He should be tougher. No, he was great. I loved him just the way he was.

AFTER WE TOOK A MILLION PICTURES, WE ALL GOT ON the party bus. We sat at the very front because we were both freshmen. Then all of Katherine's friends were at the very back. Shannon Shunton never showed up. I texted her to see if she wanted us to wait. I don't even know why. I had never texted her anything before. But she didn't text me back.

The upperclassmen started passing up plastic cups filled with alcohol as soon as we started driving toward the dance. Trevor and I had never talked about drinking. I didn't know what I was going to do if he started drinking. I guessed I should if he did. Just a sip. I knew he'd still love me even if I didn't, but I didn't want him to feel alone. Or maybe I didn't want to feel alone. But guess what? When Henry handed him a cup, Trevor said, "No, thanks."

Henry said, "You should at least hold a cup, dude, so they don't think you look like a loser."

Which I didn't think was a terrible idea, but Trevor said, "I don't care what they think." And oh my gosh, it was like Trevor had just said the coolest line in a movie, like one where the audience would cheer, and I was his girlfriend. And you should have seen the look on Peggy's face. It was like she knew. Knew Trevor was so much better than Henry. Not better. That's mean. But yes, better! Henry was a jerk and he pretended to be this leader but really he was the biggest follower and said dumb things all the time!

But as much as I loved what Trevor said and thought more than ever that I had the coolest, most amazing boyfriend in the history of the universe, after he said that to Henry, we were kind of ignored the rest of the ride to the dance. Licker asked Trevor one question about basketball. But Henry and Jake ignored him totally, and Peggy and the other freshman girls ignored me.

Then at the dance, we tried to dance with the group except it was weird to dance with people who weren't talking to you. I mean, this was the first time Trevor and I had ever danced together, and all I could think about was how Peggy wouldn't even look at me. So eventually, during a slow dance, which was my favorite, I whispered to Trevor, "Want to go dance with your friends?"

"Sure, babe," he said, which was the first time he ever called me "babe" or anything besides Carolina. I liked it. I think. He took me by the hand and we walked away from Peggy and the others and I almost cried. But not really. I think, maybe, I was done crying over Peggy. We danced with his sophomore friends and their dates, who were super nice. It felt really good to have people not ignore you, and eventually, after the dance was over, we got in their limo and went to Denny's. It was fun, but I didn't feel like I was living my own life. It was like I was this other girl who had never known Peggy or any of those freshmen. Like I was a sophomore girl who had grown up with these sophomore girls and been friends with Aaron and Tor forever and had been dating Trevor since we were born.

48
Trevor takes off Carolina's bra

THE SUNDAY AFTER HOMECOMING SOMETHING AWESOME happened. My parents took Lily downtown like she had been begging them to do for months. I was supposed to go, but I said I was too tired after the dance. I invited Carolina over and her mom dropped her off. As soon as she walked through the front door, I kissed her. I was so excited, I had to keep kissing her right there. We made out in my living room, which we had never done. It felt strange, and Carolina kept thinking my parents would come home. It felt dangerous, not dangerous, I suppose, but thrilling. Which made it more fun and made me want to keep kissing her even more. I repeated, over and over, that my parents would be gone all day. Then we took off our shirts. And she reached down my pants. Which felt incredible, like always, but . . . I don't know. I wanted a new kind of incredible too.

I said, "Can I take off your bra?"

"Why?" she asked.

"I want our skin to touch everywhere."

"Our stomachs touch."

"I want our chests to touch."

"But . . . my boobs are small."

"I love your body," I said.

"I don't want to have sex."

"Me either." Which was true. I swear. I wouldn't even know what to do.

"Okay." She reached behind her back to unlatch her bra.

"Can I do it?"

"Okay," she said, so I reached behind except I couldn't figure it out. "Want some help?" she said, and laughed. I loved when Carolina laughed, especially when we were, you know, making out and stuff. It made me think she enjoyed it as much as I did. She reached again behind and both our hands undid the bra together.

Then she slid it off and there she was, Carolina, and her naked boobs. They were small. She was right. They didn't look anything like what I saw on the internet.

"You think they're small, don't you?" she said, then I looked up and saw her eyes, and the hurt, and I wanted to never see her hurt again.

"No, they're sexy."

"They're not sexy. They're small."

"They're perfect," I said.

"You're just saying that because you love me."

"Can I touch them?"

"You've touched them before."

"Yes, but never without your bra."

"Yes, silly, you can touch them."

So I did. And then I kissed her. And then I pulled her against my chest and I loved the feel of her cool nipples against mine. I wanted our bodies so close there was not even one millimeter of air between them. "This feels so good," I said when we took a break from making out.

She said, "You're right, it does." And then Carolina said something so beautiful. "It feels like our bodies belong next to each other."

Then we kissed with even more crazy passion than usual and eventually she touched me and I came. She put her bra back on, but we left our shirts off, heated up a frozen pizza, and went down into the basement. After eating, we put on the first season of *Game of Thrones*, which we were slowly getting through, and fell asleep on the couch. But only after I asked if she'd take her bra off again.

When we woke up, I was excited again. So I kissed her and she kissed me. And then she grabbed me, but then I said, "Can I touch you?"

"I don't want to have sex," Carolina said, which is what she always said. Frustrating.

"Carolina, I don't either. But I read a lot of stuff on the internet and I talked to my mom and I don't want you to always do this for me. I want to be able to make you feel good too." This was true. But I also wanted to touch her because the thought made me excited. Was that bad?

"You do make me feel good."

"I want to make you have an orgasm."

"Oh gosh."

"You don't want to have one?"

"I . . . uh . . . don't know if I can have one."

"Why do you say that?"

"Because the internet says most girls don't have orgasms until they're over twenty years old."

I said, "That's not what I read. I read girls have orgasms even before boys. Like as young as nine or ten sometimes."

"Yes, but that's doing it themselves. What I read is that most girls

238

have a hard time having one with a boy until they are in college or later."

"Have you done it yourself?" I asked, and I don't know why, but waiting for her to answer made me feel nervous. Or maybe anxious. Or maybe even more excited than I already was. My breath got quick. And tight. My heart beat fast. And faster.

Then she said, "No . . . No. I just . . . like doing it with you."

"But before you met me?"

"I never thought about it. Not really. Does that make me sound so immature? I'm sorry, Trevor."

"Don't be sorry! You didn't do anything wrong. I'm sorry for bringing it up."

Then we sat there and didn't kiss and didn't talk and I didn't know what to say.

Carolina said, "Okay. You can touch me."

"I don't want to if you don't want me to."

"But I do want you to."

"Carolina, I think you just want me to because you want to make me happy. I don't want to be one of those boyfriends who only does sex stuff with his girlfriend that makes him feel good. I want you to like it too."

Carolina got quiet for a second, then her eyes started watering. But it was the good kind. She said, "Gosh, I love when you say stuff like that, Trevor. . . ."

"I mean it."

"I know," she said, then she grabbed my hand and pushed it toward the top of her jeans. And I reached down and felt her pubic hair and she gasped.

"Is that okay?" I asked.

"Yes. It just is sensitive when you touch it for some reason. I like it," she said. Then I tried to reach farther, except her jeans were too tight.

"Can I take off your jeans?"

"I'll be naked!"

"You'll have your underwear on."

"I'll be almost naked."

"I'll take my jeans off too."

"But no sex, right?"

"Carolina, I promise we will never have sex."

"Not never, just not for a long time, okay?"

"I promise," I said, and then I unzipped her jeans and slid them off. She was naked except for her underwear. Then she undid my jeans and pulled them off. I had to help at the end because I'm taller. So I was naked except for my underwear too. I looked at her whole body, up and down, and caressed it with my right hand. She shivered any time I got near her underwear. I didn't feel like I was real anymore. I felt like I was watching a movie of my life. "So it's okay if I touch you?"

"You are touching me," she said.

"I meant touch you there."

"I know. I was kidding. I'm nervous."

"Me too," I said.

"You're not nervous! You're a boy!" She was smiling but also kind of yelling.

"Boys can be nervous too!" So I smiled and kind of yelled too.

"But you don't have to do anything!"

"I have to do it right!"

"You do everything right," she said, then kissed me so I couldn't say anything. That's when I reached between her legs and pulled away her underwear. I'd read several articles about how to give a girl an orgasm. They said most girls can't come from putting your fingers inside but now that I had my fingers there, I wanted to go inside. So I pushed one finger inside and she clenched.

"Is that okay?"

"Yeah," she said.

"I can tell you're lying, Carolina."

"I'm not lying. It feels okay."

"Don't lie, please," I said.

"It feels weird. . . . I don't know. . . ."

"Okay. I won't do that." Then I took my finger out and tried to do what I'd read, which was find the clitoris. I had no idea what it would feel like or look like or what it was at all. Not really. So I just moved my fingers around on the outside where it was wet. Carolina seemed to shiver again, which was better than clenching up. "So how's that?" I said.

"That's better," she said, and she was lying on her back and her whole upper body was stiff, so I don't think she liked it that much. Her hands gripped on to the couch like she was afraid of what might happen next. Her legs kept twitching every time I moved around my fingers. Which maybe was good, but I couldn't really tell.

After five minutes, she said, "Okay, I feel good."

"Did you orgasm?" I asked.

"I don't know."

"How would you know?"

"I don't know. I don't think I did."

"How do you know you didn't?" I asked. I felt like such a failure.

"I don't know, Trevor. Let me touch you now."

"No, I don't want you to." Which was a big goddamn lie. She knew it was so she just grabbed me anyway. So I kissed her. She kissed me. And then, you know, she used her hand to make me go.

Afterward, as we were lying there, naked except for our underwear, I said, "I love you so much, Carolina."

"Even though I couldn't orgasm?"

"It was my fault you couldn't."

"It wasn't your fault. It was my fault."

"It was my fault, Carolina. You're perfect. I didn't know what to do."

"I didn't know what to do either."

"But you knew what to do to make me finish, so it's my job to know what to do to make you finish."

She said, "I think boys are easier to finish than girls."

"Maybe, but it's still my job to know how."

She said, "How about it's both our jobs to figure it out but neither of us can feel bad if it doesn't happen until we are twenty years old?"

This was smart, but all I could say was, "You really think it could take that long?"

"I don't know!" she yelled, but not smiling this time.

"I'm sorry."

"It's okay. This was amazing but it was fast and I'm nervous and I feel bad."

"Don't feel bad."

"Okay. I love you too, Trevor."

"I love you so much."

"I love you sooo much."

"I love you sooo much more," I said, but she didn't say it again. She just snuggled her body against mine. Which was nice. I guess.

49

Carolina hears from Shannon Shunton

ON SUNDAY NIGHT, AFTER I HAD GOTTEN INTO BED, I thought about how Trevor and I had gotten almost naked. How he had touched me. How it didn't feel that good. It did, kind of, but more weird than good. Maybe I should do it myself, but then I put my hand down there and it just felt so ridiculous to do it myself that I pulled my hand away. My phone beeped. It had to be Trevor, and I'd rather text with Trevor than, you know, do that.

Except the text was from Shannon Shunton:

> **SHANNON SHUNTON**
> **How was homecoming?**

My brain was racing. So fast. It was weird to be so excited about a text from anyone besides Trevor. I responded:

> **ME**
> **It was great! Trevor was amazing.**
> **Peggy was weird. But that's okay.**
> **Why didn't you come?**

Then I waited. Fifteen minutes. Then almost thirty. I fell asleep. Then the phone beep woke me up in the middle of the night. Like one a.m.

SHANNON SHUNTON

I like how real you are, Carolina. Sorry
I was a bitch in junior high.

Even though my brain was, like, seventy-seven percent asleep, I texted back right away:

ME

It's totally okay. You have been super
nice to me in high school. Nicer than
Peggy. I think you're the most
interesting person in school.

After I pressed send, I wish I hadn't sent it. It was too honest, too kidlike, too complimentary. It was probably better to be more elusive with Shannon Shunton, more artistic. How can you be artistic with texts? Gosh. I don't know. Then she texted again, which made me feel so much better:

SHANNON SHUNTON

You're my rock star.

Her rock star. It was the second time she called me this. I knew she didn't mean it literally. I knew she meant I was amazing, but it was a much cooler way to say I was amazing, which was amazing. It might have been the best compliment a girl had ever given me. Ever. And so I texted back:

ME

I want us to become best friends.

And then she responded:

:)

Which I knew meant she wanted to end the conversation, so I sent my own:

ME

:)

And then I lay awake in bed, thinking about all Shannon Shunton could teach me about boys and sex and, you know, everything. Trevor would love me even more when I knew all the things Shannon knew. I was smart, but more book smart, and Kendra was smart, but more life smart. Shannon was "deep" smart. I don't know what that means. Maybe I mean she just seemed to have seen things no other kids had seen. Maybe Kendra, Shannon, and I would all become best friends. All three of our smarts could be combined and we'd rule the school, but in a nice way. Maybe the three of us would go to homecoming together next year.

BUT SHANNON WASN'T AT SCHOOL ON MONDAY. I TEXTED her, but she didn't respond. On Tuesday, her sister wasn't in school either. By Tuesday afternoon, people started whispering that Shannon had run away because no one could find her. And I texted her, like, five hundred times. Not five hundred. I'm not going to exaggerate anymore. I've said this before, I know, but really, life was getting serious and I needed to be more serious. I texted Shannon six times on Tuesday night and Wednesday during school. That's exact. But she didn't respond once. She would respond to me if she could . . . wouldn't she?

By the end of the week, everyone was saying that Shannon had been killed. Murdered. But the police couldn't find her body, either alive or dead, and there wasn't any real proof. Every teenager had seen police shows on TV, so we knew there needed to be proof or a confession, but the one kid that knew anything, this junior named Dan Gassman, who was the son of a Riverbend police officer, said there was nothing, no proof at all, nothing. Then Shannon's mom and sister moved to Florida to live with Shannon's grandmother. They left the dad behind, which made it look like he was the one that murdered Shannon, but still there was no evidence and no one in the family would say anything to anyone.

When I first heard the rumors that Shannon Shunton might be dead, it was at lunch and I started crying. I tried really hard not to, but I couldn't stop and Trevor hugged me. He didn't say anything. Just hugged me. Then Peggy found me and hugged me. She was crying so loudly it almost felt fake, and she talked the whole time we hugged about how sad it was, except I didn't think Peggy knew the real Shannon like I did. I didn't think Peggy thought it was that sad, she just wanted everyone to think she was sad. When Peggy and I stopped hugging, it felt like we were bigger strangers than ever. Shannon Shunton had been better to me than her, and she was gone and Peggy was still here. I wished Peggy was dead and Shannon was alive. I felt like a horrible person for thinking that. I did. I should be arrested for thinking some of the things I think. I wondered if other people had evil thoughts like I did. Probably not. I was probably the only evil thinker in the whole school. I couldn't find out if I was the only one, obviously, because I couldn't tell people what my thoughts were in order to find out if they had bad ones too.

But two weeks after Shannon disappeared, I started thinking she wasn't dead. Those texts we shared in the middle of the night on

Sunday, weren't they the texts of someone knowing they would run away? Weren't they? I didn't tell anyone about them. Maybe I should have told the police, but I didn't want to ruin her plan if she had run away. See, Shannon was too smart, deep smart, to have been murdered.

So yeah, Shannon Shunton was alive. Had to be. Somewhere. She had probably found a cool older boy to take her to California and she changed her name, and she would become a singer or an actress and someday I'd see her on television and only I would recognize her. I wouldn't say anything to anyone. But I would tweet her, because famous people use Twitter more than Facebook, and I'd tweet, "You're a rock star," and she would know I knew but she would also know I could be trusted and she would text me, because I'd have the same number, and we'd become secret best friends. I really hoped that would happen. I really, *really* just hoped she wasn't dead. Because if Shannon Shunton could be gone forever, anyone and anything could be gone forever soon too.

50

Trevor loses his juice

COACH PASQUINI ASKED ME TO RUN VARSITY CROSS-country for the conference championships. After winning several junior varsity races, my times were better than anyone's except for the star, Todd Kishkin, and the captains, Randy Chung and Craig Billings. I had done a good job of not seeing Carolina the night before meets, or at least not kissing her much if I did. But the Friday night before the conference meet, Carolina came over and we went into my basement. Shannon Shunton had only been missing a few days. Carolina was upset, and I could tell her thoughts were only half about me. She kept saying she wanted to be closer to me than ever. So we got naked super fast. I promised Aaron I would never hook up on nights before races, but Carolina was kissing me with too much energy. It made me lose my mind. I couldn't stop her. Then, after she started touching me, she kissed my neck. Then she kissed my chest. Then my stomach. Then . . . it.

Holy . . .

It was the greatest feeling in my life. It hurt a bit because of her teeth, but I didn't care. I can't even think straight now remembering it, let alone when it was happening. Afterward, I asked Carolina why she did it.

"Did you like it?" she asked.

"It was so good I can't describe how good it was."

"Good. I'm glad. I watched videos and tried to do what they did," Carolina said. Then with a different tone in her voice, like she was possessed by a ghost, "I don't want to wait forever anymore. I don't want to wait to experience things with you because I'm afraid something bad might happen. Bad things might happen no matter what."

"I love you, Carolina."

"I know, Trevor."

THE NEXT DAY, AT THE CONFERENCE CHAMPIONSHIP MEET, I ran my worst race of the year. Well, the worst since the first one. I finished last on our team and with a worse time than three of the junior varsity guys. By a lot. Coach Pasquini asked if I was sick. So I said yes. He could tell I was lying. But I couldn't tell him I had gotten my first blow job last night and my brain and body both felt like they weighed five times as much as usual.

The next week was sectionals. But I knew he'd run someone else. My cross-country season was over.

SHANNON SHUNTON DISAPPEARING CHANGED CAROLINA. It changed everyone at school, at least a little, but Carolina . . . She suddenly seemed much older. I felt too immature for her. I was still this freshman, but now she had the air of a senior. A senior too old for high school anymore. I'd want to talk about video games or school, but Carolina would only want to talk about life. And family. And being a kid. And growing up. And not growing up. Before I met Carolina, before we fell in love, that was me . . . I was the one who could only think about the dark, depressing crap. But since Carolina, I've tried to be positive. To think about good things. But Carolina couldn't. She couldn't think about anything fun or easy. Only about Shannon Shunton. "Because if Shannon Shunton was dead, she would never grow up." Carolina said this over and over.

"We'll never see her be a sophomore," Carolina said. "And we'll never know if she would have graduated. Maybe she would have become my best friend and she would have taught me about all the horrible things in the world and I would have taught her how to be a better student. Maybe she would have gone on to a great college and she would have written books or songs or saved the environment. Maybe . . ."

"Maybe," I said.

"It's not fair, Trevor. It's not fair."

"I thought you thought she was still alive. That she ran away."

"You're right," Carolina said, "you're right. That's what I really think. But why wouldn't she text me to tell me she was okay? I wouldn't tell anyone."

"You'd tell me," I said.

"I wouldn't even tell you if she told me not to."

"You wouldn't tell me?" That hurt. Carolina would keep a secret from me. We were soul mates and we were going to spend the rest of our lives together. But she would keep a secret from me already.

"Trevor, I'd eventually tell you, of course, once Shannon trusted me. But that's not important. What's important is why isn't she texting me?"

"She will."

"You think so?" she asked.

"Yes."

"Oh, I hope you're right. Everything would be better if I knew she was okay and not dead." Then Carolina hugged me, dug her face into my chest. It was a Saturday night. A month since Shannon disappeared. We were in my basement. I really wanted to kiss, make out, hook up, get naked, have her kiss me down there, but Carolina didn't want to. I could tell. She hadn't been very excited about doing sexual stuff the last two weeks. I started to feel like I was the second most important person in her mind and the first most important person was probably dead.

51

Carolina talks to Alexander Taylor

MY BIRTHDAY WAS ON JANUARY 9. ON NOVEMBER 20 I made a decision. I was going to have sex on my birthday. I know I said I would wait until college, and then I said I would wait until I was a junior, but then Shannon Shunton disappeared and everything was different. It wasn't ruined. I didn't even think that anymore. I'd never think that again. I know I say things and then I don't always do the things I say, but this time it really was the case. So nothing was ruined. It was just changed. I was changed.

Club soccer season was over. So I didn't see Peggy at all anymore. Obviously I saw her in class, but we didn't sit next to each other and never said anything about anything. Kendra and I talked a lot. Mostly about school. We didn't even talk about Trevor that much. What was there to talk about? Trevor was amazing, I loved him, he loved me, we were going to get married someday. It was all decided. I didn't even think about it that much anymore. It just was what it was and it was going to be what it was going to be.

We went to movies with his sophomore friends, and I supposed they were my friends too, but I never felt like I really belonged. Apart from movies, we just had dinner alone, either at a restaurant in River-bend or ordered in to his house, then went to his basement, got naked, and hooked up. It was great. I still loved kissing him. And I liked that I could make him feel good, but what he did to me only felt good once in a while and, I don't know, I wanted to do stuff besides hook up in his basement. I wanted to go to parties and see people. I wanted to go to new places, like downtown Chicago, or at least outside Riverbend. I definitely wanted to marry Trevor someday, but I wanted to marry him in ten years, not right then. I still wanted to be a teenager. I'm rambling. I was just upset about Shannon. Trevor was perfect. He didn't do anything wrong. I was so lucky he was my boyfriend.

REMEMBER THAT BOY THAT TALKED TO ME, LIKE, ON THE first day of school? The junior. The weird junior that dressed in ties and acted mysterious? His name was Alexander Taylor. It still is. I just sort of forgot he existed when Trevor and I fell in love. I would see him once in a while, and he would stare at me. But I didn't think about it. He never said anything to me, and I certainly never said any-thing to him.

But then, on the Tuesday before Thanksgiving break, I went to the bathroom during study hall. I had gone every day since Shannon disappeared. Don't know why. Yes, I do. I kept thinking she'd be hid-ing there, waiting for me. But . . . obviously . . . she was never there.

Anyway, on my walk to the bathroom, through the empty alien planet that school seems when you walk around the halls alone, Alex-ander Taylor was waiting there, standing in front of the girls' bath-room door. Weird, like the first time.

"Hi, freshman," he said.

"Hi," I said. And he had that same look he'd had when he first approached me. Like he wanted to do stuff to me. Sex stuff. But I understood it better now. It didn't scare me as much. It didn't scare me at all. Okay, maybe a little. But maybe I liked being scared. Maybe everything with Trevor was so perfect and safe, I wanted to be scared right this second. I don't mean that. I don't know what I mean. Forget it.

"How's puppy love?"

"My boyfriend is amazing."

"Don't become boring or I'll lose interest in you," he said.

"I'm not boring," I said, even though I wanted to say, *I'll never be interested in you,* which was true, obviously, because I was only interested in Trevor. But for some reason I didn't say anything else.

Then Alexander Taylor said, "We'll see," and lifted up my chin with his two fingers, looked so far into my eyes I felt embarrassed, and then he walked away. I ran into the bathroom and kept telling myself what a freak he was, but I couldn't stop thinking about his face and his eyes. Trevor was sooo much better-looking. Trevor was sooo much better . . . in every way. Gosh. But, and I CAN'T BELIEVE THIS EVEN ENTERED MY HEAD, I wondered what it would be like to kiss him. Kiss Alexander. Would his lips feel the same as Trevor's? Would he move his tongue the same way? Would he taste different?

OH. MY. GOSH. I TOOK OUT MY PHONE AND TEXTED Trevor how much I loved him. How I loved him more than ever. Then I texted him that we should see each other that night, but he said he had basketball practice. Why did Trevor even try out for the basketball team? We could see each other almost every day if he hadn't made the stupid basketball team. Because now, when I needed to see him most, he was busy. It was his fault I was thinking about Alexander Taylor. Then Trevor texted:

But I'm super excited to see you
(and your beautiful naked body)
tomorrow night.

Ugh. How could Trevor only think about hooking up all the time? I was sick of his stupid basement! He was boring. Maybe I was boring. Maybe we were boring.

52

Trevor tries out for basketball

So I started thinking about sex. Anything sex. Hooking up. Hand jobs. Blow jobs. Even the real big thing. All. The. Fucking. Time. Which could be embarrassing. And a pointless waste of time. Right? Every time I saw Carolina at school, I would get, you know, a hard-on. (Not every time, but way too often, okay?) I'd text her stuff like "thinking about your sexy stomach," except she would text me back "I love you so much," which was cool, but not what I was hoping for. I don't know what I was hoping for. It's not like you could have sex over text.

I wanted to see her more than just on Friday and Saturday nights and Sunday afternoons, but she said her mom wouldn't allow her out on school nights. That might have been true, but it felt like Carolina wanted it to be true. I was glad she was a good student, but did she really want to be with me as much as I wanted to be with her if she could not see me for five days? I suppose we saw each other at school all those days. I mean, you know, no making out and hooking up.

Yeah. So. Guess what? I started looking at porn . . . more . . . and it excited me even though before it didn't. Yeah. So. I masturbated. God, I felt dumb doing it. I made sure to turn the music loud even though I only did it when no one was home. (At first at least.) So dumb. I told myself after it was over that I would never do it again.

But then I did it the next day.

I didn't do it the next day and I thought I might be cured of it.

But then I did it the next day and the next and the next.

I searched the internet for masturbation addiction, but I didn't seem to be as bad as those cases. I just felt so stupid and I hated feeling stupid. I wanted to not do it at all or only do it once a week or maybe twice. I couldn't talk to my parents about it. No way. Not to boys either. That's strange, dude. I almost talked to Carolina about it, but how can you talk to a girl about masturbation? So I could only think about not wanting to do it, which made me think about it, which made me want to do it. I was going insane! Crap! All these internet sites said masturbation was very healthy and a way to better understand your own sexuality. But what was I understanding besides the fact that I liked to make myself have orgasms? The religious sites were very judgmental and looked like they were written by zombies from the Middle Ages, so those didn't help at all.

And then . . .

My dad said something. He said, "You gonna try out for basketball?"

And I said, "No."

And he said, "I think you need to stay busy during the winter." And the way he said it? He knew. He knew what I was doing in my room all the time. He didn't say any more than that. But I knew he knew. And I felt so goddamn stupid I wanted to die. Crap. Crap. Crap. Crap.

"Yeah, okay, maybe," I said, and walked away. I signed up for basketball tryouts the next day.

So I MADE THE FRESHMAN TEAM. LICKER MADE IT AS well. My cousin Henry and Jake said they were going to wrestle, but then they decided to just lift weights for the winter. After cross-country and football ended, they had started talking to me again. Which was fine. I didn't care enough to ignore them. Aaron and Tor were much better friends than they could have ever been, so I wasn't mad anymore. I wasn't really mad about anything anymore. How could I be? I had Carolina. Every day she got more beautiful. Every day I fell more in love with her. I know how stupid that sounds. *I know*. But it's true. Yeah, I wish she thought about sex as much as me, but maybe I wouldn't respect her as much if she did. Maybe girls have to be more controlled when it comes to physical stuff or else we would all go crazy.

It's just . . . Carolina didn't seem to like it as much anymore. I couldn't make her orgasm no matter how hard I tried, and she had learned to make me orgasm in five minutes or less if she really wanted. Which wasn't as fun as when we would make out for a long time and then, you know, finish.

On the Wednesday before Thanksgiving, after we had hooked up in my basement, I asked, "What's wrong?"

"Nothing."

"Something's wrong, Carolina."

"Nothing's wrong. Let's watch TV."

"I want to talk."

"What do you want to talk about?" she asked.

"About what's wrong with you."

"Nothing's wrong, Trevor."

"I love you," I said.

"I love you too," she said, but it didn't feel like she meant it. And then I could feel myself breathing fast, and not able to concentrate. I turned on the TV so she could watch something besides me imploding. Crap. What had I done wrong? Crap. Everything was perfect and now she was acting differently. Do something. Say something. You're going to lose her. But I didn't know what to do or say so I just watched TV with her. We didn't say anything. We didn't even hold hands. Just sat there. Next to each other. Like we were strangers again. Except we were in our underwear and we were in love.

THE NEXT DAY, I FOUND MY MOM TAKING A NAP IN HER room. But her eyes were open. Just staring out the window like she was thinking deeply or she was half dead. Who knew with her? So I asked her if she could talk.

"I'm tired," she said.

"Okay," I said, and turned around.

Then she said, "What is it, Trevor?"

"We can talk about it later."

"No, I'm sorry. I'm sorry. Let's talk now. Is it about Carolina?"

I turned around and went and lay on the bed next to her. We had not done this for years. Now it felt strange. Like I was too old. But screw it. I needed advice. "Yeah," I said.

"Did you have a fight?"

"No . . . it's just . . . she doesn't seem to love me as much anymore."

"Has she said something?"

"No . . . it's just something's changed."

"Falling in love doesn't last forever. You might be transitioning from the 'falling in love' stage to the 'being in love' stage."

"What does that mean?"

"What nobody tells you is that the 'falling in love' stage is just one big pit of quicksand. . . . It's so fun, so addicting you don't notice . . . but then, once it's over, you are stuck. You're too attached to the person to leave, so you keep waiting around for the 'falling in love' feeling to start again . . . except it never really does, but if you wait around long enough, the 'being in love' stage begins and it's great in a whole other way."

"Is that what happened with Dad?"

"Yeah, of course," she said, but she looked away. Was she lying?

"How long did the 'falling in love' stage last with you and Dad?"

"We were . . . I don't know . . . a couple months. We got married before it ended."

"And how long before the 'being in love' stage started?"

"I'll let you know," she said, then laughed. "I'm kidding. I don't know. Maybe a year."

"A year?"

"Well, it all happens faster when you're young."

"But I don't feel like the 'falling in love' part is over for me. How can I make her fall in love with me again?"

"I'm sure she still is."

"Mom, but if she weren't . . . how could I?"

"Well . . . girls like to know they're worth some effort."

"What's that mean?"

"It means . . . you two spend an awful lot of time in the basement."

I. Was. Mortified. Like I could tear open my stomach and yank out my guts.

260

"Trevor, I already gave you the sex talk. I'm not going to bore you a second time with that."

"We aren't having sex!"

"Well, that's fine. You still have those condoms?"

"We aren't having sex, Mom!"

"Trevor. Great. But you're doing a lot of other stuff. Are you being nice to her? Making sure she's happy?"

"I try . . . but I'm not good at making her have orgasms. . . ." I can't believe I just said the word "orgasms" to my crazy mother. Shit.

"No teenage boy in the world is. I'm sure you are very nice and courteous. Keep communicating with her like I said, but I didn't really mean if she was happy sexually. I meant, why don't you take her somewhere special? Somewhere besides pizza in Riverbend?"

"Like what?"

"Like . . . take her downtown. Take the train downtown next weekend. Have her dress up. Make a reservation at a popular restaurant on Rush Street or Michigan Avenue or maybe ask Dad about the Metropolitan Club. Hold her hand. And then, when you get home, kiss her good night without taking her to the basement."

Goddammit, did I feel stupid! How could she presume so much? She didn't know what we were doing in the basement. She didn't know what Carolina really felt. She thought she knew everything, but she knew nothing. I hated my mom.

For a minute.

Damn. I thought about it. And I just sat there. The heat in my skull cooled. And my mom didn't say anything. I looked at her. Looked at my mom. She was pretty great. What if she had really died when she tried . . . and I started crying. I had never cried before about it. It was so dumb not to cry about it then. And so dumb to cry about it now.

"Why are you crying, Trevor?"

"I'm sorry."

"Don't be sorry."

"I'm sorry," I said, then I curled up, and laid my head near hers. She kissed my forehead. It was the first time I can remember us hugging or kissing since before she tried to kill herself.

53

Carolina takes a train ride

ON SUNDAY NIGHT, THE SUNDAY AFTER THANKSGIVING, Trevor texted me:

TREVOR

Are you free next Saturday?

Obviously I was free. I had no life but Trevor.

ME

You know I am.

But then:

TREVOR

Not just night. The whole day.

Now, this was weird. He was being weird.

ME

Yeah. Why?

And then:

Because I'm planning something
special.

And, oh my gosh, my brain got super excited. Special? Like what? So I texted him to tell me what, but he said it was a surprise. Which only made me more excited. Then I thought Trevor didn't know how to plan something special. So I demanded he tell me or I would be mad. I didn't want to spend a week getting excited and then be disappointed. He should disappoint me today! But he texted:

Then you'll have to get mad because
I'm not telling you ;)

Oh my gosh! Trevor didn't care that I would get mad! How could my boyfriend not care that I would get mad? But then I realized I was smiling. Grinning. Just a small one. Wait a minute: Did I like that he didn't care? That would be crazy. But I think I did. I liked that he was being secretive. I liked that I had to guess. Oh my gosh, am I screwed up or what? I didn't care. Being screwed up and excited about your boyfriend is much better than being normal and bored with him.

SO ON THE FOLLOWING SATURDAY, TREVOR PICKED ME UP (with his dad sitting in back) and, at first, I thought we were just driving into Riverbend to see a movie, but we drove past the theater and stopped at the train station.

"Are we going on the train?"

"How'd you figure that out?" Trevor said, smiling, but still, he

264

was being sarcastic with me. Which . . . I kind of liked. As we were waiting on the platform, I asked, "Where are we going?"

"On the train," he said. OH, HE WAS DRIVING ME CRAZY!

"WHERE on the train are we going, Trevor?"

"You'll see, babe," he said, then winked. Trevor was being so cool. Again. I mean, he was always cool, I guess. But then I fell in love with him and found out everything about him and I had seen him naked a thousand times and heard him pee and seen him sleep and seen him after he woke up and seen him with saliva on his face and smelled his farts and, I don't know, he was Trevor then and not this cool, hand-some new boy. But today . . . he was that boy again. I had to kiss him. Just had to. A big kiss. Gosh. This was amazing.

So we took the train into Chicago. And we got out at Union Station. I had never gone downtown on the train without my parents before, so it felt very grown-up. Then we took a cab to Michigan Avenue and we walked along the street and went into all the fancy shops, like Macy's and Saks Fifth Avenue, and he said, "I'd like to buy you a dress."

"Really?"

"Yes."

"But how will you pay for it?"

"I've saved money."

"But—"

"And you have to spend at least one hundred dollars."

"Trevor!"

"Carolina!" he said. Mocking me! Mocking me! And I liked it!

"Trevor, why are you being so nice?"

"Because I love you."

"Oh gosh, I love you so much."

"You do?" he said, and I could tell he wasn't joking. He was really asking. Oh my gosh. Trevor knew I had been thinking bad thoughts about us. He knew. Obviously he knew. He's my soul mate. Soul mates always know.

"I love you so much, so much, so much, so much, and I just forgot to show it the right way. I'm sorry, you are the most amazing boy ever, and I'm the luckiest girl ever, and I'm so happy I want to cry." And then I cried.

AFTER HE BOUGHT ME A YELLOW ONE-SHOULDER DRESS from Saks, we took a cab to the Willis Tower. Which used to be the Sears Tower and the tallest building in the world. We went up super high to the Metropolitan Club and he gave the hostess his name, and she said, "Right this way, Mr. Santos," and then she walked us to a table that overlooked the entire city and Lake Michigan from all the way up in the clouds. This was now my favorite day of my life, and I wanted to marry him right then and I wanted to kiss him and be close to him and do everything with him.

On the train ride home, I thought we should have sex tonight. Yes. I know I said I would wait until my birthday. But today I felt so, so grown-up. I felt eighteen. Even older maybe. Today was THE special day. It was. At the train station in Riverbend, his mom picked us up. She got in the back and let Trevor drive us.

"Did you have fun?" she asked.

"It was the best day of my life," I said.

"I'm glad. Trevor spent a lot of time thinking about it."

"My mom helped a little," Trevor said. Everything was perfect again. His mom liked me again. Trevor was cool again. I was in love again. (I had never stopped! I'm just saying I FELT it again.)

Except . . . Trevor took me straight to my house. I didn't know what to say. He didn't want to kiss me? He didn't want to go into the basement like we always did? He didn't find me attractive anymore?

At my house, he got out and walked me to the door. I finally had to ask, "You didn't want to hook up tonight?"

"I just wanted you to know I could have a great date with you without hooking up."

"Really?" I said, and I almost started crying. Gosh. But I didn't.

"Yes."

"You made me feel sooo special today, Trevor. Like we were special together too."

"I'm glad."

"So can we go back to your house now and go to the basement?"

He laughed. Laughed!

"Why are you laughing?"

"Because I thought you were tired of doing sex stuff with me."

"I'm not!" I said, even though I had been. But now I wanted it more than I ever had before. Like I needed him. Gosh. Gosh. Gosh.

"I'm glad. But I still want to wait today."

"Why are you being so different? Do you not find me attractive anymore?"

"Carolina . . . you're the sexiest girl in the universe."

"I don't believe you," I said. Why was I acting so pathetic now? BECAUSE MY BOYFRIEND DIDN'T WANT TO HOOK UP WITH ME!

"Carolina . . . I've . . . been . . . excited almost the entire day with you."

"Down there?"

"Yep."

"Even though we weren't making out?"

"Yep."

"Really?"

"Yep. Does that make me strange?"

"No," I said. "That makes me feel good."

"Really?" he said.

"Yeah. Does that make me weird?"

"No. I like it. So much. But I should go. My mom is waiting."

"Oh . . . okay," I said, then Trevor kissed me and went back to his car.

WHEN I GOT TO MY ROOM, I MISSED TREVOR SO MUCH. I wished I were with him so much. I wished we were naked in his basement. I wished I could make him feel good so he'd know how much I loved him. So . . . gosh . . . I put on my new dress, and I, uh, pulled the single strap over my shoulder and I hiked the skirt up so it was almost to my underwear. And then . . .

I took a picture in the mirror.

OH MY GOSH. I said I would never do this. You read about this stuff in the news. You read about this STUPID girl who took sexy pictures and sent them to a boy and then those pictures got sent around and everyone calls her a slut and her life is over and she has to move or something. But I ignored EVERY SMART PART OF MY BRAIN and texted Trevor the picture. I just had to. I just had to make him happy. Would that make him happy? I don't even know and I sent it anyway. And then I waited and Trevor texted me:

**You are the sexiest girl to ever walk
the earth.**

And for one second I hated myself. Hated myself that I sent the picture. But also hated that I loved his compliment so much. Why can't girls just be strong and smart and successful? Why do we have to be sexy too? But we do. Or I do. I want to be sexy. I hate that I do. But I do. And I loved that Trevor made me want to be sexy for him. Again. Or more. Or in a new way.

54
Trevor goes to dinner

MY SPECIAL TRAIN RIDE DATE INTO CHICAGO HAD WORKED. Really worked. Carolina sent me a sexy picture. She made me promise not to show anyone, which she didn't need to ask because I'd literally rather cut off my hand than show anyone a sexy picture of Carolina. Why would I want other boys to know how sexy she is? Then they would want her and I would have competition. Maybe not. But either way, no way would I show anyone. I would never betray her like that. Ever.

The next couple weeks, Carolina would text me fun stuff like "thinking of being naked with you" and "wish we were in your basement right now." She even sent me a few more pictures. Never of any actual naked private parts. You know, boobs or butt or anything. But what she sent was better. It made me have to imagine what I couldn't see. Made me think of her all the time. Made me think I'd be happy the rest of my life as long as Carolina was my girl.

The following weekend she said we should have a dinner with our parents. When she brought it up, the skin on my face sucked back all at once. Like it wanted to peel away from her even though my actual brain didn't think it was such a bad idea. Yeah, a couple months ago, it would have been the crappiest idea ever. No way would I want to expose her parents to my mom's nuttiness. But my mom had been awesome the past month. She had been a real mom. Better than a real mom. She had given me insights and truths that I bet no other mom would ever give. Because she wanted to treat me with respect. I loved it. I loved her again, maybe. I never stopped loving her. I guess I trusted her again, which is more important than love because it has to be earned.

So that's why I said yes. Yes, we could have our parents all meet. Carolina was so excited, it got me excited.

"Should we tell them we're engaged?" she yelped out.

"Yes."

"I'm serious!"

"Me too."

"You're not serious, Trevor," she said.

"You're not either," I said.

"But someday I will be."

Then I said something my old self would have fucking shot myself for saying: "Someday I'll spend the rest of my life with you, Carolina." She did that "awww" thing girls do and then leaped into my arms.

On the Friday before Christmas, my parents, Lily, and I met Carolina and her parents at an Italian restaurant called

Pontarelli's in town. My dad said the Fishers should choose the restaurant. He didn't say why, but I knew: my dad didn't want to choose a restaurant Carolina's parents might find expensive.

We got to the restaurant first. I was too stressed out not to force my family to arrive early. But the Fishers were ten minutes late. As we waited, I started obsessing about my mom seeing Carolina's dad for the first time since high school. What if they had been in love? What if they'd had sex? Would it be awkward? Crap. What if they fell back in love at first sight and tore apart our families and then Carolina and I would feel responsible, and . . . Screw it, I wasn't going to think about it.

Turns out I worried for nothing. When Carolina's parents walked in, all four adults stood up, shook hands with sort of fake smiles, then sat back down. I didn't notice one look between my mom and Scott.

Lily said, "This is all so exciting," and everyone laughed because she's the best. Carolina and I sat next to each other, but we didn't say much. All I could do was hope my mom didn't start acting like she'd rather be dead than at dinner with strangers. Carolina had this strange smile frozen on her, like she couldn't decide what she was feeling, so she would just grin through everything. After the adults talked about "how wonderful it is that we found first love" and what to order for appetizers, Carolina's mom said, "Ashley, Scott says you two knew each other in high school. What an amazingly small world we live in."

"Oh, of course . . . from Midnight Dogs, right, Scott?" my mom said, but with a very blank face. Almost too blank. She'd smiled when I first told her that Carolina's dad remembered her. Now she was acting like she didn't care. Like it was nothing. I didn't need her to smile and act excited, but I needed her to not act like it was nothing. I hated when my mom did this. So aloof and snobby, like she thought she was too good for someone. I wished, when she acted like this, that my mom would remember that if she was so goddamn perfect she wouldn't have tried to kill herself.

After we ordered, Lily asked, "Mr. and Mrs. Fisher, do you think Trevor and Carolina are soul mates? I do. But I'm only seven, so I'm not as old as adults." The Fishers laughed, of course.

Carolina's mom said, "I am happy they found something special, but I think they are very young."

Then my mom, who had been stone-faced quiet for twenty minutes, said, "But, really, does it matter that they are young? Are you any more sure Scott is your soul mate at forty-six than they could be as teenagers?"

"Ashley," my dad said, trying to shut her up. Which he should have. Because Mrs. Fisher was red-faced. But I also liked what my mom said. I've always thoughts kids knew just as much as adults. We just don't have the power to do anything about it.

"Maybe you're right," Carolina's mom said. You could tell she would rather slam her head into the table than get into an argument with my mom.

Then Scott said, "How about this answer, Lily. Yes, I think they are soul mates. But I don't necessarily think that means we only have one soul mate." And then, I swear I fucking saw this, he looked right at my mom. For, like, the shortest glance ever. Then he leaned over and kissed his wife on the cheek. But I saw that look. I saw it. I know I did. And it meant something. I'm not sure what it meant, but I'm sure it meant something and I'm goddamn sure it meant something horrible.

55

Carolina gets a Christmas present

SO THE DINNER WITH OUR PARENTS WAS A HUGE, AMAZING success. Just amazing. This is going to sound weird, but it almost felt like Lily was our child and they were the four grandparents. I know, that's crazy, but Trevor and I were so mature. We really were. I know I used to say how I wanted to act mature but deep down I knew I was still immature. Then I was bored of trying to be mature, but now it was just who we were and I loved what we were more than ever. Other kids looked at us like this super-experienced couple. Girls would ask for my advice on love and relationships. Boys didn't really ask Trevor because boys are always afraid of asking questions, but you could tell they respected him for having a serious girlfriend so fast. Really.

Anyway.

So for Christmas, which Trevor and I celebrated on the morning of Christmas Eve, I bought a picture frame that said TOGETHER FOR-EVER and put a photograph of us from our date downtown at the Metropolitan Club since that was my favorite date ever. On the back, in Sharpie, I wrote, *Merry Christmas to the love of my life —Carolina*. Then

I hid a sexy picture of me just in a towel after a shower behind the real picture. I printed it in black and white and tried to make it as artistic as possible. I also gave him a card that said how much I loved him and talked about how I could never have imagined I would have the most amazing boy ever as my boyfriend. It was really nice, and I meant every word. I told Trevor he didn't have to get me a Christmas present because he had bought me that dress at Saks Fifth Avenue, but I don't think I meant it because after he opened my present, he said, "You told me not to get one." And this huge hole exploded in my heart and dropped into my stomach, but then he laughed.

"Why are you laughing?" I screamed.

"Because of course I got you a Christmas present, Carolina."

Then I leaped into his lap even though I didn't even know what the present would be. He reached under the couch and pulled out two boxes. One big. But not clothes big. The other small. Like jewelry small. (OH MY GOSH, IS HE GOING TO PROPOSE?) I asked, "Which should I open first?"

"The big one." So I tore open the wrapping paper, then pulled open the box, and peeled back the tissue to find a notebook. It was leather. Nice leather. On it, in black Sharpie just like I'd used on his card, Trevor had written, *The Story of Carolina and Trevor.* And, oh my gosh, I got butterflies in every molecule in my body, and I opened to the first page. It said, "On the first day, she gave him two pieces of paper . . ." And there was a sketch, like a really, really, really good one, of a girl's hand laying two pieces of paper onto a desk.

"Oh my gosh, who drew this?"

"I did."

"YOU DID?"

"Yes."

"Trevor, this is amazing. You're, like, an artist. Why didn't I know you could draw like an artist?"

"I've never shown anyone. Lily, I have. But not even my parents."

"You are so talented," and tears, happy tears, formed in my eyes as I turned to the next page and the next page and the next. It was each of our most important days captured with one description and one beautiful drawing. My boyfriend was an artist. He was handsome and a great athlete and an artist. I found the perfect boy. I did. I really did.

By the time I had read through the entire notebook, my face was filled with tears and a big, silly smile. I had forgotten about the other box. Not really. But sort of. So I opened it . . .

And it wasn't a diamond ring. I guess we weren't getting married. But that was just me being crazy. I wouldn't have said yes anyway. Yes, I would have. But then I would have said we should keep it secret until we were eighteen. Anyway. It was a necklace. A gold necklace with a gold heart. It was really beautiful. But not as beautiful as the book he made. Nothing would ever be as beautiful as that.

MY BROTHER, HEATH, DIDN'T GET HOME FROM COLLEGE until late Christmas Eve. He was supposed to come home last Saturday, but then he said he was staying with his girlfriend in Denver. My mom's feelings were hurt, but Heath didn't know that because my mom never talked about her feelings.

When he walked through the door with my dad, who had picked him up at the airport, Heath looked very different. Like a stranger. Like, when did he start dressing so nicely? I didn't even think we were related anymore. We had texted and Facebooked a little bit since August, but it was always him asking the same thing: "How's Mom?"

and I would tell him Mom and Dad were in love again and tell him a long story about Trevor except he would just write back, "That's great, C," and not say anything about his life or ask anything else about mine. I guess Heath and I never talked that much about serious things. He always looked out for me, but the five years' difference between us made it hard to share much more than parents, I guess.

After we opened presents Christmas morning, we had brunch. Well, we called it brunch even though it wasn't even nine a.m. yet. We had to eat early because my mom had to work a shift at noon. She always seemed to work on Christmas so I was used to it.

Heath asked me more questions about Trevor while we ate the egg soufflé that my mom had made, which I liked. I told him we were soul mates. He laughed, but it was a supportive laugh.

My dad eventually said, "You haven't told us much about your girlfriend, Heath."

Heath looked at my dad like they shared a secret. I didn't like that they knew something I didn't. Maybe I was wrong. But then Heath reached over and grabbed my mom's hand and said, "My girlfriend is a boyfriend, and his name is Michael."

For, like, a second, I didn't know what to think. I mean, my brother was . . . gay? That's what he was telling us? Right? But he had girlfriends in high school. Well, one. And, yeah . . . they weren't like Trevor and I. Not at all. Oh. My. Gosh. I jumped up, got in my brother's lap, and hugged him. We never hugged much, but I thought he needed it. He probably didn't. My brother has always been the strongest person I know. Maybe I wanted to give him a hug anyway. While I was in his lap, I noticed my mom was crying.

My dad said, "This is a great day, Ellie. Our son is who he is meant to be. I'm so proud of him."

"Heath, do you know how difficult it is to be gay? Do you know how many people will judge you? Can you think about this before you make up your mind? I don't want your life to be so much more diffi-cult than it has to be."

"Goddamn it, Ellie," my dad said.

"It's okay, Dad," Heath said. But I was really, really mad at my mom. I mean, I never thought she would be prejudiced. She never was. She always voted for gay rights and told me everyone is equal and everything. But I guess she thought it was okay for everyone but her son.

I started crying. Gosh, I cried so much. I screamed out, "Mom, he's your son!"

"Carrie, it's okay. It's okay," Heath said. So calm. He was always so calm and wise. He guided me off his lap, back to my chair, and then took both my mom's hands in his. "Mom . . ."

"Oh, honey, I love you so much," she said, crying more than me. So much that I stopped.

"I know," he said.

"I just want you to not get hurt by people."

"I know."

"Or made fun of or anything bad. Is there any way you can like girls?"

"No," Heath said, and laughed.

"But—"

"Mom, I'll be okay."

"He'll be better than okay," my dad said.

"Dad, not now," Heath said.

"She needs to know her son is perfect the way he is."

"She knows." Heath kept holding on to my mom's hands.

"She needs to know—" my dad started.

But Heath interrupted and shot his words back, "She needs not to get a lecture from you right now."

Gosh was Heath amazing. But I couldn't believe he was gay. And then, I guess, I believed it.

MY MOM EVENTUALLY STOPPED CRYING AND APOLOGIZED one thousand times. You could tell she was still scared, like terrified, but also that she wasn't anti-gay or anything. Just anti her son having to endure anti-gay people. But Heath was really smart and explained that the world was different than when she was his age. He said that every day someone openhearted was born to replace someone closed-minded who died. (My brother should be a writer, don't you think?)

Later, after my mom had gone to work and Heath had left to meet some friends, I asked my dad how long he had known Heath was gay.

"Probably since he was eight or so."

"How could you tell?" I asked.

"If you pay attention, almost everyone will tell you who they are without saying a word. And it's your job, as their parent or sister or friend, to embrace whoever that person wants to be," he said. My dad did lecture too much, but he was also brilliant, so I didn't really mind at a moment like this.

56
Trevor puts it closer and closer

AFTER WE GOT HOME FROM MY GRANDMOTHER'S CHRIST-mas night, Carolina came over. She said hello to my parents and good night to Lily and then we went into the basement.

"Guess what?" she said. "I think we should go on a double date with Art and Bryan."

"I don't think they're a couple," I said.

"Everyone says they're a couple. It doesn't even matter. I just think we should be supportive of the gay community."

"Okay." She wasn't making a whole lot of sense.

"Guess what else?"

"What?"

"My brother's gay," she said.

"That's cool," I said. What else should I say? I had gay friends back in California. It wasn't a big deal. But I guess it was a bigger deal here.

"I mean, I just found out."

"Oh. How do you feel?"

"Good. I'm really happy for him."

"So you're happy for him for being who he is?" I asked.

"Yeah."

"Okay. Cool. I'm happy for you that you are who you are, then." I tickled her just because.

"I'm serious, Trevor."

"I am too."

"I don't want anyone to pretend they aren't themselves."

"Me either."

"So if you were gay, I would totally still love you," she said.

"Are you being serious?"

"I'm just saying, I love you for whoever you are."

"I like girls, Carolina. Well, one girl. See?" And I grabbed her hand and put it on my penis. Which was hard. It almost always was when we went into the basement. I wasn't even embarrassed about it anymore.

But Carolina didn't keep her hand there. She pulled it back and got sad. "Trevor, I want you to know everything about me."

Oh, crap. Was she about to tell me she liked girls? No. No . . . right? No. But . . . what?

She said, "My parents almost got divorced. My dad cheated on my mom. They're better now. They're more in love than ever. But I want you to know that I don't come from this perfect family. My brother's perfect. I'm not saying we're not perfect because he's gay. I'm saying we're not perfect because my dad and mom almost got divorced."

I didn't know what to say. I should have told her about my mom. About her trying to kill herself. But I couldn't. I just couldn't say it. Parents got divorced all the time. Who cares? But someone trying to kill herself was so much worse. So much harder to understand.

"Why aren't you saying anything?" she asked.

"I don't think anyone is perfect, Carolina. Besides you." I tried to smile.

"So you don't think I'm damaged now because of my parents?"

"I think you are even more awesome because you are who you are despite their crap," I said.

Carolina hugged me, then kept her head against my chest. Then she said, "So you would tell me anything I don't know about you, right?"

Crap. "I will," I said, which didn't feel like such a lie because "I will" could mean I would tell her about future stuff but also about past stuff in the future.

CAROLINA AND I SPENT ALMOST EVERY NIGHT OF CHRISTMAS break together. We studied a little for the finals that would happen a couple weeks later, but mostly we watched movies and got naked and did all sorts of sex stuff besides actual sex. I went and kissed her down there, which she liked and moaned and giggled. But she didn't orgasm. It drove me nuts that I couldn't make Carolina orgasm. I mean, I want to be a good boyfriend. I want to be able to make her happy! She said she was. She said how good she felt. She repeated how the internet said it was rare for girls to come with boys at first. But that didn't make me feel any better. It just made me feel like I wasn't even a unique failure, just an average one.

But everything Carolina did for me was amazing. She started keeping lotion in her purse, which was a lot better than just her dry hand. And she would kiss it if I asked. (I didn't ask every night or else she would think I was selfish.) We also tried a bunch of other stuff, like putting me between her breasts (which were getting bigger I think) and between her butt cheeks. (Not in her butt. But sliding . . . Forget it.) It was all good. But just for something different. Her mouth was still the best. But even then, I wished I could kiss her while she

282

was kissing it. Which I supposed was why people had sex. We were going to wait. But then we started putting "me" near "her." Just touching. Except we never put it in. Never. And we wouldn't talk about it either. I promised I was going to talk about it. But I didn't. It was too scary to talk about. So we just kept getting closer and closer and I didn't know which one of us was going to stop when the next step closer was actual sex.

57

Carolina gets a New Year's text

FOR NEW YEAR'S EVE, TREVOR AND I WENT TO A PARTY AT his sophomore friend Aaron's house. His family was rich. Richer than Trevor's. How do people get so much money? I don't understand. Anyway. They had a big indoor pool so we all brought our swimsuits even though it was cold outside. There was lots of good food and loud music but his parents were there so there was no alcohol. I didn't drink, and didn't want to drink, but parties seemed more fun when other people were drinking. Does that make me sound dumb? Maybe. I don't know. It was a great party, but it felt like a junior high party not a high school one, even though almost everyone there was older than me.

We all swam together at first. I wore a bikini and everyone said it looked nice but some of the older girls had much more developed boobs so I didn't feel that sexy. After twenty minutes where the couples sort of made out and flirted in the pool, which was cute, all the boys started showing off and doing flips and playing rough so it got boring and I got out and watched. That's when I got a text from a number I didn't recognize:

UNKNOWN

happy new year's, freshman

I almost for sure knew who it was, but I still texted back:

ME

Who IS this?

Then he texted back:

UNKNOWN

you know

Annoying! Gosh! Yes, I knew it was Alexander Taylor. The weirdo junior who wore ties and thought dirty thoughts in his eyes.

ME

Maybe I do

Then:

ALEXANDER TAYLOR

where are you? i'll come pick you up

WAIT A MINUTE! He thought I would just let him come get me? Was he crazy? Was he insane? I was with Trevor! I would never leave Trevor to go with him! I didn't know him at all! THEN WHY WAS I WISHING I COULD SAY YES? Because I'm not a good person. I'm not. I pretend I am. But I'm not. I'm such a jerk. I had the greatest boyfriend ever and I was texting some psycho junior who would probably murder me. But probably not. We probably would just drive around and talk and he would have interesting things to say and it would be weird but it would be so different. And he would try to kiss me and I wouldn't let him because I'm in love with Trevor, but I would like that he tried.

Another text:

i need an address, freshman

My heart was racing so fast I thought it would burst out of my chest and leap into the pool and Trevor would scream and I would die and he would look at my phone and see that I was text cheating on him.

"Who are you texting, babe?" Trevor said, and I quickly erased the conversation and looked up and saw that Trevor was out of the pool—I hadn't even noticed!—and drying off.

"Kendra," I said. I lied. Gosh, I should be punished for being such a liar.

"Why don't you invite her?" Trevor said.

"She never wants to come to parties, but okay," I said, and texted her just because it made it look like I'd already been texting her. Kendra asked if there was drinking and I said no and so she said she would come. My phone kept buzzing with texts as I waited for Kendra to arrive, but I knew it was Alexander Taylor not Kendra, so I pretended I wasn't dying to know what he was texting and just left it in my purse.

After Kendra arrived, I forgot about Alexander Taylor's texts, which was a relief, and remembered how nice it was to talk to real girlfriends outside school since I hadn't in so long. But then these two sophomore boys started flirting with Kendra, and Trevor was back in the pool being silly. So I was alone. No one flirted with me because Trevor and I were going to spend forever together and no boy flirts with a girl who's already promised to spend forever with another boy.

I went to the bathroom so I could look at the texts from Alexander without anyone noticing. I should be arrested. I know. But it also made me really excited, so I did it anyway. There were like a hundred texts, including:

ALEXANDER TAYLOR

answer me, freshman

don't be a tease, freshman

send me a picture

send me a sexy picture

don't be a freshman, freshman

i know you're thinking about me

That was the worst. Because it was true. Why couldn't I stop thinking about him? It was so dumb and so wrong and I wished I could think about anything besides Alexander Taylor and what it would be like to be with him somewhere, anywhere, instead of here with Trevor.

I didn't text Alexander back anything. I erased what he sent and hoped he didn't send me any more, but then I hoped he'd send me another text that very second. I'm a crazy person, aren't I? I went back out to the pool and found all the girls were back in the water, even Kendra, and Trevor was picking up and throwing this sophomore girl named Jamie, who was super short and heavy but had a pretty face and super, super, super-big boobs and I could see Trevor's eyes watch her boobs every time she jumped up after the splash. HOW COULD HE DO THAT TO ME? But then I remembered my texts with Alexander and stopped being mad, sort of, and then I jumped into the water and made sure I was the only girl Trevor picked up the rest of the party.

58
Trevor doesn't answer a call

I DON'T KNOW WHO CAROLINA WAS TEXTING WHILE I WAS in the pool, but it wasn't Kendra. She had this look on her face. This smile. It looked so . . . interested. So that's why I got out, to try to see. But then I couldn't stand the idea of seeing, so I asked. And she lied. I know she did. My mom has lied to me enough so I know when someone lies. I always know. I wish I didn't know when people lied. I hate being able to see the truth even when everyone else can't.

But who could it have been? Peggy? But why would she have lied about Peggy? Was it another boy? What boy? I had never seen her flirt with or talk to any boy at school. But I wasn't with Carolina all the time. Maybe I should follow her. Yep. Maybe I should spy on her in her classes. That sounds so creepy. Screw it. Screw it, okay? Yep. So then when she left the pool area, I started talking to this girl Jamie who I had no interest in whatsoever but was nice and clearly lonely because no other boys were talking to her. All the boys started throwing their girlfriends and dunking them so I did it to Jamie and it made her happy and . . . okay, I started looking at her chest, but only when she had her eyes closed from the water. I loved Carolina's body, but

Jamie's boobs were so . . . bouncy. Is that creepy too? Carolina had come back when I wasn't looking. Had she seen me looking at Jamie's boobs? Who cares? She lied to me so I don't care. Carolina jumped in and got all kissy and girlfriendy, so maybe she didn't. And then I got horny and didn't want to think about who she was texting, or fight about it, because I wanted to get naked with her later. Goddamn, I wish I didn't get so excited every time Carolina kissed me with tongue. I'd be a much stronger person, and if I was a stronger person she'd probably never lie to me.

IT ALWAYS SEEMED LIKE THE WORLD WAS GOING TO END when it was a new year. I didn't even know why I felt like that. Whatever. Was I getting negative again? What was wrong with me? I couldn't even tell. It was just . . . something didn't seem right anymore. Carolina lied to me, and I looked at another girl's boobs. I guess that's what wasn't right. Maybe that would cause the world to end. That sounded stupid. But I didn't fucking care.

We went back to school on Wednesday, January 2. Three days of classes, then finals the next week. What moron schedules finals after a two-week Christmas break? They expect us to remember all the crap they've been making us memorize for four months after not thinking about it for two weeks? Why was I complaining about this? Why did I feel like complaining about everything?

On Thursday night, my dad was out of town and my mom said she was seeing a play in Chicago with some girlfriends—lie!—so Lily and I ordered pizza and watched Netflix. She said, "You seem sad, Trevor."

"I'm fine."

"Are you and Carolina fighting?"

"No." Which was true. We just weren't . . . in last year anymore.

"You should tell her you're sad."

"I'm not sad, Lily!"

"You only yell at me when you're sad!" Then Lily ran to her bedroom and locked the door. I didn't care. Yes, I did. Lily always made me care.

"I'm texting Carolina!" I screamed super loud so Lily could hear me. Then I sent:

ME

I need to tell you something

Carolina texted me back a few minutes later. We hadn't been texting "I love you" as much. Texts were always right to the point, so hers was:

CAROLINA

What?

Lily returned, standing in the archway to the family room as I texted:

ME

I'll do it in person

One second later:

CAROLINA

Oh my gosh what's wrong?! Are you mad at me? Tell me now, Trevor!!!

But I didn't even know what I was going to tell her anymore. That I was sad? Screw that. About how I knew she lied on New Year's Eve? I don't know . . . maybe. But . . . I just felt dumb. I didn't want to fight with her. I wanted her to love me forever. I couldn't believe how cheesy I was. And weak. And stupid. While I was thinking what to text, Carolina called. Called. We never called. She was worried. Worried I was mad at her.

But I didn't pick up.

"Why aren't you answering, Trevor?" Lily asked. Except I still didn't answer. I just looked at her name on my phone. I liked that Carolina was worried. I liked that she thought I was mad at her and it was making her call me. "She's going to think something's really wrong, Trevor!" Lily ran over and jumped on me, trying to answer the phone for me. But I leaped to my feet and held the phone out of her reach. Then it stopped ringing. And then it buzzed with a text and another and another—

CAROLINA

Trevor! Why aren't you answering?

Trevor!

Talk to me!

Why are you mad?

What do you want to say to me?

I'm so worried!

I'm worried you hate me! Please!

Please please please please

I had never seen Carolina act like this. Never. I didn't like that she was so scared. But I also did like it, you know? I hated that she was upset . . . but I was glad she cared enough about me to be upset. I'm so fucked up. I finally texted:

ME

Carolina. I love you. We just need to

291

talk about something. We can do it
tomorrow night.

CAROLINA
You promise promise promise
you are not mad at me?

I wasn't mad at her, was I? I was sad. (Lily always knew.) But maybe I was mad that I was sad.

ME

I promise I'll love you forever. I'm going
to bed and turning off my phone.

Crap. Why did I do that? Why make her think I was mad at her? Even if I was, I shouldn't let her worry all night I was mad. I shouldn't. But . . . I wanted her to never text whoever she texted on New Year's Eve ever again. And maybe she needed to worry all night so she never would. It's a horrible thing to do, to torture your girlfriend like that, but maybe that's what you have to do so she doesn't take you for granted.

59

Carolina finds out who is sad

TREVOR KNEW. HE KNEW. OH MY GOSH. HOW COULD HE know? I quadruple-checked that I erased all of Alexander Taylor's texts. He couldn't know. But why else would he be mad at me?

He totally knew.

Oh my gosh. I was going to lose Trevor. He was going to dump me. If I were him, I would dump me. I deserved it. Even if all I did was text, it was still cheating. I knew it in my heart. I deserved to be dumped. I deserved to lose the greatest boyfriend I'd ever have. That ANY girl ANYwhere could EVER have.

At school on Friday, I tried to look really pretty. I usually didn't try so hard for school because, well, I knew Trevor would love me no matter what, but today I tried really hard because I didn't know if he loved me anymore. As soon as he arrived at biology class, I couldn't breathe. I mean, I could. But it was like I couldn't breathe. He sat down next to me.

I leaned over and I said, "Please tell me what's wrong."

"Not at school."

"Oh my God, you hate me."

"I don't hate you."

"Then why won't you tell me?"

"Because."

"Because why?" I whined. Whined. I thought I would never whine again. This is why I should never do anything wrong. I should never lie or cheat or even think bad thoughts because then I become this pathetic person. Like I was right that second.

"Carolina . . . tonight." Then Trevor took out his notebook and just ignored me the rest of class. Then he ignored me in history. And he sat with his sophomore friends at lunch. I sat with Kendra, which was fine, but, oh my gosh, Trevor and I were breaking up. Weren't we? Weren't we?

"What's wrong?" Kendra asked. She always knew when something was wrong. It was like she was Peggy, but the old Peggy.

"Trevor is breaking up with me."

"What are you talking about?" Kendra scooted close to me and whispered, "He's not really breaking up with you, is he?"

"I don't know. . . . He's not talking to me and he says we have to talk about something serious, but we have to do it not at school and I feel like I can't even see straight."

"Did you do something?" Kendra asked. Why would she ask that? Why couldn't Trevor just be being a big jerk? Because he wasn't. It was my fault.

"No!" I whispered in a yell. And lied. I just said I would never lie but I totally lied to Kendra when she was the one person in the world who never judged me.

"Carolina, it might be nothing."

"It doesn't feel like nothing." Don't cry. Don't cry. I didn't.

Kendra said, "I've never seen a boy love a girl as much as Trevor loves you. Even in movies."

"Really?" Oh my gosh. That was true, wasn't it?

"Really." Kendra gave me a hug, and I felt better. Even if Trevor found out about Alexander Taylor, he loved me too much to dump me just because I was texting another boy.

Right?

Please, please, please let that be right.

THAT NIGHT, MY DAD DROVE ME OVER TO TREVOR'S. I WORE a short skirt that was super uncomfortable, but I wanted Trevor to think sex thoughts and not mad-at-me thoughts.

"Ready for finals?" my dad asked.

"Dad, oh my gosh, what's wrong?" I didn't want to think about anything except Trevor. Yeah, I was calling him Dad again. He liked it better. And he had been amazing for so long, so he deserved it.

"Why can't a dad ask his daughter about school?"

"Because you never ask me about school."

"Your mom is worried you haven't studied as much as you used to."

"You've always told me I studied too much!"

"Is everything all right?"

"Yes, Dad. I'm fine." I couldn't tell him Trevor was mad because then I would have to tell him about Alexander Taylor. And to tell my dad that I was cheating (but just text cheating!) would make him think his REAL cheating was okay. Which it wasn't. At all. My dad parked outside Trevor's house and said, "Okay. I'm going to see a movie. Text me when you need me to pick you up."

"Trevor can drive me home." Unless he dumped me!

"Trevor doesn't have his license."

"But Trevor can drive me home with his mom or dad."

"Isn't his dad out of town?" my dad asked.

"Why would you know that? I don't know that. Gosh, Dad. Trevor will drive me, okay?" He was freaking me out!

"Okay. Text me if you need me. Just in case." Then I got out and he left.

I RANG THE SANTOSES' DOORBELL, AND LILY ANSWERED. She gave me the biggest hug ever. Oh my . . . did she know Trevor was going to dump me? She took me by the hand and led me to the kitchen. Trevor wasn't there, but his mom was unpacking takeout Chinese food.

"Hi, Carolina, you look nice," she said. Mrs. Santos was dressed in a short skirt too. She wore lots of makeup, but it looked amazing. She was so sexy. So much sexier than I was. I was such a little girl. I thought I was so mature, but I could never be mature when there were adults like Trevor's mom.

"Hi, Mrs. Santos, thanks, but you look so, so, so nice," I said.

"Very kind of you to say. Trevor's dad is out of town all weekend, so my friend Katie is taking me downtown for dinner."

"That sounds like fun."

"Why don't we all go downtown, Mom!" Lily jumped up and down at the idea.

"Not tonight, Lily," Mrs. Santos said, then yelled, "TREVOR! Get down here! I'm leaving." Footsteps slowly moved upstairs, then down the stairs, and then my heart froze and then the kitchen door swung open and there was Trevor. He always looked the most hand-some when I feared he didn't love me anymore. Was this the last night we would be boyfriend and girlfriend? Before I could say anything, Mrs. Santos said, "Call if you need anything. I'm leaving some extra money if this isn't enough food." There were, like, ten boxes of Chinese food for just the three of us. Then Mrs. Santos waved good-bye and left through the garage.

"Your mom looks so pretty," I said.

Trevor ignored me as he got out plates.

"Trevor!" Lily said. "Carolina said something."

"I heard her."

"Are you two fighting? Please tell me you aren't fighting!"

Trevor went silent again so I said, "I don't . . . I don't know if we're fighting, Lily."

"Trevor's been sad all week."

"Lily!" Trevor yelled. "None of your business."

"I'm your sister and you're sad and that makes me sad and Carolina can make you happy so stop being so mean to me!" Lily cried out. It was the most seven-year-old thing I had ever heard Lily say. Then nobody said anything for so long.

I decided to be super brave even though it was super scary and I asked, "Why . . . are you sad?" Then I waited. Waited for Trevor to tell me he knew about Alexander Taylor. Waited for him to tell me we were breaking up. That he hated me.

"I'm not . . ." Trevor started.

Lily cried out again, "You are, Trevor! You are! You have been just like Mom used to be!"

"Your mom gets sad?" I asked.

"Our mom—" Lily began.

"Lily! Don't!" Trevor yelled as he ran toward Lily to grab her.

Lily screamed really fast, "Our mom hurt herself and almost died!"

"GODDAMN IT, LILY!" Trevor yelled. So loud. So mean. So scary. It was like he was a different person. Like there was a mean boy in him this whole time and I had never seen it. Lily ran out of the kitchen. Trevor wouldn't look at me. He just stared at the ground and kept his eyes closed, like he could make it all go away if he didn't see anything. Maybe it wasn't a mean boy inside. Maybe it was a scared boy. Yes, a scared little boy. And this is going to sound so, so, so, so horrible, but I was happy. Happy that Trevor was scared because that meant he wasn't mad at me, right? If he was scared, he needed me. Oh my gosh, Trevor needed me. That's what love is. Your boyfriend needing you, and you being there for him when he needs you.

I walked over to Trevor and wrapped my arms around him and squeezed until he hugged me back, which made me feel like the best girlfriend ever and not the worst.

60

Trevor . . .

WHEN CAROLINA HUGGED ME, I STARTED CRYING. NOT crying, crying. I'm not a girl. But, you know, tears in the corners of my eyes. I didn't even know what it was about. About my mom? Maybe. Or maybe about Carolina lying about those texts. I thought I might be losing her, and now she was hugging me like she loved me more than ever and would take care of me always. After I teared up for a minute, my penis got hard. Carolina was hugging me so tight! I never thought you could cry and get an erection at the same time. Life is so complicated.

"Is that what you wanted to tell me? About your mom?" Carolina asked. No, it wasn't, of course. I had thought all day about what I would tell her because I didn't have anything I wanted to tell her. I just wanted her to think I had something.

So I said, "Yeah."

"She tried . . ."

"To kill herself. Yeah. A bunch of pills. It's been two years. It's kind of why we moved away from California."

"I'm so sorry, Trevor." And she kissed my neck and dug her hands into my back. I was so turned on. I wanted to go to the basement right now. But we had to eat dinner and I had to make sure Lily wasn't mad at me.

"It's okay," I said. Didn't want to think about this anymore.

"That must have been so hard. I'm glad you told me."

"Lily told you."

"I'm glad you were going to tell me. I don't want us to hide anything from each other," Carolina said. I didn't like her saying that. Because that meant she would have to tell me about those texts, and I didn't want to know. But now that she said we shouldn't hide anything, I did want to know. I wanted to know she wouldn't hide anything if she said she wouldn't. If we had this pact, you know, that we would hide things, that would be fine. But that's not what she said. She said we shouldn't hide anything! And now she wasn't telling me about her goddamn texts!

And then she started crying. Like girl crying. Sobbing. You know, snot and spit and I didn't know what the hell to do.

"I just texted him! He texted me first. And I never said anything bad, I don't think! I told him I had a boyfriend! But I lied to you and said it was Kendra! I lied! I lied!"

"On New Year's—" My whole brain went so dark so fast I thought I would pass out. Like all the blood stopped flowing in my body. Lava could come out of my ears and melt the whole fucking kitchen floor.

"Yes! I'm sorry! You were looking at that girl Jamie's boobs!"

"I was only swimming with her because you weren't with me!"

"He texted me! I was just answering!"

"YOU LIED!"

"I KNOW! BUT I ONLY LIED BECAUSE I DIDN'T WANT YOU TO KNOW!"

"THAT DOESN'T MAKE SENSE!"

"I know! I know! I just lied because I love you so much and I don't know why I texted him back!"

"Who is he?" I stopped yelling. Well, at least I stopped yelling as loud as I could.

"His name is Alexander and he's a junior on the stupid swim team and he's creepy and he keeps contacting me."

"Tell him to stop!"

"I will!"

"Tell him right now!"

"Okay! Okay!"

61

Carolina . . .

I TOOK OUT MY PHONE AND I FOUND ALEXANDER'S NUMBER and I started a text and . . . I almost didn't want to do it, you know, just in case . . . but in case of what? Trevor and I would never break up! I was going to marry him and we would be happy and the only reason we wouldn't be happy is if I lied to him so I texted Alexander:

ME

I love my boyfriend so, so, so much

so please don't text me anymore

And then I showed it to Trevor and then I pressed send and then I turned off my phone because I didn't want to see Alexander's response in case I liked it.

"I'm sorry, I'm so sorry," I said, and I was still crying, but now I was kissing Trevor and he started kissing me back and we grabbed at each other and it was very aggressive and so intense and I wanted to just keep grabbing each other and I wanted to eat him and I wanted him to tear off my clothes, except not really, but you know, keep being so passionate and then I reached into his pants and he moaned and I loved to make him moan and then I remembered Lily was here, some-where, so I stopped and said, "Lily . . ." We pulled away and then heard footsteps run away from the kitchen door. Oh my gosh, if she saw any of that I would die. So Trevor ran after her and I waited in the kitchen and I almost turned on my phone to see Alexander's re-sponse but instead I decided two things: one, I would never do any-thing to hurt Trevor ever again, and two, we should have sex that night.

62

Trevor . . .

"Lily!" I called out as I ran after her through the house. "Get back here!"

"Are you guys fighting?" she yelled from some hiding spot. I followed her voice.

"Not anymore."

"Are you guys having sex?"

"NO!" I said but . . . I wanted to. I wanted to be that close. I wanted Carolina to be my first and for me to be her first and for us to do it before anything could ever stop that from happening.

Lily popped out from the storage door under the stairs. "I don't think you should have sex until you are married," she said.

"Okay."

"I don't think you should fight ever."

"Okay."

"I'm hungry."

"Me too," I said, but I wasn't. I didn't want to do anything but kiss Carolina and be naked and get so close that no one and nothing could ever come between us.

63

Carolina . . .

AFTER WE ATE DINNER IN THE FAMILY ROOM, TREVOR and I cuddled under a blanket on the couch while Lily lay on the floor four feet from the television. While Lily watched TV, Trevor and I moved our hands under the blankets all over our bodies. Onto our bare skin. He even put his fingers inside me and I felt like we were being so wrong because Lily was right there but it also felt better than it ever had.

After the movie was over, Trevor made Lily go to bed even though it was early. She complained but not much. I didn't get up from the couch because my pants were undone but Lily hugged me and then Trevor walked her upstairs to her room.

I went down to the basement by myself and I waited and I thought, oh my gosh, I was about to have sex. I didn't want to think it. I just wanted it to happen so that I didn't have to think later that I could have not done it. I wanted it to just be that our bodies did it, that they loved each other so much that we had to have sex tonight even though it was still a week until my birthday and I promised I would wait until then. It sounded so much more mature to wait but I just couldn't. Trevor and I needed to have sex, we did, or else all these bad things like Alexander or his mom's sadness or the universe might pull us apart.

Wait a minute. Trevor's mom tried to commit suicide, and I hadn't even really thought what that meant. I was so happy he wasn't mad about me texting Alexander (well, he wasn't mad until I told him), that I didn't really think about how this made Mrs. Santos such a different person. She was so perfect and yet she tried to kill herself. I wanted to be just like her, so does that mean I'd want to kill myself some day? What if I'm not as perfect as she is, won't that mean I'd want to kill myself even more? Oh my gosh. Oh my gosh. This world is a horrible place and I can be a horrible person, but even if I'm a perfect person it won't matter. . . .

And then Trevor came downstairs, and he started kissing me without talking.

64

Trevor...

KISSED HER. GRABBED HER. TOOK OFF HER SHIRT. SHE took off mine. Kissed her. Bit her lip. She bit mine. Never done that so I did it again. She cried out a little but she bit me harder back. Took off her skirt. She took off my pants. I took off my underwear. She took off hers. Then I was on top of her and she was beneath me. Kissing so fast. Eyes open. Our eyes were never open. But I wanted to see her. I wanted to see if it was okay. I wasn't going to ask. I couldn't ask. If I asked, she might say no. But if we just got closer and closer and closer and she didn't say anything, then she might mean yes. . . .

65

Carolina . . .

TREVOR WAS NAKED AND I COULD FEEL HIM, HIS PENIS, the tip, I could feel it on my, you know, and it kept rubbing against me and it felt so good. So tingling. Shivers. I wanted to laugh. But not laugh out loud. I kept my eyes open because I wanted him to know it was okay. I wanted to see what he looked like when it happened.

I kept scrunching my butt lower so that I would be closer to him, so that he would know he could do it. Why can't we just talk about it? We should. We weren't wearing a condom. Oh my gosh. We didn't have a condom. But it was okay. You can't get pregnant on your first time. Obviously you can. I'm not stupid. But it wouldn't happen. We would be fine. And I didn't want to stop. I wanted to have sex. I wanted to be a woman. I wanted to be with Trevor forever.

66

Trevor . . .

"I LOVE YOU, CAROLINA," I SAID.

"I love you, Trevor."

"I love you so much, Carolina."

"I love you so, so much, Trevor."

"I'll love you forever."

"I'll love you forever."

"I . . ." I started, but then I could feel my penis slip inside so I couldn't talk. More than just the tip. It was more than just more than the tip. It was like my whole body went inside her and she was this huge warm lake and I was swimming. That's so dumb. But it felt true. Like this is exactly where my penis should be. It knew it should be. It wanted to be just like this, in Carolina, forever.

"Ah," Carolina said. I had forgotten about her. Not forgotten. I mean, I was having sex with her. But I'd forgotten to ask how it felt for her. Goddamn, I screwed up.

"Does it feel okay?"

"Yeah," she said. But she was lying.

"Do you want me to stop?" Please don't tell me to stop. Please don't tell me to stop. Please don't tell me to stop.

67

Carolina . . .

"No," I said. And I meant it. I didn't want to stop. I wanted to have sex. I *was* having sex.

Wait a minute.

Wait. A. Minute.

I was having sex. SEX.

It didn't hurt.

Everyone on the internet said it would hurt.

It didn't.

It didn't feel good. I mean, it felt great to share this moment with Trevor but physically it didn't feel good. It didn't hurt either. There wasn't, like, real pain. It just, you know, felt like it didn't belong. So weird. Like he was a round peg and I was a square hole except, I guess, he would really be a square peg and I would be a round hole. I don't even know what I'm saying.

His face was so happy. So happy. That felt nice. It felt so nice to have Trevor so happy. I thought we were going to break up, but now we were having sex and I was making him so happy we would never break up. I really hope we don't get pregnant. I want to spend forever with him, but I don't want to have a baby or an abortion. What would I do? Oh my gosh, I should tell him to stop. To get a condom. But I don't want to ruin our first time. This is so important.

Except this is not as great as I thought it would be. I mean, it's important. But it's just . . . not amazing. I shouldn't say that! It's great. It's great! It's just not a big deal. It's a HUGE deal because it's my first time and he's my soul mate. I'm just saying the feeling, the actual feeling of having a penis inside is . . . kind of boring. Oh my gosh, I just said it was boring. I don't mean that. I mean that I thought it would be this earth-shattering thing, like jumping out of an airplane in space or something, but instead it's just . . . what it is.

Trevor said, "This is the greatest feeling I've ever had."

Oh gosh, I smiled so big. I even forgot how it felt awkward and boring for a second. And for that second, our eyes were so close and so deep and our bodies were so, so, so together and it was like, if we could stay just like this forever, then everything between us would always be okay.

But then, you know, he came.

Part Four

FIGHTERS FOR
A SEMESTER

68

Trevor knows how technology works

AFTER WE FINISHED HAVING SEX, AND I PULLED OUT, I realized I wasn't wearing a condom. The thought might have crossed my mind before we started, but I ignored it. I just wanted to do it so badly I didn't think. I'm such an idiot. I can't believe how out of control I was. Everything was supposed to be perfect, but I couldn't even put on a condom.

But it felt so good. So f-ing good I don't know how people do anything but have sex if they are adults and don't have school or parents. Wouldn't Carolina and I just do it all day, every day? Maybe eat. Of course eat. And sleep. But not much. Just have sex. Feel what I just felt. It was literally, literally like I was transported into another world where your whole body can fly through a beautiful, soft, tingling cloud. Crap. I suck at describing stuff. I mean, it was the most awesome fucking thing ever, okay? It just was.

A half hour later, after we had told each other how much we loved each other over and over, I wanted to have sex again. Carolina said okay if we could wear a condom. Of course. So I got the condom box that my mom gave me from my room and we had sex again.

It didn't feel as good. But it was still great. Still incredible. And Carolina was more comfortable, and she even moaned I think. Which made me feel like I was good at sex. Which is the most important thing. I only want to have sex with Carolina if it feels good for her. If she orgasmed right now, while we were having sex the second time, I think it would be a sign that our love was more powerful and important than even I could fathom.

But she didn't. I came again. Then I threw the condom into the toilet and flushed.

SHE TEXTED HER DAD AT MIDNIGHT TO COME GET HER because my mom hadn't come home yet. He didn't respond, so she called him ten minutes later. He didn't pick up. So I called my mom. She didn't pick up either. Then her dad texted:

CAROLINA'S DAD ON HER PHONE

Be there in thirty

"You live two minutes away," I said.

"He was probably sleeping," Carolina said. And then I realized I shouldn't say anything. I knew I shouldn't even before I got a text from my mom that said:

MY MOM ON MY PHONE

on my way home

"That from your mom?" Carolina asked.

"Yeah," I said.

"What did she say?"

"She's still downtown with her friend."

I KISSED CAROLINA EVERY SECOND THAT WE WAITED FOR her dad to arrive. I loved her so much I didn't know how to talk anymore. I wished we were the only two people in the world. Or at least the only two people in our families.

When her dad arrived, she ran out to his car. I watched from the front door. It hurt so much to watch her leave I couldn't move. Not even twenty seconds after they drove out of sight my mom pulled down the street and opened the garage. Adults think they are so smart. Adults think we don't see things. Think we don't know things. But we know everything. Everything. Man, I wish we didn't. I wish I didn't. But I do. I know fucking everything, and it's going to be impossible to be happy if I know fucking everything.

I sat in the kitchen on a stool facing the door to the garage. My mom walked in. She looked worn. Tired. Stressed. I fucking hated her.

"Why are you still up?"

But I didn't say anything.

"Sorry I'm so late. Katie and I lost track of time," she said. Just talking, talking, talking her crap. Like she could fool me by talking her crap, crap, crap. Like she could fool the world with it.

Me? I just kept staring at her. Hating her. Letting her know I knew everything.

"What's wrong? You're being weird, Trevor. Go to bed."

Still didn't say a word.

"Good night, Trevor," she said, and walked past me, not looking at me. Not looking at me because I could see right into her rotten, selfish soul and she didn't want to see me seeing it.

THE NEXT DAY, I STAYED LOCKED IN MY ROOM. LILY knocked and asked how I was. I said I was tired. Which was true. Tired of all of existence. My mom knocked too, but I just ignored her.

She said, "You open this door right now and talk to me!"

Ha. Adults think they can lecture you, order you around, when they are twice as irresponsible and twice as childish as any kid. Ha. HA! She left. She knew. She knew I knew. And she didn't want to be around me any more than I wanted to be around her.

Lily said Mom was taking her to a movie. I said have fun. No way was I going. Carolina and I texted a bit, but it was just talking love stuff. She was clueless. I couldn't tell her what I knew. Not ever. Carolina wouldn't be able to handle it. She would hate me. I hate me. I hate my mom because she makes me hate me.

AFTER LILY AND MY MOM LEFT, I WENT TO MY PARENTS' bedroom and found my mom's iPad. I opened up the Messages app. See, if you have an iPhone and an iPad like my mom, messages go to both unless you disconnect them. My mom probably doesn't even remember this. Because adults are dumb when they are being pathetic.

It was there. Right at the top. Right at the goddamn top. "Midnight Dog," it said his name was. I could feel this wild black rat eating my insides one big bite at a time. I opened the messages and . . . aw, crap . . . crap, crap, crap, crap, crap, crap, crap . . . I can't look at this.

No kid should have to look at this. Ever.

There was sex talk and pictures—pictures of my mom! of my mom!—and I just threw it on the ground and almost stepped on it. To smash it. To make it all go away. But I just stumbled back. I was so weak. I couldn't stand. My head was so fuzzy. I looked down and moved fast, back to my room. I ran into the doorjamb because I couldn't look up and then I slammed my door and locked it even though I was home alone.

I flung myself face-first onto my bed and screamed into the pillow. Screamed so loud I thought I'd put a hole in it. Aw, man, what was I supposed to do now? Aw, aw, aw, this hurt so much I wanted to take the whole world in my hands and squeeze it into nothingness so no one would feel this helpless and horrible ever again.

69

Carolina goes to a motel

TREVOR ACTED WEIRD ON SATURDAY. HE WAS SO HAPPY with me during sex and after and then he was different. That's what happens in movies. Girls finally have sex with their boyfriends and then the boys become jerks. But Trevor wasn't that way. He couldn't be. He was my Prince Charming. He couldn't be a jerk from the movies.

He didn't ask if we were hanging out Saturday night all day, which he always does, so finally around two p.m., I asked if he was mad at me. He texted:

TREVOR

You are my soul mate and I would die for you.

That was intense, even more intense than we usually get. So I asked:

ME

Are you okay?

TREVOR

I'm going to walk over to your house

and then just want to walk around
and we can eat and do anything and
go anywhere but let's be by
ourselves, k?

I said okay even though it was really scary.

BUT WHEN TREVOR KNOCKED ON MY DOOR, HE LOOKED amazing and so in love with me I thought I could float off the ground. Trevor didn't want to come into the house to say hi to my dad, so I yelled good-bye and he took my hand and we started walking.

We didn't talk much at first. It was cold. Really cold, but neither of us wore gloves or hats. It was snowing for the first time all season. It was very pretty but also like we were not in real life. Like the snow was in our minds.

As we walked, Trevor would squeeze my hand whenever he looked at me, which was like him saying he loved me without words, which made me realize how happy I was that we had sex. Because you read all these stories about a girl's first time with a boy she doesn't care about or who doesn't care about her, but Trevor and I were the most-in-love first love ever. If something happened between us and we broke up—nothing would, but just if—then I'd still be happy he was my first.

Eventually, Trevor started talking and he seemed like he just needed to talk so I listened. Girls did this lots, but I'd never seen a boy need to just talk. To, you know, vent. But he was saying how the world is filled with craziness and that if you don't see how crazy it is, you'll be swept whichever way the craziness tells you to go, and if you do realize how crazy it is, you'll be so sad that none of it makes sense and you won't know how you can live.

He was being so deep and interesting and it was something I had never seen in him. I liked it. I did. I had worried he was boring. That's not true. I guess I started to think we had talked about everything we could ever talk about and WE had become boring. But now I realized there was so much more inside both of us and that we could go on forever finding out what was there.

But it was also sort of scary. I was afraid he couldn't keep breathing and walking and talking at the same time. Like he would just fall down and pass out at any second because all the ideas that were inside him were sucking his life away.

So I stopped him, and I hugged him, and I said, "I love you more than ever," and it felt different to say it today. Like not only that I meant it, but that I meant it in a way that I understood for the first time. I think Trevor could tell because he stopped talking and hugged me back and we held each other a long, long time and it felt perfect.

Then he got hard and we started kissing and we decided we could go to the golf course, which was closed because it was winter, but would have trees we could hide in. So we got there and he took off his jacket and I lay on it and took off my pants and he pulled down his and we had sex even though we didn't have a condom. I was sore, but it felt better than yesterday. I just loved him so much and, today, our bodies felt like they loved each other as much as our hearts.

"Don't go inside me," I said, and he nodded and then, as if me saying it sped him up, he pulled out and went on my stomach. It was gross but it was better than getting pregnant.

We were both freezing now so we walked to Roth's Diner and ordered hot chocolate, french fries, and soup. We sat next to each other in the booth instead of across, and I didn't notice anyone else in the restaurant even though it was filled with old people for the early bird dinners.

After Roth's, we walked to the movies and watched a horror movie that made me sick to my stomach. So I closed my eyes and went to sleep. After the movie was over, Trevor said, "Want to go to a hotel?"

"What about our parents?" I asked.

"I don't care about my parents."

"Yes, you do."

"No, I don't," he said, and I could tell he meant it.

"My parents would never let me."

"Why should our parents be able to tell us what to do?" he asked.

"Because they're our parents." I felt like such a kid saying that, but it was true even if Trevor's answer sounded cooler.

"Just because they made us doesn't mean they know what's best any more than we do."

"We can't, Trevor. Someday. But we can't. Why don't we go to your house?"

"No. How about we go to a hotel but don't spend the night?"

"But that's so much money."

"I don't care. I have my parents' credit card."

"They'll get mad."

"I don't care," he said. Gosh, he was different. It was so intense, but sexy. Yeah, sexy. Maybe I knew what sexy meant now.

"Okay," I said.

So we went to a Best Western, but they wouldn't rent to us because we weren't old enough. So we went to this local motel by the Home Depot. Trevor paid cash so they didn't ask for his

ID. We went into the hotel, which smelled like the oxygen had died and rotted, and we both went to the bathroom, got naked, and got into bed. It was the first time we had been naked in a bed.

"You're my soul mate, Trevor," I said just before we had sex again.

"You're my everything," he said.

I forgot to tell him to pull out.

70
Trevor gives a gift card

I WILL NEVER FEEL CLOSER TO CAROLINA OR ANYONE than I felt with her in the motel Saturday night. Never. You can tell me I don't know what I'm talking about. But you don't know and I do. My whole existence will never live up to that moment. It's crappy to know that, but I still know it.

My dad got home Sunday. I didn't tell him about my mom's affair. What the hell could I say? He was clueless. I think he liked being clueless. But him being home made it possible for me to be in the house without wanting to kill my mom. It's like I knew she was someone else's problem again.

FINALS SUCKED. I'M SURE I FAILED EVERY CLASS. CAROLINA was stressed out. She said she didn't study nearly as much as she planned. I felt bad but she's so smart I was sure she'd get straight As.

I had three dozen roses—pink, white, and red—sent to Carolina's house Wednesday morning for her birthday. Maybe that was too much, but it didn't feel like enough so then I left a voice mail where I sang "Happy Birthday" when I knew her phone would be off. I also told her I'd have a special present that weekend. I didn't know what it would be, but it gave me a few more days to think of something.

ALL I WANTED WAS TO BE WITH CAROLINA, SO I DIDN'T care about basketball but I couldn't quit. I should have quit. But I didn't. I had to play a tournament all night Friday after finals and all day Saturday and all I could think about was Carolina and having sex again.

That Saturday night, she came over and my parents were in the living room, which was torture. Carolina talked to them and I wanted to throw my mom outside into the snow and lock the door but I just went into the basement and let Carolina listen to their bullshit.

We had sex right away, with a condom since I had stuffed them under the couch cushion. Carolina kept saying, "This feels good," which was good, I think, but maybe that meant it didn't feel that good before. It doesn't matter. It felt good now. It turned me on her saying that and I came.

After that, I gave her a gift card to Banana Republic as her last birthday present. I didn't even know if she shopped there, but it was next to the Apple Store at the mall so I knew where it was. I probably should have drawn her something again. She liked that gift so much. I'll do it for Valentine's Day.

I wanted to have sex again later, but she was tired so we just cuddled and fell asleep. My dad woke us up at midnight by pounding on the basement door. I wish Carolina and I lived together and didn't have to be apart ever.

THE SECOND SEMESTER STARTED, AND IT WASN'T UNTIL I was walking to health class that I realized I didn't have health class anymore, I had Architectural Design as the elective now. And then when I walked into the new class, I realized Carolina wasn't there. She had another elective. We never even discussed it. Strange, right? We wouldn't finish the school day together anymore.

71

Carolina texts the unknown

W HEN I WOKE UP ON MY BIRTHDAY, THERE WAS A TEXT
waiting for me:

ALEXANDER TAYLOR

happy birthday, freshman

Alexander Taylor. He had never sent a text after I told him not to.
Until this one. I didn't know if I liked that he stopped or didn't like
that he stopped. I almost texted him back "thanks" or something else,
but then the doorbell rang and it was flowers from Trevor. I hate to
say this—hate it!—but I was more excited about the text from Alexander than the million flowers from Trevor. It's not Trevor's fault. I
expected the flowers. But the text was a surprise. It's nice to not know
something's going to happen before it happens.

I had two finals on my birthday. How terrible is it to have to take
tests on your birthday? When I got home that night, my parents took
me out to a birthday dinner at Cheesecake Factory. It was my favorite
restaurant so it's where we went every year. I was always allowed to
bring a friend to my birthday dinner and I had always brought Peggy.

But we hadn't talked in years. Not literally, obviously, but it felt like it. I thought about bringing Trevor. My mom expected me to. But I asked Kendra instead and told my mom Trevor had basketball. Which was true, but he would have been done in time to go to dinner. So I guess I lied. But I don't even feel bad about it. Am I becoming a worse person or a better person? I don't even know.

At dinner, my mom asked Kendra, "Do you have a boyfriend?"

And Kendra said, "My dad said I can't have a boyfriend until I'm a sophomore."

"That's probably smart," my mom said, which made me feel like such a slut.

My dad said, because he always knows when my mom says stuff that hurts me, "Ellie—we love Trevor. I think Carolina having Trevor will be one of the most important things to ever happen in her life." Which was true. So true. The truest thing ever. But because something's important, does that mean it's good? Yes. Right? I didn't know. I was so tired.

Kendra and I talked about soccer season and the new semester and other stuff. I didn't talk about Trevor much. I hadn't told Kendra or anyone that we had had sex. Maybe I should tell someone. No way I could tell my parents. But maybe Kendra. But later. I don't know. Kendra was amazing. But her not dating boys made her hard to relate to when it came to boys and sex things. She always said such smart things and always sounded so wise, but it's easy to be smart and wise about boys if you aren't in love with one.

So that night, after I got into bed, I texted Shannon Shunton. I hadn't texted her since a month after she disappeared. This is what I wrote:

ME

I had sex with Trevor

I was ninety-nine percent sure she wouldn't respond, but I figured it would make me feel better. You know, like writing to Santa Claus or saying a prayer. You knew no one would respond, but it felt better doing it just because.

But then someone DID respond. OH MY GOSH. Shannon Shunton was alive! Except the text was:

SHANNON SHUNTON

Who is this?

Could Shannon Shunton have forgotten about me? How could she forget about me? I would never forget about her. I didn't know what to think, so I just texted back:

ME

It's Carolina

And then I waited. So long. And then finally, another text came:

SHANNON SHUNTON'S PHONE

I don't know you. You have the wrong number. Know who you are you texting before you tell people your business.

My whole face burst into fire and I died. Not really. But gosh, did I feel like the stupidest person ever. I wanted to throw up. I couldn't sleep because I felt so sick and silly. But you know what else? Shannon Shunton's phone number had been taken over by someone else. Maybe that meant she really was dead. Maybe that meant not all stories had happy endings.

72
Trevor sends a secret note

I NEEDED TO STOP MY MOM FROM SEEING "MIDNIGHT Dog" again without telling her I knew. Or telling my dad. Or telling Carolina. So I typed up a letter that said:

STOP CHEATING ON YOUR WIFE

Then I wrote the address in block letters to hide my handwriting, took a long walk after dinner Thursday night to find a mailbox that was as far from my house as possible, and dropped it into the mail. Then I texted Carolina that I loved her because that's why I was doing all this secretive stuff. To protect her from the horrible crap adults do to their kids.

LICKER WAS BECOMING MY BEST FRIEND AT SCHOOL because of basketball. He was the best player on the team and I was the best rebounder—rebounding is just about being crazy and relentless, which I guess I was—so the two of us together played almost every minute of every game. Even though I'd rather have sex with Carolina than play basketball, if I couldn't have sex with her all the time I guess basketball was better than masturbating or studying or even playing video games. Maybe not better than video games.

Aaron and Tor were still cool, but we didn't have any classes together and I didn't see them at cross-country practice anymore. Maybe when track started in the spring we'd be closer again.

We got our first-semester grades back and I got four Bs and two Cs, which is about as good at school as I had ever done. It was because Carolina and I had spent so much time studying on Sundays through the fall, even if I would have rather been hooking up. So I owed all my good grades to her, except she had gotten two Bs, when she had always gotten straight As in junior high, and even though she didn't say it, I knew she blamed me. I felt like shit. I'm poison. Carolina was perfect and could accomplish anything she wanted, but I was this destructive meteorite with all my demons and my mom's demons and I was going to ruin her life. If I was a selfless person, I would have broken up with her so she could be free of my crap. But I loved her too much to let her go.

MY DAD WAS IN TOWN THROUGH THE REST OF JANUARY and the beginning of February, so I don't think my mom was seeing Midnight Dog anymore. Also, I think my note worked. I hope so. I wished I could tell Carolina how my plan had succeeded in saving our love and both our parents' marriages but the whole point of stopping their sicko affair was so Carolina would never find out. So I couldn't tell her or anyone. You start to go crazy when you don't tell people stuff. But I think I've always been crazy. I'm just more aware of it now. For a while, Carolina made me forget it. But now not even she could fool me into thinking I was anything but deranged.

For instance, I started walking through the halls between classes as if I were an alien. An alien with a computer in my head. I was here on earth studying humans. Downloading all this information so I could take it back to my home planet and report on whether we should take over the world or leave it alone or just blow it up. I was a goddamn brilliant alien spy. I was the James Bond of alien spies.

Yeah.

See?

Deranged.

73

Carolina has a talk with her mom

So, gosh. I mean. Really? Okay. B-minus in biology. Fine. My worst subject. Okay. I mean . . . but a B in history? I LOVED history. I was GOOD at history! But it was my other class with Trevor. (Well, and health. But everyone got an A in health. Except Trevor. He was smart. But not book smart. How could I marry someone not book smart? Never mind. That's mean. Trevor was brilliant. No one knew it. But I did. I think.)

My mom was right. I let a boy distract me. Yes, I loved him and he was my first of everything and my life was so much better with him—all that!—but shouldn't I be able to still get straight As even when I'm in love? I mean, if it was a PERFECT love I would have gotten PERFECT grades. That sounds dumb. I'd never say that out loud.

Forget it. Forget it. I just was not going to see Trevor as much this semester. I was going to make sure all my grades were perfect. I know I said I'd be happy being married to Trevor and living in the suburbs and not being a famous CEO and just being with him and having kids, but now I thought I should have both. I wanted Trevor *and* I wanted to be a famous CEO of a huge company that all sorts of girls like me—and boys too!—looked up to as a role model. But I would never tell anyone I had sex so young. I couldn't believe I'd had sex already. I wished I could go back in time and just wait a week until after my birthday. WHY COULDN'T I HAVE WAITED A WEEK?

I was one of those girls. I was so smart and then I met a boy and I became so dumb. That had to stop. When I was a famous CEO and someone asked when I lost my virginity, I was going to say eighteen. That sounds so much better. Trevor would be the only other person who knew the truth, and we'd be married so he would lie for me. My gosh, I was going to be a role model who lies. It didn't matter. They don't ask CEOs when they lost their virginity. I couldn't believe I was thinking about this.

Whenever I wasn't with Trevor, I thought we should not have sex again for a long time. Like a year. Like really wait. But then when we were alone, I'd just want to be close to him and so I didn't stop. I wanted him to do it. It was starting to feel good. Not amazing. I mean, it felt amazing to be so close. But it was still not making me go crazy like girls in porn videos. We were wearing condoms every time now because we only hooked up in his basement again and that's where he kept them. It made me feel better. My period was one day late in January, and it almost gave me a heart attack. So maybe as long as we wore condoms it'd be okay that we were having sex so young. Maybe. I don't know.

It felt so right when I was with him and so wrong when I wasn't. It was very confusing.

My dad was spending more and more nights out at campus. My mom looked depressed again. But I didn't think he was cheating. I knew he wasn't. He would never hurt us again like that. He'd been so amazing since freshman year started. He would never want to ruin that. So I thought my mom just wanted to be depressed. On a Sunday night when it was just the two of us, I said, "Did you know Trevor's mom tried to commit suicide?"

"Carrie! You shouldn't say things like that," my mom said. She still called me Carrie whenever she talked without thinking first.

"It's true."

"Even if it is, it's not our business."

"Don't you think we should talk about things?"

"Not about other people's things," she said.

"Do you ever think about killing yourself, Mom?"

"Of course not, Carrie! How can you say that?"

"I don't know."

"I would never do that."

"Why?"

"Because it's wrong."

"Why's it wrong?" I asked.

"Oh my gosh!" she screamed, and sounded just like me. "Are you sad? Is something wrong with Trevor?"

"No, Mom! I'm fine. I'm worried about you!"

"I'm fine."

"You're sad again now that Dad's not around as much."

"I like having him here. It's okay for me to be sad when he's gone."

"He's not cheating again, Mom. I know it."

But my mom didn't say anything. She just nodded. Her face lost color.

"He loves you, Mom."

"I know. But I want you to know I would never, ever hurt myself. And that it's okay to be sad, Carolina. Because if you know it's okay to be sad, then you know being sad is not a reason to hurt yourself." My mom never talked like that. I liked it. I wanted her to keep talking like that. Except we just sat there for a bit in silence, her reading and me studying. But ten minutes later, maybe more, she turned to me again and said, with this very calm voice that made me calm even though I didn't even know I wasn't calm, "Carolina, I haven't always done a great job of communicating what I am feeling with you. Especially when things first came to light with your dad last year. I know you think you have to take care of me, and while I really do appreciate how much you care about me, I want you to know that above anything else—above my job, above your dad, anything—being here for you, being your mom, is by far the most important and greatest thing in my life."

I scooted over on the couch and curled up and laid my head on her lap like I was just a kid. I wasn't just a kid anymore, I know. But my mom saying that made me feel it would be okay to be a kid again for at least tonight.

Valentine's Day was on a Thursday, a school night, and Trevor had a basketball game on the 15th so we were going to celebrate on Saturday the 16th. We were going downtown on the train and back to the Metropolitan Club. It was our favorite date, and I think we wanted to go back in time. We were so young then. And virgins. And young.

74

Trevor buys two sweaters

My parents went out on Valentine's Day. Dressed up, all that crap. Lily and I stayed home, ate sandwiches and cookies, watched cartoons. My parents came home looking so happy. Like they were in love. Like they were the perfect couple. It annoyed me—because of course they were a total sham—but it also made me smile, and it made Lily smile, which made me smile even more. Because I wanted my parents to think they could be the perfect couple even if they couldn't be.

Then my mom sat down next to us, hugged Lily, and starting watching TV.

My dad said, "Lily, time for bed. Ashley, why don't we go to bed too?"

"I want to watch cartoons with the kids for a bit. You go. I'll be there soon," she said.

My dad almost argued. You could see he was sad. He wanted sex, didn't he? Holy crap. I could tell my dad wanted sex. And he was sad his wife didn't want to have it with him. Now that I had had sex, I could see stuff like this. He turned around, disappeared up the stairs.

"I think Dad wants you to go spend the rest of Valentine's Day night with him," I said to my mom once my dad was out of sight.

"I think you should mind your own business," my mom said. Didn't even look at me. And there was something about how she said it. Like it was about more than what I'd just said. Like she knew I had sent that note or seen her texts. Her knowing and telling me to mind my own business made me want to yell, *Fuck you, Mom*, but I didn't. I would never swear like that in front of Lily. So I got up, went to my room, and debated how and when I would tell my dad his wife was having an affair. But I knew I couldn't do it. Because if my dad knew, he'd divorce my mom and we'd probably move back to California with him (because he was the only one even remotely qualified to be a parent). And I'd rather die than go to California without Carolina. I'm not even joking.

MY DAD WENT ON ANOTHER TRIP EARLY THE NEXT DAY. At breakfast, my mom said she was going to visit her friend Paula in Indianapolis Saturday night and wouldn't be back until Sunday. She said we'd be fine alone for one night, that I was more than old enough to take care of Lily by myself, and we could all go grocery shopping to make sure there was plenty of food.

I said, "I'm celebrating Valentine's Day with Carolina tomorrow. I can't babysit."

"Yes, you can. Have Carolina come here. Have her spend the night here. That will be special."

"Her parents would never let her spend the night here," I said.

"Her dad wouldn't care," she said.

"How do you know her dad wouldn't care?" I said. That shut her up. For two seconds.

"Trevor, you used to pride yourself on not being a cliché. Well, you've become the cliché of a smart-ass teenager with your attitude." Then my mom walked out of the kitchen. After she was gone, Lily came over and hugged me.

"She's sad Dad left," Lily said. Yeah, right. But I couldn't tell Lily that. I had to protect Lily from the truth just like I had to protect Carolina. Only I could handle it. Only I should have to handle it.

ON SATURDAY NIGHT, I DECIDED CAROLINA, LILY, AND I would all go downtown. We'd make it an even more special night in spite of my mom's lies.

The train station was too long of a walk in the cold, so I drove us there in my dad's car even though I only had my permit. I knew I'd be careful. And I was. Lily kept saying, "This is very wrong, but I won't tell." I knew she wouldn't. Lily was too good a person to be a tattletale.

I couldn't get reservations at the Metropolitan Club without telling my dad or mom what we were doing, so instead we took a cab from Union Station to Michigan Avenue. We window-shopped and I bought (using my dad's credit card) both Lily and Carolina sweaters from the Gap. Neither of them wanted sweaters all that much, but I wanted us to buy something. Just because. Yeah, my dad might notice the charge weeks from now. But probably not. The man was goddamn blind to everything that was around him.

If I hadn't insisted that we go to the Gap, the night downtown might have been awesome. Because I swear, right before that, Carolina and I were feeling so close. Holding hands. Or each holding one of Lily's hands. Like we were a family. We were adults. And it felt good to be adults. Because we were real adults, taking care of Lily like she was the most important thing in the world. Unlike our own parents, who took care of their own stuff first.

So. Yep. As we were walking out of the Gap, me holding a bag filled with two sweaters Carolina and Lily didn't want or need, I heard Lily yell, "Mom! Did you decide to surprise us?"

Crap.

Then I looked up. And I saw our mom standing there. Looking so terrified. Like she wished she had succeeded in killing herself two years ago.

And behind her was Midnight Dog.

Carolina's dad.

His longish hair and casual clothes didn't look cool anymore. They just made him look like he didn't know how to act his age.

I looked toward Carolina. Her brain couldn't or wouldn't put together how my mom and her dad could be standing together on Michigan Avenue when Ashley Santos was supposed to be in Indianapolis with her friend Paula and Scott Fisher was supposed to be at Northern Illinois University working on a grant all weekend.

She said, "Dad?" And that's all she had time for before I picked up Lily, grabbed Carolina by the hand, and started speed walking away from our two lying, cheating, destroying parents as fast as possible.

75

Carolina takes a shower

I DIDN'T FIGHT TREVOR AS HE PULLED ME AWAY FROM MY dad and his mom. I didn't know why I didn't fight or why I should fight, but then, as we got in the cab, I realized. My dad was cheating again. Not just cheating. Cheating with Trevor's mom.

I threw up. It was white. Chunky. I think it was some roasted peanuts we had gotten on the street. I didn't know. Maybe egg salad. But I didn't remember eating egg salad. Lily asked if I was okay, but I don't think I said yes or no. I looked down. I could see throw-up on my clothes. In my lap. Trevor was using our new Gap sweaters to wipe it up. The taxi driver was yelling at us. Trevor yelled back at him. The cab pulled over and ordered us out. We got out.

I said, "Trevor?"

He said, "Let's just get home. Okay?"

I nodded. He was so calm. How was he so calm? Trevor finished wiping the throw-up off of me, threw the new sweaters away in a garbage can, and got us into a second cab. Trevor said to the driver, "Can you drive us to Riverbend?"

"It will be, like, eighty dollars," the driver said.

"I have a credit card," Trevor said.

"Okay," the driver said, and then we drove. We got on the Kennedy Expressway and just drove. For so long. Lily kept asking why my dad was with their mom in Chicago, and Trevor kept saying they became friends because of us. Trevor was trying to lie to Lily to protect her. But it was also the truth, right? Because of us my parents' marriage would probably end for real this time. I thought my falling in love with Trevor was saving my mom and dad but really, because of us, I'd just made it a million times worse.

We went directly to their house, leaving Trevor's dad's car at the train station. We went inside. I smelled so gross. I almost threw up again just smelling myself.

"She isn't talking," Lily said about me.

"She's sick."

"Should we go to the hospital?"

"She needs to rest."

"She can rest in my room," Lily said.

"I'll have her rest in my room," Trevor said.

"But you're a boy," she said back, her eyes holding steady on us. How much did she not understand and how much did she pretend not to understand?

"We're in love, so it's okay. Okay, Lily?"

"Okay, Trevor. I think I'll rest too."

"Okay, Lily."

TREVOR LED ME TO HIS ROOM, LOCKED THE DOOR BEHIND us, and started taking off my clothes. I thought he wanted to have sex, which felt like the grossest thing I could ever imagine right now, so I twisted hard away from him and said, "No . . ."

"A shower, Carolina. You should take a shower."

I stopped fighting and let him undress me. He led me to his bathroom, turned on the shower, and let me step inside. A few seconds later, he was under the water next to me, naked. He kissed me. Not a sex kiss. But a nice kiss. I could see in his eyes he just wanted to take care of me. Just make sure I was okay. Trevor was the kindest person in history. I don't think my parents have ever taken a shower together, but we were. Because our love was real. Unlike theirs.

After the shower, he wrapped me in a huge towel. Now I was shivering. I couldn't stop. He led me to his bed, pulled back the covers, let me lie down even though I was still dripping water and the wet towel was still wrapped around me. Then he pulled the covers over me. I fell asleep within, like, two seconds.

When I woke up, Trevor was taking the towel off of me. "I don't want to have sex," I said.

"I know. But you should put some clothes on so you don't get sick." Then he put a T-shirt over my head and slid his boy boxers up to my waist. I loved Trevor more right now than ever. He was right. Adults are no smarter than we are. They're worse. Because they pretend they can tell us stuff. Like all those things my dad said to me, all those things I thought were so smart about love and my brother and life. It was all a lie. He was just a big fake who liked to talk. I'm never going to talk to him again. I'm not. I have Trevor. I don't need my dad anymore. That's what I was thinking when I fell asleep a second time.

WHEN I WOKE UP AGAIN, I COULD HEAR TALKING DOWN-stairs. It was still dark outside, but an early morning dark. I looked at my phone. It said 4:17 a.m. Trevor was getting dressed by the door to his bedroom.

"Who is that?" I asked.

"Stay here," he said, then left. But I got up and followed him downstairs. In the front foyer, my dad was standing by the door. Trevor's mom was standing by the living room couch. They looked like strangers. Like he was just my dad, picking me up, and she was just Trevor's mom, meeting him for the first time.

But Trevor started talking. "She wants to stay here. You two should leave us alone."

"She needs to go home," his mom said.

"She wants to stay," Trevor said again.

"I want to stay," I said, then put my arm through Trevor's and laid my head on his shoulder. It was us against them. It was our love against their disgustingness.

"Carrie—we need to go home. I told your mom you were here, but she'd like you home. You can call Trevor tomorrow."

"No," I said to him, to Scott, even though I'd promised to never speak to him again. I knew I would never call him Dad again. Ever. Ever. Ever.

"Carolina, I'm sorry," Trevor's mom said, "this is a bad situation, and we can't deal with it right now in this way. Go with your dad. He needs to talk to you. I need to talk to Trevor."

"No," Trevor said, holding me tighter.

"Trevor?" a voice came from atop the stairs. We all turned to find Lily. Trevor looked at me. We both knew what the right thing to do was now that Lily was there.

"Do you have a big coat?" I asked. He nodded, fetched one from the front closet, kissed me on the lips, and then opened the door for me. I walked out to my dad's car. I was freezing, but I didn't care. I got in the passenger seat. My dad got in next to me.

76
Trevor buys Lily pancakes

AFTER I WATCHED CAROLINA AND HER DAD PULL OUT OF our driveway and disappear down the street, I closed the door, looked at my mom—where I was standing, Lily couldn't see me—and mouthed *I fucking hate you.*

She said, "That's your right." What did that even mean?

I walked back upstairs, led Lily to her room, closing and locking the door behind us.

"Why'd you lock the door, Trevor?"

"Because Mom needs to be by herself for a while."

"She might need our help," Lily said. Seven years old. More concerned about her mom than her mom was about her.

"Get in bed," I said. "I'm going to sleep on the floor. Okay?"

"Okay," she said.

"I love you, Lily."

"I'm worried about Mom."

"She'll be okay."

"What if she hurts herself? We have to save her."

"She won't."

"How do you know?"

"I just do," I said. But I didn't know. I just didn't care.

IN THE MORNING, I TOLD LILY TO GET DRESSED IN WARM clothes. I did the same. Then we walked toward the train station.

"But we should check on Mom," she said as we walked outside.

"Mom will be fine. We need to eat." I wasn't even hungry, but I just had to be outside of that house until my dad's plane landed in the afternoon.

We got into my dad's BMW at the station, and I drove us to Roth's Diner. We ordered strawberry crepes and chocolate pancakes and shared them both.

"Trevor," Lily said after she took a big bite of chocolate pancakes. Her face was smeared with it.

"Yeah?" I said.

"I know I'm only seven, but I'm smart."

"I know," I said.

"You think I don't know things, but I do."

"I know," I said.

"But maybe it's better if we don't talk about it."

"Okay."

"Isn't it funny how we don't talk about the most important things?"

"Yeah."

"It's hilarious," she said, then took another bite. And, poof, it was like her brain wiped clean any bad thoughts. Nodding her head blissfully to the cheesy restaurant music. I wish I could do that. Maybe I could when I was seven. Maybe my parents' crap was just as bad back then but I wiped it clean because if I hadn't, I wouldn't have been able to live with either of them. You have to when you're seven. You can't feed yourself or go anywhere by yourself. Not really. But I was old now. Maybe I couldn't wipe it clean anymore because I knew I could take care of myself. If I really needed to, I could go get a job or hunt deer or at least go live in a shelter or something. Maybe that's it. Maybe as soon as you're old enough to survive without your parents, you're old enough to see your parents for who they really are.

77

Carolina gets into a Toyota 4Runner

As he drove me from Trevor's, my dad kept saying, "Can we talk?" But I didn't say anything back. I didn't look at him. Trevor's coat was big and long, but underneath I had on only a T-shirt and boxers. Underneath I was so cold. Underneath I was numb. So, so, so numb. But not numb enough, you know?

When my dad parked in our driveway, I said, "Don't you ever come inside, ever, ever again." I ran out of the car and took out my key, but my mom was awake and opening the front door for me.

"Are you okay?" she asked. No, I wasn't. Oh my gosh, I would never be okay again. Okay? Okay? But then I thought my mom already knew. That's why she had been so sad. I should have said, *Are you okay, Mom?* and hugged her or said nothing and hugged her or even just said nothing, but instead I said, "You picked the worst husband in history," and went to my room. So mean. I shouldn't be mean to my mom. She has a husband who's mean to her, so her daughter should be nice. But she had let him back in our life. She had let him hurt us all over again. I would never let a man hurt me like that. Never.

I CRAWLED INTO MY OWN BED. I DIDN'T EVEN TAKE
Trevor's coat off. My phone buzzed. It was Trevor. Asking if I was
okay. But I pretended I didn't see it. Why was I pretending things to
myself? I don't know. Trevor was amazing. More amazing than ever.
But . . . I don't know.

Wait a minute.

Oh. My. Gosh.

He knew.

The whole night flashed back through my brain. He wasn't even
mad when he saw them. Saw his mom and my dad together. Because
he knew. I could see his face in my memory as he took my hand and
led us away. He hated them. But he was focused. He was prepared.
Because he knew.

He knew.

How could he not tell me? HOW COULD HE NOT TELL
ME?

I picked up my phone, wanting to ask how long he had known.
Wanting to ask why he hadn't told me.

Except I saw Alexander Taylor's birthday text five messages down.
I had never written anything back. Because I was a good girlfriend. I
was. I had lied that once, but I was an amazing girlfriend. I had given
Trevor my heart and sex and my time and gotten bad grades and lost
friends and changed my whole life forever. All for him.

And he hadn't told me about my dad and his mom. I almost got
sick again. Except nothing came up. Just gross air. Empty gross air.
Nothing was left in my stomach to throw up. Nothing was left in my
insides at all.

So I texted:

ME

Hi, junior.

It wasn't to Trevor. Duh. As soon as I pressed send, I wished I hadn't. I mean, it was not even five a.m. Alexander wouldn't be up for a hundred hours, and I'd have to wait and feel bad about text cheating again and feel bad without even the excitement of actual texting from Alexander. But as I was thinking all this, my phone buzzed.

It was from Alexander:

ALEXANDER TAYLOR

it's early, freshman

And because this is what I really felt, I responded:

ME

I don't care.

ALEXANDER TAYLOR

**i'm going back to bed. i'll pick you up
at 10 for breakfast. text me your
address. wear something interesting.**

No way would I go to breakfast with him. No way would I text him my address. But then I did text him my stupid address. And then I sat in bed for the next four hours and thought about how I should cancel the breakfast and thought about my dad and thought about Trevor and thought that I had never liked my life less than at this exact moment and then I also thought about what I would wear. And then I thought about everything again but in a different order.

So at nine I took a shower and I put on a skirt and tall boots and a turtleneck and I put Trevor's coat under my bed so I wouldn't have to look at it. I put on makeup. I had never put on makeup on Sunday morning, and it felt so weird. Then I sat by my window and stared out at my driveway, waiting for Alexander Taylor to pick me up and make everything better by just making me think about something besides everything.

As soon as he pulled into the driveway, Alexander honked. He drove a big black Toyota 4Runner. It was an older model with tinted windows and a dented rear door. It looked like a truck no girl should get into unless she wanted to die. But I ran out through my house, ignored my mom's yelling from the kitchen, and jumped right into his scary truck.

"Hi, freshman," he said as he put the 4Runner in reverse. The leather seats were cracked and cold against the bare of my legs. Why did I wear a skirt? He'd tricked me. He'd said, "Wear something interesting." Why would he care what I wore? I mean, he's a boy. He cared because he wanted me to look sexy. But why would he make it so obvious he cared? To trick me. I would have worn jeans if he hadn't said that.

"Hi," I said, wishing I could jump out. But maybe not. My whole body was prickly. A good prickly. An alive prickly. My breath was fast and my heart was faster.

"What are you running away from? Mom? Dad? Both? Boyfriend? All of the above?"

"I'm not," I said. Such a lie.

"Yeah, right. It's okay. I'm glad. I like that you're running to me. I'm a good person to run away to." Then he reached over and squeezed my naked knee. I jumped. I laughed. He thought it was a fun laugh so he did it again, except higher on my leg. I didn't laugh this time. So he stopped. *Why* was I in this stupid truck?

WHEN WE PARKED AT ROTH'S DINER, I SAW TREVOR AND
Lily sitting in a booth by the window inside. Oh my gosh. Oh my
gosh. Oh my gosh.

"I don't want to go here," I said.

"Are you making decisions now, freshman?"

"Please," I said, slinking down into the seat to hide. Alexander
looked up, through the windshield, seeing Trevor in the restaurant
window.

"So I guess you're not broken up?" He smirked.

"Please," I said.

"If we go somewhere else, what do I get?"

I didn't say anything.

"Do I get a kiss?"

"Okay," I said. And then he backed out and drove away and I
could breathe again.

WE ATE AT EGG HARBOR IN GLENVIEW. IT WAS A FAR
drive, but I felt much safer. No one would see us here. I didn't know if
he would pay and I only had five dollars so I just ordered oatmeal. I
wasn't that hungry. I mean, I was starving and my head felt dizzy, but
I also felt sick so oatmeal was enough. I guess. He didn't ask about
Trevor. He mostly talked about himself. About books he had read
and TV shows he liked. It wasn't as interesting as I had always thought
it would be. Alexander knew how to act like he'd be interesting but I
was bored and it wasn't even the middle of our first date. Oh my gosh,
was this a date? It was. Maybe. I had told him I would kiss him! How

could I do that! I'd tell him I couldn't. I'd tell him I would pay him back another way. He would understand.

At the end of breakfast, I offered my five dollars. He took it.

We got back in his truck and drove to a nearby Target. "Why are we going here?" I asked.

"Because we can park here," he said, and parked on the side, facing out into an empty field. No other cars were parked anywhere close. It's not like we were in the middle of nowhere, but it was still creepy. You know? I told myself I should get out. *I should get out, go into Target, call my mom, and wait for her to pick me up.*

"Freshman?" he said. I turned away from the window and toward him, only he was already leaning close to me. I pulled back. Oh my gosh, his breath smelled weird. Not bad. I guess not bad. But not like Trevor's. Alexander said, "What about my kiss?"

"I can't," I said.

"You promised," he said. And I tried to remember if I'd promised. I didn't. I just said, "Okay." But he leaned again and I didn't move. His lips pressed into mine, and I closed my eyes and tried not to think about what was happening. He pushed his tongue into mine and moved it around but I didn't move mine, and then he ran his tongue around my lips and bit my nose. Oh my gosh, why did he bite my nose? Like, scraped it with his teeth. Weirdo! And then I could feel his hand on my leg and he was reaching up my skirt. *Oh my gosh, this is so gross. Say no. Stop him.* Then he curled his fingers under my underwear and touched me. I was so dry. He tried to press one more time, but then I pinched my legs shut and he pulled away his hand. I never wanted another boy besides Trevor to touch me ever again. Then Alexander grabbed my right hand and put it on his jeans, where I could feel his penis. I left my hand there but I just let it lie there.

Alexander stopped kissing me, pulled away, and said, "I thought you would know what to do. You know. Be experienced."

I didn't say anything. I wished I had never left Trevor's at four a.m. I should go find him and hug him and never leave him again.

"Are we going to hook up or not?"

I didn't say anything. I should have said no. I should have said this was a big mistake. But I was so afraid, not of him, maybe a little, just so afraid of everything that I didn't want to say anything.

"You know, you shouldn't leave a boy like this. It's not fair." He pointed at his groin. But I looked away, out the window. "Freshman. Fucking freshman. I should have known better." Then he put the car in reverse, left Target, put on an Eminem song really, really loud, and drove me home.

As soon as he parked, I jumped out and ran back inside. My mom was waiting on the couch. "Who was that?" But she really said it like WHO WAS THAT? except not loud. Just the effect was like that. I almost ran to my room. But instead I ran to the couch, laid my head on my mom's lap, closed my eyes, and breathed big breaths until I calmed down. I didn't cry. I didn't. I think I would have cried on every day of my life before this one. But not today. My mom didn't say anything. She just petted my head. It helped. It helped that she didn't say anything too. I didn't need advice or a lecture or even one word that would make me feel worse than I already did. I just needed her to be there.

After about ten minutes or maybe much longer, I gave her a big hug and then went to my room and checked my phone, which had been off. There were a bunch of messages from Trevor. All of them were so nice and caring and loving. Stuff like "Hope you are okay" and "I'm here for you" and "You're my soul mate." When I saw that, that's when I finally cried. Oh my gosh, why did I get in Alexander's car? How could I have been so stupid?

I texted:

ME

**I love you so much, Trevor, and I want
us to spend eternity together**

I wanted this so badly I could feel my body scream the words over
and over. Then I went and took a shower and tried to scrub everywhere that Alexander had touched me.

When I got out, I found a text from Trevor that said:

TREVOR

**I should have told you about our
parents. I was worried you'd hate me.**

ME

**It's okay. I understand. I don't want to
talk about it. I just want us to be
happy forever. Okay?**

TREVOR

Okay. I promise.

I sent a smiley face and then crawled into bed in sweatpants and
went to sleep. I was so tired. So, so, so tired. Like I couldn't even think
anymore.

When I woke up, it was dark. I had slept the whole day away.
There was a text. From Peggy. So weird. So, so, so weird. It said:

PEGGY

**Heard about Alex. Want details!
Trevor was so boring. He made you
weird. Call me.**

Oh my gosh. Oh. Oh. Oh. Oh. Oh. If Peggy knew, more people
knew, and if more people knew, Trevor would know soon . . . so soon. . . .

78
Trevor crashes the car

AFTER BREAKFAST, LILY AND I WENT TO A MOVIE. I TEXTED while we watched, even though I hate people who text during movies. At least I sat in the back so nobody behind me had to look at my phone's light.

Carolina didn't respond, but I figured she would be sleeping. Licker and I texted about basketball and about Kendra. (He had a crush on her but told me not to tell Carolina until he was sure Kendra liked him too.) Then I got a text from my mom:

MOM

Going to pick up Dad. Will have long talk. Will be home late. Please take care of Lily.

I hated seeing her name on my phone but I also liked it. Maybe I liked hating it. Hearing from her allowed me to release my frustration instead of just letting it build louder and bigger and crazier in my head. After the movie, Lily and I got hot chocolate from Starbucks even though we had just had candy at the theater and chocolate pancakes at

Roth's. It didn't even taste good. It made me feel sick. Maybe I wanted to feel sick. Who the hell knows? Life makes no sense.

As we were driving home, we stopped at a light. A police car stopped right next to us.

"Trevor," Lily said, then pointed at the police. Which only made it worse.

"Don't point," I said. The police officer looked right at me. Crap. We were going to get arrested for me driving without a license. We were. I'd be thrown in jail. But then the light turned and the officer drove on. I guess I fooled him. Everyone was so stupid.

As I opened the garage door, my phone buzzed. I reached for it because I wanted it to be from Carolina but instead it was from Licker:

LICKER

Sorry about Carolina, dude.

Huh? He couldn't know about our parents and that text wouldn't make sense even if he did. So I texted:

ME

What about her?

LICKER

About Alex Taylor. What a dick. You could totally beat the shit out of him.

The texts. He was talking about her New Year's Eve texts. This seemed strange. And then I got a text from my cousin Henry:

HENRY

Told you not to go out with her.

What the fuck? So I texted Licker:

**I know what happened but you tell
me what you think happened**

I didn't know. Maybe I did. But my gut said I didn't. But I didn't
want anyone to know I didn't. Licker texted:

LICKER

**She gave him a hj in his car this
morning**

"TREVOR!" Lily yelled as the BMW crashed into the back of the
garage and my mom's hanging bicycle, which she had never used once,
dropped from the ceiling onto the car's roof and made a dent so big
you could probably sit in it.

Shit.

But then I looked back at the text. From Licker.

It couldn't be.

It couldn't be.

It couldn't be.

Everything inside me twisted tighter. Tighter. Tighter. So goddamn tight I couldn't breathe. My skin everywhere broke and shattered. Fuck. Fuck. Fuck.

"Why are we leaving again?" Lily screamed, but I didn't respond.
I just backed out of the garage, let the bike fall off the car and lay
crumpled in the middle of the garage floor. "Trevor!" Lily said every
few minutes as I sped faster and faster toward Carolina's.

I PARKED IN HER DRIVEWAY, TOLD LILY TO STAY, OPENED the door to Carolina's house without knocking, walked past her mom, who was watching TV, and maybe yelled at me, and then opened her bedroom door and there she was, crying, phone to her ear. She was calling me. My phone was ringing. I looked at it, saw her name, saw the picture of us at the Metropolitan Club, then pressed ignore.

"Did . . . ?" But I couldn't say any more.

"I didn't!"

"AAAAAAAAAHHHHH!" I screamed even though she said she didn't. Because I just knew. Knew. Crap. I hated knowing every goddamn thing ever.

"He kissed me! And he tried to touch me! And tried to make me touch him! But I didn't! And then he took me home! And I want to only kiss you forever! I hate myself! I hate myself! Please, Trevor, don't hate me too!" She ran into my arms and sobbed into my chest and her whole body went limp and I caught her but I didn't want to so I let her down on her bed. She looked terrible. So red-faced and snotty and boyish in her sweatpants. But I was still excited. My penis was still hard. That makes no sense! And I still wanted to kiss her so bad. But I wasn't going to. I was never, ever going to kiss her again.

"I hate you as much as I hate my mom," I said, and then I screamed again and then I grabbed the notebook I had made for Christmas and ripped out five pages just because and then I threw it against the wall and I left.

79

Carolina's brain goes to mush

I WANTED TO RUN AFTER TREVOR, I THINK, BUT I WAS crying so loudly it made my legs wobbly so I crawled along my bedroom floor, yelling his name, I think, but maybe I wasn't saying anything, not any real words, just loud yells and wails and crazy noises that people make right before they die from so much pain no person could survive it. No person would want to.

And then my mom was standing there, then she was on the floor, opening her hands, and I crawled the last few feet and collapsed into her lap.

"TREVOR!" I yelled. I think. Something like that. A word like his name. But filled with all this spit and snot and tears.

"He's gone," my mom said. And then she squeezed me tight against her, and my brain stopped knowing what to think or do so it just went to mush.

LATER. I DON'T HOW MUCH LATER. BUT LATER. MY MOM led me back to my bed and laid me down. I slept. I think. But can you sleep when your brain is mush? Wouldn't it be impossible? I don't know. I should look that up. People in comas must sleep. Right? But my brain was more mush than a coma. I swear. It was worthless. Just worthless. I think. I suppose I'm kind of having these thoughts or kind of remember having these thoughts so maybe it wasn't one hundred percent mush. Who knows? Maybe we are all two different people. One person who feels and one person who thinks. And the person who feels can think a little and the person who thinks can feel a little, but sometimes one of those people dies or gets hurt and can't do what she is supposed to do. So maybe the person in me who feels died or at least went into a coma and the person who thinks just kind of lies there because she has never been so alone and afraid before.

So many people texted me that night. Even gross, disgusting Alexander Taylor. So many people. But not Trevor. I texted him five hundred times. That's not even an exaggeration. I mean, maybe. But it was close. It felt like ten million . . . ten million texts to the one person I could ever love and no texts back. I even sent him a sexy picture. Except I looked so sad it wasn't even sexy. I shouldn't have sent it. But I had to. I would have done anything to have him back. I'd have done anything he asked. Anything. But Trevor is so nice he'd never ask me to do anything gross or dumb. Unlike Alexander Taylor and every other boy on earth. See? SEE? I had the most amazing boyfriend in history and I kissed another boy in his dumb truck just because . . . just because . . . I don't even know anymore. Just because I'm a horrible person, I guess.

So I had to take the bus Monday morning. My mom had an early shift. My dad was gone because I told him to be gone. Peggy and Katherine had stopped driving me to school after homecoming. And Trevor, whose parents had driven me the most this year, was not going to pick me up. Not ever. Not ever again. Oh my gosh, I have no Trevor, no Peggy, no Dad. And I have to ride the bus with a bunch of people who look at me like I'm a psycho slut. And it smells like plastic and it's slow and it's loud and I need to transfer schools.

Biology was like torture. No, not like. It *was* torture. GIRLS SHOULD BE ABLE TO STAY HOME WHEN THEIR BOY-FRIENDS DUMP THEM! Or at least not go to classes they have with them! He sat on the other side of the room. Like, one desk away from Peggy. Peggy talked to him. Smiled at him. She'd texted me that he was boring, and now she was flirting with him? Humans are all terrible people. I cried the whole class. Not loudly. I would have been kicked out. But this low, shaking cry that I tried to keep quiet, but everyone knew. Everyone in class knew. And they kept looking at me, either like I was so pathetic or funny-looking. But not Trevor. He didn't look at me once. If he looked at me, wouldn't he fall back in love? Wouldn't he remember all the good things and forgive me and take me back and then everything would be amazing again?

But he didn't. He didn't want to remember, I guess. I don't blame him. I wanted to forget.

So that's how all of school went. History was almost as bad as biology, and my other non-Trevor classes were terrible in a different way because I couldn't see him there and dream he would look at me and love me again.

Lunch was terrible too. Duh. Boys laughed at me, and girls

whispered stuff. Only the soccer girls sat with me. Kendra sat the closest. She kept saying, "It will be okay," over and over. I knew it wouldn't be. I knew my whole life was ruined—YES, RUINED! IT'S FINALLY TRUE! SO I CAN SAY IT AND IT'S NOT ME BEING IMMATURE OR EXAGGERATING AT ALL! CUZ IT'S TRUE! RUINED! RUINED! RUINED!—but anyway... gosh ... anyway ... yes, so it was nice of Kendra to say it would be okay even though it was a horrible, terrible lie.

I SENT TREVOR TEXTS, LIKE, EVERY FIVE SECONDS I HAD MY phone on. He didn't respond. Even if he had cheated on me, I would have responded. I would have wanted to yell at him! Why wouldn't he yell at me? Why? WHY? WHY? WHY? WHY? If he yelled at me, I'd know he still loved me. But he doesn't. He doesn't look at me or talk to me or text me or think about me. I bet he doesn't even have one thought about me. I bet someone today said, "What's happened with you and Carolina?" and he said back, "Who?" Yep, I bet he's forgotten every beautiful thing we ever did and having sex and saying we loved each other. I bet he's already looking at new girls and thinking about them and kissing them and he'll probably think the new girl is his real soul mate. But I am. I'm his real soul mate. And he doesn't remember. He has amnesia. He has to remember. If he would just remember, he'd forgive me. He would. Then everything would go back to normal. My life would be fine. I don't need Peggy or my dad or good grades or a job or anything besides Trevor. Just him. Oh, please, please, please, please let me have him back.

80
Trevor has pizza with his dad

AFTER I GOT BACK IN THE CAR WITH LILY SUNDAY NIGHT, she asked, "What happened, Trevor? What happened?" She was so scared. She cried a little. Not a big cry. But a real cry. Our parents sucked. She knew it. But I think she, maybe me too, wanted Carolina and me to be her real parents. The real couple. The couple who loved each other so much we could take care of anyone else too. Like Lily. So Lily didn't have to be so goddamn old when she was just seven.

"We broke up," I said. Face twitched. Twitched bad. Like my skin was about to peel off and this monster was going to take over. Like I was always a monster. Like only Carolina kept the monster from taking control.

"Get her back, okay? Please! Please!"

"I hate her."

"You love her! You love her! Trevor! Don't say that! You love her!" And she just kept saying I had to get her back, but I pulled out of the driveway and started driving.

Eventually Lily stopped talking. Eventually my body stopped feeling like it was just one huge raging piece of flesh, and I realized I had driven halfway to Wisconsin. I pulled over into the next gas station. Lily, who looked like a ghost, said, "Where are we?"

"I don't know."

"Dad should be home by now," she said. "Can we go see Dad?"

"I think Dad and Mom are going to talk by themselves all night, Lily."

"What are we supposed to do?"

"I don't know."

"I'll think of something," Lily said, and she closed her eyes. Like the idea of how to fix all this crap would come to her if she just concentrated.

"How about we pick up McDonald's, go home, and watch TV?" I said.

"That's a good plan, Trevor. Except can we go to Sonic? They have better milk shakes."

"Okay."

I didn't sleep that night. Sometimes people say that, but I know they're making it up. I really didn't sleep. I just lay there and thought about Carolina kissing and touching another boy. Like, each time the image of that would hit my brain it was like this giant bird dinosaur would tear into my chest with its giant dinosaur claws. Here's what I had to do. Fucking had to do: Pretend she didn't exist. Ignore her. Ignore people who talked to me about her. Not look at her. Not think about her.

I was thinking about her every goddamn second. Crap. But I

would keep yelling at my brain until I stopped. Or something. Just ignore her, Trevor. Just ignore her until your brain can forget her.

That's what I did Monday. Didn't look at her. Not once. My whole stupid body wanted to look at her. For her to see me and tell me it didn't happen. Even if that was a lie, I wanted her to convince me. Maybe. Crap. I don't know. What the hell happened? How did this happen? My mom. My mom and her dad and their bullshit.

MY DAD PICKED ME UP FROM PRACTICE MONDAY NIGHT.

He said, "Let's go talk." I nodded. He drove. We went to this pizza and bar place near the train tracks. They gave you peanuts to eat and had no real menus, just big chalkboards with pizza toppings. My dad got a beer and I got a Coke. We ordered a pepperoni pizza.

"How are you doing?" my dad said.

I shrugged my shoulders. He knew about Carolina. Lily had told him this morning when my dad started yelling at me about the BMW having a dent. Lily was the smartest, best person ever.

"Sorry about Carolina."

"I want to go back to California," I said.

"We're not going back to California."

"You're leaving Mom, right? You're getting a divorce, right? No way Lily and I can stay with her. No fucking way."

"Watch your language."

I wanted to yell, *Yeah? Yeah? I should watch my language? Yeah! How about you watch your wife?* But I didn't say anything.

"Trevor . . . we're not getting divorced. You get married, you make promises. You make promises to the Church and God—"

"I don't believe in God."

"He still believes in you."

"Mom doesn't believe in God," I said.

"And she's not very happy because of it."

My dad was a lunatic. In a different way from Mom or me, but still a lunatic.

"Trevor, listen . . . sorry . . . I didn't want this to be combative. I want this to be a grown-up talk. Your mom and I will keep working on things. But you have to let us work on them. If you unleash that wrath of yours on her every time she steps into a room, she won't be able to take it. She's fragile. She needs our strength."

"Isn't a mom supposed to give her kids strength?" I said, and as I did I almost lost it. Not mad. But emotions. I held it. Barely.

"Yes . . . you're right. Your mom gave you lots of talent, and brains, and passion. But she needs strength from you. I'm sorry about that."

"How can you stay with her?"

"I love her."

"Well, she doesn't love you!" I said.

That smacked across his face. Then he breathed for a second and said, "I'm not a perfect husband either."

And—f-ing unbelievable—I saw it in his eyes. Man. He had done the same to her. Before? Before she tried to kill herself? Or after? Now? "When?" I asked.

"What you think you know, you don't. You shouldn't have to know any of this. But you do, and we have to deal with it."

"Kids know everything. You both suck."

"Don't use that language."

"AAAAH!" I yelled out, and the whole restaurant looked at us and I felt so fucking stupid, so I just started mumbling in this whisper that didn't even sound like me, "Aw, Dad . . . God . . . you tell me that . . . you tell me that . . . and you and Mom . . . my language . . .

you're worried about me swearing . . . I don't know, Dad. You're worried about me saying words, and you two do all this crap. . . ." Then I stopped talking. And he didn't talk. He always filled silence. Always. He could be quiet for days, but he always filled those strange silences. Not today. Not now. The pizza came. We ate. We watched *Sports-Center* on the TV above the bar. He kept opening his mouth, had something he wanted to say. But nothing. Nothing.

We got back in his car, started driving home. Then he pulled over into the parking lot of a closed bank.

"I'm sorry, Trev. Really sorry. You're right. I'm going to be better. Your mom is going to try and be better. I promise. Let us try. Give us that?"

Can't say anything to that besides "Okay."

THAT NIGHT I WAS SUPER TIRED. SO TIRED. BUT MY BRAIN kept obsessing about Carolina and wishing I could kiss her and have sex and spend forever happy with her. I couldn't stop, could I? I was so mad at her. So mad. So goddamn mad. But I loved her. I loved her so much. And if I moved away or I died, maybe I'd be able to keep myself from wanting to be with her. But she's in school and she's a five-minute drive away and I had to be with her again. I had to. I just had to beat the shit out of Alexander Taylor first.

81

Carolina attends a fight

KENDRA TOLD ME AT LUNCH ON TUESDAY.

She said, "Trevor and Alexander are going to fight after school."

"Really?" I said, and, oh my gosh, I was so sad and excited at the same time. Like, I can't believe I hurt Trevor and I can't believe I kissed stupid Alexander and it was my fault and I'm a horrible person . . . but also, like, two boys would fight over me? ME? In junior high, boys wouldn't even look at me, and now two boys were going to fight because of me.

And then I decided that as amazing as that was for the dumb girl in my head who wants to be important, it's a very bad thing for the person I'm supposed to be. You know, the nice, mature, good person.

So I started texting both Alexander and Trevor, pleading both not to fight. Alexander texted me back right away, saying he wouldn't fight Trevor if I kissed him "for real" next time. I think he meant sex or a hand job or something that made me want to throw up. But I almost said yes because I didn't want Trevor to get hurt. But kissing Alexander because he tricked me was how I ruined my life in the first place, so I texted back to him, "I hope you lose."

Trevor didn't respond to any of my texts, and when I tried to talk to him in the hall, he just walked by like I wasn't even there. Worse. Like he would get a disease if I touched him or if he even looked at me.

THE FIGHT WAS SUPPOSED TO TAKE PLACE IN THE PARKING lot of Riverbend Community Center Pool. It was closed because it was winter, so there would be no grown-ups there. Kendra and I got a ride with some sophomore she knew because of her mom. It seemed like the whole school was going because all these cars drove in a big line, and people were honking, and leaning out the windows and screaming just to scream.

There was already a big circle of people there when we arrived. It wasn't the whole school, I exaggerated again, closer to, like, fifty people. But that's still a lot to watch a fight between two boys fighting over me.

Trevor was standing there, in the center of the circle, looking at the ground. He was so still. So intense. I swear, he was like a monk. He seemed like he couldn't see or hear anything except his own mind.

Alexander Taylor wasn't there, and I hoped he wouldn't show up. That would be the best. Trevor would be the hero because he was brave enough to fight but he also wouldn't have to fight. See, Trevor is tall and strong, I think, for being a freshman and kind of thin, but Alexander Taylor is on the swim team and he has very broad shoulders and he's a junior, so he's thicker and probably has more experience fighting because he's an asshole. I never swear. But he is. I hate him. I feel so disgusting thinking about him. It's not like he molested me. I didn't say no. I didn't run away. I even said I'd kiss him. But the way he did it, the way he did everything, was so wrong. Boys who trick girls into doing sex stuff with them are the worst boys in the universe.

They are gross and stupid and so uncool. I know I screwed up. I know. I should have been smarter. But that doesn't mean Alexander Taylor isn't a worse person than me. Because he is.

So . . . just when people started whispering that Alexander Taylor wasn't going to show up, these five SUVs arrive, including that dumb black 4Runner, and out of all these trucks jump twenty juniors and seniors from the swim team. All wearing their team blue-and-gold sweatpants and jackets. Oh. My. Gosh. This was SO unfair! Trevor had Licker and two other freshman basketball players and then Aaron and Tor from the cross-country team. And they were all, like, half the size of these swim people. (Henry and Jake were there, but I knew they would never defend Trevor because you can tell when someone's a wimp inside even when he acts tough outside.) So Trevor only had, like, five people and they were thin and young. And Alexander had TWENTY friends. Twenty big upperclassmen.

"Trevor!" I yelled because I didn't want him to die. But he didn't look at me. He was about to die and he hated me so much that he still wouldn't look at me. Henry mocked me by yelling, "Trevor," in a girl's voice. I don't care. I know he's just trying to be funny because he knows he's a wuss.

AFTER ALEXANDER TAYLOR MOVED INTO THE CIRCLE AND the whole swim team pushed people aside to form this wall behind him, people started chanting, "FIGHT, FIGHT, FIGHT."

Alexander paced, back and forth, one step toward Trevor, then back toward his friends; he kept smiling but you could tell he was nervous. He didn't want to leave his friends and go toward the center.

Trevor still hadn't moved from the middle. Not even one step. It was actually freaky. Like he was possessed. Who wouldn't move?

Who wouldn't at least look up or look back? OR LOOK AT THE GIRL WHO LOVES YOU? But no, Trevor just stayed so still. So, so, so still I thought maybe he was a statue. Not really. But at least, like, not human. Oh my gosh, Trevor is so weird . . . and I love him. I love him so much. He's so different. Look at Alexander, acting all cocky with a million friends, but really he was so nervous and jumpy and boring. He was like five million other boys. But not Trevor. Trevor was so weird and unique and special. Trevor was like this super-spiritual master who could concentrate even when everything around him was crazy. He was so intense. His brain, you could tell just looking at him right now, was so much faster and deeper than anyone else's. Oh. My. Gosh. Trevor has a fast brain like me. Not that we're smarter than everyone. What I'm saying is, I didn't really understand what made Trevor and I love each other until right now, when I saw him so silent and about to get beat up. It's all the thoughts we don't tell anyone else. All the thoughts that move so fast through our whole bodies. I should have told him more. I should have told him every time I ever thought of another boy or about my dad or about when I was afraid or bored and everything. We should have just opened up our brains and put all our thoughts out there. Even if those thoughts hurt the other person, we would have been even closer. I wanted that. I wanted that with him. I wanted him to know everything I ever thought and felt and I wanted to know everything he ever thought and felt. Everything, no matter how bad or scary or weird. Everything. Love needs to know everything.

ALEXANDER TAYLOR YELLED OUT, "YOU SURE YOU WANT to fight?"

Trevor didn't say anything.

Alexander yelled again, "Too scared to say anything, freshman?" His swim team friends laughed.

Trevor still didn't say anything.

Alexander then said, "You don't want to fight. This is a waste of my time. We're leaving." Then Alexander turned back toward the trucks.

Only Trevor finally said something, even though he hadn't looked up. He didn't say it. It was like he bellowed it. Just so, so loud you could feel the words hit your chest. Trevor bellowed, "I'M THE ONE STANDING HERE IN THE CENTER, AND YOU'RE THE ONE STANDING BY YOUR FUCKING FRIENDS!"

OH. MYYYYYYY. GOSSSSSSHHHHHHH. TREVOR WAS SO cool. That was the coolest thing anyone has ever said ever. Oh my gosh. Oh my gosh. People were laughing at Alexander. Even some of his team. Oh my gosh. Trevor was so amazing. How did he even think to say that? How could he say something so perfect and so cool at the exact right moment? Oh my gosh. This was like a movie. But . . . wait . . . if this were a movie, would the audience be rooting for me or against me? I mean, they would definitely be rooting for Trevor, but gosh, was I the bad girl the audience hated for cheating? Oh my gosh, I wasn't. I kissed another boy because my dad was having sex with Trevor's mom and Trevor didn't tell me and I was scared and I made a huge mistake. . . . Oh, I wanted to be the one they root for too. I did. So I yelled, "I LOVE YOU, TREVOR!" So loud. As loud as Trevor yelled. My gosh. I just had to. And I was crying. I couldn't even tell if they were happy tears or sad tears. I don't know. I just loved him so much I had to yell and cry and guess what? GUESS WHAT? He turned. Everyone turned toward me. But most important by a trillion, Trevor turned. And he looked at me. And he smiled. Not a big smile. I don't even think he moved his lips. But his eyes. I could see the smile in his eyes. Because we're soul mates, and soul mates can see those things.

Then Trevor turned back toward Alexander, looking right at him. And Trevor's eyes were so intense again. Like terrifying. Like he was insane. But I knew he wasn't. Maybe he was. But I loved him anyway. Maybe I loved him because I was insane too.

The crowd chanted, "FIGHT, FIGHT, FIGHT," again and Alexander Taylor finally took a few steps toward Trevor, though you could tell he didn't want to go. I wouldn't either. There was something in Trevor's eyes that would make the strongest person in the universe scared to fight him, I think.

Alexander yelled, "You're dead, freshman!" But it was kind of lame-sounding and then he ran at Trevor and Trevor ran at him, but Trevor crouched low at the last second and, like a football player making a tackle, lowered his shoulder into Alexander's stomach, wrapped his arms under Alexander's butt, and then Trevor screamed, "AAAAAAAAAHHHHHHHH!" like a wild animal, except animals couldn't make that noise, and then Trevor lifted up for a second and slammed Alexander down into the parking lot cement. Alexander's head whiplashed against the ground and he cried out. Like really cried out. Like a little boy.

Alexander held up his hands, saying, "Wait, wait, I hit my head . . . wait . . ."

Trevor screamed another "AAAAAAAHHHHH," and then he turned and walked away.

Alexander managed to stand, wobbly, but still trying to be tough. He yelled, "I didn't say we were finished, freshman!"

Trevor turned fast, like super fast, like Superman fast, and started charging right at Alexander, only Alexander ran away, ran to his swim team and hid behind them. And everyone laughed. Even all his swim team. And Trevor stopped, turned, found me, and walked right toward me.

Oh my gosh. It was like a movie star was walking toward me. And those eyes. It was so sexy. I was so excited. You know, excited down there. That had never happened when I had my clothes on. Oh my gosh, this is love. I didn't say anything; he didn't say anything. He just grabbed my hand and he started walking across the parking lot, and I went with him, obviously, and I didn't turn around and he didn't turn around and we just kept walking and then there was this path and we walked down it and suddenly we were alone. And I tried to look at him and say something, but I was too nervous. I didn't want to say anything wrong. I know I said Trevor and I should share everything. But that was before, when he was so far away. But now I had him again. He was so close. I couldn't say or tell him anything that might ruin anything. This was the greatest moment of my life, I just knew it was.

And then, when were in the middle of some trees, Trevor let go of my hand and collapsed to the ground, right in some mud, and he started hyperventilating and his eyes filled with tears. And my superhero movie star became this shaking mess and I got so confused so fast and, oh, why can't life be a movie where the hero girl never makes horrible mistakes and the hero boy never hyperventilates in the mud?

He said, his chest heaving up and down, "I fucking hate you, Carolina."

And I almost cried and yelled at him, I don't even know what I would yell, but instead I sat on the ground next to him and started kissing him. All over his face. His eyes and his tears and ears. I said, "I'm so, so, so sorry, Trevor."

"Why . . . ?" he said, but I knew what he was asking.

"I was mad at you for not telling me about my dad and your mom, I think."

"I'll tell you everything forever, okay?"

"Okay."

"Just never hurt me ever again, okay?"

"Never," I said. "Never, ever, ever."

A WHILE LATER, WE WERE BOTH SO COLD, SO WE STOOD UP and we walked all the way to his house. His dad was out of town, but Lily and his mom were reading in the living room.

"I'M SO HAPPY!" Lily screamed and ran and leaped into my arms. Even though it had only been three days since I found out Mrs. Santos was having sex with my dad, it felt like five lifetimes. Plus . . . I had cheated. I was like her. Gosh. Maybe I would try to kill myself like her someday. But I don't think so. That sounds so impossible no matter how sad you feel.

Trevor's mom said, "You two look cold and dirty. Why don't you clean up. I'll take Lily out for pizza. We'll bring you back a fresh pizza in about an hour. Okay?"

"But, Mom, let's wait for them so they can go with!" Lily said.

"I think they should be alone, Lily," his mom said.

"Thanks," Trevor said. Mrs. Santos took the still-protesting Lily by the hand and led her toward the kitchen and out into the garage.

I FOLLOWED TREVOR UP TO HIS ROOM. WE WENT INTO HIS bathroom and started kissing and took off each other's clothes. We got under the hot shower and he was excited and I wanted to have sex with him more than ever in my life and we tried but it was really hard to make the angle work standing up so then we tried to lie down in the tub and I was on bottom and it was super uncomfortable except it was also amazing to be having sex in the shower with the love of my life. We didn't use a condom. Can you even use condoms in a shower? Duh. Obviously you can. But neither of us would have ever stopped to put one on. We wanted to be together forever, and you can't stop to put a condom on if you want to be together forever. That makes no sense, I know, but it made sense at the moment to me.

82
Trevor passes a test

CAROLINA AND I ARE BACK TOGETHER.

It's great.

It's better than any other dimension of existence in which we are broken up or where we had never met.

But it's not better than the dimension where she never cheated. I believe her that she didn't plan on kissing him. Didn't really kiss him back. Didn't really touch him. I do. Maybe I have to. But I do believe her. Carolina has talked a lot since we were back together about telling each other every single thought that goes through our brains. She said it would prevent me from hiding stuff from her (like our parents' affair and stuff) and it would prevent her from ever hurting me again. It would be pretty nutty to talk about telling each other every thought and then lie about what happened with Alexander Taylor. So yeah. I believe her. I still hate her sometimes when I think about it. But I believe her.

So. Yeah. Being with Carolina is better than not being with her. I love her. So fucking much I double over from feeling how much

I love her sometimes. But I can feel this really angry voice in my head that wants to yell at her every time I see her. I don't do it. It goes away after we kiss and I smell her. I'm just saying it's there. This voice. And I don't know how I'm going to get rid of it. If there was a way to go to other dimensions, one where Carolina never cheated, I'd go. In a heartbeat. Even if I go to one where she did it but I never found out, I think I'd go. Because knowing she betrayed me feels like it's never going to become unknown. Never forgotten. Never even made smaller in my head. It's just going to tick, tick, tick away like a bomb until it explodes. I hope it doesn't explode. Because I love Carolina so much and if it explodes, it will probably kill us both.

Two weeks after we got back together, I took the driver's test, passed, and got my license. My dad and I went car shopping and he bought me a Ford Edge. It's nice. I got a blue one. I always liked black best, but Carolina didn't want me to get a black truck so I didn't. I'm super spoiled and lucky. My parents are totally screwed up, but all kids' parents are probably screwed up and not all kids get a new car for their birthday. I wish I was so cool and strong that I could tell my dad I didn't want a car. But I'm not.

Carolina and I drove downtown to celebrate, just the two of us. On the way home, she said she wanted to give me my birthday present but that I couldn't drive on the highway while she gave it to me. That's when we pulled off to drive on neighborhood streets without much traffic. She undid her seat belt, leaned over, and unzipped my pants. Eventually I had to pull my pants down. She used her mouth. You know, road head. I had never really thought about it before but now I don't know if I can ever be in a car with Carolina without thinking about it.

ONE WEEK AFTER MY BIRTHDAY AND THREE WEEKS AFTER
we got back together, Carolina came over after my first indoor track
meet. I had run well. Won the freshman mile. Coach Pasquini said,
"You seem even tougher now," and patted me on the head.

It was March 16. Carolina had been strange in texts the past
couple days. I worried she didn't love me as much anymore. I hadn't
been the same since we got back together. I tried. I tried to be so nice.
But it's hard to be nice sometimes if you've got that angry voice inside
you, and Carolina was the one who put it there. Or made it come back.
But when she came over on that Saturday, you could tell she loved
me still. She was scared. But different than I had ever seen her. She
could barely look Lily in the eyes, told Lily she was sick, but I knew
she wasn't.

We went in the basement, and she lay down and said, "Cuddle
with me," and so I did even though I wasn't sure what the hell was
going on. Carolina couldn't look at me. She was shaking even though
it had been super warm that day for March and it was almost stuffy
hot in the basement. Someone must have died. Her dad. She hadn't
talked to or seen her dad in three weeks. Now she had found out he
was dead. . . .

"What's wrong, Carolina?" I asked.

She tried to open her mouth, she tried to look at me, but her face
quivered and—what the fuck was going on?

"Carolina? Did I do something? Man, I'm sorry. Was I mean? I
love you. Tell me what's wrong."

"I think, I think . . ." she started. Her whole throat shook and her
lips vibrated with all this intense emotion. "I haven't . . . gotten my,
you know, period."

I didn't really know what this meant for about two seconds. Just confused. Like, why is she telling me about her chick stuff? But then I remembered. I'm not a moron. Holy. Crap. She's . . .

She's pregnant.

"You're pregnant?" I said.

"I don't know!" she wailed, and that "I don't know" felt like a yes. And. Pregnant. Pregnant. Baby. I just turned learned to drive! My life was over. Over. Carolina and I would be together forever now. We would have to be. She was stuck with me! No. I don't like that. I do. But not really. We'd both be stuck. For the baby. I'm too young. Crap. I love her. I love everything about her. I don't even care now that she cheated. I love her. But a baby . . . pregnant . . .

"Have you taken a test?" I asked after a whole long time of just trying to make sense of what might be happening. I couldn't really think straight. Baby. Pregnant. I wanted to play video games. . . .

She shook her head. "It's been a week. It's never been late a week. I looked online, and everything says I'm pregnant."

"But how?" I asked.

"Trevor! We never use a condom half the time!"

"But . . ." I started. But what was I going to say? She was right. We only used it if it was convenient. And . . . crap . . . I'm that guy. I'm that idiot who got his high school girlfriend pregnant. I couldn't go to college now. I'd have to work. What would I do? I had to support a baby. I had to get married. For real. Not imaginary. For real. And raise a baby. What the hell did I know about raising a baby?

Crap. Crap. Crap. Crap. Crap.

Abortion. My mom did it. We should do that. Yeah.

"We can get an abortion," I said before thinking it through.

"Oh, Trevor, don't you love me?"

"I love you, Carolina! But you're so young and our lives will be over!"

"I KNOW! DON'T YELL!"

"Do you want to have it?"

"I don't want to be pregnant! But I don't know! Like, I'm supposed to know better! I'm supposed to be the girl that knows better! And if I just get an abortion because I was stupid, I don't know! It doesn't seem right! I feel like I should have to have it and my life will be changed but it's what I'm supposed to do!"

Crap. "Yeah . . ." I said.

"What?" she said as she wiped the corners of her eyes.

"You're right."

"Really?" she said.

"Yeah. I knew what to do. To use condoms. But we didn't. I knew I should talk about sex more. But I didn't. And we screwed up so much. And now this happened. And we have to accept it."

"So?"

"I don't know," I said.

"I don't want to be pregnant, Trevor. I want to be just in high school and in love and go to classes. I don't want to be mature. I don't. I want to be a kid. OH MY GOSH, I JUST WANT TO BE A KID! But I've thought about it so much and I don't want to get an abortion."

"Okay."

"You won't leave me?"

"I just want to go to high school too, Carolina. But I could never leave you," I said. And I meant it more than I had meant anything I had said in my life.

THAT EVENING, WE WENT TO THE DRUGSTORE, BOUGHT A pregnancy test, then went to TGI Fridays and she peed on the test in the bathroom. She came back crying, and I thought that meant we were having a baby.

"It was negative," she said.

"What's that mean?"

"I don't know." We spent all of dinner on our phones reading about pregnancy tests and how accurate they were. It was a really strange dinner.

THE NEXT MORNING, CAROLINA CALLED ME UP SUPER early. Like, seven a.m.

"I got it," she said.

"Got what?" I asked, but I knew. I just didn't want my heart to know it unless it was one hundred percent true.

"My period."

"Carolina . . ." I said, really soft, but my whole body screamed with so much relief. My whole life was handed back to me. It had been gone. Changed. Gone. But now it was back. I was alive. That teenage dad-boy was dead. Stay dead. I don't want to be you ever.

"We get to be kids again," she said, and laughed. Not a happy laugh. Like an *I'm glad that roller coaster didn't fall off the tracks and kill us* laugh.

Fuck. I'm free. I think.

83

Carolina names a baby

I WOULD HAVE NAMED A GIRL ISABELLA. I DON'T KNOW
what I would have named a boy. Maybe Scott. I know this is my dad's
name and I hate my dad! But I also love him. I love him but I want
him to be different. So maybe if I had a boy, I could have named him
Scott and then made him to be a better person than my dad. I don't
know. Is my dad a bad person? I don't think so anymore. I should say
I don't know. It's all so complicated. Like, I'm such a good person,
right? I think so. But I cheated on Trevor. I wasn't married! I didn't
do it, like, a hundred times! But I still cheated. Trevor's my soul mate, I
know he is. Which is even more important than your wife or husband,
so . . . Never mind. I'm just trying to say that I might have named a
boy Scott. Especially if my dad died in a plane crash or something
before the baby was born. Then for sure.

I CAN'T BELIEVE FOR TWENTY-FOUR HOURS I THOUGHT I
would have a baby. It's so weird because I suddenly feel sooo young
again. Like such a little girl. Like I don't know anything again. Like

I don't want to get married or have babies until I'm sooo old. But for a couple days, especially the night after I told Trevor, which made it so real, I thought I was going to be a mom. I thought I was this adult woman. Like you see on television. Like, as old as my mom. High school and being popular and even school and college and everything any kid thinks about ever felt so, so, so, so silly. Oh my gosh, so silly.

Now that I know we're not pregnant, I guess I care about school again. I do. But I care in such a different way. I like it because it's fun and easy and simple. It's not, like, this huge life-or-death thing anymore. I'll still try really hard, I will, but it will just be different.

I might never have a baby or get married. I really do want to be a CEO and a great leader, and I just know if I had gotten pregnant, that wouldn't have happened. How many teenage moms grow up to be super successful and on TV and respected? I don't know one. Maybe there is. But I think it would be on their Wikipedia page. And I've never read about one.

I mean, yes, okay, maybe I'll want a baby and a husband some-day. But only after I'm successful for sure. But if you made me choose right now between having a baby now and NEVER having a baby at all . . . gosh . . . yeah, I would choose never. I'm too young to be old.

So after I had my period and Trevor and I went back to being just boyfriend and girlfriend and not stuck-with-me-forever soul mates because of a baby, something changed in him. Probably in me too. But something changed in how he looked at me. Maybe it was everything. You know, Alexander and our parents and the almost-baby, but he didn't look at me with those eyes anymore. Those eyes that just looked like they never looked at or even thought about another girl.

At lunch, I could see him look at other girls. Not like in that creepy sex way like Alexander. But just for an extra moment. Just that tiny little moment that told me I wasn't everything to him anymore.

"Do you wish I dressed like her?" I said one day when Trevor watched this sophomore Penn Vadire enter the lunchroom.

"What are you talking about?" he said, even though he knew exactly what I was talking about. I mean, how could he find both me *and* Penn attractive? She looked like she should live in New York with her leather jacket and her black jeans and her high-heeled black boots and her dark eyes and her thin arms and her sultry everything. And I was none of that. I was just, you know, me.

"Forget it," I said, because I didn't want to think about it for even one more second.

All through April and most of May, he still acted like the best boyfriend ever. We would text "I love you" almost as much as ever. And I totally believed he still loved me. But, you know, it was different.

Trevor came to my soccer games. (I made varsity. So did Kendra. Peggy didn't make varsity. She played with the freshmen and kept saying soccer was a waste of time.) Trevor and I would still see each other at least once a weekend. You know, go into his basement. We didn't have sex as much. I mean, we still did. (And ALWAYS, ALWAYS, ALWAYS with a condom.) But it wasn't as much. I actually liked it more than ever, but Trevor . . . I mean, he still liked it and stuff. Obviously. He's a boy. But you could tell he didn't love it so much he would die without it like before. That's another reason I knew Trevor was . . . I don't even want to say it.

And Trevor would go out with his friends more. I mean, when we were first falling in love and in the winter, oh my gosh, he would never choose to hang out with boys instead of me. But now, he'd say, "The guys and I are going to a movie," or "Just gonna play video games over at Licker's." And I wouldn't be invited. Not that I would want to go, but I guess I would have liked to be invited.

It made me start hanging out with Kendra more. And the other soccer girls. Peggy and I still weren't really friends anymore. I mean, we would talk a little. But it was always about soccer or school. Never about boys. Never about our feelings. Never about anything that best friends would talk about. When I think about how we spent our whole lives as the best friends ever, it makes me sad. But when I look at her as just high school Peggy, I can't be sad. I don't think we would have been friends at all if we met now. Weird. So weird. But it's true. It's like the bubble that only Trevor was inside. Peggy was now two bubbles away. Never mind.

When I see Katherine now and she is being this crazy bitch (oh, I hate that word, but it's just who she is), I don't get scared or even worried. I just laugh in my head. All that stuff I went through with Trevor makes Katherine just the most ridiculous person ever, and you can't be scared of ridiculous people. You can't take them seriously at all.

I STUDIED SUPER HARD FOR FINALS. NOT STRESSED ABOUT it. You know, not this panic of I have to get good grades or I'm going to explode. I just wanted to do really well. (And I did. I won't brag, but I got all As. Well, an A-minus in biology.)

Before I found out my grades, on the Friday night after finals and school were over, Trevor and I had a date planned. I felt so good and so calm and I was so excited to spend the summer with Trevor, maybe getting a job together at the movie theater or at Lou Malnati's or something since we went there so often. There was a party that night. Trevor wanted to go to the party. He never wanted to go to parties, but he wanted to go that Friday night. I should have known something was wrong just by that.

84
Trevor talks to a hurdler

THERE WAS THIS SOPHOMORE GIRL ON THE TRACK TEAM. She was a hurdler. Her name was Betsy Kwon. She was Korean. She had the longest legs. Like six inches taller than both her parents, she said. She ran so fast and chewed gum at the same time. It was magic.

When we were stretching as a team before every track practice, she would always sit by me. She was really funny. She would always talk to me, laugh at what I said, smile at everything. Then right before we would run, she would say, "This is going to suck," and wink at me. I'm not sure if she was being sexual. But in my brain, it was sexual. I masturbated to pictures of her in a bathing suit on Facebook. That's so wrong, but fuck, I did it, so I have to admit it.

I didn't flirt with Betsy. I don't I think I did. But we became friends, and I liked talking to her at every practice. Listen. I loved Carolina. She was my goddamn soul mate. She was. But there was so much crap between us. So heavy. Even though I had forgiven her for kissing Alexander, I had not forgotten. I couldn't. And even though she had forgiven me for not telling her about our parents, she never quite believed me that I was telling her everything. So we'd have fights about stupid small new stuff even though it was really about big old stuff.

And then there was that day and night when we thought we were pregnant. You can't go back in time and pretend you almost weren't going to be a mom and dad together. It's like we were living this life as teenage kids in love while at the same time living that life as kids having a baby at the same time. It was so much. Too much. We carried both those lives everywhere.

With Betsy, it was only fun. It was only smiles and jokes. There was nothing sad or mad or exhausting about talking to her and hanging with her, ever.

Yeah. Okay. A few weeks before finals, Carolina and I were in my basement and we started having sex and I couldn't stop closing my eyes and imagining she was Betsy Kwon. Just couldn't stop. It made me so excited I came super fast.

Crap. So. Yeah. I felt like such a fake. Such a liar. Such a cheat even if I hadn't actually cheated. I hated myself again. Carolina is my soul mate, right, and I'm picturing another girl when we are having sex?

Maybe . . . maybe . . . that means she's not my soul mate. Does it? Can you imagine another girl during sex and still be in love with your girlfriend? I asked Google. I hated all the answers. Nobody knows anything. Man.

When it happened a second time, you know, me imagining Betsy while I was with Carolina, I knew I couldn't do it anymore. I couldn't keep kissing Carolina when I couldn't stop thinking of another girl. I didn't mind being miserable or mad or alone . . . but I couldn't be a liar. And whenever I thought of Betsy when I was with Carolina, I felt like such a liar I wanted to bash my head against the wall until I passed out.

I DECIDED TO WAIT UNTIL AFTER FINALS. IT WAS THE NICE thing to do. If I broke up with Carolina before finals, she might have cried and been so upset, she would fail her tests. Probably not fail. She's too smart for that. But maybe get a B again. I wanted her to get straight As. I wanted her to go to Stanford or Harvard and then do these awesome things in life. I just didn't think I could be with her while she did it. Because even when we are forty years old, wouldn't I look at her and think: "She kissed Alexander Taylor in his goddamn 4Runner"? I didn't want to think about that the rest of my life.

I wanted to be a kid again. Just a teenager. I'd been grown-up so long. Even before Carolina. With my mom and her crap and moving and then all the Carolina stuff. Damn. I just wanted to be a kid. Just laugh and smile with Betsy Kwon.

I loved Carolina. I still loved her so much my stomach got cramps. But it was so much work loving her. We were so old together. I wanted to be young with someone else. I wanted to be a kid. And you can't be a kid with your soul mate, not forever.

85

Carolina can walk alone

"CAROLINA," TREVOR SAID AFTER WE ORDERED AT A SAND-wich place called Uncle Josh's. He had a look on his face. Oh my gosh, he had this look.

"Yeah?"

"I think . . ." But he couldn't say any more.

"I love you," I said.

"I love you too," he said back, "but . . . I think . . ."

"Don't, Trevor," I said. I shouldn't have said that. It makes me so weak. I shouldn't have.

"Don't what?" he said.

"I don't know," I said.

"I . . . don't think we should be boyfriend and girlfriend anymore."

I started nodding. Oh my gosh. Don't cry. Don't cry. Don't cry. But I cried. Not like this pathetic crazy cry. Just, you know, tears and sniffling. But I stopped not too long after I started.

"I love you," he said again.

"Then why are you breaking up with me?"

"Because you cheated on me."

"You said you forgave me! If you didn't forgive me, you shouldn't have gotten back with me!" I don't even know why I was saying this. Really. I didn't mean any of it. It just came out because.

"You're right. . . ."

"I'm sorry," I said.

"It's . . . I love you so much it doesn't feel good anymore," Trevor said. That didn't make any sense but I loved it. It felt like a poem. Trevor should be an artist. He should. He's deep and crazy like that. I'll be CEO of a huge company and he'll be a famous artist or writer or something. Except we're breaking up. So we won't know each other. We'll be strangers. We'll never think about each other ever again. Except I'll think about him every day until I die.

THE SANDWICHES ARRIVED AND HE ATE, AND I LOOKED AT the sandwich and I looked at him and I could see he didn't want to go to the party with me. So I said, "You go to the party."

"I want to go with you."

"I don't want to go with you," I said. Which was true. But only true because I knew he didn't really want to go with me.

"Want me to drop you at home?"

"No."

"You can't stay here," he said.

"Why not?"

"How will you get home?"

"I'll walk," I said.

"You can't walk by yourself," he said.

"Yes, I can." And I tried to smile so I looked amazing.

He left. I didn't think he would. I guess I hoped he wouldn't. But it's okay. I'll be okay. I lost the greatest love of my life, but I'll be okay. I'm really smart and strong. I forgot I was for a while because I was so in love. But I remember again.

I sat there in Uncle Josh's for an hour, staring at my uneaten sandwich. I had nowhere to go. No person to go anywhere with. My mom was working. Kendra left for Nashville on a family vacation an hour ago. Peggy . . . oh, I don't know . . . my best friend Peggy was back in junior high forever and high school Peggy was a stranger.

And then . . . my phone beeped. It was sitting on the table, just sitting there. I hadn't even been looking at it. Who could text me? Who could I text? But then there was this beep, this text:

UNKNOWN NUMBER
Miss ya, rock star

Oh, oh, oh, oh, my eyes started watering. Oh, oh . . .

ME
Shannon?
SHANNON SHUNTON'S NEW NUMBER
Yep ;)

I wanted to ask a million things, like why and how and where, and then tell her all about Trevor, and I almost just started letting it all out, like the old Carolina would. But the new Carolina, the new, *new* Carolina with the broken heart, she just wanted to say:

ME
I miss you too
SHANNON SHUNTON'S NEW NUMBER
Sorry I disappeared. Just had to

make a big change so I could

breathe again

ME

I understand. I so understand.

You okay now?

SHANNON SHUNTON'S NEW NUMBER

Yeah, better. Still want to

be best friends?

ME

Yes :)

SHANNON SHUNTON'S NEW NUMBER

Cool ;)

And then we started texting back and forth like we had been best friends for years and not ten seconds. She told me after taking a train to New York by herself to meet a girl she'd met online, she was now down in Florida with her mom and sister. I told her about Trevor. *Everything* about Trevor and sex and everything. Even told Shannon about my dad and Trevor's mom. She then texted, "Parents try to pretend they aren't, but they're just humans," and as soon as I read that, I knew it was time for me to make a big change too.

So after Shannon and I stopped texting, I called him.

"Carolina?" he answered after one ring, saying my name right even.

"Hi, Dad." Big breath. "Trevor broke up with me." It was the first time I had called him or anything since I found out about his affair with Mrs. Santos. He had never come by the house. He had never tried to contact me.

He said, "Can I take you to dinner so we can talk about it?"

I said, "Okay."

86
Trevor goes for frozen yogurt

WHEN I GOT INTO MY CAR AFTER BREAKING UP WITH Carolina, I thought I could fly. Seriously. As I was driving down the street, it felt like my car was a spaceship and I could blast off into space and visit other planets and stars and anywhere in the universe that I could imagine. I had never felt so free in my existence. Never.

After I parked at the party, I texted Betsy Kwon and she texted back before I even got to the front door. I felt a little slimy texting a new girl five minutes after breaking up with Carolina . . . but I still didn't stop. I only stayed at the party for an hour. I was texting Betsy the whole time. She eventually texted:

BETSY KWON

I have a taste for froyo

That was a signal, wasn't it? It was. Damn. She was aggressive. I liked it. I texted:

ME

me too

BETSY KWON

Pick me up?

ME

Okay ;)

And then she texted me five emoticons that made me laugh. Everything about Betsy Kwon made me smile and feel good. Well, everything except that I thought I was stabbing Carolina in the back. But we were broken up. I wasn't doing anything wrong. We were broken up. I didn't cheat. She did. Right. Yeah.

I PICKED UP BETSY, WE WENT AND GOT FROZEN YOGURT, and then we drove around and ate it in the car. Then we parked in the movie theater parking lot but didn't go in. Then she got quiet. She looked at me very directly. Man. She wanted me to kiss her. She didn't leave any doubt. So I kissed her.

And . . . I thought about Carolina the whole time.

WE STOPPED AFTER A BIT. I THINK SHE WOULD HAVE DONE more stuff, but, I don't know, I didn't feel that horny. I know that's . . . I just didn't. So we drove around some more. It was a lot of fun. Betsy was such an awesome girl. So nice and funny. I know I've said this a lot. But, God, I just needed that. I didn't need a soul mate or love or any heavy crap. I just wanted to laugh and not think too much about how serious life could get.

I dropped Betsy off pretty late and we made plans to go see a movie the next day. It felt so strange and weird to make plans with a different girl than Carolina, but I think it was good. I think if I didn't make plans I would have called up Carolina and made plans with her. I'd probably think about Carolina during the movie with Betsy tomorrow. But that didn't feel wrong. Not like when it was the opposite. Because I loved Carolina. Man. I did. But I didn't want to go out with a girl I loved anymore; I wanted to go out with a girl I just liked.

When I got home, my mom was sitting on the couch in the living room reading her Kindle.

"Where's Dad?" I asked.

"Asleep."

"Why are you up?"

"I like this book."

"Okay."

"How was your night?" she asked. Which was weird. She usually didn't ask.

"Fine."

"Why was it just fine?"

"Why are you asking questions?" I asked. Like, with attitude. My mom and I had ignored each other for months and now she was curious?

"I'm sorry," she said. Which made me feel like crap. I'm an asshole.

"Carolina and I broke up."

"I'm sorry," she said. "Do you want to talk about it?" What the hell? Why was she being so nice and normal? I couldn't say yes. I just couldn't. It would have been too easy on her.

So I said, "Why'd you cheat?" because that question was anything but easy.

She put down her Kindle, looked right at me, didn't say anything for a while but I could tell she was thinking some massive thoughts. So I waited. Then my mom finally said, "Sometimes you run to something new because it's easier than sitting with something old."

Man. *Man.* I mean, it's like she knew everything, right? She, my mom, she basically just explained . . . Never mind. I just said, "Okay," and nodded.

"Do you want to talk about it more?"

I said, "No," because I just had to. But then I said, "Maybe tomorrow." And then I started walking toward the stairs to go to bed.

"I'm proud of you, Trevor," she said, which made me turn around.

"Why?" I said. With attitude.

"For being real." And she smiled, then picked back up her Kindle. That was the goddamn best thing she had ever said to me. Crap. Just like I was tired of loving Carolina, maybe I was tired of hating my mom. Maybe.

87

Carolina doesn't cry

I THREW AWAY THE SANDWICH TREVOR BOUGHT FOR ME. It felt wasteful. I know. But I wanted to eat dinner with my dad, not eat a sandwich alone that my ex-boyfriend paid for. EX-BOYFRIEND. Oh my . . . but I didn't cry. I just imagined I did. I think in a movie, the girl would cry. Then the audience would feel sorry for her. But this wasn't a movie. It was just me, and I didn't want to feel sorry for myself.

My dad picked me up at the sandwich shop, and we drove to a sushi restaurant in Northbrook. I told him everything that had happened from the time I told him I never wanted to see him again. (Well, I left out the sex stuff and almost being pregnant.) My dad listened better than he ever had. Then he said the best thing.

He said, "I don't think the Carolina and Trevor story is over."

"Really?" I said.

"My gut says it's not."

"Mine too," I said. Except I didn't know if that was my gut or my hope, and I didn't know how I could tell the difference. Then I said, and I don't even know why I said this, maybe because I wanted to say something nice to him, "I think Mom would take you back."

"Do you want her to take me back?" he asked.

What a weirdly strange question. Right? I didn't know. Kind of. I wanted my dad back in my life. But I didn't want him to hurt my mom ever again. And now . . . now, after all I had gone through, I don't know if he couldn't. I understand love too much to think anything is easy. So instead I asked, "Why did you cheat on Mom?" I said it in a whisper so the other people at the restaurant couldn't hear us.

"That answer is so complicated, Carolina."

"I'm mature, Dad."

"You are, aren't you?"

"Yeah," I said, and I knew I was even though I was also still a kid.

"Okay . . . well. First of all. Your mom and I fell in love really fast. Almost as fast as you and Trevor. Except we were in our twenties, and people get married and have kids when they are in their twenties even if they don't know a whole lot more than they did when they were teenagers. By the time I realized I didn't want to be married, we were pregnant with Heath. I talked to your mom about it. She said we could get divorced. She's always been practical. But then Heath was born and all I wanted to be was a dad. Until one day I wanted more again. But then your mom was pregnant with you. And then all I wanted to be was a dad again. And then when you were five or so, I got fired from Northwestern and realized I was a failure. . . ."

"You're not a failure." I don't know if it's true or not, but I don't want my dad to think it's true.

"Thanks, Carolina. But I thought I was going to do some pretty great things in life. And I haven't done any. I helped make you guys. And you are the best things in the world. But I haven't done anything that I dreamed of when I was your age. I'm not dead. There's time. But I went through a phase where the only way I could feel good about myself was to . . . be with other women. It made me feel young. It made me feel special. Your mom is so on top of everything I never felt good enough around her. That's not her fault. But . . . Is this too much, me telling you this?"

"No," I said, though I wasn't sure if I meant it.

My dad kept talking. He needed to say this, I think. "Your mom and I made you and your brother, and this is what all parents say, but it's true—it's the greatest choice I ever made. But your mom wanted someone a bit more stable, I believe, and I wanted someone a bit more crazy. We had you two, so we tried and we tried. I didn't try as hard as her. But I tried. And when it worked, it mostly worked because of you. And when it didn't work, it hurt you the most. So really, that means it doesn't really work at all . . . so . . . ." Then he stopped. But I knew.

"You're getting divorced?"

My dad nodded.

Wait a minute. Gosh. I breathed in deep. Was I going to cry? I don't think so. Maybe later. But not right now. Okay.

"Your mom said I should tell you because if she told you, you'd worry more about her than yourself. You do know your mom is probably the most mature, wisest person either of us will ever know, right?"

"I know."

"You're taking this awfully well, Carolina. It scares me a bit."

"Dad," I said—yeah, I called him Dad—"I'm really sad. But just because I'm sad doesn't mean I don't understand."

WE TALKED A LOT MORE. WE TALKED UNTIL THEY CLOSED the restaurant. Then we went and got milk shakes at Sonic and he drove me home. I hugged him good-bye and told him I was glad he was my dad again. Because he's a not a bad dad. He's a bad husband. Gosh, yes. But maybe now that he doesn't have to be a husband, he'll be an even better dad. I don't know what I'm talking about. It doesn't matter.

When I got in my bed, I realized that Trevor and I broke up on the same day my parents got divorced. (That's not literally true since they have to do paperwork and stuff. But it was the same day I found out, so that's really my point. Okay?)

Anyway. I'm not sure what that's supposed to mean. But it probably does mean something.

Part Five

EXES FOR EVER

88

Trevor...

ON THE SUNDAY MORNING BEFORE SOPHOMORE YEAR
started, I was lying in bed, and I don't know why—crap, really, I
couldn't explain why—but I just had to text her. Carolina. I hadn't
texted her the whole summer. I texted Betsy Kwon every day. But
never Carolina. I thought about Carolina every day. Of course I did. I
mean, every stupid day. Really. But I never, not once, texted her. But
today . . . I just had to.

89

Carolina . . .

Hi.

That's it. That's all he texted me. I had been waiting the whole summer for him to text me. I knew he had been dating a sophomore girl. Wait a minute. I guess she was a junior now. Because I was a sophomore. So strange! Sophomore. Sounds so old. Anyway. I decided I wouldn't text Trevor back until he texted me something more. Better. At least asked me a question.

Oh. No way could I wait. I didn't love him anymore. Okay. I did. But it wasn't like that. I had met a boy at soccer camp. His name's Greg. He's really nice. And really good at soccer and school. We've kissed a bunch of times but nothing else.

(Okay, well, one time after I drank my first beer Greg and I got, like, in our underwear and touched each other but nothing really finished, if you know what I mean. Yes, I drank a few times. I don't know why. I don't like it that much, but it's nice not to be the only one who doesn't. I hope Trevor never drinks. Nothing really happens to me.

I just smile more. But for Trevor—it might make his darkness so much darker.)

Anyway. I just don't want to have sex or do anything really with Greg. Kissing is much simpler. And it's so easy to only kiss when I don't love him. I did learn to, you know, do it to myself by myself but the only way I could have an orgasm was if I imagined Trevor. Maybe that's why I was fine never doing anything more with Greg. I don't know. Never mind.

So, anyway, the longest minute ever later, I texted him just because.

ME

Hi back.

TREVOR

Hi again ;)

Annoying! But also kind of cute. My heart was racing.

90

Trevor...

THIS IS GOING SO SOUND FUCKING STUPID, BUT TEXTS FROM Carolina felt like they were three-dimensional while texts from everyone else were just one dimension. Even Betsy's. Betsy's were funny and nice. But just . . . not like Carolina's.

CAROLINA

Hi. Again. Back.

I could do this all day. I'm not kidding. I could sit here in my bed all day and just text one or two words to Carolina at a time. Cute, harmless stuff that made me think of her sitting there texting me. Man, that would actually be fun. It is the dumbest thing I've ever thought, but it's true. But instead of doing that, I did the dumbest thing I've ever done and texted:

ME

I miss you

91

Carolina . . .

HE MISSES ME. OH. MY. GOSH. MY DAD WAS RIGHT. OUR story wasn't over. It was just a chapter break. That was clever. I'm funny. Greg doesn't think I'm funny. Greg doesn't have my brain. Trevor has my brain. I miss him so much I want to die.

ME

I miss you. Back.

Maybe I shouldn't have texted that so fast. I was winning. I had him saying he missed me, and I should have made him wait. I should have. But no. I'm glad I didn't. Because I don't want to play games with Trevor. Not any boy ever. But one hundred million percent never Trevor. I want to be better than that. I want to be amazing. Always.

TREVOR

Can I come pick you up?

ME

Yes.

92

Trevor . . .

I DRESSED SO FRICKING FAST I DON'T THINK I BREATHED until I was out of the house and driving to Carolina. Entering her neighborhood was like entering a video from my past life. I couldn't tell what was real and now and what was past and then I was parking. As I got out to go knock on her door, she was opening it up and there she was and—

93

Carolina . . .

HE'S LOOKING AT ME LIKE HE USED TO. LIKE I'M THE only girl in the world. This is happening. My whole body is floating over the ground. That's not true. But you know what I mean. I smiled at him. And I think my smile must have reminded him of all of who I was because Trevor just shook his head. A shake that said, "You are my soul mate." I know this because I am. And he's mine.

94

Trevor . . .

WHEN WE GOT INTO THE CAR AND CLOSED THE DOORS, I could smell her. Goddamn. It was her. Her smell. Betsy had been riding along all summer in my car but it never smelled right. Carolina. She smelled right. Because she smelled like Carolina. I don't know how to say this other than to just say it but that smell gave me the hardest hard-on I have ever had. Betsy and I hooked up and it was okay, I mean, it was fun . . . but it was never this. Just sitting in the car looking at Carolina, smelling Carolina, was better than getting naked with Betsy.

95

Carolina . . .

TREVOR STARTED DRIVING, BUT HE COULDN'T STOP TURNING and looking at me. And I couldn't stop smiling from him looking at me. So we didn't drive more than four or five blocks before he stopped his car and put it in park and I was moving toward him as he was moving toward me and we kissed. Oh my gosh, we kissed. Nobody kisses like Trevor. He tastes perfect and our mouths just eat each other up, but in a beautiful, amazing way that's passionate and a bit crazy but also so comfortable and safe. So perfect. We kissed and we kissed and my head got light and I grabbed him and he grabbed me and we pulled each other so close. So close. I wanted to be naked and in his basement. I wanted to have sex. My body wanted to have sex. Oh my gosh. We really were soul mates.

And then I stopped kissing him. I don't know why. I thought of Greg maybe. Or maybe I thought of my dad. Of his story. My dad was ready. Then not. Then ready. Then not. Where was I? Where was Trevor? Don't think, Carolina! But I had already stopped. So then I pulled away. And I looked at Trevor. His mouth was wet and red. There was spit on his chin. I didn't want to wipe it off.

96

Trevor . . .

CAROLINA STOPPED. NOTHING COULD HAVE STOPPED ME. Nothing. I only wanted Carolina. I didn't care about our crap or our heaviness or anything. There was no one like her in the world. But she stopped.

"Is something wrong?" I asked.

"I don't know. . . ."

"I want to kiss you so bad," I said.

"I've been dating a boy," she said.

"Don't tell me that! I don't want to hear that!" Bam. Bam. Bam. Images blasted through my head of Carolina kissing a boy. Images of Alexander, even though it wasn't him, I'm sure. Oh. Oh. Oh. Why did she have to tell me that?

"But we were going to tell each other everything," she said.

97

Carolina . . .

I SHOULDN'T HAVE MENTIONED GREG. BUT I SHOULD HAVE. I didn't want secrets. Not from Trevor. Not if he was my soul mate.

"Trevor . . ."

"I've been dating a girl." He couldn't look at me. At least he didn't want secrets either.

"I know."

"I don't love her."

"I don't love Greg."

"I love you, Carolina."

"I love you too." And then I had to ask. "Have you had sex with Betsy?"

He didn't speak right away. But I knew. Then he said, "I'm sorry."

Oh. Gosh. Then I cried. I cried my first big cry since we broke up. My breath became fast and short.

Trevor tried to console me. Patting my arm and shoulder. But I just needed to let it out. I'd be okay. I just needed to let it go. He kept saying, "I'm so, so, so sorry."

I shook my head. I didn't want him to be sorry. I didn't. It's okay.

Boys have sex with girls even when they don't love them. Maybe girls do too. Maybe I would someday. But I think if a boy has sex with a girl he doesn't love, it also means he doesn't still love the girl he used to love. Maybe that's not true. Maybe it's all so complex you can't really tell what love really is. But I knew I didn't want to have sex with Trevor. Not now. I didn't even want to kiss him. Not now. If he could have sex with another girl . . . I don't know. I really don't. I just knew our story wasn't just on a chapter break.

98
Trevor . . .

I DIDN'T HAVE A HARD-ON ANYMORE. THAT MIGHT SOUND weird to state, but it's just that two minutes ago I had never been more excited and now . . .

"I wish . . ." I started.

"Yeah?" she said.

"I wish . . ." But I couldn't say anything else. I looked at her face, and I loved that face so much that it hurt again. It hurt everywhere. It hurt so much I couldn't talk. I could only look at her and wish I loved her just a little less so . . . I don't even know. It's all so fucking complicated and tragic and life sucks because you find someone like Carolina and it's all so perfect and life tricks you into thinking it will always be perfect and then when it's not, you're just supposed to accept that it never will be. But it was. Goddamn it. It was perfect. And you can't forget that it's not anymore.

INFINITY

Carolina AND Trevor

TREVOR?

Yes?

I love you.

I love you too, Carolina.

I can see into your eyes right now, and I can see everything you're
thinking.

I can see your thoughts too.

What do you think that means?

I don't know.

Are you mad at me, Trevor?

No. Are you mad at me?

No, I'm just so, so, so sad.

Are we over forever, Carolina?

I don't know.

I don't know either.

I miss you so much, Trevor.

Me too, Carolina.

So then why can't we be together?

Maybe someday?

Maybe . . .

Maybe not . . .

Oh gosh.

Crap.

You're my soul mate, Trevor.

And you're mine, Carolina.

Even if we never kiss again.

Even if.

THE END

ACKNOWLEDGMENTS

Since Carolina helped out with the dedication, I invited Trevor to assist with the acknowledgments. But then Carolina heard we were getting together and asked (pleaded, really) if she could join us. It had been over a year since they last talked, so I expected it to be awkward having them in the same room again. And it was . . . awkward. Very awkward. But it was also something else.

"Hi, Trevor," Carolina said the moment she saw him, with a confident smile, like the smile of a woman who knows a man's secrets. It was very mature. Almost sexual. Which I really didn't think Carolina was capable of, but, like I said, it had been a year. A lot can happen in a year.

"Carolina," Trevor responded, not looking at her. He kept his focus down on the circular table we had gathered around.

"Thanks for assisting me on this," I said.

"Oh my gosh! Obviously! It's so amazing that our story got published!" It was nice to know Carolina hadn't changed completely.

"Yeah, man, congrats," Trevor said. "But people won't be, like, showing up at school asking us if all that crap you wrote is true, will they?"

"No," I said, but didn't explain why. Trevor was brewing hotter than usual. I needed to get this done before he blew. I got to the point. "So, you two know me about as well as anyone. Who do you think I should thank?"

Carolina shouted out first. Of course she did. "Your wife, obviously! She's smart and beautiful AND she's your soul mate and this is about soul mates!"

"This is about soul mates who break up, Carolina!" Trevor said. "So he should only thank her if they get divorced."

"Trevor!"

"Okay, my wife. How's *Thank you first to Danica. You provided a foundation that gave my creativity the freedom to fly.*"

Trevor hated that. "So cheesy."

"It's adorable! But also tell her you love her." *(I love you, wife.)*

"Fine, whatever. Just move on to the next person."

"Your parents. You have to thank your parents, B. Your mom made you love books and your dad loves your books even though he doesn't love any other books, and of course, they made you," Carolina said.

I nodded. "Yep, yep, so, *To my parents—*"

Trevor interrupted, "And your sisters, Pam and Lindsey, because Lily would be super mad if you didn't mention your sisters."

I started again, *"To my parents and my sisters for their unconditional love and unwavering support even when they thought I was crazy."*

"That's funny," Trevor said. He almost smiled too. Almost.

Carolina tapped the table with inspiration. "You have to thank Jessica Brody; she totally mentored you through every step of writing the book and finding an agent and everything."

"Perfectly said, Carolina."

"Man, wow," Trevor said, "talk about your agent. A lot. Because no offense to your wife, but come on, without Jill Grinberg, you would be nowhere. She's the best agent out there, and for reasons I still don't understand, she chose to represent you. *And* she gives great notes, *and* she's nice, like, cool, *and* she calls you back super fast, *and* she even liked your sci-fi crap that was never going to sell."

"I like his sci-fi stuff!" Carolina shouted. "And so did Jill's assistant, Katelyn Detweiler, so you have to thank her too."

"So how's: *To Jill, the first gatekeeper who believed I was worth holding open the gate for.*"

Trevor shook his head. "That's sounds like you're trying to show off. But I don't care. Let's get this over with. I have somewhere to be."

"Where do you have to be?" Carolina asked.

"None of your business."

"WHY WON'T YOU BE MY FRIEND, TREVOR?!" Oh boy. Carolina cracked first.

"YOU KNOW WHY, CAROLINA!"

"OH MY GOSH, YOU BROKE UP WITH ME!"

Trevor stood to leave. I spoke up. "Trevor, sorry, I know this is hard. But we're almost done. A few more minutes?" He didn't say yes, but he didn't leave either. Just turned and leaned back against the wall. The glare he leveled at Carolina would have knocked over a lesser girl.

Carolina was not a lesser girl.

As they spoke to each other in their heads, I said, "I should mention Jennifer Hunt—she encouraged me to concentrate on character voices, not plot concepts. And Jessa Zarubica for reading the first draft in two days and getting me excited about you two."

"Cool," Trevor said, mostly because he wanted to get through this.

Carolina winked at Trevor. Winked! When did she learn to wink at boys? She then turned to me. "B! You should start talking about your editor, Kate Farrell. She made the book better without making it worse."

Trevor said, "That makes no sense."

"Kate will know what I mean because she is obviously so amazing!"

"You're only saying that because she was the only one who liked you as much as me."

"Which makes her a genius! In fact, I think she liked me more. Can you ask her if she liked me more?"

"She liked you both the same," I said. "How about I thank her like this: *To Kate, for believing Carolina and Trevor were worth showing to the world.*"

"Amazing!"

"Yeah, awesome, but I would have shown the world who I was on my own eventually."

Carolina stood up from the table. "Trevor, you can't do everything by yourself."

He ignored her. "Are we done?"

"I think so."

"Oh my gosh, you have to thank your baby, Axel! He's sooooooooo cute!"

"Yeah," Trevor said, "you're totally going to screw him up like all parents screw up their kids, so you should thank him for loving you anyway."

I laughed. "You said it better than I could have, Trevor."

"Trevor . . ." Carolina stood up. She inched toward him. He wanted to look away. But he couldn't. He was still in love with her. "I'm still in love with you too," she said.

"You have a boyfriend, Carolina!"

"You have a girlfriend!"

"We broke up six months ago."

"I didn't know," she said.

"Which just proves you know nothing about me. Are we done or what?" Trevor asked me, but *to* Carolina.

My eyes started tearing up. Goddamn. I didn't realize how much I missed them until right this second. Not just missed them. Missed them together. I said, "I should thank you two, right? I should say, *To Carolina and Trevor, for being soul mates.*"

"For a year," Trevor said. "We were only soul mates for a year."

"Or . . ." Carolina said, and that smile of hers was back. That smile that said she knew things now that I didn't think she would ever know. *"To Carolina and Trevor, for being soul mates for a year AND forever."*

I wasn't quite sure what she meant, but they started talking to each other in their heads again. Like I wasn't even in the room.

So I left.

Maybe, without me there, they'll work something out.

Maybe.

FOREVER
FOR A YEAR

BONUS MATERIALS

GOFISH

B. T. GOTTFRED

What was your inspiration for the concept of *Forever for a Year*? What made you want to write about this time of life—starting high school, falling in love for the first time, and growing up and into yourself?
I believe first love—first great, romantic, sensual love—serves as a model for all relationships that come after. Some elements of that first love you try to duplicate, some elements you try to run away from. So I wanted to find two characters that I loved and watch them journey through this. To see how they would change as individuals and as a couple.

Carolina and Trevor are such vivid, memorable characters—can you tell us a little about how you came up with their characters? And how you developed their distinctive voices?
I have no elaborate process. The voices just start talking. There are hundreds in my head right now. Eventually a voice becomes insistent on being heard and so I start to seriously consider where it belongs. A book? A play? A movie? In a straitjacket? And once Carolina and Trevor let me know they were ready, I just let them start talking and tried to keep up. (And maybe edited out a few of their long-winded tangents.)

The book is split into two points of view—some chapters are Carolina's and some are Trevor's. What was most important to you about telling the story in this way and getting inside these two characters' heads?

Love is a two-way connection. (At least two ways.) Love stories only told from one POV end up (often) feeling as if one side of that relationship is one-dimensional. This then renders the love itself one-dimensional. Going forward, I can't think of a love story I'd want to tell any other way than from both people's perspectives.

What was the most challenging part of writing *Forever for a Year*? What did you find most enjoyable?

The most challenging aspect was staying loyal to where Carolina and Trevor were going, what they were feeling, and not giving in to this writerly idea of where I thought they should go and what they should feel. It's also the most rewarding because you end up being surprised by how much more they know about themselves (and their true story) than you do.

What did you want to be when you grew up?

Mostly I wanted to be just like my dad until I realized I needed to be me instead. My dad's a great person. But he's a great him and I needed to be a great me.

When did you realize you wanted to be a writer?

When the voices and ideas in my head needed somewhere to live (the page) besides my head.

What's your most embarrassing childhood memory?
Talking to a supercute girl and a huge booger flying out of my nose. (The girl—Allison Bradbury—laughed and she remains a friend. Even came to the book signing.)

What's your favorite childhood memory?
Getting the *Millennium Falcon* on the same day my baby sister came home from the hospital.

What was your favorite thing about school?
When it was over. ;) (I also liked my friends and a few teachers and even, once in a great while, actual things being taught.)

What were your hobbies as a kid? What are your hobbies now?
I liked sports, video games, and girls. Now, I like sports, video games, and my wife.

What was your first job, and what was your "worst" job?
First paying job was as an umpire for Little League Baseball. I was probably twelve. I literally fell asleep standing up, missed a call, and got yelled at by one of the coaches.

What book is on your nightstand now?
Reading Philip K. Dick's *The Man in the High Castle* because the TV series got me addicted.

How did you celebrate publishing your first book?
Food with Family and Friends. (The three most important *F*s! Well, there's one other.)

What challenges do you face in the writing process, and how do you overcome them?
Crippling fear and delusional overconfidence. I tend to let these two balance each other out over time.

What is your favorite word?
And . . . .

If you could live in any fictional world, what would it be?
In Riverbend with my characters.

What was your favorite book when you were a kid? Do you have a favorite book now?
Catcher in the Rye and *Siddhartha* . . . and it's probably those two now.

What's the best advice you have ever received about writing?
All writing advice is bad because it suggests one way is the right way. So my advice is: There's no one right way. Follow your own gut, your own path.

What would you do if you ever stopped writing?
Be dead. ;)

A quiet girl with secret urges and a nerdy boy end up at
the same resort for winter break. They're drawn to each other.

BUT IS THERE SUCH A THING AS HAPPILY EVER AFTER FOR THIS UNLIKELY PAIR?

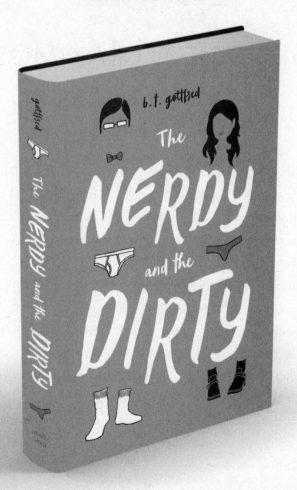

KEEP READING FOR A SNEAK PEEK.

— 1 —

BENEDICT MAXIMUS PENDLETON

"I'M VERY HANDSOME. I DON'T REALLY THINK this is a question of opinion. I am objectively handsome," I said to Robert, who was staring at his roast-beef sandwich. He always stared at his sandwiches. This made it difficult to have conversations. I've talked to him about it. He's working on the problem.

"I agree, Benedict," Robert said to me. Toward the roast beef but to me.

"Of course you agree. You are a logical person. I am six feet one inch tall, slender but not skinny because I do fifty push-ups every morning and every night. My eyes and nose are proportional. My ears might be slightly large for my head, but my thick head of hair, which I style every day, should more than compensate. I also dress very well. Not trendy. I dress with sophistication."

"I like how you dress," Robert said.

"Thank you. I know you do. Sport jackets are woefully under-represented in the wardrobes of today's teenagers. Do you know why I am telling you this, Robert?"

"No."

"I am telling you this, Robert, because I think it is time I get a girlfriend."

"You've never had a girlfriend."

"I know! Obviously. But only because my dad told me I could not date until I was sixteen. He wanted me to concentrate on school. This was great advice."

"Your dad is very smart."

"He is. Obviously. But I turn seventeen in six days and not one girl has expressed interest in me the past year, and though some of the fault must lie in the female student population of Riverbend High School, I must also admit that, with my having been on the proverbial sidelines of the dating scene until a year ago, they might not be aware of my availability and interest."

———

In the several seconds it took Robert to respond, Evil Benny started talking in my head. Evil Benny is not real. I'm not crazy. It's just self-doubt. I call this voice, this self-doubt, Evil Benny because I want to make sure my better self differentiates itself from my lesser self. And Evil Benny, obviously, is my lesser self. It is easier to ignore Evil Benny if I make him a separate person. I don't actually think he's a separate person. That would make me crazy, which I have already stated I am not. I just make him separate in my head. Evil Benny says very untrue, very destructive things like "You don't have a girlfriend because you are very unlikable." So, obviously, destructive thoughts are not productive. That's why he's Evil Benny and must be ignored. I will expunge him, and self-doubt entirely, from my head someday soon. I am sure of it.

———

"I'd like a girlfriend," Robert said, which made me happy since it was easier to ignore Evil Benny when I could talk.

"Robert . . ." I started, but then stopped. I was about to tell him that he was not objectively handsome. Robert wouldn't have minded me telling him this. He enjoyed that I was always honest with him. But I fear my practice of being blunt with Robert since we were twelve has led me to be blunt with others, which may be a third reason for my current lack of girlfriend. Girls, see, prefer that you lie to them. So I have decided to start lying to Robert about certain things. As practice for when I have a girlfriend. Thus I said to Robert, "Yes, I agree. You and I both should get a girlfriend." Though, obviously, I would get a girlfriend first, and then my girlfriend would provide one of her less attractive friends for Robert to date.

2

pen

Let's say I was writing a book about my life.

I'm not. My real life is boring and all the crazy fantasy stuff in my brain should never, ever, ever, ever be public. So no way would I ever write a book.

But, because I read a lot and can't help thinking about this sometimes, let's say I was. And I had to figure out a way to start the book, a totally honest/unique/mind-blowing opening that would make some sixteen-year-old girl like me want to read the whole thing after they downloaded the sample on their phone. But I also had to figure out a not-too-girly beginning so boys would want to read it too, even though they're usually too lazy to read books not assigned for school. Oh, and I guess it couldn't be too honest or sexy or anything that would make parents burn my book before any kid even saw it.

So . . . never mind. I can't think of anything that could do all that. All I guess I could say was, "My name is Pen. I pretend I'm normal. The end." So, yeah, NEVER MIND. This is a stupid thing to think about.

I'm stupid.

I'm boring.

Stupid.

Boring.

Oh, and fake.

So fake. Not fake like you see on TV where the girls are all snotty yet saying nice things like "You are so pretty" even though it's clear the girls hate everyone including themselves. No, fake because I wish I could be real. I wish I could just come out tell everyone who I really am. I could just come out and say stuff like:

I masturbate a ton.

I would never, ever, ever tell anyone that. NEVER. But I wish I could. Every inch of my stupid/boring/fake body wishes I could. If I was a guy, talking about how much you masturbate would be pointless to mention. But I'm a girl in high school, so maybe it's interesting. As far as I know I'm the only girl at Riverbend who masturbates. I wish I wasn't. I wish all my friends masturbated as much as me because then I wouldn't feel like a freak.

So, yeah . . . I guess if I was going to write a book, I'd write a book about anything or anyone but me. I'd make it about someone who's actually interesting. Someone so interesting even boys would want to read my book.

So maybe it should be about a boy.

A really, *really* interesting boy.

Probably too interesting for someone boring and fake like me, but at least he'd be fun to write about. Not that I'll write anything ever. I don't even know why I'm thinking about this. Other than because math class is even more boring than thinking about how boring my life is.

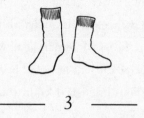

— 3 —

BENEDICT MAXIMUS PENDLETON

JUST AS I WAS CONVINCED ROBERT COULD BE a good ally in helping me find my first girlfriend, he said, "I want to date Pen Lupo."

"Robert, please, we have to take this seriously."

"What's wrong with Pen?" He actually put down his sandwich to say this. Having all his attention on me made me uncomfortable. For only a moment. I can handle almost any confrontation. Obviously.

I explained, "Penelope Lupo is not even in the top one hundred of class rank. In fact, she's probably in the bottom one hundred. We should set up rules for our girlfriend search. And one of the rules, obviously, is that they are smart."

"Pen is very smart."

"Robert!" I yelled. Sometimes I yelled when people were not logical.

"She is, Benedict. We used to talk all the time in seventh grade."

"Robert . . ." I calmed myself. I was good at calming myself most of the time. I had been enduring him talking about Penelope Lupo since we were in junior high and I had been, understandably, dismissive of his interest. But if I were going to get a girlfriend, I would have to learn to be patient with a girl's irrational thinking. Though Robert was usually very smart, he was not smart at all when it came to discussing Penelope Lupo, which meant he could be a good practice subject on this issue as well. Thus I stated, "I know you and Penelope—"

"No one calls her Penelope anymore."

Do not yell at him Benedict! I didn't. It was very difficult. "Fine. Pen. I know you two were lab partners in seventh-grade science class, but you haven't spoken since we got to high school."

"She always says hi in the halls."

"But you haven't actually discussed anything at length, correct?"

Robert shook his head and picked up his roast beef again.

I continued, "That's because you have nothing in common anymore. You and I are in the top ten smartest kids at Riverbend." Technically, he was twelfth in class rank. I was third. Being third, it's my duty to be generous in praise of those lower than me. "Both of us will attend nationally ranked universities." I'll attend Northwestern. My dad went there. He's famous. I would, obviously, get into Northwestern even if my father were not a famous legacy. I would get into an Ivy League school if I wanted! But that's not important right now. What's important is, "Penelope—"

"Pen."

"Pen, sorry, is a stoner and a loser. She might not attend college at all. She will drag you down to her level. And you being my best friend, if you were dragged down to her level, you might then drag me down. We have to protect each other from making bad choices." Obviously, I just needed to protect Robert. I didn't make bad choices.